François de Salignac de La Mothe Fénelon

The Adventures of Telemachus

François de Salignac de La Mothe Fénelon

The Adventures of Telemachus

ISBN/EAN: 9783337342845

Printed in Europe, USA, Canada, Australia, Japan

Cover: Foto ©Andreas Hilbeck / pixelio.de

More available books at **www.hansebooks.com**

THE
ADVENTURES
OF
TELEMACHUS,
THE
SON of ULYSSES.

BY THE

ARCHBISHOP of CAMBRAY.

Tranflated into ENGLISH by

Mr. DES MAIZEAUX, F. R. S.

The SEVENTH EDITION, corrected.

LONDON:

Printed for J. F. and C. RIVINGTON, S. CROWDER,
T. LONGMAN, T. CASLON, G. KEITH, B. LAW,
T. LOWNDES, J. JOHNSON, F. NEWBERY
W. GOLDSMITH, and T. BEECROFT.
MDCCLXXIX.

A
DISCOURSE*
OF
EPIC POETRY,
AND OF THE
EXCELLENCE
Of the POEM of
TELEMACHUS.

IF we could relish naked truth, she would not want, to gain our love, the ornaments which imagination lends her; *(The origin and end of poetry.)* but her pure and delicate light does not sufficiently sooth the senses of man; she requires an attention which is too troublesome to his natural levity. To instruct him, it is necessary to give him not only pure ideas which enlighten his mind; but also images which strike his senses, and keep his eyes stedfastly fixed on the truth. This is the source of eloquence, of poetry, and of all the sciences which belong to the imagination: It is the weakness of man which makes these sciences necessary. The plain and unchangeable beauty of virtue does not always affect him; it is not sufficient to shew him truth; she must be painted amiable (a).

We shall examine the poem of Telemachus in these two views, of instructing and pleasing; and we shall endeavour to shew that the author has instructed more than the ancients by the sublimity of his moral, and

---

* This discourse has been revised, altered and improved in many places, according to corrections communicated by Mr. Ramsey, who is the author of it.
(a) *Omne tulit punctum, qui miscuit utile dulci,*
Lectorem delectando, pariterque monendo.
Hor. Art. Poet.

that

that he has pleafed as much as they by imitating all their beauties.

There are two ways of inftructing men in order to render them good: The firft, by shewing them the deformity of vice, and its fatal confequences, which is the chief defign of tragedy: The fecond, by difcovering the beauty of virtue, and its happy end, which is the proper character of the Epopœa or epic poem. The paffions which belong to the former, are terror and pity; thofe which agree to the latter, are admiration and love. In one, the actors fpeak; in the other, the poet makes the narration. *Two forts of heroic poetry.*

The Epic poem may be defined, *A fable related by a poet to raife the admiration, and infpire the love of virtue, by the reprefentation of the action of a hero favoured of heaven, who executes a great defign by triumphing over all obftacles that oppofe it.* There are therefore three things in the Epopœa, the *action*, the *moral*, and the *poetry*. *The definition and division of epic poetry.*

I. Of the EPIC ACTION.

The action muft be *great, one, entire, marvellous,* but yet *probable,* and *of a due length.* The Telemachus has all thefe qualifications. Let us compare it with the models of epic poetry, Homer and Virgil, and we shall be convinced of it. *The qualities of the epic action.*

We shall only fpeak of the Odyffey, whofe plan has a greater refemblance of this of Telemachus. In that poem Homer introduces a wife king returning from a foreign war, wherein he had given fignal proofs of his wifdom and valour. Tempefts ftop him by the way, and caft him on divers countries, whofe manners, laws and politics he learns. Hence naturally arife an infinite number of incidents and dangers. But knowing how many diforders his abfence caufed in his kingdom, he furmounts all thefe obftacles, defpifes all the pleafures of life, *The defign of the Odyffey.*

life, and is unmoved even by immortality itfelf: he renounces every thing in order to relieve his people, and to fee his family again (a).

(b) In the Æneid, a pious and valiant hero, having efcaped from the ruins of a powerful ftate, is deftined by the Gods to preferve its religion, and to found an empire more great and more glorious than the firft.   This prince being chofen king by the unfortunate remains of his fellow-citizens, wanders a long while with them in feveral countries, where he learns every thing that is necef-fary to a king, to a legiflator, to an high-prieft.   He at laft finds an afylum in a remote country, from whence his anceftors came.   He defeats feveral power-ful enemies who oppofe his fettlement, and lays the foundation of an empire, which was afterwards to be the mafter of the univerfe. **The fubject of the Æneid.**

The action of Telemachus comprehends what is great in both thefe poems.   We there fee a young prince, animated by the love of his country, going in queft of his father, whofe abfence caufed the misfortunes of his family and kingdom. He expofes himfelf to all forts of danger; he fignalizes himfelf by heroic virtues; he refufes royalty, and crowns more confiderable than his own; and, paffing thro' feveral unknown countries, learns every thing that is neceffary to govern afterwards ac-cording to the wifdom of Ulyffes, the piety of Æneas, and the valour of both, like a wife politician, a reli-gious prince, and an accomplished hero. **The plan of Telema-chus.**

The action of the Epopœa ought to be one.   The epic poem is not a hiftory, like the Pharfalia of Lucan and the Punic war of Silius Italicus; nor the entire life of an hero, like the Achilleid of Statius: the unity of the hero does not conftitute the unity of the action.   The life of man is full of inequalities; he is continually changing his defigns, either thro' the inconftancy of his paffions, or **The action ought to be one.**

(a) See father Boffu, B. I. chap. 10.
(b) Ibid. chap. 11.

the unforeseen accidents of life. Whoever should describe the whole man, would draw but a fantastical picture, a contrast of opposite passions, without coherence or order. It is for this reason that the Epopœa is not the panegyric of an hero who is proposed for a pattern, but the recital of a great and illustrious action which is exhibited for imitation.

It is in poetry as in painting; the unity of the principal action does not hinder the inserting of many particular incidents. *Of Episodes.* The design is formed in the beginning of the poem, and the hero accomplishes it by surmounting all difficulties. It is the recital of these obstacles which makes the episodes; but all these episodes depend on the principal action, and are so interwoven in it, and so connected together, that the whole presents but one single picture, composed of several figures in a beautiful disposition and in a just proportion.

I do not here inquire, if it is true that Homer sometimes drowns his main action in the length and number of his episodes; if his action is double; if he often loses sight of his principal personages. It is sufficient to remark, that the author of Telemachus has every where imitated the *The unity of the action of Telemachus, and the continuity of the episodes.* regularity of Virgil, by avoiding the faults which are imputed to the Greek poet. All our author's episodes are connected, and so artfully interwoven into each other, that the former brings on that which follows. His chief personages do not disappear, and his transitions from the episode to the principal action, always makes us sensible of the unity of the design. In the first six books, Telemachus speaks, and makes a recital of his adventure to Calypso; and yet this long episode, in imitation of that of Dido, is related with so much art, that the unity of the principal action remains perfect. The reader is there in suspense, and perceives from the beginning that the abode of the hero in that island, and what passes there, is only an

obstacle

obstacle that is to be surmounted. In the XIIIth and XIVth books, where Mentor instructs Idomeneus, Telemachus is not present, being at that time in the army : but then it is Mentor, one of the principal persons of the poem, who does every thing with a view to Telemachus, and for his instruction after his return from the camp. It is also great art in our author, to introduce episodes into his poem which do not arise from the principal fable, without breaking either the unity or continuity of the action. These episodes are placed there, not only as important instructions for a young prince (which is the great design of the poet) but because they are recounted to his hero during a time of inaction, to fill up a vacuity. Thus Adoam informs Telemachus of the manners and laws of Betica, during the calm of a voyage ; and Philoctetes relates his misfortunes to him, while the young prince is in the confederate camp waiting for the day of battle.

The epic action ought to be *entire.* This integrity supposes three things, the cause, the intrigue, and the unravelling.

> The action ought to be entire.

The cause of the action ought to be worthy of the hero, and conformable to his character. Such is the design of Telemachus, which we have seen already.

The intrigue must be natural, and drawn from the action itself. In the Odyssey, Neptune forms it ; in the Æneid, it is the anger of Juno ; and in Telemachus, the hatred of Venus. The intrigue in the Odyssey is natural, because there is naturally no obstacle more to be dreaded by those who go to sea, than the sea itself (*a*). The opposition of Juno in the Æneid, as an enemy of the Trojans, is a beautiful fiction. But the hatred of Venus against a young prince, who despises pleasure through a love of virtue, and subdues his passions by the assistance of wisdom, is a fable which is drawn from nature, and at the same time includes a sublime moral.

> The intrigue.

(*a*) See father Bossu, B. II. chap. 13.

A 3

the

The unravelling muſt be as natural as the intrigue. In the Odyſſey, Ulyſſes arrives among the Phæacians, relates to them his adventures, and thoſe iſlanders, fond of the marvellous, and charmed with his ſtories, furnish him with a ship to return home: the unravelling is plain and natural. In the Æneid, Turnus is the only obſtacle to the ſettlement of Æneas. This hero, to ſave the blood of his Trojans, and that of the Latins, whoſe king he was ſoon to be, decides the quarrel by a ſingle combat (*a*). This unravelling is noble. That of Telemachus is at once natural and great. This young hero, in obedience to the commands of heaven, conquers his love for Antiope, and his friendship for Idomeneus, who offered him his crown and his daughter. He ſacrifices the moſt violent paſſions, and even the moſt innocent pleaſures, to the pure love of virtue. He embarks for Ithaca on ships with which he was furnished by Idomeneus, for whom he had performed many ſervices. When he is near his own country, Minerva cauſes him to put in at a little deſert iſland, where she diſcovers herſelf to him. Having accompanied him, without his knowing her, through ſtormy ſeas, unknown countries, bloody wars, and all the evils that can try the heart of man, wiſdom at length conducts him to a ſolitary place, where she ſpeaks to him, informs him of the end of his labours, and of his future good fortune, and then leaves him. As ſoon as he is going to enjoy happineſs and repoſe, the Divinity withdraws, the marvellous ceaſes, and the epic action ends. It is in adverſity that man shews himſelf a hero, and needs a divine ſupport. It is only after he has ſuffered, that he is able to walk alone, to conduct himſelf, and to govern others. In the poem of Telemachus, the obſervation of the minuteſt rules of art is accompanied with a profound moral.

(*a*) See father Boſſu, B. II. chap. 13.

Beſides

(marginal note: The unravelling.)

Besides the plot and general solution of the main action, each episode has its own plot and solution, which ought to have all the same qualities. In the Epopœa, we do not look for the surprising intrigues of modern romances : surprise alone raises but a very imperfect and transitory passion. The sublime is to imitate simple nature, to prepare the incidents in so delicate a manner, that they may not be foreseen, and to conduct them with such art that the whole may appear natural. We are not uneasy, suspended, diverted from the chief end of heroic poesy, which is instruction, to attend to a fabulous unravelling, and an imaginary intrigue. This is allowable, when the sole design is to amuse ; but in an epic poem, which is a kind of moral philosophy, these intrigues are only witty conceits beneath its gravity and dignity.

The general qualifications of the intrigue and unravelling of the epic poem.

As the author of Telemachus has avoided the intrigues of modern romances, so has he not fallen into the marvellous with which some reproach the ancients ; he neither makes horses speak, nor tripods walk, nor statues work : not that this kind of the marvellous shocks reason, when it is supposed to be the effect of a divine power that can do every thing. The ancients introduced the Gods in their poems, not only to bring about great events by their interposition, and to unite the probable and the marvellous ; but to teach men, that the most valiant and most wise can do nothing without the help of the Gods. In our poem, Minerva continually conducts Telemachus. Thereby the poet makes every thing possible to his hero, and intimates, that man can do nothing without the assistance of divine wisdom. This is not all his art : the sublime consists in the concealing the Goddess under an human form. Not only the probable, but the natural also, is here united to the marvellous. All is divine, and yet all appears human. And this is not yet all : if Telemachus had known that he was conducted

The action must be marvellous.

by

by a Goddess, his merit would have been less ; he would have had too great a support in her. Homer's heroes almost always know what the Gods do for them. Our poet, by concealing the marvellous part of his fiction from his hero, exercises his virtue and his courage.

Tho' the action must be probable, it is not necessary that it be true ; because the end of the epic poem is not to make a panegyric or satire upon any particular man, but to instruct and please by the recital of an action, which leaves the poet at liberty to feign whatever characters, personages, and episodes he pleases, which are proper to the moral he designs to insinuate.

The truth of the action is not contrary to the nature of the epic poem, provided it does not hinder the variety of the characters, the beauty of the descriptions, the enthusiasm, fire, invention, and other parts of the poetry ; and provided that the hero be made for the action, and not the action for the hero. An epic poem may be built on a true as well as on a fabulous action.

The nearness of times should be no check upon the poet in the choice of his subject, provided he supplies this defect by the distance of places, or by probable and natural events, the detail of which has escaped the historians, and which it is supposed could not be known but by the persons who are actors in them. Thus an epic poem and an excellent fable may be built on an action of Henry IV. or of Montezuma, because it is not essential to the epic action, as F. Bossu observes, that it be true or false, but that it be moral, and teach important truths.

The duration of the epic poem is longer than that of tragedy. In the former, the poet relates the continued triumph of virtue : in the latter, he shews the unexpected mischiefs which arise from the passions. The action of the one ought consequently to have a greater length than

Of the duration of the epic poem.

that

that of the other. The Epopœa may take in the actions of several years; but, according to the critics, the time of the principal action, from the place where the poet begins his narration, cannot exceed a year; as the time of the tragic action ought at most to be but one day. However, Aristotle and Horace say nothing about it, and Homer and Virgil have observed no certain rule as to this particular. The action of the Iliad in all its parts takes up but fifty days, that of the Odyssey, from the place where the poet begins his narration, but about two months; that of the Æneid, one year; and a single campaign suffices Telemachus, from his departure from the Islands of Calypso to his return to Ithaca. Our poet has shewn the mid way between the impetuosity and vehemence with which the Greek poet runs towards his end, and the majestic and even pace of the Latin poet, who sometimes seems to flag, and to lengthen out his narration too much.

(a) When the epic action is long and not continued, the poet divides his fable into two parts; in the former, the hero speaks, and relates his past adventures; in the latter, the poet only makes a relation of what afterwards happens to his hero. Thus Homer does not begin his narration till after Ulysses is departed from the isle of Ogygia; nor Virgil his, till after Æneas is arrived at Carthage. The author of Telemachus has perfectly imitated these two great models. He divides his action, like them, into two parts. The principal contains what he himself relates, and begins where Telemachus concludes the recital of his adventures to Calypso. He takes only a little matter, but he treats it at large: eighteen books are employed upon it. The other part is much more extended as to the number of the incidents and the time; but it is much more contracted as to the circumstances: it contains only the six first books. By this division of what our poet relates himself, and of what he makes Telemachus relate,

Of the epic narration.

(a) See F. Boffu, B. II. chap. 18.

be

A difcourfe on Epic Poetry.

he recalls the whole life of the hero, and collects all
the events of it together, without prejudicing the
unity of the principal action, and without giving too
great a duration to his poem. He joins variety and
continuity of adventures together : all is motion, all
is action in his poem. One never fees his perfonages
idle, nor does his hero ever difappear.

II. Of the MORAL.

Virtue may be recommended by examples and by
inftructions, by manners and by precepts ; and in this
refpect our author greatly excels all other poets.

We are indebted to Homer for the no-   Of the
ble invention of perfonalizing the divine   manners.
attributes, human paffions, and phyfical
caufes; a fruitful fource of beautiful fictions which
animate and enliven every thing in poetry. But his
religion is reduced to a texture of fables, which reprefent the divine nature under images by no means
proper to make it beloved and revered.

Every one knows the tafte which all antiquity, facred and profane, Greek and Barbarian, had for fimi-
litudes and allegories. The Greeks derived their mythology from Egypt. Now hieroglyphic characters
were, among the Egyptians, the chief, not to fay the
moft ancient, way of writing. Thefe hieroglyphics
were figures of men, birds, animals, reptiles, and various productions of nature, which denoted, as em-
blems, the divine attributes and the qualities of fpirits.
This fymbolical ftyle was founded upon a very ancient
opinion, that the univerfe is only a picture which reprefents the divine perfections; that the vifible world
is only an imperfect copy of the invifible; that there is
confequently a hidden analogy between the original and
the pictures, between fpiritual and corporeal beings,
between the properties of one and thofe of the other.

This manner of *painting words, and of giving body
to thoughts*, was the true fource of mythology and of
all poetic fictions : but in procefs of time, efpecially
when

when the hieroglyphical ſtyle was turned into the alphabetical and vulgar, men having forgotten the primitive meaning of theſe ſymbols, fell into the groſſeſt idolatry. The poets debaſed every thing by giving a looſe to their imagination. By their appetite for the marvellous, they turned theology and the ancient traditions into a real chaos, and a monſtrous jumble of fictions and all the human paſſions. The hiſtorians and poets of after-ages, as Herodotus, Diodorus the Sicilian, Lucian, Pliny, Cicero, who did not go back to the original deſign of this allegorical theology, underſtood every thing according to the letter, and equally derided the myſteries of their religion and the fable. But when we conſult among the Perſians, Phœnicians, Greeks and Romans, thoſe who have left us ſome imperfect fragments of the ancient theology, as Sanconiathan and Zoroaſter, Euſebius, Philo and Manetho, Apuleius, Damaſcius, Horus-Apollo, Origen, St. Clement of Alexandria, they all tell us that theſe hieroglyphic and ſymbolical characters devote the myſteries of the inviſible world, the doctrines of the moſt profound theology, *the heavens and the faces of the Gods.*

The Phrygian fable invented by Æſop, or according to ſome by Socrates himſelf, gives us at firſt ſight to underſtand that we muſt not adhere to the letter, ſince the actors, who are made to ſpeak and reaſon, are animals void of ſpeech and reaſon: why then ſhould we adhere to the letter only in the Ægyptian fable and the mythology of Homer? The Phrygian fable exalts the nature of the brute, by giving him underſtanding and virtues. The Ægyptian fable ſeems indeed to degrade the divine nature, by giving it body and paſſions. But one cannot read Homer with attention, without being convinced that he underſtood many great truths, which are diametrically oppoſite to the ſenſeleſs religion with which the letter of his fiction preſents us. This poet lays it down as a principle in

ſeveral

several places of his poems, (*a*) that it is a weakness
to believe that the Gods ressemble men, that they are
inconstant, and pass from one passion to another; (*b*)
that all the Gods enjoy is eternal, and that all we possess passes away and perishes; (*c*) that the state of
souls after death, is a state of punishment, suffering,
and expiation; but that the soul of the hero does not
remain in hell; that it takes its flight to the stars, and
sits down at the table of the Gods, where it enjoys a
happy immortality; that there is a continual intercourse between men and the inhabitants of the invisible world; that without the Deity, mortals can do
nothing; (*d*) that true virtue is a divine power that
comes from heaven, which transforms the most brutal,
the most cruel and passionate men, and makes them
humane, tender and pitiful. When I see these sublime
truths in Homer, inculcated, particularized, insinuated
by a thousand different examples and a thousand various images, I cannot believe that this poet is to be
understood according to the letter in other places,
where he seems to attribute to the supreme Deity prejudices, passions and vices.

I know that several moderns, in imitation of Pythagoras and Plato, have censured Homer for having
thus debased the divine nature, and having declaimed
with much wit and force against the absurdity of re-
presenting the mysteries of theology by impious actions attributed to the celestial powers, and of teaching
morality by allegories whose letter presents nothing
but vice. But without any breach of the regard due
to the judgment and taste of these critics, may we
not respectfully represent to them, that their anger
against the allegorical taste of antiquity may be carried too far?

However, I do not pretend to justify Homer in the
extravagant sense of his blind admirers; he lived in a
time when the ancient traditions concerning the ori-

(*a*) Odyss. B. III.   (*b*) Ibid. B. IV.   (*c*) Ibid.
(*d*) Iliad. B. XXIV.

ental

ental theology began to be forgotten. Our moderns
therefore have some reason to shew no great regard
for Homer's theology; and they who endeavour to
vindicate him in every thing under pretence of a perpetual allegory, discover that they are not sufficiently acquainted with the spirit of these true ancients, in
respect of whom, the bard who sings of Troy is himself but a modern.

Not to continue this discussion any longer, I shall
content myself with remarking that the author of Telemachus, in imitating what is beautiful in the fables
of the Greek poet, has avoided two great faults which
are imputed to him. He personalizes like him the divine attributes, and makes subordinate Deities of them;
but he never introduces them but on occasions that deserve their presence. He never makes them speak or
act but in a manner that is worthy of them. He artfully joins together *the poetry of Homer and the philosophy of Pythagoras.* He says nothing but what the pa-
gans might have said, and yet he has put into their
mouths what is most sublime in the Christian morality,
and has hereby shewn that this morality is written in
indelible characters in the heart of man, and that he
would infallibly discover them there, if he obeyed the
voice of pure and simple reason, in order to give himself wholly up to that sovereign and universal truth,
which enlightens all spirits, as the sun enlightens all
bodies, and without which the reason of every particular man is nothing but darkness and error.

The ideas our poet gives us of the Deity are not
only worthy of him, but infinitely amiable with regard to man. Every thing inspires confidence and
love; a gentle piety, a noble and free adoration, due
to the absolute perfection of the infinite Being; and
not a superstitious, gloomy, slavish worship, which
oppresses and dejects the heart, when God is considered only as a powerful legislator, who punishes with
rigour the violation of his laws.

He

He represents God as a lover of men; His ideas of
but his love and goodness towards us are the deity.
not directed by the blind decrees of a fatal destiny,
nor merited by the pompous show of an exterior worship, nor subject to the whimsical caprices of the pa-
gan Deities, but always regulated by the immutable
law of wisdom, which cannot but love virtue, and
treat men, not according to the number of the animals which they slay, but of the passions which they
sacrifice.

We may more easily vindicate the cha- Of the
racters which Homer gives to his heroes manners of
than those which he gives to his Gods. It Homer's
is certain that he paints men with simpli- heroes.
city, strength, variety and passion.   Our ignorance of
the customs of a country, of the ceremonies of its religion, of the genius of its language; the fault, whereof
most men are guilty, of judging of every thing by
the taste of their age and nation; the love of pomp
and false magnificence, which has corrupted pure and
primitive nature; all these things may mislead us, and
give us an unreasonable disgust of things that were
most esteemed in ancient Greece.

There are, according to Aristotle,
two sorts of Epopœas, one *pathetic*, the Of the two
other *moral*; one, where the great pas- sorts of
sions reign; the other, where the great epic poems,
virtues triumph.   The Iliad and Odys- the pathetic
sey afford examples of both these kinds. and the
In the former, Achilles is represented moral.
naturally with all his faults; sometimes so transported, as to preserve no dignity in his anger;
sometimes so furious, as to sacrifice his country to his
resentment.   Tho' the hero of the Odyssey be more
regular than the young, hot, and impetuous Achilles;
yet the wise Ulysses is often false and deceitful: And
the reason is, because the poet paints men with simplicity, and such as they generally are.   Valour is
often

often united to a furious and brutal violence. Policy is almost always joined with lying and diffimulation. To paint after nature, is to paint like Homer.

Without pretending to criticife on the different views of the Iliad and Odyf-fey, thefe remarks by the way on their different beauties, are fufficient to make us admire the art with which our author unites in his poem thefe two forts of Epopœas, the *pathetic* and the *moral.* There is an admirable mixture and contraft of virtues and paffions in this wonderful picture. It shows nothing too great, but equally reprefents to us the excellence and meannefs of man. It is dangerous to shew us one without the other, and nothing is more ufeful than to let us fee them both together; for perfect juftice and virtue require that we should efteem and defpife, that we should love and hate ourfelves. Our poet does not raife Telemachus above humanity: he makes him fall into the weaknefses which are compatible with a fincere love of virtue : and his weaknefses ferve to reclaim him, by infpiring him with a diffidence of himfelf, and his own ftrength. He does not make the imitation of him impoffible, by giving him a fpotlefs perfection; but he excites our emulation, by fetting before our eyes the example of a young man, who, with the fame imperfections which every one feels in himfelf, performs the moft noble and the moft virtuous actions. He has joined together, in the character of his hero, the courage of Achilles, the wifdom of Ulyffes, and the tender difpofition of Æneas. Telemachus is wrathful like the firft, without being brutal ; politic like the fecond , without being deceitful ; and tender-hearted like the third, without being voluptuous.

I own that there is a great variety in Homer's characters. The courage of Achilles and that of Hector, the valour of Diomede and that of Ajax, the wifdom of Neftor and that of Ulyffes, the love of Helen and that of Brifeïs, the fidelity of Andromache and that

of

Thefe two forts in Telemachus.

of Penelope, are by no means alike. There is wonderful judgment and nicety in the characters of the
Greek poet. But what is there of this kind which
we do not find in the poem of Telemachus, in the so
varied and always so well supported characters of
Sefoftris and Pygmalion, of Idomeneus and Adaftrus,
of Protefilaus and Philocles, of Calypfo and Antiope,
of Telemachus and Bocchoris? I even dare to affirm
that there is in this inftructive poem not only a variety
in the colouring of the fame virtues and paffions, but
fo great a diverfity alfo of oppofite characters, that we
find in this work the entire anatomy of the human
mind and heart : for the author know *man* and *men*.
He had ftudied one within himfelf, and the other
amidft a flourifhing court. He divided his life between folitude and fociety : he lived continually attentive to the truth which inftructs us within, and
never went out of himfelf but to ftudy characters, in
order to cure the paffions of fome, and to perfect the
virtues of others. He knew how to fuit himfelf to
all men in order to found them, and to affume all
forts of forms without ever departing from his real
character.

Another way of inftructing is by precepts. The author of Telemachus joins
the moft important inftructions with heroic examples, the morality of Homer
with the manners of Virgil. His morality however
has three qualifications, which are not found in the
fame degree in any of the ancients, whether poets or
philofophers : It is *fublime* in its principles, *noble* in
its motives, and *univerfal* in its ufes.

Of moral precepts and inftruc- tions.

1. Sublime in its principles. It arifes
from a profound knowledge of man. The
poet lets the reader into his own heart ; he
shews him the fecret fprings of his paffions,
the latent windings of felf-love, the difference between falfe and folid virtues.

The quali- ties of the morality of Telema- chus.

From the
knowledge

knowledge of Man, he afcends to that of God himfelf. He every where makes us fenfible, that the infinite Being inceffantly acts in us, in order to make us good and happy: that he is the immediate fource of all our knowledge, and of all our virtues: that we are not lefs indebted to him for reafon, than for life: that his fovereign truth ought to be our only light, and his fupreme will the rule of all our affections: that for want of confulting his univerfal and unchangeable wifdom, man fees nothing but feducing phantoms, and for want of hearkening to it, hears nothing but the confufed noife of his paffions: that folid virtues are fomething foreign, as it were, that is infufed into us; that they are not the effects of our own endeavours, but of a power fuperior to man, which works in us when we do not obftruct it, and of whofe working we are not always fenfible, by reafon of its delicacy. He at length shews us, that without this firft and fovereign power, which raifes man above himfelf, the moft shining virtues are only the refinements of felf-love, which confines all its views to itfelf, makes itfelf its own Deity, and becomes at the fame time the idolator and the idol. Nothing is more admirable than the picture of the philofopher, whom Telemachus fees in hell, and whofe only crime was his having been enamoured of his own virtue.

It is thus that the morality of our author tends to make us forget ourfelves, in order to refer every thing to the fupreme Being, and to make us adore him; as the end of his politics is to make us prefer the good of the public to private advantage, and to induce us to love the human Race. The fyftems of Machiavel, Hobbes, and the two more moderate authors, Puffendorf and Grotius, are well known. The two firft lay down, as the only maxims in the art of government, craft, artifice, ftratagem, defpotic power, injuftice, and irreligion. The two laft build their politics upon maxims of government, which are not even equal to thofe of Plato's Republic, or Tully's Offices.

Thefe

These two modern authors laboured indeed with a view of being useful to society, and directed almost every thing to the happiness of man considered in a civil Capacity. But the author of Telemachus is an original, in that he has joined the most perfect politics to the ideas of the most consummate virtue. The grand principle on which the whole turns is, that all the world is but one republic, of which God is the common father, and every nation as it were one great family. From this beauteous and delightful idea arise what politicians call *the Laws of nature and nations,* equitable, generous, full of humanity. Each country is no longer considered as independent on others, but the human race is an indivisible whole. We are no longer limited to the love of our own country; the heart enlarges itself, grows immense, and by an universal friendship embraces all mankind. Hence arise a love for strangers, a mutual confidence between neighbouring nations, integrity, justice, and peace between the princes of the universe as well as between the private men of every state. Our author also shews us, that the glory of royalty is to govern men, in order to render them good and happy; that the authority of the prince is never better established, than when it is founded in the love of the people; and that the true riches of a state consist in retrenching all the imaginary wants of life, and in being satisfied with necessaries, and with simple and innocent pleasures. He hereby shews that virtue not only contributes to the fitting of men for future felicity; but that it actually renders society as happy as it can be in this life.

2. The morality of Telemachus is noble in its motives. Its grand principle is, that the love of *beauty* ought to be preferred to the love of *pleasure*, as Socrates and Plato express themselves: the *honest* to the *agreeable*, according to the expression of Cicero. Lo! the source of noble sentiments, greatness of soul, and all heroic virtues. It is by these pure and elevated

The morality of Telemachus is noble in its motives.

vated

vated ideas, that he deſtroys, in a manner infinitely more affecting than by diſpute, the falſe philoſophy of thoſe *who make pleaſure the only ſpring of the human heart.* Our poet ſhews by the excellent morality which he puts in the mouth of his heroes, and the generous actions which he makes them perform, what an effect the pure love of virtue may have on a noble heart. I know that this heroic virtue paſſes among vulgar ſouls for a phantom, and that men of a lively imagination have inveighed againſt this ſublime and ſolid truth by many frivolous and deſpicable witti-ciſms: for finding nothing in themſelves that may be compared to theſe noble ſentiments, they conclude that humanity is not capable of them. They are dwarfs, that judge of the ſtrength of giants by their own. Minds that continually grovel within the bounds of ſelf-love, will never comprehend the power and extent of a virtue which raiſes a man above himſelf. Some philoſophers, who in other reſpects have made fine diſcoveries in Philoſophy, have been ſo far carried away by their prejudices, as not ſufficiently to diſtinguiſh between the love of order and the love of pleaſure, and to deny that the will may be as ſtrongly moved *by the clear view of truth,* as *by the natural taſte of pleaſure.*

A man cannot read Telemachus with attention without getting over theſe prejudices. He there ſees the generous ſentiments of a noble ſoul whoſe concep-tions are all great: of a diſintereſted heart that con-tinually forgets itſelf; of a philoſopher who does not confine his views to himſelf, nor to his own country, nor to any thing in particular, but directs every thing to the common good of mankind, and all mankind to the ſupreme Being.

3. The morality of Telemachus is uni-verſal in its uſes, extenſive, fruitful, ſuited to all times, to all nations, and all con-dition. We there learn the duties of a prince, who is at the ſame time a king, a warrior, a philoſopher and legiſlator.

The mora-lity of Tele-machus is univerſal in its uſes.

We there ſee

see the art of governing different nations; the way to
maintain peace abroad with our neighbours, and yet
always to have in our own kingdom a warlike youth
that is ready to defend it; to enrich our dominions
without falling into luxury: to find the medium between the excess of despotic power, and the disorders
of anarchy. Here are given precepts for agriculture,
trade, arts, government, the education of children.
Our author introduces into his poem not only heroic
and royal virtues, but those also which are suitable to
all sorts of condition. While he is forming the
heart of his prince, he teaches every private man his
duty.

The design of the Iliad is to represent the fatal consequences of discord among the commanders of an
army. The Odyssey shews us what prudence and
valour in a king may effect. In the Æneid the actions of a pious and valiant hero are described. But
all these particular virtues do not constitute the happiness of mankind. Telemachus goes far beyond all
these plans, by the greatness, number and extent of
his moral views; so that one may say with the philosophical critic upon Homer, * *The most useful present*
which the Muses have made to Men, is the Telemachus;
for if the happiness of mankind could arise from a poem,
it would arise from it.

Of the POETRY.

It is a fine remark of Sir William Temple, *That*
in poetry are assembled all the powers of eloquence, of
music, and of picture. But as poetry only differs from
eloquence, in that it paints with enthusiasm; we rather chuse to say that poetry borrows its harmony
from music, its passion from painting, its force and
justness from philosophy.

* L'Abbé Terrasson's Dissertation on the Iliad.

The

The ſtyle of Telemachus is polite, clear, flowing, magnificent; it has all the richneſs of Homer, without his redundancy of words. Our author is never guilty of repetitions; when he ſpeaks of the ſame things, he does not recall the ſame images. All his periods fill the ear by their numbers and cadence; there is nothing shocking, no hard words, no abſtruſe terms, nor affected turns. He never ſpeaks for the ſake of ſpeaking, nor even barely to pleaſe : all his words make us think, and all his thoughts tend to make us virtuous.

The harmony of the ſtyle of Telemachus.

The images of our poet are as perfect as his ſtyle is harmonious. To paint is not only to deſcribe things, but to repreſent the circumſtances of them in ſo lively and affecting a manner, that we may imagine we ſee them. The author of Telemachus paints the paſſions with art; he had ſtudied the heart of man, and knew all its ſprings. When we read his poem we ſee nothing but what he shows us, nor do we hear any but thoſe whom he directs to ſpeak : he warms, he moves, he tranſports; we feel all the paſſions he deſcribes.

The excellence of the painting of Telemachus.

The poets uſually make uſe of two ſorts of painting, ſimilies and deſcriptions. The ſimilies of Telemachus are juſt and noble. The author does not raiſe the mind too much above his ſubject by extravagant metaphors, nor does he perplex it by too great a crowd of images. He has imitated all that is great and beautiful in the deſcriptions of the ancients, as their battles, games, shipwrecks, ſacrifices, &c. without expatiating on trifling particulars that make the narration languish, and without debaſing the majeſty of the epic poem by the deſcription of things that are low and beneath the dignity of the work. He ſometimes deſcends to particulars; but he ſays nothing that does not merit attention, and that does not contribute towards the idea which he deſigns

Of the compariſons and deſcriptions of Telemachus.

to

to give. He follows nature in all her varieties. He knew that all discourses ought to have their inequalities, and be sometimes sublime without swelling into bombast, and sometimes plain without being low. It is a false taste always to aim at embellishment. His descriptions are magnificent but natural; simple, and yet agreeable. He does not only paint after nature, for his pictures moreover are always amiable. He joins together the truth of design, and the beauty of colouring; the fire of Homer and the dignity of Virgil. Nor is this all; the descriptions of this poem are not designed only to please: for they are all likewise instructive. If the author speaks of the pastoral life, it is to recommend an amiable simplicity of manners. If he describes games and combats, it is not solely to celebrate the funeral rites of a friend or a father; it is also to chuse a king who excels all others in strength of mind and body, and who is equally capable of bearing the fatigues of both. If he represents to us the horrors of a shipwreck, it is to inspire his hero with firmness of soul, and resignation to the Gods, in the greatest dangers. I could run through all his descriptions, and find the like beauties in them: but I shall content myself in observing, that in this new edition the sculpture of the formidable Ægis, which Minerva sent to Telemachus, is full of art, and includes this sublime moral: that the shield of the prince, and the support of the state, are good manners, sciences and agriculture: that a king armed by wisdom, always seeks for peace; and finds fruitful resources against all the evils of war, in a well disciplined and laborious people, whose minds and bodies are equally inured to labour.

Poetry derives its strength and justness from philosophy. In Telemachus, we every where see a rich, a lively, an agreeable imagination, and yet a just and a profound judgment: two qualifications which are rarely found in the same author. The soul must be in an

The philosophy of Telemachus.

almost

almost continual motion, to invent, to raise the paſſions, to imitate, and at the ſame time in a perfect tranquility, to judge as it produces, and out of a thouſand thoughts which offer themſelves to ſelect the moſt proper. The imagination muſt undergo a kind of rapture and enthuſiaſm; while the mind, at peace in its empire, checks and turns it where it pleaſes. Without this pathos which animates the whole, the diſcourſe is cold, languid, abſtracted, hiſtorical; without this judgment which regulates the whole, it has no juſtneſs nor true beauty.

The fire of Homer, eſpecially in the Iliad, is impetuous and violent like a ſtorm of flames which ſets every thing in a blaze. The fire of Virgil has more light than heat, and always shines in an uniform and equal manner. That of Telemachus warms and enlightens all at once, *The poetry of Telemachus compared with that of Homer and Virgil.* according as it is neceſſary to convince the mind, or to move the paſſions. When this flame enlightens, it makes us feel a gentle heat, which gives no uncaſineſs. Such are the diſcourſes of Mentor upon politics, and of Telemachus on the ſenſe of the laws of Minos, &c. Theſe pure ideas fill the mind with their gentle light. There the enthuſiaſm and poetic fire would be hurtful, like the too fierce rays of the ſun which dazzle the eye. When the buſineſs is no longer to reaſon, but to act: when a man has clearly ſeen the truth, and his reflections ariſe only from irreſolution, then the poet raiſes a fire and pathos which determine and bear away the enfeebled ſoul, which has not the courage to yield to the truth. The epiſode of Telemachus's amour in the iſland of Calypſo, is full of this fire.

This mixture of light and heat diſtinguiſhes our poet from Homer and Virgil. The enthuſiaſm of the former ſometimes makes him forget art, neglect order, and paſs the bounds of nature; the ſtrength and flight of his great genius bore him away in ſpite of himſelf. The pompous magnificence, the judgment
and

and conduct of Virgil sometimes degenerate into too formal a regularity and he then seems rather an historian than a poet. The latter pleases philosophical and modern poets much more than the former. Is it not because they are sensible that they can more easily imitate by *art* the great judgment of the Latin poet, than the noble fire of the Greek, which *nature* alone can bestow?

Our author must needs please all sorts of poets, as well those who are philosophers, as those who admire nothing but enthusiasm. He has united the perfections of the mind with the charms of the imagination. He proves the truth like a philosopher, and he forces us to love the truth he has proved, by the sensations he excites. All is solid, true, proper to persuade; no points of wit, no glittering thoughts, whose only design is to make the author admired. He has followed this great precept of Plato, which says, That a writer ought always to conceal himself, to keep out of sight, and make himself forgotten, in order to produce nothing but the truths he designs to inculcate, and the passions he designs to purify.

In Telemachus all is reason, all is passion. It is this which makes a poem for all nations and all ages. All foreigners are equally affected with it. The translations which have been made of it into languages less delicate than the French, do not efface its original beauties. The † learned lady who apologizes for Homer, assures us, that the Greek poet is an infinite loser by a translation; that it is not possible to transfuse into it the strength, dignity, and soul of his poetry. But one may venture to affirm that Telemachus will always preserve, in all languages, its strength, dignity, soul, and essential beauties. And the reason is because the excellence of this poem does not consist in the happy and harmonious arrangement of words, nor even in the charms which it borrows from the imagination; but in a sublime taste of the

† Madam DACIER.

truth,

truth, in noble and elevated sentiments, and in the natural, delicate and judicious manner of treating them. Such beauties are of all languages, of all times, of all countries, and equally strike good wits and great souls throughout the world.

Several objections have been made against Telemachus: 1. That it is not in verse. First objection against Telemachus

Versification, according to Aristotle, Dionysius of Halicarnassus, and Strabo, is not essential to the Epopœa. It may be written in prose, as some tragedies are written without rhyme. A man may make verses without poetry, and be very poetical without making verses according to the rules of art: but he must be born a poet. What constitutes poetry, is not the fixed number and regular cadence of the syllables; but the sentiment which animates the whole, the lively fiction, the bold figures, the beauty and variety of the images. It is the enthusiasm, the fire, the impetuosity, the energy, and I know not what, in the words and thoughts, which nature alone can give. All these qualifications are found in Telemachus. The author has therefore performed what Strabo says of Cadmus, Pherecides and Hecateus: *He has perfectly imitated poetry; he has indeed broken the measure of it, but he has preserved all the other poetical beauties.* **Answer.**

> Lo! Homer lives and sings again
> In Cambray's more instructive strain,
>   Which glowing virtue warms.
> Nor clogg'd with jingling chains the Nine
> The soaring bard, that truth might shine
>   In all her native charms *.

And indeed I know not whether the constraint of rhyme and the scrupulous regularity of our European construction, together with the fixed and measured number of feet, would not very much lower the flight

* *Ode to the Gentlemen of the Academy, by Mr. de la Motte,* First Ode.

and

and pathos of heroic poesy. To move the passions
strongly, we must often neglect order and connection.
It was for this reason that the Greeks and Romans,
who painted every thing with life and taste, used to
invert their phrases; their words had no certain place;
they ranged them as they pleased. The languages of
Europe are a composition of Latin, and of the jar-
gon of all the barbarous nations which subverted the
Roman empire. These northern people froze every
thing, like their climate, by a cold regularity of syn-
tax. They knew nothing of the beautiful variety of
long and short syllables, which so well imitates the
delicate motions of the soul; they pronounced every
thing with the same coldness, and knew at first no
other harmony in their words than a vain jingling of
final syllables of the same sound. Some Italians and
Spaniards have endeavoured to free their verse from
the constraint of rhyme. An English poet * has done
it with wonderful success, and has even happily begun
to introduce inversions of phrases into his language.
Perhaps the French in time may resume this noble
freedom of the Greeks and Romans.

Some, through a gross ignorance of the
noble liberty of the epic poem, have reproached Telemachus with being full of
anachronisms.

Second objection against Telemachus.

The author of this poem has only imitated the prince of the Latin poets, who

A N S W E R.

could not but know that Dido was not contemporary
with Æneas †. The Pygmalion of Telemachus the
brother of this Dido, Sesostris, who is said to have
lived about the same time, &c. are no more faults
than the anachronism of Virgil. Why should we
censure a poet for sometimes breaking through the order of time, since it is sometimes a beauty to break
through the order of nature? It would not indeed be
allowable to contradict an historical fact that happened

* Milton, and many others since.
† According to the chronology of the famous Sir ISAAC NEW-
TON, they were contemporary.

not long since; but in remote antiquity, whose annals
are so uncertain, and involved in so much obscurity, a
poet may adapt ancient traditions to his subject. This
is Aristotle's opinion, and Horace confirms it. Some
historians have written, that Dido was chaste, and
Penelope a strumpet; that Helen never saw Troy, nor
Æneas Italy : And yet Homer and Virgil made no
scruple to depart from history, to make their fables
more instructive. Why shall not the Author of Telemachus be allowed for the instruction of a young
prince, to bring the heroes of antiquity together,
Telemachus, Sesostris, Nestor, Idomeneus, Pygmalion, Adrastus, in order to unite in the same picture
the different characters of good and bad princes, whose
virtues were to be imitated and vices avoided ?

Some censure the author of Telema-
chus for having inserted the loves of Ca-   Third ob-
lypso and Eucharis in his poem, and se-   jection a-
veral other descriptions of the same kind,   gainst Te-
which seem, they say, too full of passion.   lemachus.

The best answer to this objection, is the   ANSWER.
effect which Telemachus produced in the
heart of the young prince for whom it was written.
Persons of a lower rank have not the same need to be
cautioned against the dangers to which elevation and
authority expose those who are destined to reign. If
our poet had written for a man who was to have passed his life in obscurity, these descriptions would have
been less necessary. But for a young prince, in the
midst of a court where gallantry passes for politeness,
where every object infallibly awakens a taste of pleasure, and where all that surrounds him is employed to
seduce him ; for such a prince, I say, nothing was
more necessary than to represent to him with that
amiable modesty, that innocence and wisdom which
are found in Telemachus, all the seducing wiles
of an extravagant passion ; than to paint this vice in
its imaginary beauty, in order afterwards to make him
sensible of its real deformity; and to shew him the

utmost

utmoſt depth of the abyſs, to prevent his falling into
it, and even to remove him far from the brink of ſo
dreadful a precipice. It was therefore wiſe and worthy of our author, to caution his pupil againſt the
extravagant paſſions of youth, by the fable of Calypſo;
and to give him, in the hiſtory of Antiope, an example of a chaſte and lawful love. By thus repreſenting this paſſion to us, ſometimes as a weakneſs
unworthy of a great ſoul, ſometimes as a virtue worthy of a hero, he ſhews us that love is not beneath the
majeſty of the Epopœa, and thereby unites in his
poem the tender paſſions of modern romances, and
the heroic virtues of the ancient poetry.

Some think that the author of Telema-
chus too much exhauſts his ſubject, by the   Fourth ob-
fertility and richneſs of his genius. He   jection a-
ſays every thing, and leaves nothing to   gainſt Te-
the thoughts of others. Like Homer, he   lemachus.
ſets all nature before our eyes. We are better pleaſed
with an author who, like Horace, includes a great
deal in a few words, and gives us the pleaſure of un-
folding the extent of them.

It is true that the imagination can add   Answer.
nothing to the pictures of our poet; but
the mind by purſuing his ideas opens and extends itſelf. When his buſineſs is to paint, his pictures are
perfect, and want nothing; when it is to inſtruct, his
inſtructions are fruitful, and we diſcover in them a
vaſt extent of thoughts. He leaves nothing to the
imagination, but he furniſhes infinite matter for thinking. This was ſuitable to the character of the prince
for whom alone the work was written. He diſcovered
in his infancy a happy and fruitful imagination, an
elevated and extenſive genius, which made him reliſh
the beautiful parts of Homer and Virgil. It was this
which ſuggeſted to our author the deſign of a poem,
which might equally contain the beauties of both thoſe
poets. This plenty of beautiful images was neceſſary
to employ the imagination, and form the taſte of the
prince. It is evident that theſe graces might have
been

been as eafily fuppreffed as produced, and that they arife as much from defign as fecundity, in order to anfwer the wants of the prince and the views of the author.

It has been objected, that the hero and fable of this poem have no relation to the French nation; whereas Homer and Virgil have interefted the Greeks and Romans, by making choice of actions and actors from the hiftories of their countries.

Fifth objec-
tion againft
Telema-
chus.

If the author has not interefted the French in particular, he has done more; he has interefted all mankind. His plan is more extenfive than that of either of the two old poets. It is greater to inftruct all mankind at once, than to confine one's precepts to a particular country. Self-love bids us direct every thing to it, and is difcovered even in the love of our country; but a generous foul ought to have more extenfive views.

Answer.

Befides was not France greatly interefted in a work, which had formed for her a prince the moft proper one day to govern her according to her wants and defires, like a father of his people and a Chriftian hero? What was feen of this prince gave hopes, and was the firft fruits of what was to follow; the neighbours of France were already interefted in it as in an univerfal bleffing, and the fable of the *Greek*, became the hiftory of the *French* prince.

The author had a greater defign than that of pleafing his own country; he defigned to ferve it, without its knowledge, by helping to form for it a prince, who even in the fports of his infancy feemed born to crown it with happinefs and glory. This auguft child loved fables and mythology; it was neceffary to take an advantage of his tafte, and to fhew him in what he was fond of, the folid and the beautiful, the fimple and the great, and to imprint upon his mind by affecting actions, generous principles, which might caution him againft the dangers of the higheft birth and

　　　　　　　　fupreme

supreme power. With this view, a Greek hero, and a poem in imitation of Homer and Virgil, the histories of foreign countries, times and actions, were extremely proper, and perhaps the only means of setting the author at full liberty to paint, with truth and force, all the rocks which threaten princes in all ages.

It happens by a natural and necessary consequence, that these universal truths may sometimes seem to relate to the histories of the present time, and the actual state of things; but these are only general relations, which have no particular applications; it was necessary that the fictions which were designed to form the infancy of the young prince, should comprehend precepts for all the moments of his life.

This suitableness of general maxims of morality to all sorts of circumstances, raises our admiration of the fertility, depth and wisdom of the author; but it does not excuse the injustice of his enemies, who have endeavoured to find in his Telemachus certain odious allegories, and to pervert the wisest and most sober designs into the most outrageous satires against all he most respected. They have inverted the characters, to find imaginary relations, and to poison the purest intentions. Should the author have suppressed these fundamental maxims of such sound and seasonable morality and politics, because the most discreet manner of saying them, could not shelter them from the misconstructions of those who delight in the basest malice?

Our illustrious author has therefore united in his poem the greatest beauties of the ancients. He has all the enthusiasm and profusion of Homer, and all the magnificence and regularity of Virgil. Like the Greek poet, he paints every thing with strength, simplicity and life, and has variety in his fable and diversity in his characters; his reflections are moral, his descriptions lively, his imagination fruitful, and every where that beautiful fire which nature alone can bestow. Like the Latin poet, he perfectly observes the unity of action, the uniformity of character, the order

order and rules of art. His judgment is profound and his thoughts elevated, while he at the same time unites the natural to the noble, and the simple to the sublime. Art every where becomes nature. But the hero of our poet is more perfect than those of Homer and Virgil, his morality more pure, and his sentiments more noble. From all this let us conclude, that the author of Telemachus has shewn by this poem, that the French nation is capable of all the delicacy of the Greeks, and of all the great sentiments of the Romans. The elogium of the author is that of his country.

End of Mr. Ramsay's Discourse.

THE

ADVENTURES

OF

TELEMACHUS,

SON of ULYSSES.

BOOK the FIRST.

The ARGUMENT.

Telemachus guided by Minerva, in the shape of Mentor, gets on shore after a shipwreck in the island of the Goddess Calypso, who was still bewailing the departure of Ulysses. The Goddess gives him a kind reception, conceives a passion for him, offers him immortality, and desires of him an account of his adventures. He relates to her his voyage to Pylos and Lacedæmon; his shipwreck on the coast of Sicily; the danger he was in of being sacrificed to the manes of Anchises; the assistance which Mentor and he gave Acestes in an incursion of Barbarians, and the care which this King took to requite their service, by giving them a Tyrian ship to return to their own country.

CALYPSO could not be comforted for the departure of Ulysses: in her grief she found herself unhappy by being immortal. Her grotto no longer echoed with the sweet music of her voice: the nymphs who attended her dared not speak to her. She often walked alone on the flowery turf,

with

with which an eternal fpring furrounded her ifland :. but thefe beautiful fcenes, far from alleviating her forrow, did but recall to her the fad remembrance of Ulyffes, whom she there had feen fo many times with her.   She often ftood motionlefs on the fea-shore, which she watered with her tears, and was continually turned towards the part where the ship of Ulyffes, ploughing the waves, had difappeared from her eyes.   On a fudden she perceived the fragments of a veffel that had juft been wrecked, rowers benches broken in pieces, oars. fcattered here and there on the fand, a rudder, a maft and cordage floating on the shore.   Then she defcried two men at a diftance; one of them feemed in years, the other, though young, refembled Ulyffes. . . He had his fweet and noble afpect, with his ftature and majeftic port.   The Goddefs knew him to be Telemachus, the fon of that hero : but though the Gods far furpafs all men in knowledge, she could not difcover who the venerable perfon was by whom Telemachus was attended; becaufe the fuperior Gods conceal from the inferior whatever they pleafe; and Minerva, who accompanied Telemachus in the shape of Mentor, would not be known by Calypfo.   Mean time Calypfo rejoiced at a wreck which brought the fon of Ulyffes, fo like his father, into her ifland.   She advances towards him and without feeming to know who he is, What infpires you, fays she to him, with the prefumption to land in my ifland? Know, young ftranger, that none enters my empire unpunished.   She endeavoured to hide under thefe threatening words the joy of her heart, which in fpite of her appeared in her face.

Telemachus anfwered, O ! whoever you are, whether a mortal or a Goddefs (though none can fee and not take you for a deity) can you be infenfible to the misfortunes of a fon, who, feeking his father through perils of winds and waves, has feen his veffel fplit againft your rocks? Who then is the father you are in queft of, replied the Goddefs ?. He

is.

is called Ulysses, said Telemachus; he is one of
the kings, who have, after a ten years siege, subverted the famous Troy.   His name was renowned
through all Greece and Asia for his valour in combat, and yet more so for his wisdom in council. Now
wandering o'er the whole extent of seas, he runs
through all the most terrible dangers. His country
seems to fly before him. Penelope his wife, and I
his son, have lost all hopes of ever seeing him again.
I am running the same hazards as he, to learn where
he is.   But, what do I say! perhaps he is now buried
in the profound abysses of the sea.   Pity our woes;
and, O Goddess! if you know what the destinies
have done either to save or destroy Ulysses, deign to
inform his son Telemachus of it.

Calypso, surprized and moved at finding so much
wisdom and eloquence in such blooming youth,
could not satisfy her eyes with looking upon him,
and remained silent.   At length she said to him, We
will inform you, Telemachus, what has befallen
your father; but the history of it is long, and it is
time for you to refresh yourself after your toils.
Come into the place of my abode, where I will receive you as my son; come, you shall be my comfort in this solitude; and I will procure you happiness, if you know how to enjoy it.

Telemachus followed the Goddess, incircled by a
crowd of young nymphs, above whom she raised
her whole head, as a large oak in a forest raises its
thick branches above all the surrounding trees.   He
admired the lustre of her beauty, the rich purple of
her long flowing robe, her hair tied with graceful negligence behind, the fire which flashed from her eyes,
and the mildness which tempered its vivacity.   Mentor, with downcast eyes and a modest silence, followed
Telemachus.

They came to the entrance of Calypso's grotto,
where Telemachus was surprized to see, with an appearance of a rural simplicity, all that can charm the
eye.   There was seen indeed neither gold, nor silver,

por marble, nor columns, nor pictures, nor statues:
the grotto was hewn out of the rock, in arches lined
with shells and pebbles; its tapestry was a young vine
which extended its pliant branches equally on all
sides. Gentle Zephirs here maintained, in spite of
the beams of the Sun, a delightful coolness. Fountains, sweetly purling through meadows sown with
amaranths and violets, formed, in various places,
baths as pure and clear as chrystal. A thousand
springing flowers enamelled the verdant carpets which
surrounded the grotto. There was found a whole
wood of wose tufted trees which bear apples of gold,
and whose blossoms, which are renewed in all seasons, shed the sweetest of all perfumes. This wood
seemed to crown those beautiful meads, and formed
a shade which the rays of the Sun could not penetrate. Here nothing was ever heard but the warbling
of birds, or the murmurs of a brook, which, rushing from the top of a rock, fell in large and frothy
streams, and fled across the meadow.

The Goddess's grotto was on the declivity of a
hill, from whence one beheld the sea, sometimes
clear and smooth as glass, sometimes idly irritated
against the rocks on which it broke, bellowing and
swelling its waves like mountains. From another
side was seen a river, in which were islands bordered with blooming limes, and lofty poplars, which
raised their haughty heads even to the clouds. The
several channels, which formed those islands, seemed sporting in the plain. Some rolled their limpid
waters with rapidity; some had a peaceful and sleepy
stream; others by long windings ran back again, to
re-ascend as it were to their source, and seemed not
to have power to leave these enchanting borders.
At a distance were seen hills and mountains, which
lost themselves in the clouds, and formed, by their
fantastic figures, as delightful an horizon as the eye
could wish to behold. The neighbouring mountains
were covered with verdant vine branches, hanging

in

in feſtoons; the grapes, brighter than purple, could
not conceal themſelves under the leaves, and the
vine was over-loaded with its fruit.   The fig, the
olive, the pomgranate, and all other trees, overſpread the plain, and made it a large garden.

Calypſo, having shewn Telemachus all theſe natural beauties, ſaid to him, Repoſe yourſelf, your
garments are wet, it is time for you to change them:
afterwards I will ſee you again, and relate things
with which your heart will be touched.   The Goddeſs then cauſed him and Mentor to enter into the
moſt ſecret and retired part of a grotto, next to that
in which she herſelf reſided.   In this appartment the
nymphs had taken care to light a great fire of cedar-
wood, whoſe fragrant odor diffuſed itſelf on all ſides,
and had left veſtments in it for their new gueſts.
Telemachus, ſeeing they had allotted him a tunic of
fine wool, whoſe whiteneſs eclipſed that of ſnow,
and a purple robe embroidered with gold, took the
pleaſure which is natural to youth, in viewing their
magnificence.

Mentor ſaid to him in a grave tone, Are theſe,
Telemachus, the thoughts which ought to poſſeſs
the heart of the ſon of Ulyſſes? Think rather of
ſupporting your father's reputation, and of conquering the fortune which perſecutes you.   A young man
who loves to deck himſelf vainly like a woman, is
unworthy of wiſdom and glory: glory is due only
to a ſoul which knows to bear pain, and trample
pleaſures under foot.

Telemachus anſwered, ſighing, May the Gods deſtroy me rather than ſuffer luxury and voluptuouf-
neſs to take poſſeſſion of my heart: no, no, the ſon
of Ulyſſes shall never be vanquished by the charms
of a ſoft and an effeminate life.   But how gracious
is heaven in directing us after our shipwreck to this
Goddeſs, or this mortal, who loads us with benefits!

Fear,

Fear, replied Mentor, left she load you with evils :
fear the fweet, deceitful words more than the rocks
which dashed your veffel in pieces. Shipwreck and
death are lefs fatal than pleafures which attack virtue. Take heed not to credit what she will relate
to you. Youth is prefumptuous ; it hopes every
thing from itfelf; though frail, it thinks itfelf all-
fufficient, and that it has never any thing to fear ;
it is credulous and unwary. Be fure not to regard
Calypfo's fweet and flattering words, which will in-
finuate themfelves like a ferpent under flowers. Suf-
pect their hidden poifon, miftruft yourfelf, and always
wait for my advice.

After this, they returned to Calypfo, who was
waiting for them. The nymphs with braided hair
and white veftments immediately ferved up a plain
repaft, but exquifite with regard to its tafte and ele-
gance. There was no flesh but that of birds which
they had taken in their nets, or of beafts which they
had killed with their arrows in the chace. Wine,
more delicious than nectar, flowed from large filver
vafes into golden cups crowned with flowers. There
were brought in baskets all the fruits which the
fpring promifes, and autumn lavishes on the earth.
At the fame time four young nymphs began to fing.
They firft fung the war of the Gods againft the
giants; then the loves of Jupiter and Semele ; the
birth of Bacchus, and his education under old Si-
lenus; the race of Atalanta and Hippomenes, who
was conqueror by means of the golden apples gathered in the gardens of the Hefperides : at laft the
Trojan war was likewife fung, and the combats and
wifdom of Ulyffes extolled to the skies. The chief
of the nymphs, whofe name was Leucothoë, joined
the harmony of her lyre to the fweet voices of all
the others. When Telemachus heard the name of
his father, the tears which ran down his cheeks gave
a new luftre to his beauty. But as Calypfo perceiv-

ed

ed that he could not eat, and that he vas seized with grief, she made a sign to the nymphs; upon which they sung the battle of the Centaurs with the Lapithæ, and descent of Orpheus to hell to fetch his dear Eurydice from thence.

When the repast was ended, the Goddess took Telemachus aside, and bespoke him thus: You see, son of the great Ulysses, with what favour I receive you; I am immortal; no man can enter this Island without being punished for his temerity; and even your shipwreck could not save you from my indignation, if I did not moreover love you. Your father had the same good fortune as you; but alas! he was not wise enough to turn it to his advantage. I detained him a long while in this Island; he might here have lived with me in a state of immortality; but the blind passion of returning to his wretched country, made him reject all these advantages. You see all he has lost for Ithaca, which he will never see again. He was resolved to leave me; he departed, and I was revenged by the tempest: his vessel, having long been the sport of the winds, was buried in the waves. Make a right use of so sad an example. After his shipwreck you can have no hopes of either seeing him again, or of ever reigning in the Island of Ithaca after him; be not afflicted at his loss, since you find a Goddess ready to make you happy, and a kingdom which she offers you. To these words Calypso added a long discourse, to shew how happy Ulysses had been with her. She recited his adventures in the cave of Polyphemus the Cyclop, and in the country of Antiphates king of the Lestrigons. She forgot not what happened to him in the Island of Circe the daughter of the Sun, and the dangers he was in between Scilla and Charybdis. She described the last storm which Neptune had raised against him when he departed from her; and designing to make Telemachus think that he perished in this tempest, she suppressed his arrival in the islands of the Phæacians.

Telemachus,

Telemachus, who had at firſt too haſtily abandoned himſelf to joy at being ſo well treated by Calypſo, at length perceived her artifice, and the wiſdom of the counſels which Mentor had juſt given him. He replied in a few words, O Goddeſs, excuſe my ſorrow. I cannot at preſent but grieve. Perhaps hereafter I may be more able to reliſh the happineſs you offer me. Permit me now to weep for my father. You know better than I how much he deſerves to be lamented.

Calypſo, not daring to urge him further at firſt, pretended even to ſympathiſe with him in his grief, and to pity Ulyſſes. But the better to know the means of winning the heart of the youth, ſhe asked him how he was wrecked, and by what accidents he was on her coaſt. The relation of my misfortunes, ſaid he, would be too tedious. No, no, replied ſhe, I long to know them; make haſte to relate them to me. She preſſed him a long while: at length, not being able to deny her, he began thus:

I left Ithaca in order to go and enquire of the other kings returned from the ſiege of Troy news of my father. My mother Penelope's ſuitors were ſurpriſed at my departure; for knowing their treachery, I had taken care to conceal it from them. Neſtor, whom I ſaw at Pylos, nor Menelaus, who received me in a friendly manner at Lacedæmon, could inform me whether my father was ſtill alive. Weary of living continually in ſuſpenſe and uncertainty, I reſolved to go into Sicily, where I had heard that my father had been driven by the winds. But the ſage Mentor, whom you ſee here preſent, oppoſed this rash deſign; repreſenting to me the Cyclops, monſtrous giants who devour men, on the one ſide; on the other, the fleet of Æneas and the Trojans who were on thoſe coaſts. The Trojans, ſaid he, are exaſperated againſt all the Greeks, and would take a ſingular pleaſure in ſhedding the blood
of

of the fon of Ulyffes. Return, continued he, to
Ithaca; perhaps your father, beloved of the Gods,
will be there as foon as you; but if the Gods have
decreed his deftruction, if he muft never fee his country again, you should at leaft go to revenge him, to
fet your mother at liberty, to manifeft your wifdom
to the world, and to let all Greece fee in you a king
as worthy of reigning as ever Ulyffes himfelf was.
Thefe were falutary words; but I was not wife
enough to liften to them; I liftened only to my paffions. The fage Mentor loved me fo well as to attend me in this rash voyage, which I undertook contrary to his counfel; and the Gods permitted me to
commit a fault, which was to cure me of my prefumption.

Whilft Telemachus was fpeaking, Calypfo gazed
at Mentor. She was aftonished; and fancied she
perceived in him fomething divine; but she could
not clear up the confufion of her thoughts. She remained therefore full of fear and fufpicion at the
fight of this ftranger. And being apprehenfive that
she should difcover her diforder, Go on, faid she to
Telemachus, and fatisfy my curiofity. Telemachus
thus refumed his ftory:

We had for a long time a favourable wind for failing to Sicily; but at laft a black tempeft ravished the
heavens from our eyes, and we were involved in a
profound night. By the flashes of lightning we difcovered other ships expofed to the fame danger, and
prefently knew that they were Æneas's fleet; no
lefs formidable to us than the rocks themfelves.
Then I perceived, but too late, what the heat of
my imprudent youth had hindered me from confidering with attention. Mentor appeared in this
danger not only firm and intrepid, but more gay
than ufual. It was he who encouraged me, and I
was fenfible that he infpired me with an invincible
fortitude. He gave out all orders with tranquillity, while the pilot was at a lofs what to do. Dear
                                        Mentor;

Mentor, said I, why did I refuse to yield to your counsel? How wretched am I in following my own, at an age when one has no foresight of the future, no experience of the past, nor wisdom to govern the present! O! should we ever escape this tempest, I will mistrust myself as my most dangerous Enemy; you, Mentor, shall always rule me.

Mentor replied with a smile, I am far from reproaching you with the fault you have committed; it suffices that you are sensible of it, and that it will teach you another time to cub your desires. But when the danger is over, your presomption perhaps will return. We must however at present support ourselves by our courage. Before we run into danger, we should foresee and apprehend it; but when one is in it, we have nothing to do but to despise it. Be therefore the worthy son of Ulysses, and manifest a courage superior to all the dangers which threaten you.

The good-nature and courage of Mentor charmed me; but I was still much more surprised, when I saw with what dexterity he delivered us from the Trojans. The moment the heavens began to clear up, and the Trojans seeing us near could not but have known us, he observed one of their ships, which nearly resembled ours, and had been separated by the storm, whose stern was crowned with certain flowers. He immediately placed garlands of the like flowers upon our stern; he tied them himself with ribbands of the same colour as those of the Trojans, and ordered all our rowers to stoop as close as possible to their benches, that they might not be known by the enemy In this condition we passed through the midst of their fleet, while they shouted for joy at seeing us, as though they had seen their companions whom they thought they had lost: nay, we were constrained, by the violence of the Sea, to sail a good while along with them. At last we staid a little behind; and whilst the impetuous

petuous winds drove them towards Africa, we made
our utmoft efforts to land by dint of rowing on the
neighbouring coaft of Sicily.

We indeed arrived there, but what we fought
vas no lefs fatal than the fleet which occafioned
our flight. We found on this coaft of Sicily other
Trojans, and confequently enemies of the Greeks.
Here reigned old Aceftes, who fprung from Troy.
We had hardly reached the shore, but the Inhabitants, fuppofing us either other people of the
Ifland who had taken arms to furprife them, or
foreigners who came to feize their lands, burnt our
veffel in the firft tranfport of their rage, and murdered all our companions; referving only Mentor
and myfelf to prefent us to Aceftes, that he might
learn from us what were our defigns, and from
whence we came. We entered the city with our
hands tied behind our backs, and our death was
deferred only that we might ferve for a fight to a
cruel people, when they should know that we were
Greeks.

We were immediately prefented to Aceftes, who
holding his golden fceptre in his hand, was admi-
niftering juftice among the people, and preparing
for a grand facrifice. He asked us, in a ftern
voice, of what country we were, and the occafion
of our voyage. Mentor immediately replied, and
faid to him, We come from the coaft of great
Hefperia, and our country is not far from thence.
Thus he avoided faying that we were Greeks. But
Aceftes, without hearing any thing more, and taking
us for foreigners who concealed our defign, ordered
us to be fent into a neighbouring foreft, to ferve as
flaves under thofe who tended his flocks. This condition appearing to me more intolerable than death,
O king, cried I, put us to death rather than treat
us thus unworthily. Know that I am Telemachus,
the fon of the fage Ulyffes, king of the Ithacans;
I am feeking my father in every fea : if I can
neither find him, nor return to my native country,

try, nor avoid flavery, take from me a life which I cannot fupport.

I had hardly uttered thefe words, when all the enraged people cried out, that they ought to put to death the fon of the cruel Ulyffes, whofe artifices had overthrown the city of Troy. O fon of Ulyffes, faid Aceftes to me, I cannot refufe your blood to the manes of the many Trojans, whom your father has fent to the banks of black Cocytus ; you, and he who conducts you, shall die. At the fame time an old man of the company advifed the king to facrifice us on the tomb of Anchifes. Their blood, faid he, will be grateful to the shade of that hero ; Æneas himfelf, when he shall hear of fuch a facrifice, will rejoice to fee how much you love what of all things in the world was the deareft to him. All the people applauded this propofition, and thought of nothing but of facrificing us. They were already leading us to the tomb of Anchifes ; they had there erected two altars, on which the holy fire was kindled ; the knife which was to flay us was before our eyes ; we were crowned with flowers ; no pity could fave our lives ; our fate was determined, when Mentor, calmly defiring leave to fpeak to the king, faid to him :

O Aceftes, if the misfortunes of the youthful Telemachus, who never bore arms againft the Trojans, cannot move you ; at leaft let your own intereft move you. The knowledge I have obtained of prefages and the will of the Gods, inform me, that before three days are elapfed, you will be attacked by barbarous nations, which are coming like a torrent from the tops of the mountains to overflow your city, and to ravage all your country. Make hafte to prevent them ; put your fubjects under arms, and delay not a moment to drive within your walls the rich flocks and herds which you have in the fields. If my prediction is falfe, you will be at liberty to facrifice us in three days ; if

on

on the contrary it is true, you will remember that you ought not to take away the life of those to whom you owe your own.

Acestes was astonished at these words, which Mentor pronounced with a confidence which he had never found in any man. I plainly perceive, O stranger, replied he, that the Gods, who have allotted you so small a portion of the gifts of fortune, have given you a wisdom which is more valuable than the greatest prosperity. At the same time he put off the sacrifice, and immediately gave the orders which were necessary to prevent the attack, with which Mentor had threatened him. Nothing was seen on every side but trembling women, men bowed down with age, and little children with tears in their eyes, retiring into the city. Herds of lowing oxen and flocks of bleating sheep came in crowds, quitting their fat pastures, and unable to find stabling enough to receive them. There was in all parts a confused noise of men, who pressed upon and could not understand each other, who took in this confusion a stranger for their friend, and who run without knowing whither they were going. But the chiefs of the city, conceiting themselves wiser than the rest, imagined that Mentor was an impostor, who had made a false prediction to save his life.

Before the end of the third day, whilst they were full of these thoughts, there was seen on the descent of the neighbouring mountains a curling cloud of dust; then they perceived an innumerable host of armed barbarians. They were the Hymerians, a savage people, with the nations which inhabit the Nebrodian mountains, and the top of Agragas, where a winter reigns, which was never softened by the Zephirs. They who had despised Mentor's prediction, lost their slaves and their flocks. The king said to Mentor, I forget that you are Greeks; our enemies are become our faithful friends; the Gods have sent you to save us; I do not expect less from

your

your valour than from the wifdom of your counfels ;
make hafte to fuccour us.

Mentor difcovers in his eyes an intrepidity which
aftonishes the fierceft warriors. He takes a buckler,
a helmet, a fword and a lance ; he marshals the foldiers of Aceftes; he marches at their head, and advances in good order towards the enemy. Aceftes,
though full of courage, can by reafon of his age only
follow him at a diftance. I follow him clofer, but
cannot equal his valour. In the battle his cuirafs refembled the immortal Ægis. Death ran from rank
to rank wherever his blows defcended : fo a Numi-
dian lion, ftung with hunger, falls on a flock of feeble
sheep; he rends, he flays, he fwims in blood, and
the shepherds, inftead of fuccouring the flock, fly
trembling to efcape his fury.

The Barbarians, who hoped to furprife the city,
were themfelves furprifed and thrown into diforder.
The fubjects of Aceftes, animated by Mentor's words
and valour, felt a vigour of which they thought
themfelves incapable. With my lance I killed the
fon of the enemy's king ; he was of my age, but he
was taller than I ; for thefe people are defcended from
a race of giants of the fame origin as the Cyclops.
He defpifed fo weak an adverfary as me. But without being alarmed at his prodigious ftrength or favage
and brutal air, I thruft my lance againft his breaft,
and made him as he expired vomit forth torrents of
black blood. He had like to have crushed me in
his fall. The clattering of his arms refounded in the
mountains. I took the fpoils, and returned to find
Aceftes. Mentor, having intirely routed the enemy,
cut them in pieces, and purfued the fugitives even
into the woods.

This fo unexpected a fuccefs made Mentor looked
upon as a man beloved and infpired by the Gods.
Aceftes, touched with gratitude, told us, that he
should be in the greateft fear for us, if Æneas's fleet
                                                    should

should return to Sicily.   He gave us a ship to return
without delay to our own country, loaded us with
prefents, and preffed us to depart, in order to prevent the evils he forefaw.   But not caring to give us
either a pilot or rowers of his own nation, for fear
they should be too much expofed upon the coaft of
Greece, he provided for us fome Phœnician merchants, who, trading with all the nations of the
world, had nothing to fear, and were to bring back
the veffel to Aceftes, when they had left us in Ithaca:
But the Gods, who fport with the defigns of men,
referved us for other misfortunes.

End of the Firft Book.

THE
ADVENTURES
OF
TELEMACHUS,
SON of ULYSSES.

BOOK the SECOND.

The ARGUMENT.

Telemachus relates how he was taken in the Tyrian vessel by the fleet of Sesostris, and carried captive into Egypt. He describes the beauty of the country, and the wise government of its king. He adds, that Mentor was sent a slave into Ethiopia; that he himself was reduced to tend a flock in the desart of Oasis; that Termosiris, a priest of Apollo, comforted him, by teaching him to imitate Apollo, who had formerly been a shepherd to king Admetus; that Sesostris was at last informed of all the wonders which he did among the shepherds; that being convinced of his innocence he recalled him, and promised to send him back to Ithaca; but that the death of this king plunged him again in fresh misfortunes; that he was imprisoned in a tower on the sea-shore, from whence he saw the new king Boccoris, who perished in a battle against his own subjects, who had rebelled, and were assisted by the Tyrians.

THE Tyrians, by their pride, had irritated against them king Sesostris, who reigned in Egypt, and had conquered many kingdoms. The riches they had acquired by commerce, and the

strength

ftrength of their impregnable city of Tyre, which is fituated in the fea, having puffed up the heart of thefe people, they had refufed to pay Sefoftris the tribute he impofed upon them in his return from his conquefts, and had fent fome troops to his brother, who had attempted to affaffinate him at his return, in the midft of the rejoicings of a grand feftival.

Sefoftris had refolved, in order to humble their pride, to interrupt their commerce in every fea. His ships went to all parts in fearch of the Phœnicians. An Egyptian fleet met us, as we began to lofe fight of the mountains of Sicily. The port and the land feemed to fly from us, and to lofe themfelves in the clouds. At the fame time we faw the Egyptian ships, like a floating city, approaching. The Phœnicians knew, and endeavoured to get clear of, them: but it was too late. Their fails were better than ours; the wind favoured them; their rowers were more numerous. They board, take, and carry us prifoners into Egypt.

In vain did I reprefent to them that we were not Phœnicians; they hardly deigned to hear me. They took us for flaves in whom the Phœnicians traded, and thought only of the profit of fuch a prize. We now obferve the waves of the fea to whiten by their confluence with thofe of the Nile, and perceive the coaft of Egypt almoft as low as the fea. We afterwards arrive at the ifle of Pharos which is near to the city of No, and from thence fail up the Nile as at as Memphis.

If grief for our captivity had not rendered us infenfible to all pleafures, our eyes would have been charmed with feeing this fertile country of Egypt, like a delightful garden, watered by an infinite number of canals. We could not caft our eyes on either shore without feeing opulent cities, country houfes agreeably fituated, lands yearly covered with a golden harveft without ever lying fallow, meadows

C   full

full of flocks and herds, husbandmen bending under the weight of the fruits which the earth had poured out of her bosom, and shepherds who made all the echoes round them repeat the sweet sounds of their flutes and their pipes.

Happy the people, said Mentor, who are governed by a wise king! They abound; they live happy, and love him to whom they owe all their happiness. It is thus, added he, O Telemachus! that you ought to reign, and to cause the joy of your people, if ever the Gods put you in possession of the kingdom of your father. Love your subjects as your children, relish the pleasure of being beloved by them, and act so that they may never be sensible of peace and joy, without remembering that it is a good king who made them these rich presents. Kings who think only of making themselves feared, and of humbling their people in order to render them more submissive, are the scourges of human kind. They are feared as they desire to be; but then they are hated, detested, and have more to apprehend from their subjects than their subjects have to apprehend from them.

I answered Mentor, Alas! it is not our business to think of the maxims by which we ought to reign. There is no Ithaca for us, we shall never see our country nor Penelope again. And though even Ulysses should return, full of glory, to his kingdom, he will never have the pleasure of seeing me there: never shall I have that of obeying him, in order to learn how to command. Let us die, my dear Mentor; other thoughts are no longer allowed us: let us die, since the Gods have no pity of us.

As I spoke thus, profound sighs interrupted all my words. But Mentor, who was apprehensive of evils before they happened, no longer knew what it was to fear them when they were present. Unworthy son of wise Ulysses! cried he, what! do
you

you suffer yourself to be vanquished by your misfortunes! Know that you will one day see again the isle of Ithaca and Penelope : you shall see, even in his former glory, him whom you never knew, the invincible Ulysses ; whom fortune cannot subdue, and who, in his calamities, yet greater than yours, teaches you never to despair.   O! if he should hear, in the remote country on which the tempest has thrown him, that his son knows to imitate neither his patience nor his fortitude, the news would overwhelm him with shame, and be more grievous to him than all the evils he has so long endured.

Mentor afterwards made me take notice of the joy and plenty which overspread the whole country of Egypt, in which were reckoned two-and-twenty thousand cities.   He admired the good government of these cities ; the justice exercised in favour of the poor against the rich ; the good education of children, who were trained up to obedience, labour, sobriety, the love of arts or letters ; the exact observation of all religious ceremonies, the disinterested spirit, the thirst of honour, the fidelity towards men, and the reverence of the Gods which every father instilled into his children.   He was never weary of admiring this beautiful order.   Happy the people, was he continually saying to me, who are thus governed by a wise king! but still more happy the king who causes the felicity of such multitudes, and finds his own in his virtue! He holds men by a chain an hundred times stronger than that of fear, namely, that of love. Men not only obey, but even delight to obey him.   He reigns in all hearts ; every one, instead of wishing to get rid of him, is afraid of losing him, and would lay down his life for him.

I was attentive to what Mentor said, and perceived that my courage revived from the bottom of my heart as my wise friend was talking to me. As soon as we arrived at Memphis, a rich and magnificent city, the governor ordered that we should

go

go as far as Thebes, to be presented to king Sesostris, who was desirous of inspecting into things
himself, and was greatly exasperated against the
Tyrians. We therefore still proceeded up the Nile,
as far as the famous Thebes, which has an hundred
gates, and was the place of this great prince's re-
sidence. This city appeared to us of a prodigious
extent, and more populous than the most flourishing
cities of Greece. Its policy is perfect with regard
to the neatness of the streets, water courses, the
conveniency of baths, the culture of arts, and the
public safety. The squares are adorned with fountains and obelisks; the temples are of marble, and
of a plain but majestic architecture, The prince's
palace alone is like a great city: nothing is seen there
but marble columns, pyramids and obelisks, Colos-
sean statues, and furniture of solid gold and silver.

Those who had taken us told the king, that we
were found on board a Phœnician ship. He gave
audience every day, at certain stated hours, to all
his subjects, who had any complaints to make, or
informations to give him. He neither despised nor
repulsed any man, and thought himself a king only
to do good to his subjects, whom he loved as his
children. As for strangers, he received them with
indulgence, and was desirous of seeing them, because he thought that one always learns something
useful, by informing one's self of the customs and
maxims of distant nations. This curiosity of the
king was the occasion of our being brought before
him. He was on an ivory throne, holding a golden scepter in his hand. He was now in years,
but agreeable, full of sweetness and majesty. He
administered justice daily among his people with a
patience and wisdom which all admired without
flattery. After having toiled all the day in settling
public affairs, and in rendering impartial justice, he
refreshed himself in the evening in hearing of the
learned, or in conversing with the best of men,
whom he well knew how to select and admit into
his

his familiarity. He could not be reproached in all his life, but with having triumphed with too much oftentation over the kings he conquered, and with repofing too much confidence in one of his fubjects, whofe picture I shall prefently give you.

When he faw me, he pitied my youth; he asked me my name and my country, and we were aftonished at the wifdom which flowed from his mouth. I anfwered him, O mighty prince, you are no ftranger to the fiege of Troy which lafted ten years, and its deftruction which coft all Greece fo much blood. Ulyffes my father was one of the principal kings who deftroyed that city. He wanders through every fea without being able to find the ifle of Ithaca, his kingdom. I am in fearch of him, and a misfortune like his was the occafion of my being taken. Reftore me to my father and to my country: fo may the Gods preferve you to your children, and make them fenfible of the happinefs of living under fo good a father.

Sefoftris continued to behold me with an eye of compaffion: but defiring to know if what I faid was true, he referred us to one of his officers, who was commanded to inform himfelf of thofe who had taken our ship, whether we were really Greeks or Phœnicians. If they are Phœnicians, faid the king, they muft be doubly punished, for being our enemies, and ftill more for having endeavoured to deceive us by a bafe lye. If on the contrary they are Greeks, I would have them treated kindly, and fent back to their own country in one of my ships; for I love Greece: feveral Egyptians have been legiflators there. I am no ftranger to the virtue of Hercules; the fame of Achilles had reached even to us, and I admire what has been told me of the wifdom of the unhappy Ulyffes. It is a pleafure to me to relieve virtue in diftrefs.

The officer to whom the king committed the inquiry into our affair, had a foul as corrupted and artful, as Sefoftris was fincere and generous. This

C 3   officer

officer was called Metophis. He endeavoured to
enfnare us by his queftions, and perceiving that Mentor anfwered with more wifdom than I, he looked
upon him with averfion and jealoufy; for the bad
are provoked at the good. He feparated us, and
from that time I knew not what was become of
Mentor. This feparation was a thunder-bolt to me.
Metophis always hoped that by examining us fe-
parately, he should make us fay contrary things;
he hoped efpecially to dazzle me by flattering promifes, and to make me confefs what Mentor might
have concealed from him. In short, he did not really
feek for the truth, but endeavoured to find fome
pretence to tell the king that we were Phœnicians,
in order to make us his flaves. In fact, notwithftanding our innocence and the king's fagacity, he
found the means of deceiving him. Alas! to what
are kings expofed! Even the wifeft are frequently
abufed. Artful and felfish men furround them; the
good retire, becaufe they are neither importunate
nor flatterers: the good wait till they are fought
after, and princes do not often feek after them.
On the contrary, the wicked are impudent, treacherous, infinuating and officious, artful diffemblers,
ready to do any thing againft honour and confcience,
to gratify the paffions of him who reigns. O! how
unhappy is a king in being expofed to the artifices
of the wicked! He is ruined if he does not repulfe
flattery, and if he loves not thofe who boldly tell
him the truth. Thefe were the reflections I made
in my diftrefs; I recollected all that I had heard from
Mentor.

In the mean time Metophis fent me towards the
mountains of the defert of Oafis with his flaves,
that I might be a flave with them, and look after
his numerous flocks. Here Calypfo interrupted
Telemachus, faying, Well, what did you do then,
you who in Sicily preferred death to flavery? Telemachus replied, My misfortunes continually increafed; I had no longer the fad confolation of chufing
                                                    fervitude

fervitude or death; I was forced to be a flave, and
to exhauft, if I may ufe the expreffion, all the rigors
of fortune. I had no hope left, and I could not
fpeak even one word in order to work out my deliverance.   Mentor has fince told me that he was
fold to Ethiopians, and that he went with them into
Ethiopia.

As for me I arrived in horrible deferts : here
burning fands are feen in the midft of the plains;
fnows which never diffolve, and make an eternal
winter on the tops of the mountains; and paftures
for cattle are only found amongft the rocks. Towards the middle of thefe fteep mountains, the vallies are fo deep, that the rays of the fun can hardly
reach them.

The only perfons I found in this country, were
fhepherds as favage as the country itfelf.   There I
paffed the nights in bewailing my misfortune, and
the days in tending a flock, to avoid the brutal fury
of the chief flave; who, hoping to obtain his liberty, was continually accufing the reft, in order to
make a merit to his mafter of his zeal and attachment to his interefts.   The name of this flave was
Butis : I was ready to fink on this occafion.   Oppreft with grief, I one day forgot my flock, and
ftretched myfelf on the grafs near a cave, where I
expected death, unable longer to fupport my pains.
The fame moment I perceived that the whole mountain trembled; the oaks and pines feemed to defcend
from its fummit; the winds retained their breath,
and a hollow voice iffuing out of the cave, uttered
thefe words : " Son of fage Ulyffes, you, like him,
muft become great by patience. Princes who have
always been happy, are feldom worthy of being
fo ; luxury corrupts, and pride intoxicates them.
Happy will you be if you furmount your misfortunes, and if you never forget them. You fhall fee
Ithaca again, and your glory fhall afcend to the ftars.
When you are the mafter of others, remember that
you yourfelf have been weak, poor, and in trouble
                                                   like

like them; take a pleasure in relieving them; love your subjects, detest flattery, and know that you will be great only in proportion to your moderation and resolution in subduing your passions."

These divine words penetrated even to the bottom of my heart, and caused joy and courage to revive in it. I did not feel that horror which makes the hair rise upright on the head, and chills the blood in the veins, when the Gods reveal themselves to mortals: I rose in tranquillity; I fell on my knees, and lifting up my hands to heaven, worshipped Minerva, to whom I believed myself indebted for this oracle. At the same time I found myself a new man; wisdom enlightened my mind; I felt a pleasing power to moderate all my passions, and to check the impetuosity of my youth. I made myself beloved by all the shepherds of the desert. My meekness, my patience, my diligence, at last appeased the cruel Butis, who was in authority over the other slaves, and at first took a pleasure in tormenting me.

The better to bear the irksomeness of captivity and solitude, I sought for books; for I was overwhelmed with melancholy, for want of some instructions to cherish and support my mind. Happy they, said I, who are disgusted with violent pleasures, and know how to be contented with the sweets of an innocent life! Happy they who delight in being instructed, and who take a pleasure in cultivating their minds with knowledge! On whatever part adverse fortune may throw them, they always carry entertainment with them; and the disquiet which preys upon others, even in the midst of pleasures, is unknown to those who can employ themselves in reading. Happy they who love to read, and are not like me deprived of it. As these thoughts were revolving in my mind, I went into a gloomy forest, where I immediately perceived an old man holding a book in his hand.

The

The forehead of this old man was large, bald, and a little wrinkled: a white beard hung down to his girdle; his stature was tall and majestic, his complexion still fresh and ruddy, his eyes lively and piercing, his voice sweet, his words plain and charming. I never saw so venerable an old man. His name was Termosiris: he was a priest of Apollo, and officiated in a marble temple, which the kings of Egypt had dedicated to that God in this forest. The book which he held in his hand was a collection of hymns in honour of the Gods. He accosts me in a friendly manner, and we discourse together. He related things past so well, that they seemed present, and yet with such brevity that his accounts never tired me. He foresaw the future by his profound knowledge, which made him know men, and the designs of which they were capable. With all this wisdom he was chearful and complaisant, and the sprightliest youth has not so many graces as this man had in so advanced an age. He accordingly loved young men, when they were tractable, and had a relish for virtue.

He soon tenderly loved me; he furnished me with books for my confolation, and called me his son. I often said to him, O my father! the Gods who deprived me of Mentor, have had pity on me; they have given me another support in you. This man, like Orpheus or Linus, was, without doubt, inspired by the Gods. He recited to me the verses he had made, and gave me those of several excellents poets who were favourites of the Muses. When he was clad in his long robe of a shining white, and took his ivory lyre in his hand, the tygers, the bears, the lions, came to fawn upon him, and to lick his feet. The Satyrs came out of the woods to dance around him, the trees themselves seemed to be moved, and one would have thought the affected rocks were going to descend from the tops of the mountains at the charms of his melodious accents. He sung but the majesty of the Gods, the

C 5   virtue

virtue of heroes, and the wisdom of men who prefer glory to pleasure.

He often told me that I ought to take courage,
and that the Gods would not abandon either Ulysses
or his son.   At last he assured me that I ought, after the example of Apollo, to teach the shepherds
to cultivate the Muses.   Apollo, said he, provoked
at Jupiter's disturbing the heavens with his thunder
in the brightest days, determined to revenge himself on the Cyclops who forged the bolts, and slew
them with his arrows.   Mount Etna immediately
ceased to disgorge its storms of curling flames; no
longer were heard the strokes of the terrible hammers, which striking the anvil excited the groans
of the deep caverns of the earth, and of the abysses
of the sea.   Iron and brass being no longer polished
by the Cyclops, began to rust.   Vulcan quits his
forge in a rage, mounts though lame with speed towards Olympus, arrives sweating and covered with
dust, in the assembly of the Gods, and makes bitter
complaints.   Jupiter is provoked at Appollo, drives
him out of heaven; and hurls him headlong to
the earth.   His empty chariot performs of itself
its usual course, to give the day and night to men
with a regular change of the seasons.   Apollo, stript
of his rays, was forced to turn shepherd, and tend
the flocks of king Admetus.   He played on the
flute, and all the other swains came to shady elms
on the border of a limpid fountain, to hear his songs.
Till then they had led a savage and brutal life; they
knew but to tend, to sheer and milk their sheep, and
make cheeses: the whole country was like a frightful
desert.

Apollo quickly taught all the shepherds the arts
which can render their life agreeable.   He sung the
flowers with which the spring is crowned, the perfumes she sheds, and the verdure which rises under
her steps.   He afterwards sung the delightful nights
of summer, when the Zephirs revive mankind, and
the dew quenches the thirst of the earth.   He likewise

wife mingled in his songs the golden fruits with which autumn rewards the husbandman's toils, and the repose of winter, when the sportful youth dance before the fire. At last he reprefented the gloomy woods which cover the mountains, and the hollow vallies, where rivers by a thoufand windings feem to fport amidft the laughing meadows. Thus he taught the fwains what are the charms of a country life, when we know how to tafte the bounties of fimple nature. The shepherds with their pipes foon faw themfelves happier than kings, and their cottages attracted in crowds the uncorrupted joys which fly the gilded palace: the fports, the fmiles, the graces, every where attended the innocent shepherdeffes. Every day was a feftival. Nothing now was heard but the warbling of birds, or the foft breath of the Zephirs fporting in the branches of the trees, or the murmurs of a lucid rill falling from the rocks, or the fongs with which the mufes infpired the fwains who attended Apollo. This God taught them to obtain the prize in the race, and to pierce with arrows the hinds and the ftags. The Gods themfelves grew jealous of the shepherds, and thinking their life fweeter than all their own glory, recalled Apollo to Olympus.

This hiftory, my fon, should inftruct you: fince you are in the condition in which Apollo was, till this uncultivated earth; like him make the defert bloom; teach all thefe shepherds the charms of harmony; foften their favage hearts; shew them the beauty of virtue, and make them fenfible how fweet it is in folitude to enjoy the innocent pleafures, which nothing can take from shepherds. A day, my fon, a day will come, when the pains and cruel cares which befiege kings, will make you regret on a throne the life of a shepherd.

This faid, Termofiris gave me fo fweet a flute, that the echoes of the mountains, which made it heard on every fide, foon drew all the neighbouring fwains around me. My voice had a divine har-

C 6   mony;

mony; I was moved and rapt as it were out of myself, to sing the charms with which nature has a-
dorned the country. We passed whole days and a
part of the nights in singing together. All the shepherds, forgetting their huts and their flocks, stood
motionless around me, whilst I gave them their lessons. These deserts appeared no longer savage; all
was pleasant and smiling; the courteous manners of
the inhabitants seemed to meliorate the soil.

We often assembled to offer sacrifices in the temple
of Apollo, of which Termosiris was priest. The
shepherds went thither, crowned with laurels in
honour of the God; the shepherdesses likewise went
thither, dancing and bearing garlands of flowers and
baskets of sacred offerings on their heads. After
the sacrifice we made a rural feast. Our greatest
dainties were the milk of our goats and our sheep,
which we took care to milk ourselves, with fruits
fresh gathered with our own hands, such as dates, figs
and grapes; our seats were the verdant turf, and
the thick trees afforded us a pleasanter shade than
the gilded roofs of the palaces of kings.

But what crowned my fame among the shepherds
was, that an hungry lion one day came and fell on
my flock. He was already beginning an horrible
slaughter; I had only my crook in my hand, but I advanced boldly. The lion bristles up his mane, shews
me his teeth and his claws, and opens his parched
and flaming mouth. His eyes seemed very red and
fiery; he beats his sides with his long tail: I fell
him to the ground. The little coat of mail which
I wore according to the custom of the shepherds of
Egypt, prevented his tearing me in pieces. Thrice I
threw him down, and thrice he rose again, making
all the forest ring with his roarings. At last I strangled
him in my arms; and the shepherds, witnesses of my
victory, insisted on my wearing the skin of this terrible animal.

The

The fame of this action, and of the happy refor-
mation of all our shepherds, spread throughout Egypt,
and reached even the ears of Sesostris. He was informed that one of the captives, who had been
taken for Phœnicians, had restored the golden age in
these almost uninhabitable deserts. He desired to see
me, for he loved the muses; and every thing which
could instruct mankind charmed his noble heart.
He saw me, he heard me with pleasure, and found
that Metophis had deceived him through avarice.
He condemned him to perpetual imprisonment, and
stript him of all the riches which he unjustly possessed.
O how unhappy, said he, is the man who is exalted
above others! He cannot often see the truth with his
own eyes: he is encompassed by men who hinder it
from arriving at him; every one has an interest to
deceive him; every one, under an appearance of
zeal, hides his ambition. They pretend to love the
king, but they love only the riches he bestows; they
are so far from loving him, that to obtain his favour
they flatter and betray him.

After this Sesostris treated me with a tender friendship, and resolved to send me back to Ithaca with
ships and troops, to deliver Penelope from all her
suitors. The fleet was now ready, and we thought
only of embarking. I admired the turns of fortune,
who suddenly exalts whom she has the most deprest.
This experience made me hope that Ulysses might
probably return at length to his kingdom after long
sufferings. I thought also within myself that I might
yet see Mentor again, though he had been carried
into the most unknown countries of Ethiopia. Whilst
I delayed my departure a little, to endeavour to learn
some news of him, Sesostris, who was very old, died
suddenly, and his death plunged me again into new
misfortunes.

All Egypt seemed inconsolable for this loss. Every
family thought it had lost its best friend, its protec-
tor, its father. The old men, lifting up their hands

to heaven, cried, Never had Egypt fo good a king,
never will she have the like! O ye Gods! ye should
never have shewn him to men, or never have taken
him from them! Why muſt we furvive the great
Sefoftris? The young men faid, The hope of Egypt
is loſt; our fathers have been happy in living under
fo good a king; as for us, we have feen him only
to feel his lofs. His domeſtics wept night and
day. When the king's funeral was performed, during forty days the moſt diſtant people ran in crowds
to it. Every one defired yet once more to fee the
body of Sefoftris; every one defired to preferve an
idea of him, and feveral to be laid in the fepulchre
with him.

What ſtill increafed their forrow for his lofs was,
that his fon Bocchoris had neither humanity for
ſtrangers, nor curiofity with regard to the fciences,
nor efteem for men of virtue, nor love of glory.
His father's greatnefs had contributed to render him
thus unworthy of reigning. He had been bred up
in luxury, and a brutal pride; he looked upon men
as nothing, believing that they were made only for
him, and that he was of a nature different from
theirs. He minded only to gratify his paffions, to
fquander away the immenfe treafures which his father had husbanded with fo much care, to harrafs
the people, and to fuck the blood of the unfortunate; in a word, to follow the flattering counfels
of the giddy youths who furrounded him, whilſt he
difcarded with difdain all the wife old men who had
fhared his father's confidence: he was a monſter,
and not a king. All Egypt groaned; and though
the name of Sefoftris, fo dear to the Egyptians,
made them bear with the shameful and cruel conduct of his fon, yet the fon haſtened to his ruin:
and indeed a prince fo unworthy of a throne could
not reign long.

I was no longer allowed to hope for my return to
Ithaca; I remained in a tower on the fea-shore near
Pelufium, where our embarkation was to have been
made,

made, if Sefoftris had not died. Metophis, having
had art enough to get out of prifon, and to eftablish
himfelf in the good graces of the new king, had caufed
me to be confined in this tower, to revenge himfelf for
the difgrace I had occafioned him. I fpent the days
and the nights in a deep melancholy. All Termofiris
had foretold me, and all I had heard from the cave,
appeared to me no more than a dream. I was overwhelmed with the bittereft forrow: I viewed the billows which came and beat againft the foot of the
tower where I was a prifoner. I often employed myfelf in contemplating veffels toft by tempeft, and
in danger of fplitting on the rocks on which the
tower was built; but inftead of bewailing men threatened with shipwreck, I envied their lot. Soon, faid
I to myfelf, will they end the misfortunes of their
life, or arrive in their own country: I, alas! can
hope for neither.

Whilft I was thus pining away in fruitlefs grief,
I perceived as it were a foreft of ship-mafts. The
fea was covered with fails which were fwelled by
the winds, and the waves foamed beneath innumerable oars. I heard from all parts a confufed noife,
and perceived on the shore a party of affrighted
Egyptians running to arms, and others who feemed
going to meet the fleet which they faw arriving. I
foon perceived that thefe foreign ships were fome of
Phœnicia, and others of the ifle of Cyprus; for my
misfortunes began to render me skilful in what relates
to navigation. The Egyptians feemed to me to be
divided among themfelves. I had no difficulty in believing that the thoughtlefs Bocchoris had by his vi-
olences caufed a revolt of his fubjects, and kindled a
civil war. I was from the top of the tower a fpectator of a bloody battle.

The Egyptians, who had called in foreigners to
their affiftance, having favoured their defcent, attacked the other Egyptians who had the king at their
head. I faw this prince animating his fubjects by
his

his example, and looking like the God of war. Rivers of blood flowed around him; his chariot wheels were dyed with a black, thick and frothy gore, and could hardly pass over the heaps of mangled dead.

This young king, well made, robust, of an high and haughty mien, had fury and despair in his eyes. He was like a fine headstrong horse; his courage pushed him into dangers, but wisdom did not temper his valour. He knew neither how to retrieve his errors, nor to give proper orders, nor to foresee the evils which threatened him, nor to save his men of whom he had the greatest need: Not that he wanted a genius, for his understanding was equal to his courage; but he had never been instructed by adversity. His governors had poisoned his naturally good disposition by flattery. He was intoxicated with his power and his fortune; he thought that every thing ought to give way to his impetuous desires; the least resistance enflamed his anger; he then no longer reasoned; he was as it were beside himself; his furious pride transformed him into a wild beast; his natural gentleness and good sense forsook him in an instant; his most faithful servants were forced to fly from him, and he no longer liked any but those who soothed his passions. He was thus, contrary to his true interest, always in extremes, and forced all good men to detest his extravagant conduct. His courage supported him a long while against a multitude of enemies, but he was at last overpowered. I saw him fall: the dart of a Phœnician pierced his breast; the reins slipped out of his hands, and he fell from his chariot under his horses feet. A soldier of the island of Cyprus cut off his head; and, taking it by the hair, showed it as it were in triumph to the victorious army.

I shall all my life remember my having seen his head swimming in blood, his eyes shut and extinguished, his face pale and disfigured, his mouth half opened, and seeming still desirous of finishing
the

the fpeech it had began, his haughty and threatening air, which death itfelf could not efface.   As long as I live, his image will be before my eyes; and if ever the God's permit me to reign, I shall not forget, after fo terrible an example, that a king is not worthy of commanding, nor happy in his power, but in proportion as he fubjects it to reafon.   Alas! what a misfortune ! for a man defigned to caufe the public happinefs, to be the mafter of fuch multitudes only to render them wretched!

End of the Second Book.

THE

THE
ADVENTURES
OF
TELEMACHUS,
SON of ULYSSES.

BOOK the THIRD.

The ARGUMENT.

Telemachus relates, that the successor of Bocchoris restoring all the Tyrian prisoners, he himself was carried with them to Tyre in Narbal's ship, who commanded the Tyrian fleet; that Narbal gave him the character of their king Pygmalion, whose cruel avarice was to be feared; that he was afterwards instructed by Narbal in the Maxims of the Tyrian commerce, and was going to embark on board a Cyprian ship, in order to go by the island of Cyprus to Ithaca, when Pygmalion discovered that he was a stranger, and ordered him to be apprehended; that he was then on the brink of ruin, but that Astarba, the tyrant's mistress, saved him, in order to put to death in his stead a youth, whose disdain had provoked her.

CALYPSO heard such wise reflections with astonishment. What charmed her most was to observe, that Telemachus ingenuously related the errors he had committed through precipitation, and a want of docility with regard to the sage Mentor's counsels. She found a surprising nobleness and grandeur in the youth, who accused himself, and
who

who seemed to have made so good an use of his failings, as to render himself wise, provident and moderate. Go on, said she, my dear Telemachus, I long to know how you got out of Egypt, and where you found the sage Mentor again, of whose loss you was with so much reason sensible.

Telemachus thus resumed his story. The Egyptians the most virtuous and the most faithful to the king, being the weakest, and seeing their king dead, were constrained to yield to the others. Another king was appointed, whose name was Turmutis. The Phœnicians with the troops of the Island of Cyprus, departed after they had made an alliance with the new prince, who restored all the Phœnician prisoners. I was reckoned as one of the number; and being released from the tower and embarking with the rest, hope began to dawn again in the bottom of my heart.

A favourable gale already filled our sails; the rowers cleft the frothy waves; the wide sea was covered with ships; the mariners shouted for joy; the shores of Egypt flew far from us; the hills and the mountains grew level by degrees; we began to see nothing but the heavens and the waters, while the rising sun seemed to dart his sparkling fires out of the bosom of the deep: his rays gilt the tops of the mountains, which we still discovered a little above the horizon; and the whole heaven, painted with a deep azure, promised us an happy voyage.

Though I was dismissed as a Phœnician, none of the Phœnicians with whom I was, knew me. Narbal, who commanded the ship on board of which I was put, asked me my name and my country. Of what city of Phœnicia are you, said he to me? I am not a Phœnician, said I, but the Egyptians took me at sea in a Phœnician vessel. I have been a captive in Egypt as a Phœnician; it is under this name that I have suffered a long while; it is under this name that I was set at liberty. Of what country

try are you then, replied Narbal? I am Telemachus, said I, the son of Ulysses, king of Ithaca in
Greece; my father rendered himself famous among
all the kings who besieged the city of Troy; but
the Gods have not permitted him to see his country
again. I have sought him in various countries; fortune persecutes me as well as him. You see a wretch,
who wishes only for the happiness of returning to
his own country; and of finding his father.

Narbal looked upon me with surprise, and thought
he observed in me I know not what of fortunate,
which is one of the gifts of heaven, and is not found
in common men. He was naturally sincere and generous; he was touched with my misfortunes; and
talked to me with a confidence, with which the Gods
inspired him, for my preservation, in an imminent
danger.

Telemachus, said he, I do not, I cannot doubt
of what you tell me. The sweetness and virtue
visible in your countenance, do not permit me to
mistrust you: nay, I feel that the Gods whom I
have always served, love you; and that they would
have me love you as if you were my son. I will
give you wholesome advice, and ask nothing of you
in return but secresy. Fear not, said I, that it will
be any pain to me to be silent with regard to the
things with which you shall be pleased to entrust me.
Though I am so young, I am already grown old in
the habit of never disclosing my secrets, and more especially in never betraying, under any pretence
whatever, those of another. How can you, said he,
have accustomed yourself to secresy in so tender an
age? I shall be glad to hear by what means you
have acquired this quality, which is the foundation
of the wisest conduct, and without which all talents
are useless.

When Ulysses, said I, departed to go to the siege
of Troy, he took me on his knees, and in his arms,
as I have been informed. Having kissed me with
tenderness, he said these words to me, though I could
                                                    not

not underſtand them ; O my ſon ! may the Gods
preſerve me from ever ſeeing thee again : may the
ſciſſars of the fatal Siſters rather cut the thread of
thy days when it is hardly formed , as a reaper with
his ſickle cuts down a tender flower which is beginning to blow : may my Enemies daſh thee in pieces
before thy mother's eyes and mine , if thou art one
day to be corrupted and to abandon virtue ! O my
friends ! continued he , I leave you this ſon who is
ſo dear to me , take care of his infancy ; if you love
me , remove pernicious flattery far from him ; teach
him to vanquiſh himſelf ; let him be like a young
tree , which is only bent in order to be made ſtraight.
Above all, forget nothing in order to render him juſt,
beneficent, ſincere, and faithful in keeping a ſecret.
Whoever is capable of lying, is unworthy of being
reckoned in the number of men ; and whoever knows
not to be ſilent , is unworthy of ruling.

I relate to you the very words, becauſe care was
taken frequently to repeat them to me , they penetrated even to the bottom of my heart ; and I often repeat them to myſelf. My father's friends were careful to exerciſe me betimes in ſecreſy. I was in the
tendereſt ſtate of childhood, when they intruſted me
with all their uneaſineſs, at ſeeing my mother expoſed
to a great number of raſh ſuitors who ſought to
marry her. Thus they treated me from that time as
a reaſonable and truſty man ; they often conferred
with me about the moſt important affairs ; and informed me of what they had reſolved on to remove
theſe ſuitors. I was tranſported at their having
ſuch a confidence in me ; I thereby thought myſelf
already a perfect man. I never abuſed it ; I never
let ſlip a ſingle word which could diſcover the leaſt
ſecret. The ſuitors often endeavoured to make me
talk, hoping, that a child, who had ſeen or heard
any thing of importance, could not contain himſelf ;
but I well knew how to anſwer them without lying,
and

and without informing them of any thing which I ought not to tell them.

Hereupon Narbal said to me, You see, Telemachus, the power of the Phœnicians. They are formidable to all their neighbours by their innumerable ships. The trade they carry on as far as the pillars of Hercules, yields them riches surpassing those of the most flourishing nations. The great king Sesostris, who could never have conquered them by sea, had great difficulty in conquering them by land, with his armies which had subdued all the east. He imposed a tribute upon us which we did not long pay. The Phœnicians were too rich and too powerful to bear the yoke of servitude with patience: we recovered our liberty. Death did not allow Sesostris time to finish the war against us. It is true that we had every thing to fear from his wisdom, even more than from his power; but his power passing into the hands of his son, wholly destitute of wisdom, we concluded that we had nothing to fear. And indeed the Egyptians, instead of returning in arms to our country to subdue us once again, were constrained to invite us to their assistance, to deliver them from that impious and outrageous prince. We have been their deliverers. What glory added to the liberty and opulence of the Phœnicians!

But whilst we deliver others, we ourselves are slaves. O Telemachus! beware of falling into the hands of Pygmalion our king. He has dipt his hands, his cruel hands, in the blood of Sichæus, the husband of Dido his sister. Dido, greatly desirous of revenge, fled from Tyre with many ships. Most of those who love virtue and liberty, accompanied her: she has founded on the coast of Africa a stately city, which she calls Carthage. Pygmalion, tormented by an insatiable thirst of wealth, renders himself more and more miserable and odious to his subjects. It is a crime at Tyre to have great riches. Avarice makes him mistrustful, suspicious, cruel;

cruel; he perfecutes the rich, and he fears the
poor.

It is a ftill greater crime at Tyre to be virtuous:
for Pygmalion fuppofes, that good men cannot fuffer his unjuft and infamous actions. Virtue condemns him, and he is exafperated and irritated
againft her. Every thing moves him, difquiets
him, gnaws him; he is afraid of his shadow, and
fleeps neither night nor day. The Gods, to plague
him, load him with treafures, which he dares not
enjoy. What he feeks in order to be happy, is the
very thing which hinders him from being fo. He
repines at all he gives, he is always afraid of lofing,
and tortures himfelf for gain. He is hardly ever
feen; he continues folitary, fad, dejected, in the
moft fecret parts of his palace: even his friends
dare not approach him for fear of being fufpected
by him. A frightful guard, with naked fwords
and pikes erected, continually inveft his palace.
Thirty chambers, which have a communication one
with another, and each of them an iron door with
fix huge bolts, are the places where he shuts himfelf up. It is never known in which of thefe chambers he lies; and it is affirmed, that he never lies
two nights fucceffively in the fame, for fear of being murdered in it. He is a ftranger to the fweets
of pleafure, and the yet greater fweets of friendship. If any one talks to him of purfuing pleafure, he is fenfible that it flies far from him, and
that it refufes to enter his heart. His hollow eyes
are full of a fierce and favage fire, and inceffantly ftraying on all fides. He liftens to, and is alarmed at, the leaft noife. He is pale, emaciated, and
gloomy cares are pictured on his ever-wrinkled vifage. He is mute; he fighs; he groans from the
bottom of his heart, and cannot conceal the remorfe which preys on his bowels. The moft exquifite dishes difguft him. His children, inftead of
being his hope, are the objects of his fear; he has
made them his moft dangerous enemies. He has
                                             not

not had all his life a secure moment; he preserves himself only by shedding the blood of all those he fears.
A fool! who does not see that the cruelty in which he
confides, will cause his destruction. Some one of his
domestics, as suspicious as himself, will quickly rid
the world of this monster.

As for me, I fear the Gods; whatever it may cost
me, I will be faithful to the king they have given me.
I had rather that he should take away my life than I
his, or even than be wanting in my duty to defend
him. As for you Telemachus, be sure not to tell
him that you are the son of Ulysses : he would hope
that Ulysses, returning to Ithaca, would pay him a
large sum for your ransom, and he would keep you
in prison.

When we arrived at Tyre, I followed Narbal's
advice, and perceived the truth of every thing which
he had told me. I was not able to conceive that a
man could render himself so miserable as Pygmalion
seemed to be. Astonished at a sight so terrible and
new to me, I said to myself, Lo! a man who only
sought to make himself happy, and imagined that
he should accomplish it by riches and absolute power;
he possesses all he can desire, and yet he is wretched
even by his riches and his power. Were he a shepherd, as not long since I was, he would be as happy
as I have been; he would enjoy the innocent pleasures of the country, and enjoy them without remorse.
He would dread neither daggers nor poison ; he
would love men, and be loved by them. He would
not have these immense riches which are as useless to
him as sand, since he dares not touch them; but
he would freely enjoy the fruits of the earth, and suffer
no real want. This man seems to do all he desires,
but is far from doing it ; he does every thing his
brutal passions command. He is continually hurried
away by his avarice, his fears, and his suspicions.
He seems the master of all other men, but is not

master

mafter of himfelf; for he has as many mafters and.
tormentors, as he has violent defires.

I reafoned thus of Pygmalion without feeing him;
for he was not to be feen : one only beheld with
awe the lofty towers which were night and day furrounded by guards, wherein he immured himfelf as
in a prifon, shutting himfelf up with his treafures. I
compared this invifible king with Sefoftris, fo gentle, fo eafy of accefs, fo affable, fo curious to fee
ftrangers, fo attentive to hear every body, and to
draw out of the hearts of men the truth they conceal
from kings. Sefoftris, faid I, feared nothing, and
had nothing to fear; he shewed himfelf to all his
fubjects as to his own children : this man fears every
thing, and has every thing to fear. This wicked
king is continually expofed to a tragical death, even
in his inacceffible palace, in the midft of his guards.
On the contrary, the good king Sefoftris was fafe
in the midft of a crowd of his people, like an indulgent father in his own houfe, furrounded by his
family.

Pygmalion gave orders to fend home the troops
of the ifle of Cyprus, that came to affift his in confequence of an alliance which was between the two
nations. Narbal took this opportunity to fet me at
liberty : he caufed me to be muftered among the
Cyprian foldiers; for the king was fufpicious even
in the minuteft things. The failing of eafy and indolent princes is to give themfelves up, with a blind
confidence, to crafty and corrupt favourites ; the failing of this man was, on the contrary, to miftruft
the worthieft men. He knew not to difcern upright and frank men who act without difguife; he
had accordingly never converfed with men of probity; for fuch men never make their court to fo
corrupted a king Befides, he had feen, fince his
acceffion to the throne, in the men by whom he was
ferved, fo much diffimulation, perfidy, and shocking
vices, difguifed under the appearances of virtue, that
he looked upon all men without exception as if they

D   had

had been masked; he suppofed that there was no real virtue on the earth, and fo regarded all men as being nearly alike. When he found a man falfe and corrupt, he did not give himfelf the trouble to feek for another, fuppofing that another would not be better: the good feemed to him worfe than the moft openly wicked, becaufe he thought them as wicked and more deceitful.

To return to myfelf. I was blended with the Cyprians, and efcaped the piercing jealoufy of the king. Narbal trembled for fear I fhould be difcovered, which would have coft him his life, and me mine. His impatience to fee us depart was incredible, but contrary winds detained us a good while at Tyre.

I made ufe of this opportunity to inform myfelf of the manners of the Phœnicians, fo famous in all the known nations. I admired the happy fituation of this great city, which ftands in an ifland in the midft of the fea. The neighbouring coaft is delightful for its fertility, for the exquifite fruits it bears, for the number of cities and villages which almoft touch each other, and laftly for the mildnefs of its climate; for the mountains fcreen this coaft from the burning winds of the fouth, and it is refreshed by the north wind which blows from the fea. This country lies at the foot of Libanus; whofe fummit cleaves the clouds, and almoft touches the ftars; eternal ice covers its brow, and rivers of fnow pour like torrents from the tops of the rocks which environ its head. Beneath is feen a vaft foreft of ancient cedars, that feem as old as the earth in which they grow, and extend their thick branches even to the clouds. This foreft has at its foot fat paftures on the fide of the mountain. Here bellowing bulls are feen to ftray, and bleating fheep and tender lambkins fkipping over the grafs. There glide a thoufand rills of limpid water. Laftly, beneath thefe paftures appears the foot of the mountain, refembling a garden. Spring and autumn here reign at the fame time, in order to join fruits and flowers together.

together. Neither the peftilent breath of the fouth, which blafts and burns up all things, nor the bleak north wind, did ever prefume to fully the lively colours which adorn this garden.

It is near this beautiful coaft that the ifland on which Tyre is built emerges out of the fea. This great city feems to float upon the water, and to be the queen of all the fea. The merchants refort to it from all parts of the world, and its inhabitants themfelves are the moft famous merchants in the univerfe. When one enters into this city, one imagines at firft that it is not a city which belongs to any particular people, but that it is the common city of all nations, and the center of their commerce. It has two great moles, like arms, that ftretch themfelves into the fea, and embrace an immenfe harbour, where the winds cannot enter. In this port is feen as it were a wood of the mafts of ships, and thefe ships are fo numerous that one can hardly perceive the fea which fupports them. All the citizens apply themfelves to commerce, and their great riches never give them a diftafte to the pains neceffary to increafe them. Here on all fides is feen the fine linen of Egypt, and twice dyed Tyrian purple of a marvellous luftre. This double tincture is fo lively that time cannot efface it : it is ufed for fine cloths, enriched with embroideries of gold and filver. The Phœnicians trade with all nations as far as the ftreights of Gades, and have penetrated even into the vaft ocean which furrounds the whole earth. They have alfo made long voyages on the red fea ; it is this way they go to unknown iflands in queft of gold, perfumes, and divers animals which are not found elfewhere.

I could not fatisfy my eyes with the magnificent fight of this great city, where every thing was in motion. I did not fee here, as in the cities of Greece, idle and inquifitive perfons, who go to hear news in public places, or to ftare at foreigners who arrive in the port. The men are employed in unlading their ships, in fending away or felling their merchandifes, in putting their warehoufes in order, and in keeping an exact account of what is owing to them by foreign merchants.   The women never ceafe either to fpin wool, or to draw patterns of embroidery, or to fold up rich ftuffs.

Whence comes it, faid I to Narbal, that the Phœnicians have rendered themfelves mafters of the commerce of the whole earth, and thus enrich themfelves at the expence of all other nations? You fee the caufe, faid he: the fituation of Tyre is happy for trade ; it is our country which has the honour of having invented navigation.   For the Tyrians were the firft (if we may credit what is related of the darkeft antiquity) who tamed the waves, long before the time of Typhis and the Argonauts, fo much vaunted of in Greece: They, fay I, were the firft who ventured to commit themfelves in a feeble bark to the mercy of waves and tempeft, who founded the depths of the fea, who obferved the ftars at a great diftance from the land, according to the fcience of the Egyptians and Babylonians, and joined together fo many nations whom the fea had feparated. The Tyrians are induftrious, patient, laborious, neat, fober, and frugal ; they have a regular form of government, they are perfectly united among themfelves, and never was a nation more conftant, more fincere, more faithful, more trufty, more courteous to all ftrangers.

This, without feeking for any other caufe, is what gives them the dominion of the fea, and makes fo profitable a trade flourish in their port.   If divifions and jealoufies should creep in among them ; if they should begin to foften in pleafures and idlenefs : if the chiefs of the nation should defpife labour and frugality ; if arts should ceafe to be honourable in their city ; if they should be wanting in honefty to ftrangers ; if they should alter ever fo little their maxims of a free trade ; if they should neglect their

manufactures,

manufactures, and cease to advance the large sums
which are necessary to render all their commodities
perfect each in its kind, you would soon see the fall
of the power you admire.

But explain to me, said I, the true means of establishing hereafter a like trade in Ithaca. Do, replied
he, as is done here : treat all strangers in a kind
and condescending manner; let them find in your
ports, safety, conveniency, and an entire freedom;
never suffer yourself to be drawn away either by
avarice or by pride. The true way to gain a great
deal is never to aim at gaining too much, and to
know the proper times of losing. Make yourself
beloved by all strangers, and even suffer in some
things by them ; beware of exciting their jealousy
by your haughtiness; be steady in the rules of commerce, and let them be plain and easy; accustom
your subjects to observe them inviolably ; punish
with severity the frauds and even the negligence or
extravagance of merchants, which ruin trade in ruining those who carry it on. Above all, never attempt
to cramp commerce, in order to turn it according to
your own views. It is most proper for the prince
not to be concerned in it, but to leave the whole
profit to his subjects who have all the trouble of it ;
otherwise he will discourage them. He will draw
sufficient advantages from it by the great riches
which will enter into his dominions. Commerce
is like certain springs ; if you endeavour to divert
their course, you dry them up. It is only profit and
conveniency which attract strangers to you. If you
render trade less easy and less beneficial to them,
they insensibly retire, and never return; because other
nations, making their advantage of your imprudence,
allure them to their country, and accustom them to
live without you. I must even own to you, that for
some time the glory of Tyre has been greatly ob-
scured. O! had you seen it, my dear Telemachus,
before Pygmalion's reign, you would have been much
more astonished. You now find here only the sad

D 3   remains

remains of a grandeur which haftens to its ruin. O wretched Tyre! into what hands art thou fallen! The fea formerly brought thee the tribute of all the nations of the earth.

Pygmalion fears every thing both from foreigners and his own fubjects. Inftead of opening his ports, according to our ancient cuftom, to all the moft dif- tant nations with an entire freedom, he infifts on knowing the number of the ships which arrive, their country, the names of perfons on board them, their kind of trade, the nature and price of their merchan- difes, and the time they are to ftay here. He does ftill worfe, for he ufes artifice to enfnare the mer- chants, and confifcate their effects. He haraffes the merchants whom he thinks the richeft; he eftablishes under various pretences new impofts: he will enter into trade himfelf, and every one is afraid of having to do with him. Trade therefore languishes; fo- reigners by degrees forget the way to Tyre, which was formerly fo well known to them; and if Pygma- lion does not change his conduct, our glory and power will foon be tranfported to fome other people better governed than we.

I then asked Narbal how the Tyrians had rendered themfelves fo powerful by fea; for I was unwilling to be ignorant of any thing which conduces to the good government of a kingdom. We have, anfwer- ed he, the forefts of Libanus, which furnish us with timber for our shipping, and we carefully referve them for this ufe; we never fell any of them but for the fervice of the public. As for the building of ships, we have the advantage of having skilful workmen. How, faid I to him, were you able to find thefe workmen? He replied, they were trained up by de- grees in our own country. When we well reward thofe who excel in arts, we are fure of foon having men who carry them to their higheft perfection; for men who have the moft knowledge and genius, do not fail to apply themfelves to thofe arts to which the

the greateſt rewards are annexed. Here we treat with honour all thoſe who ſucceed in the arts and ſciences uſeful in navigation. We reſpect a good geometrician ; we highly eſteem a skilful aſtronomer ; we load with riches a pilot who excels others in his function ; we do not deſpiſe a good carpenter ; on the contrary, he is well paid and well treated : even good rowers have rewards ſure and proportioned to their ſervice ; we feed them well ; we take care of them when they are ſick ; in their abſence we take care of their wives and their children. If they periſh in a ſhipwreck, we indemnify their family, and we diſmiſs thoſe who have ſerved a certain time. By theſe means we have as many of them as we pleaſe. The father is glad to bring up his ſon in ſo good a trade, and from his earlieſt youth is diligent to teach him to handle an oar, to manage the cordage, and to deſpiſe ſtorms. It is thus that we lead men, without compulſion, by rewards and good regulations. Power alone never does well ; the ſubmiſſion of inferiors is not ſufficient ; we muſt win their hearts, and make men find their account in the things wherein we deſign to make uſe of their induſtry.

After this diſcourſe, Narbal conducted me to viſit all the magazines, the arſenals, and all the trades which are ſubſervient to the building of ships. I asked a detail of the minuteſt things, and wrote down all I heard, for fear of forgetting ſome uſeful circumſtance.

Mean while Narbal, who knew Pygmalion and loved me, waited with impatience for my departure, fearing I ſhould be diſcovered by the king's ſpies, who paſſed night and day thro' all parts of the city ; but the winds did not yet permit us to embark. Whilſt we were employed in curiouſly viewing the port, and in asking queſtions of ſeveral merchants, we ſaw coming towards us one of Pygmalion's officers, who ſaid to Narbal, the king has juſt heard from one of the captains of the ships which returned with you from Egypt, that you have brought a ſtranger

who

who paſſes for a Cyprian: it is his majeſty's pleaſure that he be apprehended, and that he may know for certain of what country he is; you are to anſwer for him on peril of your head. At this inſtant I was gone to a ſmall diſtance to take a nearer view of the proportions which the Tyrians had obſerved in building an almoſt new ship, (which was, they ſaid, by this exact proportion of all its parts, the beſt ſailor which had ever been ſeen in the port) and I was asking ſome queſtions of the builder who had adjuſted thoſe proportions.

Narbal, ſurpriſed and terrified, anſwered, I will go and ſeek this ſtranger, who is of the iſle of Cyprus. But when he had loſt ſight of the officer, he run to me to inform me of the danger I was in. I but too well foreſaw it, my dear Telemachus, ſaid he; we are loſt. The king, whom his jealouſy tortures day and night, ſuſpects that you are not of the iſle of Cyprus; he orders me to apprehend you, and will put me to death if I do not deliver you into his hands. What ſhall we do? O God! give us wiſdom, to extricate ourſelves out of this danger. I muſt lead you, Telemachus, to the king's palace. You ſhall maintain that you are a Cyprian of the city of Amathus, and the ſon of a ſtatuary of Venus: I will aver, that I formerly knew your father, and perhaps the king, without further inquiry, will ſuffer you to depart. I ſee no other way to ſave your life and mine.

I replied to Narbal: Let a wretch periſh whom his deſtiny deſires to deſtroy; I can die, Narbal, and I owe you too much to draw you into my ruin. I cannot reſolve to tell a lye; I am not a Cyprian, and cannot ſay that I am. The Gods ſee my ſincerity: it is theirs to ſave my life by their power, if they pleaſe; but I will not ſave it by an untruth.

Narbal anſwered, This untruth, Telemachus, has nothing which is not innocent; the Gods themſelves cannot condemn it; it does no injury to any one;

one; it faves the lives of two innocent perfons; it deceives the king only to hinder him from committing a great crime. You carry too far the love of virtue, and the fear of wounding religion.

It is enough, faid I, that a lye is a lye, to be unworthy of a man who fpeaks in the prefence of the Gods, and owes every thing to truth. He who violates the truth offends the Gods, and commits a violence on himfelf; for he fpeaks againft his confcience. Ceafe, Narbal, to propofe what is unworthy of you and of me. If the Gods have pity of us, they well know how to deliver us; if they are pleafed to leave us to perifh, we shall die the victims of truth, and leave men an example to prefer unfpotted virtue to length of life : mine is already but too long, being fo miferable. It is you alone, O my dear Narbal ! for whom my heart is melted. Muft your friendfhip for a wretched ftranger be thus fatal to you !

We continued a good while in this kind of combat; but at length perceived a man, quite out of breath, running towards us. He was another of the king's officers, and came from Aftarba. This woman was beautiful as a Goddefs; she joined to the charms of the body all thofe of difpofition and genius; she was gay, flattering, infinuating. With fo many delufive charms, she had, like the Syrens, a heart full of cruelty and malice ; but she knew how to hide her corrupt affections by deep artifice. She had won Pygmalion's heart by her beauty, her wit, her fweet voice, and the harmony of her lyre. Pygmalion, blinded by his violent love for her, had abandoned queen Topha his confort, and only ftudied how to gratify the paffions of the ambitious Aftarba. His love of this woman was little lefs fatal to him than his infamous avarice. But though he had fo great a paffion for her, she only defpifed and loathed him. However she concealed her real fentiments, and

seemed to desire to live only for him, at the same
time that she could not endure him.

There was at Tyre a young Cretan, whose name
was Malachon, of a marvellous beauty, but voluptuous, effeminate, and immersed in pleasures. He
minded but to preserve the delicacy of his complection, to comb his flaxen locks which flowed over
his shoulders, to perfume himself, to give a graceful turn to the folds of his gown, and to sing his
amours to his lyre. Astarba saw him, loved him,
and grows distracted for him. He slighted her
because he had a passion for another woman. Besides,
he was afraid to expose himself to the cruel jealousy
of the king. Astarba, finding herself disdained,
gave way to her resentment. In her despair she
fancied that she could make Malachon pass for the
stranger whom the king was enquiring after, and
who was said to have come with Narbal. And indeed she made Pygmalion believe it, and bribed all
those who could undeceive him. As he loved not
virtuous men, and could not discern them, he was
surrounded by such only as were selfish, artful, and
ready to execute his unjust and bloody commands.
These people were afraid of Astarba's power, and
assisted her to deceive the king, for fear of displeas-
ing this haughty woman, who had his whole confidence. Thus Malachon, tho' known for a Cretan
thro' all the city, passed for a young stranger whom
Narbal had brought from Egypt, and was thrown
into prison.

Astarba, who was afraid lest Narbal should go and
speak to the king, and discover the imposture, sent
in haste to Narbal this officer, who spoke these words
to him : Astarba forbids you to discover to the king
who your stranger is ; she asks nothing of you but
silence, and will so order matters that the king shall
be satisfied with you. In the mean time, be expediti-
ous in causing to embark with the Cyprians the young
stranger whom you brought with you from Egypt,
that

that he may be no more feen in the city. Narbal, overjoyed at being able thus to fave his own life and mine, promifed to be filent; and the officer, fatisfied with having obtained what he asked, returned to give Aftarba an account of his commiffion.

Narbal and I admired the goodnefs of the Gods, who rewarded our fincerity, and have fo tender a care of thofe who hazard all for virtue. We looked with horror upon a king given up to avarice and voluptuoufnefs. He who is fo exceffively afraid of being deceived, faid we, deferves to be, and is almoft always grofsly deceived. He miftrufts men of probity, and abandons himfelf to villains: he is the only one who is ignorant of what is tranfacting. Lo, Pygmalion! he is the fport of a shamelefs woman. Mean time the Gods make ufe of the falshood of the wicked to fave the good, who had rather lofe their life than tell an untruth.

We now perceived the winds change, and become favourable to the Cyprian fleet. The Gods declare themfelves, cried Narbal, they, my dear Telêmachus, will provide for your fafety; fly this cruel and accurfed land. Happy he who might follow you to the moft unknown shores! Happy he who might live and die with you! But cruel fate ties me down to this my unhappy country; I muft fuffer with her; perhaps muft be buried in her ruins: no matter, provided I always fpeak the truth, and my heart love nothing but juftice. As for you, my dear Telemachus, pray the Gods, who lead you as it were by the hand, to grant you the moft precious of all gifts, which is a pure and fpotlefs virtue until death. Long may you live! may you return to Ithaca, comfort Penelope, and deliver her from her rash fuitors! may your eyes fee, may your hands embrace, the fage Ulyffes, and may he find in you a fon equal to his wifdom! But in your good fortune remember the unhappy Narbal, and never ceafe to love me.

D 6 When

When he had ended thefe words, I bedewed him with my tears without replying: Profound fighs prevented my fpeaking: we embraced in filence. He conducted me to the ship: he remained on the shore, and when the bark failed, we did not, as long as we could fee, ceafe to look at each other.

End of the Third Book.

THE

THE
ADVENTURES
OF
TELEMACHUS,
SON of ULYSSES.

BOOK the FOURTH.

The ARGUMENT.

Calypſo interrupts Telemachus that he may repoſe him-
ſelf. Mentor blames him in private for having under-
taken the relation of his adventures, but adviſes him
to conclude ſince he has begun it. Telemachus relates
that in his voyage from Tyre to the iſle of Cyprus, he
had a dream wherein he ſaw Venus and Cupid,
againſt whom Minerva protected him; that he after-
wards fancied he ſaw mentor likewiſe, exhorting him
to fly from the iſle of Cyprus; that when he awaked,
the ship would have been loſt in a ſtorm, if he had
not himſelf taken the helm, becauſe the Cyprians, be-
ing drowned in wine, were not in a condition to ſave
it ; that at his arrival in the iſland he beheld with
horror the moſt contagious examples of vice ; that
Hazaël the Syrian, whoſe ſlave Mentor was now
become, happening to be at Cyprus at the ſame time,
reſtored him his wiſe guide, and took them both on
board his ship to carry them to Crete, and that in this
paſſage they ſaw the glorious ſight of Amphitrite
drawn in her chariot by ſea-horſes.

AND now Calypſo , who had hitherto continued
motionleſs and tranſported with pleaſure in
hearing Telemachus's adventures, interrupted him,
that he might take ſome repoſe. It is time for you,
said

said she, to go and enjoy the sweets of sleep after so
many toils. You have nothing to apprehend here;
every thing is favourable to you; give a loose therefore to joy, and taste of peace, and of all the other
blessings which the Gods are ready to heap upon you.
To-morrow when Aurora with her rosy fingers opens
the golden gates of the east, and the steeds of the
sun, springing from the briny waves, spread the flames
of day, and chace before them all the stars of heaven,
we will resume, my dear Telemachus, the story of
your misfortunes. Never did your father equal you
in wisdom and courage. Neither Achilles who conquered Hector, nor Theseus who returned from hell,
nor even the great Alcides who purged the earth of
so many monsters, ever discovered such fortitude and
virtue. May a sound sleep make the night seem short
to you; but alas! how tedious will it be to me! How
shall I long to see you, to hear you again, to make
you repeat what I know already, and to ask you what
I know not yet! Go, my dear Telemachus, with the
wise Mentor whom the Gods have restored to you,
go into this retired grotto, where every thing is prepared for your repose. May Morpheus shed his
sweetest charms on your heavy eye-lids! may he
cause a heavenly vapour to glide thro' all your weary
limbs, and send you pleasant dreams, which, hovering around you, may sooth your senses by the most
smiling images, and chace far from you whatever
might awake you too early.

The goddess herself conducted Telemachus to
this grotto, which was separated from her own, but
altogether as rural and pleasant. A fountain, gliding in a corner, gently murmured, and invited sleep.
The nymphs had here prepared two soft and verdant
beds, and covered them with two large skins; one
with a lion's for Telemachus, the other with a bear's
for Mentor.

Mentor, before he suffered sleep to close his eyes,
thus addressed Telemachus. The pleasure of relating
your story has carried you too far; you have charmed
the

the Goddess by displaying the dangers from which
your courage and dexterity have delivered you; you
have thereby only the more enflamed her heart, and
prepared a more dangerous captivity for yourself.
How can you expect that she will let you depart
from her island now you have enchanted her by the
recital of your adventures? Vanity has made you
speak imprudently. She promised to relate some
adventures to you, and to inform you of the fortunes
of Ulysses; but she found the means of talking a
great while without saying any thing and engaged you to tell her all she desires to know : Such is
the art of flattering and enamoured women. When,
Telemachus, will you be so wise as never to talk
out of vanity, and to conceal the shining parts of
your story, when it is of no service to reveal them?
Others admire your wisdom at an age when it is
excusable to want it, but, as for me, I can pardon
you nothing; I am the only one who knows
and loves you enough to tell you of all your faults.
How far are you still from being as wise as your
father?

How, replied Telemachus, could I refuse to relate my misfortunes to Calypso? No, answered
Mentor, it was necessary to relate them; but you
should have mentioned such things only as might
have inspired her with pity. You might have told her
that you was one while a wanderer, then a captive
in Sicily, and afterwards in Egypt. This would
have been sufficient, and all the rest served but to
enflame the poison which already rages in her heart.
The Gods grant that your's may be preserved from it!

But what shall I do now? continued Telemachus
in a modest and submissive manner. It is now too
late, replied Mentor, to conceal the sequel of your
adventures; she knows too much of them already
to be capable of being deceived in what is to come;
your reserve would only provoke her. To-morrow
therefore conclude your narrative of all that the Gods
have done in your favour; and learn another time to
speak

speak with more reserve of things which may tend to
your own praise. Telemachus received this good
advice kindly; and they both betook themselves to
rest.

As soon as Phœbus had shed his earliest rays on the
earth, Mentor, hearing the voice of the Goddess
calling her nymphs in the grove, awakened Telemachus. It is time, said he, to shake off sleep. Come,
let us return to Calypso, but be upon your guard
against the honey of her words; let the door of your
heart be continually shut against her, and dread the
insinuating poison of her praises. She yesterday extolled you above your wise father, the invincible
Achilles, the famous Theseus, and Hercules, who is
become immortal. Did you not perceive how excef-
sive such commendations are? Or did you believe what
she said? Know that she does not believe it herself.
She praises you only because she thinks you weak and
vain enough to be imposed upon by praises which bear
no proportion to your actions.

This said, they went where the Goddess was waiting for them. She smiled when she saw them, concealing under an appearance of joy the fear and inquietude of her heart; for she foresaw that Telemachus,
conducted by Mentor, would escape from her as Ulysses
had done. Make haste, said she, my dear Telemachus, to satisfy my curiosity; I saw you, methought,
all the night departing from Phœnicia, and going to
try your fortune in the island of Cyprus. Give me an
account therefore of your voyage, and let us not lose
a moment. They then sat down, in a shady grove,
on the grass enamelled with violets.

Calypso could not forbear continually casting tender and passionate looks on Telemachus, nor see
without indignation that Mentor watched even the
least motion of her eyes. Mean while all the
nymphs were silent, and leaning forwards to listen,
formed a kind of semi-circle in order to hear and see
the better. The eyes of the assembly were immoveable, and fixed on Telemachus, who with down-

cast

caſt eyes and graceful bluſhes, thus reſumed the thread
of his ſtory.

The gentle breath of a favourable wind had hardly
filled our ſails, when the coaſt of Phœnicia diſap-
peared. As I was with Cyprians, whoſe manners I
was a ſtranger to, I reſolved to ſay nothing, to make
my remarks on every thing, and obſerve all the rules
of diſcretion to gain their eſteem. But, during my
ſilence, I was ſeized with a ſweet and powerful
ſleep. My ſenſes were bound up and ſuſpended, my
ſoul was ſerene, and my heart overflowed with joy.
All of a ſudden methought I ſaw Venus cleave the
clouds in her flying chariot drawn by a pair of doves.
She had all that radiant beauty, that lively youth,
thoſe tender graces which were ſeen in her when ſhe
ſprung from the froth of the ocean, and dazzled the
eyes of Jupiter himſelf. She deſcended all at once
with the utmoſt rapidity, laid her hand upon my
ſhoulder with a ſmile, and calling me by my name,
uttered theſe words: Young Greek, you are going to
enter my empire, you will ſoon arrive at the happy
Iſland, where pleaſures, ſmiles, and wanton ſports,
ſpring up under my footſteps. There ſhall you
burn perfumes on my altars, there ſhall you plunge
into rivers of delight. Let the ſweeteſt hopes di-
late your heart, and beware of refiſting the moſt potent of all the Goddeſs, who deſigns to make you
happy.

At the ſame time I perceived her ſon Cupid fluttering his little wings, and hovering round his mother. Though he had the fondneſs, the graces, the
ſprightlineſs of a child in his face, yet had he I know
not what in his piercing eyes which made me tremble.
He ſmiled when he looked upon me, but his ſmiles
were malicious, ſcornful and cruel. He drew out
of his golden quiver the ſharpeſt of his arrows, he
bent his bow, and was aiming at my heart, when
Minerva ſuddenly appeared and covered me with her
Ægis. The countenance of this Goddeſs has not
thoſe effeminate charms, and that amorous languor,
                                                    which

which I obferved in Venus's face and air. On the contrary Minerva was a plain, carelefs, modeft beauty ; all was grave, manly, noble, full of ftrength and majefty. Cupid's arrow not being able to pierce the Ægis, and falling to the ground, he fighed bitterly through indignation, and was ashamed to fee himfelf vanquished. Begone, Minerva cried, begone, rash boy ; thou never wilt conquer but ignoble fouls, who prize thy shameful pleafures more than wifdom, virtue, and glory. The God of love, provoked at thefe words, betook himfelf to flight ; and, Venus re-afcending to Olympus, I faw her chariot and doves a long while in a gold and azure cloud; at length she difappeared, and then turning my eyes to the earth, I beheld Minerva no more.

I was, methought, afterwards tranfported into fuch a delightful garden as men defcribe the Elyfian fields to be. There I found Mentor, who faid : Fly this cruel country, this infectious Ifland, where all breathe nothing but voluptuoufnefs ; where the moft heroic virtue has reafon to tremble, and can fave itfelf only by flight. As foon as I faw him, I attempted to throw myfelf on his neck and embrace him ; but I perceived that my feet were not able to move, that my knees failed under me, and that my hands, endeavouring to lay hold of Mentor, purfued an empty shadow, which continually eluded my grafp. As I was making this effort, I awaked, and perceived that this myfterious dream was a divine admonition. I felt myfelf infpired with a firm refolution againft pleafure, with a diffidence of myfelf, and a deteftation of the effeminate life of the Cyprians. But what pierced me to the heart, was my thinking that Mentor was dead, that he had paffed the Stygian lake and was become an inhabitant of the happy manfions of the juft.

This thought made me shed a torrent of tears. I was asked why I wept. Tears, faid I, but too well become a wretched ftranger, who wanders without hopes of ever feeing his country again. In the mean time

time all the Cyprians who were in the ship, abandoned themfelves to the moft extravagant mirth. The rowers, averfe to labour, flept on their oars; the pilot crowned with flowers, left the helm; and, holding in his hand an enormous bowl of wine which he had almoft emptied, he and all the reft of the crew, tranfported with the fury of Bacchus, fung fuch fongs in honour of Venus and Cupid as would excite horror in all lovers of Virtue.

While they were thus forgetful of the dangers of the fea, a fudden ftorm troubled the heavens and the waters. The loofened winds furioufly bellowed in the fails, and the black billows beat againft the fides of the bark which groaned beneath their ftrokes. Sometimes we rode on the backs of the fwelling waves; fometimes the fea, feeming to flip from under the veffel, plunged us down a bottomlefs gulph, and clofe by us we beheld feveral rocks, on which the angry furge broke with an horrible roar. Then I learnt by experience what Mentor had often told me, that men of diffolute and pleafurable lives are cowards in time of danger. All our dejected Cyprians wept like women; I heard but woful cries, but fad laments for the loft fweets of life, and vain vows of facrifices to the Gods, if they arrived at their port. No one had prefence of mind enough either to work the ship himfelf, or to command others to do it. Thinking it my duty to fave the lives of all the reft as well as my own, I took the helm in my hand, becaufe the pilot, difordered with wine, like a Bacchanal, was not in a condition to be fenfible of the danger the veffel was in; I encouraged the affrighted fea-men, and ordered them to take down their fails. They plyed their oars with great vigour; we fteered between the rocks and had a near profpect of all the horrors of death.

This adventure feemed like a dream to all thofe who owed the prefervation of their lives to me, they looked upon me with aftonishment. We arrived at the ifle of Cyprus in the vernal month, which is facred to Venus.

This

This ſeaſon, ſay the Cyprians, properly belongs to this Goddeſs ; for it ſeems to animate all nature, and to give birth to pleaſures and flowers together.

On my arrival at this iſland, I perceived a mildneſs in the air, which rendered the body ſlothful and inactive, but inſpired gaiety and wantonneſs. The country, tho' naturally fruitful and pleaſant, was, I obſerved, almoſt wholly uncultivated, ſo greatly were the inhabitants averſe to labour. I ſaw on all ſides women and maidens gorgeouſly attired, ſinging the praiſes of Venus, and going to devote themſelves to the ſervice of her temple. Beauty, the graces, joy, pleaſure ſhone equally in their faces ; but their charms were too affected, and there was none of that noble ſimplicity, that amiable modeſty, which is the greateſt allurement of beauty. Their ſoft air, the ſtudied adjuſtment of their looks, their vain attire, their languiſhing gait, their eyes which ſeemed to purſue thoſe of the men, the jealouſies among themſelves about kindling the greateſt paſſions ; in a word, all that I ſaw in theſe women appeared to me vile and contemptible : their immoderate deſires to pleaſe excited my averſion.

I was conducted to the Goddeſs's temple : ſhe has ſeveral in that iſland ; for ſhe is particularly worſhipped at Cythera, Idalia, and Paphos ; it was to Cythera that I was conducted. The temple is all marble, and a perfect periſtyle. Its large and lofty pillars render the fabric exceedingly majeſtic. On each front, above the architrave and freeze, are large pediments, on which are repreſented in bas-relief all the moſt agreeable adventures of the Goddeſs. At the gate there is continually a crowd of people who come to make their offerings. Within the encloſure of this ſacred place no victim is ever ſlain, no fat of bulls and heifers is burnt as elſewhere, nor is their blood ever ſpilt there : the beaſts which are offered, are only preſented before the altar, and none can be offered which are not young, white, and without blemiſh or
                                    imperfection

imperfection : they are crowned with purple fillets embroidered with gold ; their horns are gilt and adorned with nosegays of odoriferous flowers, and when they have been presented before the altar, they are sent back to a retired place, where they are slain for the banquets of the Goddess's priests.

Here also are offered all sorts of perfumed liquors, and wine more delicious than nectar. The priests are clad in long white robes with girdles of gold, and fringes of the same at the bottom of their vestments. The most exquisite perfumes of the east are burning night and day on the altars, and form a kind of cloud which ascends to heaven. All the columns of the temple are adorned with pendant festoons ; all the vases which are used in the sacrifices, are gold, and a sacred grove of myrtle surrounds the edifice. None but boys and girls of extraordinary beauty may present the victims to the priest, or presume to kindle the fire of the altars. But immodesty and lasciviousness dishonour this magnificent temple.

At first I was struck with horror at what I saw ; but I insensibly began to grow familiar with it. I was no longer startled at vice ; all companies inspired me with I know not what inclination to intemperance ; my innocence was laughed at, and my sobriety and modesty served for a jest to this shameless people. They tried all arts to stir up my passions, to ensnare me, and to awaken my appetite for pleasure. I found that I lost strength daily ; my good education could scarce sustain me any longer ; all my virtuous resolutions vanished ; I had no longer power to resist the evil which pressed me on all sides, and was even ashamed of virtue : I was like a man swimming in a deep and rapid river ; at first he cleaves the waves and ascends against the stream, but if the banks are steep, and he cannot rest himself on the shore, he at length tires by degrees, his strength forsakes him, his limbs stiffen with fatigue, and the torrent hurries him away :

thus

thus my eyes began to grow dim, my heart failed within me, and I no longer summoned my reason to my aid, nor the memory of my father's virtues. The dream wherein I thought I saw Mentor in the Elysian fields, completed my dejection ; a silent, soothing languor possessed me entirely. I already cherished the flattering poison, which glided from vein to vein, and penetrated even to the marrow in my bones. I fetched however the profoundest sighs ; I shed the bitterest tears, and roared like a lion in his fury. O wretched condition of youth, said I ! Ye Gods, who cruelly sport with men, why do you make them pass through that age which is a time of folly, or a burning fever ? O ! why am I not covered with silver hairs, bowed down and dropping into the grave, like my grandsire Laertes ! Death would be welcomer to me than the shameful weakness I now feel.

I had hardly spoken thus but my grief began to abate, and my heart, intoxicated with extravagant passion, shook off almost all sense of shame ; I was afterwards plunged into an abyss of remorse. In this disorder I wandered up and down the sacred grove, like a hind which the hunter has wounded : she flies through the spacious forest to ease her pain ; but the arrow which sticks in her side, pursues her every where : she every where bears the murderous shaft. Thus did I vainly run to forget myself, for nothing could sooth the wound in my heart.

In the dark shade of this grove I suddenly perceived at some distance from me the form of the sage Mentor ; but his visage seemed so pale, so sad and austere, that I felt no joy from it. Is it you then, my dear friend, my only hope ? Is it you ? What ! you yourself ? Does not a flattering image delude my eyes ? Is it you, Mentor ? Is it not your shade, still sensible to my woes ? Are you not in the number of happy souls, who enjoy the fruits of their virtue,

tue, and on whom the Gods beftow uncorrupted pleafures, and an eternal peace in the Elyfian fields; Say, Mentor, do you ftill live? Am I fo happy as to poffefs you, or are you only the shade of my friend? As I fpoke thefe words, I ran towards him with fuch eagernefs and tranfport that I was quite out of breath: he calmly waited for me, without taking a fingle ftep to meet me. Ye know, ye Gods! how great was my joy, when I found that my hands touched him! No, 'tis not an empty shadow; I hold him, I embrace him, my dear Mentor! 'Twas thus that I exclaimed; I bedewed his face with a flood of tears, and hung about his neck without being able to fpeak. He beheld me with eyes of fadnefs and tender compaffion.

At length I faid, Alas! whence come you? What dangers have I not been expofed to in your abfence, and what could I now do without you? But he, without anfwering my queftions, cried with a terrible voice, Fly, fly hence with fpeed: this earth bears no fruit but poifon; the air you breathe is tainted; the men are infectious and fpeak not but to communicate their deadly venom. Bafe and infamous voluptuoufnefs, the moft horrible evil which iffued from Pandora's box, enervates the foul and fuffers no virtue here. Fly; what do you wait for? Do not fo much as look behind you in your flight? efface even the flighteft remembrance of this execrable ifland.

He faid; and I immediately perceived as it were a thick cloud difperfing from before my eyes, and beheld the pure light. Serene joy and manly fortitude revived in my heart; a joy very different from that effeminate and wanton joy which had poifoned my fenfes: one is the joy of drunkennefs and diforder, and is interrupted by raging paffions and ftinging remorfe; the other is the joy of reafon, and is accompanied with fomething bleffed and celeftial; it is always pure, equal, and

inexhauftible;

inexhauſtible; the deeper one plunges into it, the ſweeter it is; it raviſhes the ſoul without diſcompoſing it. I then ſhed tears of joy, and found that nothing is ſo delightful as ſuch tears. O happy they, ſaid I, to whom virtue reveals herſelf in all her beauty; Can they ſee her, and not love her? Can they love her, and not be happy?

Mentor ſaid, I muſt leave you; I muſt depart this moment; I am not permitted to ſtay. Where are you going, cried I? To what uninhabitable country will I not follow you? Think not that you can eſcape me; I will rather die in purſuing you. As I ſpoke theſe words, I held him locked in my arms with all my ſtrength. You hope in vain, ſaid he, to detain me. The cruel Metophis ſold me to certain Æthiopians or Arabs, and they, going to trade at Damaſcus in Syria, determined to ſell me again, imagining they could get a large ſum for me of one Hazaël, who was enquiring for a Greek ſlave to teach him the manners of Greece, and to inſtruct him in our ſciences. And indeed Hazaël bought me at a great price. What I have taught him of our cuſtoms, excited his curioſity to go to the iſland of Crete, to ſtudy the wiſe laws of Minos. During our voyage the winds conſtrained us to put in at the iſle of Cyprus; while we were waiting for a favourable gale, he came to make his offerings in the temple : lo! he is coming out of it. The winds call us, and already ſwell our ſails. Adieu, my dear Telemachus; a ſlave who fears the Gods ought faithfully to attend his maſter. The Gods no longer permit me to be at my own diſpoſal; they know, if I were, that I ſhould be wholly at yours. Farewel, remember the toils of Ulyſſes, Penelope's tears, and the righteous Gods. O ye immortal protectors of innocence, in what a clime am I conſtrained to leave Telemachus!

No, no, ſaid I, my dear Mentor, it ſhall not be in your power to leave me here; I will ſooner die than ſee you depart without me. Is this Syrian maſter inexorable?

exorable ? Was he fuckled by a tygrefs in his infancy ? Will he tear you out of my arms ? He muſt kill me, or fuffer me to go with you. You yourſelf exhort me to fly, and yet will not let me fly by following you. I will go and ſpeak to Hazaël, who perhaps will pity my youth and my tears : ſince he loves wiſdom, and is going ſo far in ſearch of it, he cannot have a ſavage and infenfible heart. I will throw myſelf at his feet, I will embrace his knees, I will not ſuffer him to go, 'till he has given me leave to attend you. My dear Mentor, I will make myſelf a flave with you, I will offer myſelf to him ; if he rejects me, my fate is determined ; I will lay down the burthen of life.

Hazaël at this inſtant called Mentor ; I proſtrated myſelf before him, and he was ſurpriſed to ſee a ſtranger in this poſture. What would you have, ſaid he ? Life, replied I ; for I cannot live, unleſs you permit me to accompany your flave Mentor. I am the ſon of the great Ulyſſes, wifeſt of all the kings of Greece, who deſtroyed the haughty city of Troy, ſo famous throughout all Aſia. I tell you my birth not out of vanity, but only to move you to pity my misfortunes. I have fought my father in every ſea, accompanied by this man, who was another father to me. Fortune, to fill up the meaſure of my woes, tore him from me, and made him your flave ; ſuffer me to be ſo too. If it be true that you are a lover of juſtice, and going to Crete to learn the laws of good king Minos, harden not your heart againſt my fighs and my tears. You ſee the ſon of a prince, reduced to ſue for flavery as his only refuge, tho' in Sicily he heretofore deſired death to avoid it ; but my former calamities were only faint eſſays of the outrages of fortune : I now tremble left I ſhould not be received into the number of flaves. Ye Gods ! behold my diſtreſs, and O Hazaël ! remember that Minos, whoſe wiſdom

you

you admire, will adjudge us both in the kingdom of Pluto.

Hazaël, viewing me with a benign and humane aspect, stretched forth his hand and raised me up. I am no stranger, said he, to the wisdom and virtue of Ulysses; Mentor has often mentioned the glory he acquired among the Greeks, and besides, swift-winged fame has sounded his renown thro' all the nations of the east. Follow me, thou son of Ulysses, I will be your father till you find him who gave you life. Though I were not moved with your father's glory, with his calamities nor yours, yet would my friendship for Mentor engage me to take care of you. I purchased him indeed as a slave, but I detain him as my faithful friend: the money he cost me, has gained me the dearest and most valuable friend I have in the world. In him I have found wisdom; to him I owe whatever I may have of love for virtue. From this moment he is free, you shall be so too; I ask nothing of either of you but your hearts.

I passed in an instant from the bitterest woe to the most ravishing joy that mortals are capable of feeling. I saw myself delivered from a most dreadful danger; I was approaching my country; I was assisted in my return to it, and had the consolation of being with a man, who already loved me thro' a pure affection for virtue. In short, I found every thing in finding Mentor, and in not being to part with him again.

Hazaël advances towards the shore; we follow and embark with him. The rowers cleave the peaceful waves; a gentle zephir plays in our sails, animates the whole bark, and gives it a pleasing motion. The isle of Cyprus quickly disappears. Hazaël, impatient to know my sentiments, asked me what I thought of the manners of this island. I ingenuously told him to what dangers my youth had been exposed, and the conflict I had endured in my own bosom. He was touched with my abhorrence of vice, and spoke these words: O Venus, I own your power, and that of your son: I have burnt incense on your

altars;

altars; but give me leave to detest the infamous effeminacy of the inhabitants of your island, and the brutish impudence with which they celebrate your festivals.

Afterwards he discoursed with Mentor of the first cause which formed the heavens and the earth; of that infinite unchangeable light, which is communicated to all without being divided; of that sovereign universal truth which illuminates all spirits, as the sun illuminates all bodies. The man, added he, who has never seen this pure light, is as blind as one who is born blind; he passes his life in profound darkness, like the nations which the sun enlightens not for several months in the year. He thinks himself wise, and, is a fool; he thinks he sees all things, and sees nothing, and dies without having seen any thing: At most he perceives but glimmering and false lights, vain shadows, and phantoms that have nothing of reality. Such is the condition of all who are carried away by the pleasures of sense, and the allurements of imagination. There are in the world no men really rational, except those who consult, who love, who obey this eternal reason. It is that which inspires us with good thoughts; it is that which reproves us for our ill ones. We are indebted to it for our understanding as well as for our lives; it is like a great ocean of light; our souls are like rivulets which flow from it, and return into, and are lost in it again.

Tho' I did not perfectly comprehend the wisdom of this discourse, yet I tasted in it I know not what of pure and sublime; my heart was warmed with it, and truth methought shone in every word. They proceeded to speak of the origin of the Gods, of heroes, of poets, of the golden age, of the deluge, of the earliest histories of mankind, of the river of oblivion in which the souls of the dead are plunged, of the eternal pains prepared for the wicked in the dismal gulph of Tartarus, and of the blessed tranquillity which the just enjoy in the Elysian fields, without any apprehension of losing it.

E 2

While

While Hazaël and Mentor were discoursing together, we perceived several dolphins, whose scales seemed gold and azure, swelling the waves and making them foam with their sportings. After them came Tritons blowing their writhen shells, and surrounding Amphitrite's chariot, which was drawn by sea-horses that were whiter than snow, that ploughed the briny waves, and left a deep furrow far behind them in the sea. Their eyes flamed, and foam issued from their mouths. The Goddess's car was a shell of a marvellous form ; it was of a more shining white than ivory; its wheels were of gold, and it seemed to skim the peaceful surface of the deep. Nymphs crowned with flowers, whose lovely tresses flowed over their shoulders and waved with the winds, swam in shoals behind it. The Goddess had in one hand a sceptre of gold to command the waves, and with the other held on her knees the little God Palemon her son, who hung at her breast. She had such serenity, such sweetness and majesty in her countenance, that every seditious wind and lowering tempest fled before her. Tritons guided the steeds, and held the golden reins. A large purple sail waved in the air above the car, and was gently swelled by a multitude of little zephirs, who strove to blow it forwards with their breath. In the midst of the air Æolus was seen busy, restless, vehement. His wrinkled face and sour looks, his threatening voice, his long bushy eye-brows, and the gloomy fire and severity of his eyes, silenced the fierce north-winds, and drove back all the clouds. Immense whales and all the monsters of the deep, whose nostrils made the briny wave to ebb and flow, issued in haste from their profound grots to view the Goddess.

End of the Fourth Book.

THE

THE
ADVENTURES
OF
TELEMACHUS,
SON of ULYSSES.

BOOK the FIFTH.

The ARGUMENT.

Telemachus relates that he was informed, on his arrival in Crete, that Idomeneus, king of that island, had sacrificed his only son to fulfil a rash vow ; that the Cretans resolving to revenge the son's blood, had constrained the father to quit their country, and were after long debates actually assembled to elect another king. Telemachus adds that he was admitted into this assembly ; that he there obtained the prizes in several games; that he solved the questions left by Minos in his book of laws, and that the old men, who were the rulers of the island, and all the people seeing his wisdom, would have made him their king.

AFTER we had admired this sight, we began to discover the mountains of Crete, which we could yet hardly distinguish from the clouds of the heaven and the billows of the sea. We soon discovered the top of mount Ida above the other mountains of the island : So an old stag in a forest carries his branchy head above those of the surrounding fawns. By degrees we saw more distinctly the coast of the island, which presented itself to us like an amphitheatre. As much as the lands of Cy-

prus

prus had appeared uncultivated and neglected, did these of Crete seem fertile and adorned with all sorts of fruits by the labour of the inhabitants.

On all sides we observed well built villages, stately cities, and towns which were equal to cities. We found no field on which the hand of the industrious husbandman was not imprinted; the plough had every where left indented furrows: briars, thorns and all plants that unprofitably incumber the ground, are unknown in this country. We viewed with pleasure the hollow vallies, where herds of oxen were lowing in fat pastures along the banks of the rivers; the sheep feeding on the side of the hills; the spacious plains covered with golden ears, the rich presents of fruitful Ceres; and the mountains adorned with vines, whose clustering grapes, already of a bluish hue, promised the vintagers the delicious gifts of Bacchus to sooth the cares of men.

Mentor said that he had formerly been in Crete, and informed us of all he knew of it. This island, said he, admired by all strangers and famous for its hundred cities, easily maintains all its inhabitants, tho' they are innumerable; for the earth is never weary of pouring her blessings on those who cultivate her: her fruitful bosom is inexhaustible; the more inhabitants there are in a country, the more they abound, provided they are industrious; they have never any occasion to be jealous of each other. Our bountiful mother earth multiplies her gifts according to the number of her children, that merit her fruits by their labour. The ambition and avarice of men are the only sources of their misery. Men covet all, and make themselves wretched by their desires of superfluities; if they would live in a plain and simple manner, and be contented with satisfying their real wants, we should every where see plenty, joy, peace, and concord.

This is what Minos, the wisest and best of kings, understood. All that you will see most admirable in this island is the fruit of his laws. The education he
                                                    prescribed

prescribed for children, renders their bodies healthful
and robust: they are accustomed betimes to a plain,
frugal and laborious life; it is a maxim among the
Cretans, that all pleasures enervate both the body and
the mind, and the only pleasure which they ever propose to their children is that of being invincible in
virtue, and of acquiring glory.   Courage is not solely
placed in despising death amidst the dangers of war,
but also in trampling great riches and shameful pleasures under foot. Three vices are punished here, which
are not punished in other nations, ingratitude, dissimulation, and avarice.

As for extravagance and luxury, there is no need
to suppress them; for they are unknown in Crete;
here every one works without studying to enrich himself, and thinks that he is sufficiently recompensed for
his pains by an easy and regular way of living, wherein
he enjoys in peace and plenty all that is really necessary to life. Costly furniture is not allowed here,
nor magnificent attire, nor sumptuous feasts, nor gilded palaces. Their cloaths are of fine wool and of a
beautiful colour, but quite plain and without embroidery. Their meals are temperate; they drink but little
wine at them, and their chief ingredient is good bread,
together with the fruits which the trees yield as it
were spontaneously, and the milk of their flocks and
herds: at most they only eat coarse meat, and that
too is plainly dressed; for they carefully reserve the
best of their oxen for the improvement of agriculture.
Their houses are neat, convenient, pleasant; but without ornaments: not that magnificent architecture is
unknown to them, but they apply it only to the temples
of the Gods: men are not allowed to have mansions
like those of the immortals. The great riches of the
Cretans are health, strength, courage, the peace and
union of families, the liberty of all the citizens, a
plenty of necessaries, a contempt of superfluities, an
habit of labour, an abhorrence of idleness, an emulation in virtue, a submission to the laws, and a fear
of the righteous Gods.

E 4   I asked

I asked him in what the king's authority confifted·
The king, replied he, is abfolute over the people,
but the laws are abfolute over him.   He has an un-
limited power to do good, but his hands are tied
when he would do evil.   The laws commit the
people as the moft precious of all trufts to his care,
on condition that he shall be their father.   They
ordain that a fingle perfon shall by his wifdom and
moderation promote the felicity of multitudes, and
not that multitudes by their mifery and bafe flavery
should ferve to flatter the pride and luxury of a
fingle perfon.   The king is to have nothing more
than others, except what is neceffary either to relieve him in his painful duties, or to imprint on
the people a refpect for him who is to maintain
the laws.   Nay, the king is to be more temperate,
more averfe to luxury, to pomp and pride than
any other.   He is not to have more riches or pleafures, but more wifdom, virtue and glory than the
reft of men.   Abroad he is to be the defender of
his country, by commanding its armies; and to be
the judge of the people at home, in order to render
them good, wife and happy.   It is not for his own
fake that the Gods made him king; he is fo only
to be the fervant of the people; to them he owes
all his time, all his cares, all his affection; and he is
only fo far worthy of royalty, as he forgets and facrifices himfelf to the good of the public.   Minos or-
dained that his children should not reign after him,
unlefs they reigned according to thefe maxims; for
he loved his people more than his family.   It was by
this wife conduct that he rendered Crete fo powerful
and happy; it was by this moderation that he eclipfed
the glory of all the conquerous, who aim at making
the people fubfervient to their own grandeur, that is
to fay to their vanity : in a word, it was by his juftice
that he deferved to be in hell the fupreme judge of
the dead.

   Whilft Mentor was difcourfing thus, we arrived
at the ifland where we faw the famous labyrinth
                                                made

made by the ingenious Dedalus, in imitation of
the great one which he had seen in Egypt. Whilst
we were viewing this curious edifice, we observed
multitudes of people on the shore running to a place
near the sea-side; we asked the cause of their hurry,
and the following account was given us by one Nauli-
crates a Cretan.

Idomeneus, the son of Deucalion and grandson of
Minos, said he, went like the other kings of Greece
to the siege of Troy. After the destruction of that
city, he set sail to return to Crete; but he was over-
taken by so violent a storm, that the pilot of the
ship, and all other experienced navigators, thought
that they should inevitably be wrecked. Every one
had death before his eyes; every one saw the abyss
gaping to swallow him up; every one deplored his
fate, despairing even of the sad consolation of souls
which cross the Styx after their bodies have been
buried. Idomeneus, lifting up his hands and eyes
to heaven, invoked Neptune : O powerful God!
cried he, thou who swayest the wavy empire, deign
to hear a wretched mortal! If thou givest me to see
the island of Crete again in spite of the raging winds,
to thee will I sacrifice the first head which shall present itself to my eyes.

Mean while his son, impatient to see his father
again, hastened to meet and embrace him. Unhappy youth! who knew not that he was running to
his destruction. The father having escaped the tempest, arrived at the desired port, and thanked Neptune
for hearing his vows; but he soon found how fatal
they were to be to him. A foreboding of his misfortune made him bitterly repent of his indiscreet
vow; he was afraid of arriving amongst his own subjects, and apprehensive of seeing what was dearest to
him in this world. But cruel Nemesis, an inexorable Goddess, who lies in wait to punish men, and
especially haughty kings, pushed Idomeneus on with a
fatal and invisible hand. He arrives; he hardly dares
to lift up his eyes; he sees his son: he starts back

E 5.   with

with horror, and vainly looks about for some other less dear head to serve him for a victim. Mean while the son threw himself on his neck, and is quite astonished at his father's cold returns to his fondness, and at seeing him dissolve into tears.

O my father, said he, whence this sadness? After so long an absence are you sorry to see your kingdom again, and to be the joy of your son? What have I done? You turn away your eyes lest you should see me. The father, opprest with grief, made no reply. At last after many profound sighs, he said, Ah! Neptune, what have I promised you? At what a price have you saved me from shipwreck? Give me back to the waves and the rocks, which dashing me in pieces, should have ended my wretched life; let my son live. O cruel God! here take my blood and spare his. As he spoke thus, he drew his sword to kill himself: but those about him held his hand. Old Sophronymus, an interpreter of the will of the Gods, assuring him that he might satisfy Neptune without putting his son to death. Your vow, said he, was imprudent: the Gods will not be honoured by cruelty; beware of adding to your criminal promise the crime of fulfilling it contrary to the laws of nature; offer to Neptune an hundred bulls whiter than snow; let their blood stream around his altar crowned with flowers; let sweet incense smoke in honour of the Gods.

Idomeneus heard these words, hanging down his head and without replying. Fury was kindled in his eyes: his pale and disfigured countenance changed its colour every moment, and his limbs trembled. Mean time his son said, Lo! father, here I am, your son is ready to die to appease the God of the sea; draw not his wrath upon you: I die contented, since my death has prevented yours. O my father! strike, nor fear to find me unworthy of you, or afraid to die.

Idomeneus at the same instant, quite frantick and like one torn by the infernal furies, astonishes all who

were

were near him; he plunges his sword into his son's heart; he draws it out again, all reeking and bloody, to thrust it into his own bowels: he is once more with-held by those about him. The youth falls down in his blood; the shades of death overspread his eyes; he half-opens them to the light, but as soon as he finds it, he can bear it no longer. As a beautiful lily of the fields, that is wounded in its root by the plough-share, droops and can support itself no longer, tho' it has not yet lost its lively white and the lustre which charms the eye, yet as the earth nourishes it no more, its life is extinguished: so the son of Idomeneus, like a young and tender flower, is cruelly mowed down in his bloom of life. The father grows stupid thro' excess of grief; he knows not where he is, nor what he does, nor what he ought to do; he goes staggering towards the city, and asks for his son.

Mean while the people, moved with compassion for the son, and with horror at the barbarous action of the father, cry out, the just Gods have delivered him up to the furies. Rage furnishes them with arms; they seize on sticks and stones, and discord breathes its deadly venom into all their hearts. The Cretans, the wise Cretans, forget the wisdom they so much loved, and no longer acknowledge the grandson of the sage Minos. Idomeneus's friends find no safety for him but in leading him back to his ships; they embark with him, and commit themselves to the mercy of the waves. Idomeneus, coming to himself, thanks them for snatching him from a country which he had watered with his son's blood, and could no longer inhabit. The winds waft them to Hesperia, where they are going to found a new kingdom in the country of the Salentines.

Mean while the Cretans having no king to govern them, are come to a resolution to elect one who will maintain the established laws in all their purity; and the measures they have taken in order to make this choice, are these. All the chief inhabitants of the hundred cities are here met together; they have already opened the assembly by sacrifices; they have convened all the most famous sages of the neighbouring countries, to inquire into the wisdom of those who shall appear worthy to command; they have made preparations for exhibiting public games, wherein all the candidates are to contend; for they will give the crown as a prize to him who shall be judged superior to all others both in body and mind. They will have a king whose body is robust and active, and whose mind is adorned with wisdom and virtue. All strangers are invited hither.

Nausicrates, having related this surprising story, said, Hasten, strangers, to our assembly; you shall contend with the rest, and if the Gods decree the victory to one of you, he shall reign in this country. We followed him, not with any desire of conquest, but only out of curiosity to see so extraordinary an affair.

We came to a sort of circus, which was very large, and compassed with a thick wood. The middle of the circus was an arena, which was prepared for the combatants, and was surrounded by an amphitheatre of verdant turf, on which innumerable spectators were seated in rows. On our arrival we were received with honour; for the Cretans of all nations in the world are the most generous and religious observers of hospitality. They caused us to be seated, and invited us to engage in the combats. Mentor excused himself on account of his age, and Hazaël on account of his ill health. My youth and vigour left me no excuse. I glanced my eyes however upon Mentor to discover his thoughts, and perceived that he would have me engage. I accordingly accepted of their offer; I stripped myself of my cloaths; floods of sweet and shining oil were poured on all my limbs, and I mingled with the combatants. It was said on all sides, That is the son of Ulysses, who is come to contend for the prize, and several Cretans, who had seen me during my infancy in Ithaca, knew me again.

The

The firſt exerciſe was wreſtling. A Rhodian about five and thirty years old, threw all who ventured to engage him. He ſtill retained all the vigour of youth ; his arms were nervous and brawny ; at the leaſt motion he made, all his muſcles appeared, and all his activity was equal to his ſtrength. Not thinking me worthy of being conquered, and beholding my tender youth with eyes of compaſſion, he was going away ; but I went up to him : whereupon we ſeized each other, and preſſed the breath almoſt out of our bodies ; we ſtood ſhoulder to ſhoulder, and foot to foot; all our nerves were on the ſtretch, and our arms twiſted together like ſerpents, each endeavouring to lift his antagoniſt from the ground. Sometimes he attempted to throw me by ſurpriſe, by puſhing me to the right ſide, and ſometimes he endeavoured to bend me to the left. Whilſt he was trying me in this manner, I ſhoved him with ſo much violence, that his loins gave way ; he fell on the ſand, and drew me upon him. In vain did he endeavour to get me under him ; for I held him immoveable beneath me. All the people cried, Victory to the ſon of Ulyſſes; and I helped the confounded Rhodian to get up again.

The combat of the Cæſtus was more difficult. The ſon of a rich citizen of Samos had acquired ſo high a reputation in this kind of conflict, that all others yielded to him, and there was none but I, who hoped for victory. At firſt he ſtruck me ſeveral blows on the head, and then on the ſtomach, which made me vomit blood, and ſpread a thick cloud over my eyes. I reeled, he preſſed upon me, and my breath was gone ; but I was re-animated by Mentor's crying out, O ſon of Ulyſſes, will you be vanquiſhed ? Anger gave me new ſtrength, and I avoided ſeveral blows which I muſt otherwiſe have ſunk under. The Samian failing in a blow he made at me, and extending his arm in vain, I ſurpriſed him in that ſtooping poſture : he was drawing back when I lifted up my cæſtus in order to fall upon him with
more

more force; he endeavoured to avoid me, but losing his balance, he gave me an opportunity to throw him down. He was hardly stretched on the earth, when I held out my hand to raise him up; he got up himself, besmeared with dust and blood, and in the utmost confusion, but he did not dare to renew the combat.

Immediately after begun the chariot-races; the cars were distributed by lot, and mine happened to be the worst, both as to the lightness of the wheels and the strength of the horses. We start, and clouds of rising dust obscure the heavens. At first I let others go before me. A young Lacedæmonian, whose name was Crantor, presently left all the rest behind him. A Cretan, named Polycletus, followed him close. Hippomachus, a relation of Idomeneus, who aspired to succeed him, giving the reins to his foaming coursers, hung over their flowing manes, and the motion of his chariot wheels was so rapid, that they seemed like the wings of an eagle cleaving the air, not to move at all. My steeds being warmed and brought to their wind by degrees, I left far behind me almost all those who had set out with so much ardor. Hippomachus, Idomeneus's kinsman, driving his coursers with too much fury, the most vigorous of them fell down, and by his fall deprived his master of the hopes of a crown.

Polycletus, leaning too much over his horses, could not keep himself fast in a shock which his chariot received; he fell, the reins slipped out of his hands, and he was very fortunate in being able to avoid death. Crantor seeing, with eyes full of indignation, that I was close by him, redoubled his ardor; sometimes invoking the Gods and promising them rich offerings, and sometimes encouraging his steeds with words. He was apprehensive lest I should pass between the goal and him; for my horses having been more favoured than his, were in a condition to get before him, and he could no way prevent it but by obstructing my passage. To effect this, he run the risk of

breaking

breaking his car against the goal, and indeed he broke his wheel against it. My sole care was to make a sudden turn that I might not be involved in his disorder, and was in a moment at the end of the course. The people once again cried, Victory to the son of Ulysses ; 'tis he whom the Gods appoint to reign over us.

Then the most illustrious and wisest of the Cretans conducted us into an ancient and sacred wood, sequestered from the sight of the profane, where the elders, whom Minos had appointed judges of the people and guardians of the laws, assembled us together. We were the same who had contended in the games ; nobody else was admitted. The sages opened the books wherein all the laws of Minos were collected together. I felt myself stricken with respect and awe as I approached these seniors, whom age had rendered venerable, without depriving them of their vigour of mind. They were seated in order, and motionless in their places; their hairs were white, and several of them had hardly any. A serene and engaged wisdom was conspicuous in their grave countenances. They were not eager to speak, and said nothing but what they had weighed before. When they were of different opinions, they were so moderate in maintaining what they thought on either side, that one would have imagined they were of the same mind. A long experience of things past, and application of business, gave them a great insight into all things ; but what most contributed to the perfecting of their judgment, was the tranquillity of their minds, which were free from the extravagant flights and caprices of youth. Wisdom alone operated in them, and the fruit of their long virtue was to have so thoroughly subdued their passions, that they tasted without alloy the sweet sublime pleasure of hearkening to reason. While I was admiring them, I wished that my life could be contracted that I might once arrive at so valuable an old age, and thought that youth was unhappy in being so impetuous and so far distant from this enlightened and serene virtue.

The

The chief of these elders opened the book of the laws of Minos. It was a large volume, and was usually locked up in a golden box with perfumes. All these seniors kissed it with respect; for they say that next to the Gods from whom good laws proceed, nothing ought to be so sacred to men as laws designed to render them good, wise, and happy. Those who are entrusted with the execution of the Laws for the government of the people, ought always to be governed by the laws themselves: 'tis the law, and not the man, which ought to reign. Such was the discourse of these sages. The president then proposed three questions, which were to be resolved by the maxims of Minos

The first question was, Who is the freest of all men? Some answered, that it was a king who had an absolute dominion over his subjects, and was victorious over all his enemies. Others maintained, that it was a man who was so rich, that he could gratify all his desires. Others said, that it was one who was not married, and was continually travelling during his whole life thro' divers countries, without ever being subject to the laws of any. Others imagined, that it was a barbarian, who, living by hunting in the midst of the woods, was independant of all government, and free from every want. Others believed that it was a man lately made free, because by passing from the rigours of slavery, he had a quicker relish than any body else of the sweets of liberty. And lastly, others bethought themselves to say, that it was a dying person, because death freed him from every thing, and all mankind united had no longer any power over him.

When my turn was come, I was at no loss for an answer, because I had not forgot what Mentor had often told me. The freest of all Men, said I, is he who can be free even in slavery itself. In what country or condition soever a man may be, he is perfectly free, provided he fears the Gods, and fears nothing but them; in a word, the truly free man

is

is he, who, void of all fears and all defires, is fubject only to the Gods and reafon. The elders looked on each other with a fmile, and were furprifed to fee that my anfwer was precifely the fame as that of Minos.

They then propofed the fecond queftion in thefe words, who is the moft unhappy of all men? Every one faid what occurred to his mind. One faid, It is a man who had neither money, nor health, nor honour. Another faid, It is one who hath no friend. Others maintained that it was a man who has ungrateful and degenerate children. There came a fage of the ifle of Lesbos, who faid, The moft unhappy of all men, is he who thinks himfelf fo; for unhappinefs arifes lefs from what we fuffer, than from the impatience with which we aggravate our mifery. At thefe words the whole affembly fhouted and applauded the fage Lesbian; believing that he would carry the prize as to this queftion. But my opinion being asked, I anfwered according to Mentor's maxims. The moft unhappy of all men is a prince who thinks to be happy by rendering other men miferable: his blindnefs doubles his unhappinefs; for not knowing his misfortune, he cannot cure himfelf of it; nay, he is afraid even to know it. Truth cannot pierce thro' his crowds of flatterers to arrive at him. His paffions are his tyrants; he knows not his duty; he has never tafted the pleafure of doing good, nor been fenfible of the charms of uncorrupted virtue; he is wretched, and deferves to be fo; his wretchednefs encreafes daily; he runs to his deftruction, and the Gods are preparing eternal punishment for him. The whole affembly owned that I had outdone the Lesbian fage, and the elders declared that I had hit upon the true fenfe of Minos.

For the third queftion, they asked, Which of the two is preferable, a king victorious and invincible in a war, or a king without experience of war, but qualified to govern his people wifely in peace. The majority anfwered, that a king who was invincible in

war

war was to be preferred. What profits it, said
they, to have a king who knows to govern well in
peace, if he knows not to defend his country in times
of war? his enemies will vanquish him, and reduce
his people to slavery. Others on the contrary maintained, that a pacific king would be better, because
he would be apprehensive of war, and take care to
avoid it. Others said, that a victorious king would
labour to advance his subjects glory as well as his
own, and would render them masters of other nations; whereas a pacific king would keep them in
a shameful cowardice. My opinion was asked, and I
answered thus:

A king who knows to govern only in peace or
only in war, and is not capable of conducting his
people in both these circumstances, is but half a king.
But if you compare a king who understands nothing
but war to a wise king, who, without understanding
war himself, is capable of maintaining it on occasion
by his generals, I think him preferable to the other.
A king entirely turned to war would be so continually
making it, in order to extend his dominions and
glory, that he would ruin his own people: And
what boots it them that their prince subdues other
nations, if they themselves are miserable under his
reign? Besides, long wars always draw after them
many disorders: the victors themselves grow licen-
tious in these times of confusion. Consider how dear
the triumphing over Troy has cost Greece; she was
deprived of her kings for more than ten years.
Whilst every thing is enflamed by war, laws, agriculture, arts, languish. Even the best princes, while
they are engaged in it, are constrained to commit
the greatest of evils, which is, to wink at licentiouf-
ness and to employ wicked men. How many profligate wretches are there whom one would punish in
times of peace, whose audacious villainies we are
obliged to reward during the disorders of war? Never had any nation a conquering prince, without
having much to suffer from his ambition. A conqueror

queror intoxicated with his glory, ruins his own victorious nation almoſt as much as the nations he conquers. A king who has not the qualifications requiſite
for peace, is not able to make his ſubjects taſte the
fruits of a war happily ended : he reſembles a man
who can defend his own field, and perhaps uſurp his
neighbour's, but can neither plough nor ſow, in
order to reap the harveſt. Such a man ſeems born
to deſtroy, to ravage, to overturn the world, and not
to render a nation happy by the wiſdom of his government.

Let us come now to the pacific king. He is not
indeed qualified to make great conqueſts, that is,
he is not born to trouble the repoſe of his own people,
by ſeeking to vanquish others whom juſtice has not
ſubjected to him ; but if he is really adapted to govern, in peace, he has all the qualifications which are
neceſſary to ſecure his ſubjects againſt their enemies.
For he is juſt, moderate and eaſy with regard to his
neighbours ; he never undertakes any thing againſt
them which may diſturb the publick peace, and he is
faithful to his alliances. His allies love him, do not
fear him, and have an entire confidence in him. If
he has a reſtleſs, haughty and ambitious neighbour,
all the adjacent princes, who fear the turbulent, and
have no jealouſy of the peaceful king, join themſelves to the latter, in order to hinder him from being oppreſſed. His probity, his ſincerity, his moderation, make him the arbiter of all the neighbouring
nations. Whilſt the enterpriſing monarch is hated
by all the reſt, and continually in danger of their
leagues, the peaceful prince has the glory to be as it
were the father and guardian of all others. Theſe
are the advantages which he has abroad ; thoſe he
enjoys at home are ſtill more ſolid. Since he is qualified to govern in peace, I ſuppoſe that he governs
by the wiſeſt laws. He ſuppreſſes pomp, luxury,
and all arts which ſerve only to cherish vice ; he
makes thoſe flourish which are ſubſervient to the
real wants of life ; above all, he cauſes his ſubjects
to

to apply themselves to agriculture, and he thereby
procures them a plenty of all necessaries. This laborious people, plain in their manners, accustomed to
live on a little, and easily getting their livelihood by
the culture of their lands, increase daily. Thus the
people of this kingdom are innumerable ; but they
are a healthful, a vigorous, a robust people, who are
not enervated by pleasure, who are inured to virtue,
who are not addicted to a soft, effeminate and luxurious life, who despise death, and would rather lose
their lives than the liberty they enjoy under their wife
king, who reigns only to make reason reign. Let a
neighbouring conqueror attack this people, and he
will find them perhaps not very expert in forming of
camps, in ranging themselves in order of battle, or in
erecting machines to besiege a city ; but he will find
them invincible by their numbers, by their courage,
by their patience in fatigues, by their habit of bearing poverty, by the vigour of the combatants, and
by a virtue which ill success itself cannot abate. Besides, if the king has not sufficient experience to command his armies himself, he will cause them to be
commanded by men who are capable of it, and will
know how to make use of them without losing his
own authority. He will in the mean while obtain
assistance from his allies ; his subjects will rather die
than submit to the yoke of a violent and unjust prince,
and even the Gods themselves will fight for him. Lo,
the resources he will have amidst the greatest dangers.
I conclude therefore that a pacific king, who is ignorant of war is a very imperfect king, since he knows
not to discharge one of his greatest duties, the subduing of his Enemies ; but I add, that he is however
infinitely superior to a conqueror, who wants the ac-
complishments which are necessary in peace, and is
qualified only for war.

I perceived that many persons in the assembly
could not relish my opinion ; for most men, dazzled
by glaring objects, as victories and conquests, prefer
them to what is simple, calm and solid, as the peace
and

and good government of a people. But all the elders declared that I had spoken like Minos.

The chief of these seniors cried out, I see the accomplishment of an oracle of Apollo, which is known thro' all our Island. Minos having consulted this God, to know how long his offspring would reign according to the laws which he had established, Apollo answered him : Thy race will cease to reign, when a stranger shall enter thy island and cause thy laws to reign there. We were afraid that some stranger would come and conquer the Island of Crete; but Idomeneus's misfortune, and the wisdom of the son of Ulysses, who better than any man understands the Laws of Minos, shew us the sense of the oracle. Why do we delay to crown him whom the Gods give us for our king?

End of the fifth Book.

THE
ADVENTURES
OF
TELEMACHUS,
SON of ULYSSES.

BOOK the SIXTH.

The ARGUMENT.

Telemachus relates that he refused the crown of Crete to return to Ithaca ; that he proposed the Election of Mentor, who also refused the diadem; that the assembly at last pressing Mentor to choose for the whole nation, he told them what he had heard of the virtues of Aristodemus, who was the same moment proclamed king; that Mentor and he afterwards embarked for Ithaca: but that Neptune, to gratify the resentment of Venus, had caused them to be wrecked, after which the Goddess Calypso received them into her island.

HEreupon the elders went out of the sacred wood, and their president taking me by the hand, told the people, who waited with impatience for their determination, that I had obtained the prize. He had hardly done speaking, when a confused noise was heard thro' the whole assembly. Every one shouted for joy. The shores and all the neighbouring mountains rung with this acclamation. Let the son of Ulysses, who resembles Minos, reign over the Cretans.

I waited a while, and then making a sign with my hand, desired to be heard. Mean time Mentor said in a whisper, Will you renounce your country ? Will the ambition of reigning make you forget Penelope, who expects you as her last hope, and the

great

great Ulyſſes, whom the gods have determined to
reſtore to you? Theſe words pierced my very heart,
and ſupported me againſt the vain deſire of reigning.
And now a profound ſilence of all this tumultuous
aſſembly gave me an opportunity to ſpeak thus : O
illuſtrious Cretans, I am not worthy to command
you. The oracle you mention plainly ſhews indeed,
that the race of minos ſhall ceaſe to reign when a
ſtranger ſhall enter this iſland, and cauſe the laws of
that wiſe king to reign therein ; but it is not ſaid that
this ſtranger himſelf ſhall reign. I am willing to believe that I am the ſtranger pointed at by the oracle ;
I have fulfilled the prediction ; I am come into this
Iſland ; I have diſcovered the true ſenſe of the laws,
and I wiſh that my explanation may cauſe them to reign
with him whom you ſhall elect. As for me, I prefer
my own country, the poor little Iſland of Ithaca, to
the hundred cities of Crete, and all the glory and opulence of this fine kingdom. Give me leave to purſue
the courſe which deſtiny has marked out for me. If
I contended in your games, it was not in hopes of
reigning here ; it was to merit your eſteem, and compaſſion : it was that you might furniſh me with the
means of a ſpeedy return to the place of my nativity.
I had rather obey my father Ulyſſes, and comfort my
mother Penelope, than reign over all the nations of
the univerſe. O Cretans! you ſee the bottom of my
heart ; I muſt leave you, but death only ſhall put a
period to my gratitude. Yes, even to his lateſt breath
will Telemachus love the Cretans, and be as much
concerned for their glory as for his own.

I had hardly done ſpeaking, when a hollow murmur aroſe, like that of the billows daſhing againſt
each other in a tempeſt. Some ſaid, is he a God
in an human ſhape? Others averred, that they had
ſeen me in other countries, and knew me again.
Others cried, He muſt be compelled to reign here.
At length I reſumed the diſcourſe, and every one
was immediately ſilent, not knowing but that I was
                                                                      about

about to accept of what I had refufed at firft. The words I fpoke were thefe :

Give me leave, ye Cretans, to fpeak what I think. You are the wifeft of all nations; but wifdom, methinks, requires a precaution to which you do not feem to attend. You fhould choofe not the man who reafons the beft concerning the laws, but him who practices them with the fteady virtue. As for me, I am young, and of confequence, unexperienced, fubject to violent paffions, and fitter to learn by obeying how to command hereafter, than to command at prefent. Seek not therefore a man who has conquered others in exercifes of the mind and body, but who has conquered himfelf; feek one who has your laws written on the table of his heart, and has, all his life, been punctual in obeying them ; let his actions rather than his words induce you to choofe him.

All the old men, charmed with this difcourfe, and feeing the applaufes of the affembly continually encreafing, faid : Since the Gods deprive us of the hopes of feeing you reign among us, at leaft affift us to find a king who may caufe our laws to reign. Do you know any one who can command with this moderation; I know, faid I immediately, a man from whom I derive all that you efteem in me; 'tis his wifdom, and not mine which has fpoken to you ; he infpired me with all the anfwers you have heard.

At the fame time the whole affembly caft their eyes upon Mentor, whom I fhewed to them, holding him by the hand. I related the care he had taken of my infancy, the dangers from which he had delivered me, and the evils which were poured down upon me, when I ceafed to follow his counfels. They had not at firft taken notice of him by reafon of his plain and negligent drefs, his modeft looks, his almoft continual filence, and his cold and referved air. But when they viewed him with attention, they difcovered in his face I know not what of firm-

nefs

neſs and elevation; they obſerved the vivacity of
his eyes, and the vigour with which he performed
even the minuteſt actions; they asked him ſeveral
queſtions; they admired him, and reſolved to make
him their king. He calmly excuſed himſelf, and
ſaid, that he preferred the ſweets of a private life to
the ſplendor of a crown; that the beſt of kings were
unhappy, becauſe they hardly ever did the good
which they deſired to do, and often did, thro' the
miſrepreſentations of flatterers, the evils which they
did not deſign. He added, that if ſervitude is miſerable, royalty is not leſs ſo, ſince it is only ſervitude
in diſguiſe. When one is a king, ſaid he, one is de-
pendant on all thoſe whom we need to make ourſelves obeyed. Happy he who is not obliged to command! We owe to our own country, only when she
entruſts us with authority, the ſacrifice of our liberty,
in order to toil for the publick good.

Upon this the Cretans not being able to recover
from their ſurprise, asked him whom they ought to
chooſe. A man, replied he, who knows you well, ſince
he muſt govern you, and who is afraid to take the
reins in his hands. Whoever deſires a crown, knows
not what it is; and how can he perform the duties
which he does not know? he ſeeks it for his own
ſake, and you ought to deſire one who accepts it only
for yours.

All the Cretans being ſtrangely aſtoniſhed to ſee
two ſtrangers refuſe the crown which was courted by
ſo many others, deſired to know with whom they
came thither. Nauſicrates, who had conducted us
from the port to the circus, where the games were
celebrated, pointed to Hazaël with whom Mentor
and I came from the Iſland of Cyprus. But their
aſtoniſhment was ſtill greater, when they knew that
Mentor had been Hazaël's ſlave; that Hazaël,
touched with his ſlave's wiſdom and virtue, had made
him his counſellor and his boſom friend; that this
ſlave, being ſet at liberty, was the ſame perſon who
had refuſed to be their king, and that Hazaël was ſo

enamoured

énamoured of wisdom as to come from Damascus in
Syria, to be instructed in the laws of Minos.

The elders said to Hazaël, We dare not desire you
to reign over us, for we suppose that you have the
same thoughts as Mentor. You despise men too
much to be willing to burden yourself with the care
of them ; besides, you think too lightly of riches and
the splendors of royalty, to be willing to purchase
their lustre with the pains which are inseparable from
the government of kingdoms. Hazaël replied, Believe not, Cretans, that I despise men : No, no, I am
sensible how glorious it is to toil to make them virtuous and happy : but these toils are full of anxieties
and dangers. The splendor which is annexed to
them, is false, and can dazzle none but vain-glorious
souls. Life is short ; greatness raises the passions
above its power to gratify them ; it was to learn to be
contented without these chimerical blessings, and not
to obtain them, that I came so far. Farewell : all
my thoughts are fixt on returning to a quiet and retired way of life, where wisdom will cherish my heart,
and where the hopes which I derive from virtue of
another better life after death, shall comfort me under
the miseries of old age. Were I to wish for any
thing, it would not be to be a king ; it would be,
never to be separated from these two men whom you
see before you.

At length the Cretans, addressing themselves to
Mentor, cried, Tell us, O wisest and greatest of
all mortals, tell us then whom we can choose for our
king ? We will not let you go 'till you have told us
the choice which we ought to make. He answered,
While I was in the crowd of spectators, I observed a
man who discovered not the least sollicitude nor eager-
ness. He is a hail old man ; I asked his name, and
was told that it is Aristodemus. I afterwards heard
somebody tell him that his two sons were in the
number of the combatants, which seemed to give
him no joy at all, He said, that as for one, he did
not wish him the dangers of a crown, and that he
                                                    loved

loved his country too well ever to confent that the other should reign. By this I underftood, that the father loved with a rational fondnefs one of his fons who has virtue, and that he did not indulge the other in his vices. My curiofity encreafing, I enquired what fort of a life this old man had led, and one of your citizens told me, that he bore arms a long while, and is covered with wounds; but that his fincere virtue and his averfion to flattery rendered him obnoxious to Idomeneus, which hindered the king from employing him at the fiege of Troy. Idomeneus was afraid of a man who would give him wife counfels, which he was not inclined to follow: nay, he was jealous of the glory which Ariftodemus would be fure foon to acquire; he forgot all his fervices, and left him here, indigent, and defpifed by rude and fordid wretches, who efteem nothing but riches. But contented with his poverty, he lives chearfully in a fequeftered part of the ifland, where he cultivates his fields with his own hands. One of his fons toils with him; they tenderly love each other; they are happy by their frugality, and have, by their labour, procured themfelves a plenty of all things which are neceffary to a plain way of life. The wife old man gives to the fick poor of his neighbourhood all that remains above a fufficiency for his own and his fon's wants. He caufes all the young men to work; he encourages and inftructs them; he determines all the difputes among his neighbours, and is the father of every family. The misfortune of his own is to have a fecond fon, who would never follow any of his counfels. The father, having long born with him in order to reclaim him from his vices, at laft difcarded him, and he has fince abandoned himfelf to vain ambition, and all kind of pleafures.

This, O Cretans, is what I have been told; you should know if this account be true. But if this man be fuch as he is defcribed to be, why do you exhibit games? Why do you affemble fo many ftrangers? You have in the midft of you a man who knows you,

and

and whom you know ; who understands war ; who has given proofs of his courage, not only against darts and arrows, but against frightful poverty itself ; who has despised riches acquired by flatteries ; who loves labour ; who knows how useful agriculture is to a nation ; who detests pomp ; who does not suffer himself to be unmanned by a blind fondness for his children ; who loves the virtue of the one, and condemns the vices of the other ; in a word, a man, who is already the father of the people. This man is your king, if it be true that you desire to make the laws of the wise Minos reign amongst you.

All the people cried out, Aristodemus is indeed what you represent him : he is worthy to reign. The elders ordered him to be called. He was sought for in the crowd, where he was confounded with the meanest of the people. He seemed perfectly calm. They told him that they would make him their king. He replied, I can consent to it only on three conditions. First, that I shall resign the crown in two years, if I do not render you better than you are, and if you disobey the laws. Secondly, that I shall have the liberty to continue my plain and frugal way of life. Thirdly, that my children shall have no precedence, and that they shall be treated, after my death, without distinction, according to their merit, like the rest of the citizens.

At these words, the air was rent with a thousand acclamations. The crown was placed by the chief of the elders, who are the guardians of the laws, on the head of Aristodemus. Sacrifices were offered to Jupiter and the other superior Gods. Aristodemus made us presents, not with the magnificence which is usual to kings, but with a noble simplicity. He gave Hazaël the laws of Minos written by the hand of Minos himself. He gave him also a collection of the whole history of Crete from the time of Saturn and the golden age ; he sent on board his ship all the choicest fruits that grow in Crete, and are unknown in Syria, and offered to supply him with every thing he might want.

As

As we were eager to depart, he ordered a bark to be got ready for us with a great number of good rowers and soldiers, and he sent cloaths and provisions for us on board it. The same instant a wind arose which was fair for sailing to Ithaca; but this wind being contrary to Hazaël, obliged him to wait. He saw us depart; he embraced us as friends he was never to see again. The Gods are just, said he; they are witnesses to a friendship which is founded only on virtue: they will one day bring us together again, and the happy fields, where it is said the just enjoy an eternal peace after death, shall see our souls meet each other again, never to be parted more. O could my ashes also but be collected with yours! — As he spoke these words, he shed torrents of tears, and sighs choaked his voice. We wept not less than Hazaël; he attended us to the ship.

As for Aristodemus, he said, you have made me a king; remember the dangerous situation in which you have placed me; beseech the Gods to inspire me with true wisdom, and that I may as much exceed other men in moderation, as I exceed them in power. As for me, I beseech them to conduct you happily to your own country, to baffle the insolence of your enemies, and to grant that you may see Ulysses reigning there in peace with his dear Penelope. I present you, Telemachus, with a good ship, well provided with rowers and soldiers; they may be useful to you against the unjust persecutors of your mother. O Mentor, your wisdom, which needs nothing, leaves me nothing to desire for you. Depart, and may you live happy together; remember Aristodemus; and if the Ithacans should ever have need of the Cretans, depend upon me to my latest breath. He embraced us, and we could not, as we thanked him, suppress our tears.

Mean while the wind which swelled our sails, promised us a pleasant voyage. Already mount Ida looked to us like a little hill; all the shores disappeared, and the coast of Peloponesus seemed to

advance

advance into the fea to met us. But a black tempeft fuddenly overfpread the heavens, and irritated
all the billows of the Sea ; day was turned into night,
and death prefented itfelf to us. 'Twas you, O Neptune, who with your haughty trident ftirred up all
the waters of your empire ! Venus, to revenge herfelf for our having defpifed her even in her temple of
Cythera, went to this God ; she addreffed him with
grief ; her lovely eyes were bathed in tears : at
leaft, Mentor, who is well skilled in things divine,
told me fo. Will you, Neptune, faid she, fuffer
thefe impious wretches to mock my power with impunity ? The Gods themfelves feel it, and yet thefe
rash mortals prefume to cenfure every thing which
is done in my ifland. They pretend to a wifdom
which is proof againft all temptations, and treat love
as a weaknefs. Have you forgot that I was born in
your empire ? Why do you delay to bury in your
profound abyffes thefe two wretches whom I cannot
endure ?

She had hardly fpoken, when Neptune lifted the
waves even to the very skies. — Venus fmiled, believing that we should inevitably be wrecked. Our affrighted pilot cried out, that he could no longer
withftand the winds which drove us with violence
towards the rocks. A fudden guft broke our maft,
and a moment after we heard the points of the rocks
breaking thro' the bottom of the ship. The water
enters on all fides ; the veffel finks, and all our rowers fend up loud laments to heaven. I embrace Mentor, and cry, Lo! death is here, we muft meet it
with courage. The Gods have delivered us from fo
many dangers only to deftroy us now. Let us die ,
Mentor, let us die. 'Tis fome confolation to me to
die with you ; it were in vain to contend with the
ftorm for our lives.

Mentor anfwered, True courage always finds fome
refource. 'Tis not enough to receive death with
tranquillity ; we muft without fearing it, make our
utmoft efforts to repel it. Let us take one of thefe
                                                    great

great benches of the rowers; and whilst this timorous and troubled multitude are regretting life, without seeking the means of preserving it, let us not
lose a moment to save ours. Upon this he takes a
hatchet; he cuts the mast quite off, which being
already broken, and hanging in the sea, had laid the
vessel on one side; he throws it over-board; he
jumps upon it amidst the furious billows; he calls
me by my name, and encourages me to follow him.
As a mighty tree, which all the conspiring winds
attack, remains so immoveable on its deep roots that
the tempest can only shake its leaves; so Mentor,
who was not only firm and courageous but calm and
easy, seemed to command the winds and the sea. I
followed him; and who could but have followed,
encouraged by him? We steered ourselves on the
floating mast, which was very serviceable to us; for
we could sit upon it. Had we been obliged to swim
without resting, our strength would soon have been
exhausted. But the storm often turned this huge
piece of timber round, and we were plunged into
the sea; we then drank the briny surge, which
poured from our mouths, our nostrils and our ears,
and were forced to struggle with the billows, in order to get on the upper part of the mast again. Sometimes also a wave as high as a mountain rolled over
us, and then we clung close, for fear the mast, which
was our only hope, should in such a violent shock get
from us.

While we were in this terrible condition, Mentor,
as calm as he is now on this turfy seat, said, Do you
think, Telemachus, that your life is left to the mercy
of the winds and the waves? Do you think that they
can destroy you without a command from the Gods?
No, no, the Gods determine every thing. It is the
Gods therefore, and not the Sea, who are to be
feared. Were you at the bottom of the deep, the
hand of Jupiter could draw you from it; were you
in Olympus, viewing the stars beneath your feet, Jupiter could plunge you to the bottom of the abyss, or

hurl

hurl you headlong into the flames of dreary Tartarus. I heard and admired thefe words, which comforted me a little ; but my mind was not free enough to make him a reply. He faw me not, neither could I fee him. We paffed the whole night shivering and half dead with cold, without knowing whither the tempeft would drive us. At laft the winds began to abate, and the bellowing fea refembled a perfon, who having been long in a rage, is grown tired of his fury, and feels but fome remains of his trouble and emotion ; its growlings were hollow, and its waves hardly higher than the ridges between the furrows of a ploughed field.

Mean while Aurora opened the gates of heaven to the fun, and promifed us a fine day. The eaft was all on fire, and the ftars which had fo long been hid, appeared again, but fled at the approach of Phœbus. We defcried land at diftance, and the winds wafted us towards it. Hope then began to revive in my heart ; but we faw none of our companions ; their fpirits probably failed, and the tempeft overwhelmed them and the ship together. When we were near land, the fea drove us againft craggy rocks, which would have dashed us in pieces, had we not fteered the end of the maft againft them, of which Mentor made as good a ufe as a skilful pilot makes of the beft rudder. Thus we avoided thefe dreadful rocks, and at laft found a pleafant level coaft, where fwimming without any difficulty, we got a-shore on the fand. It was there you faw us, O mighty Goddefs, who inhabit this ifland ; it was there you vouchfafed us a kind reception.

End of the Sixth Book.

THE

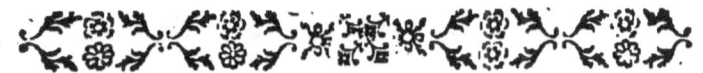

THE
ADVENTURES
OF
TELEMACHUS,
SON of ULYSSES.

BOOK the SEVENTH.

· The ARGUMENT.

Calypfo admires Telemachus in his adventures, and does all she can to detain him in her ifland, by engaging him to return her paffion. Mentor fupports Telemachus by his remonftrances againft the Goddefs's artifices, and againft Cupid whom Venus had brought to her affiftance. Telemachus however and the nymph Eucharis foon feel a mutual paffion, which at firft excites Calypfo's jealoufy, and afterwards her refentment againft the two lovers. She fwears by Styx that Telemachus shall depart from her ifland. Cupid goes to comfort her, and prevails on her nymphs to burn a ship which Mentor had built, at the time that Mentor was dragging Telemachus along to embark on board it. Telemachus feels a fecret joy at feeing the veffel on fire. Mentor perceiving it throws him headlong into the fea, and leaps into it himfelf, in order to fwim to another ship, which he faw near the coaft.

WHEN Telemachus had concluded his narrative, all the nymphs, who had been motionlefs, and kept their eyes fixt upon him, looked on each other, and faid with aftonishment, Who are thefe men, fo beloved of the Gods? Did you

eyes

ever hear of such marvellous adventures? The son of Ulysses already excels his father in eloquence, in wisdom and valour. What an air! what beauty! what sweetness! what modesty! But then, what nobleness and elevation of soul! did we not know that he is the son of a mortal, one might easily take him for Bacchus, for Mercury, or even for the great Apollo. But who is this Mentor who seems a plain, obscure and ordinary man? When one views him near, one finds in him I know not what that is more than human.

Calypso heard this discourse with an uneasiness which she could not hide. Her eyes were incessantly straying from Mentor to Telemachus, and from Telemachus to Mentor. Sometimes she desired that Telemachus would begin the long history of his adventures again; then she would suddenly interrupt herself. At last rising abruptly, and leading him aside into a myrtle grove, she tried all arts to learn of him, if Mentor were not a God concealed under the form of a man. It was not in Telemachus's power to resolve her; for Minerva, who accompanied him in the shape of Mentor, had not discovered herself to him, by reason of his youth: She was not yet sufficiently assured of his secrecy to entrust him with her designs. Besides, she was desirous to try him by the greatest dangers: Now had he known that Minerva was with him, such a support would have buoyed him up too much, and he would without difficulty have braved the most terrible accidents. He really therefore took Minerva for Mentor, and all Calypso's artifices to discover what she desired to know, were in vain.

Mean while all the nymphs gathered around Mentor, and took a pleasure in asking him questions. One enquired the particulars of his journey into Ethiopia; another desired to know what he had seen at Damascus; and a third asked him if he knew Ulysses before the siege of Troy. He answered them all in a courteous manner; and his words, though plain, were
very

very graceful. Calypſo did not leave them long in this converſation ; she returned, and while the nymphs began to gather flowers, ſingirg all the while, to amuſe Telemachus, she took Mentor aſide, in order to make him diſcover who he was. The balmy vapours of ſleep do not glide more ſweetly through the weary eyes and all the limbs of a man who is quite exhauſted by labour, than the Goddeſs's ſoothing words inſinuated themſelves, in order to enchant the heart of Mentor ; but she continually perceived I know not what which baffled all her efforts, and derided her charms : Like a ſteep rock which hides its head in the clouds, and laughs at the rage of the winds, Mentor was ſteadfaſt in his wiſe deſigns, and unshaken by Calypſo's importunities. He would ſometimes even permit her to hope that she should enſnare him by her queſtions, and draw the truth from the bottom of his heart ; but the moment she expected to ſatisfy her curioſity, her hopes vanished : All that she thought she held faſt, ſlipt from her on a ſudden, and a short anſwer of Mentor plunged her again in her doubts.

Thus she paſſed the days, ſometimes flattering Telemachus, and ſometimes ſeeking the means of ſeparating him from Mentor, from whom she no longer hoped for a diſcovery. She employed her moſt beautiful nymphs to kindle the fires of love in young Telemachus's heart ; and a Goddeſs, more powerful than herſelf, came to her aſſiſtance.

Venus ſtill highly reſenting the contempt which Mentor and Telemachus had expreſſed for the worship which is paid her in the iſle of Cyprus, was inconſolable when she ſaw that theſe two rash mortals had eſcaped from the winds and the ſeas, in the ſtorm which Neptune excited She made bitter complaints of it to Jupiter ; but the father of the Gods ſmiling, and unwilling to let her know that Minerva, in the shape of Mentor , had ſaved the ſon of Ulyſſes, gave Venus leave to ſeek the means of being revenged on theſe two men. She quits Olympus ; forgets the

ſweet

sweet perfumes, which are burnt on her altars at Paphos, Cythera, and Idalia ; flyes in her chariot drawn by doves ; calls her son, and grief diffusing itself over her face, which was adorned with new graces, she bespoke him thus :

Beholdest thou, my son, those two mortals who scorn thy power and mine ? Who will worship us for the future ? Go, pierce their insensible hearts with thy arrows ; descend with me to that island, and I will talk with Calypso. She said, and cleaving the air in a golden cloud, presented herself before Calypso, who was then all alone, on the brink of a fountain, at some distance from her grotto.

Unhappy Goddess ! said she, the ungrateful Ulysses disdained you. His son, still more insensible than he, is ready to treat you with the like contempt; but Love himself is come to revenge you. I leave him with you ; he shall remain among your nymphs, as the boy Bacchus was formerly educated by the nymphs of the island of Naxos. Telemachus will look upon him as a common child ; he will not suspect him, and will quickly feel his power. She said, and re-ascending in the golden cloud from which she alighted, left ambrosial odours behind her, which perfumed all the groves of Calypso.

Cupid remained in Calypso's arms. Though a Goddess, she presently felt his flames spreading in her bosom. To ease herself, she immediately gave him to Eucharis, a nymph, who happened to be by her. But alas ! how often did she afterwards repent her doing it ! At first nothing seemed more innocent, more sweet, more lovely, more ingenuous, more obliging than this child. When one saw his sprightliness, his wheedling, his perpetual smiles, one would have thought that he could inspire nothing but pleasure ; but as soon as one trusted his caresses, one felt I know not what of poison. The false malicious boy caressed but to deceive, and never laughed but at the cruel mischiefs he had done, or designed to do. He durst not approach Mentor, whose severity affrighted him ;

him ; he perceived that this unknown perfon was invulnerable, and that none of his arrows could pierce
him. As for the nymphs, they quickly felt the
fires the treacherous boy enkindles ; but they carefully concealed the deep wounds which feftered in
their hearts.

Mean while Telemachus, feeing the child play
with the nymphs, was furprized at his beauty and
fweetnefs. He embraces him ; he takes him fometimes on his knees, and fometimes in his arms, and
finds an inquietude in his own bofom of which he
can affign no caufe : The more he feeks for innocent
diverfions, the more reftlefs and languid he grows.
Do you fee thefe nymphs, faid he to Mentor ? How
different they are from the Cyprian women, whofe
charms were difguftful by reafon of their immodefty ?
Thefe immortal beauties difplay an innocence, a
modefty, a fimplicity that is enchanting. He blufhed,
without knowing why, as he fpoke ; he could not
forbear fpeaking, and yet had he hardly begun but
he was unable to proceed ; his words were broken,
obfcure, and fometimes had no meaning at all.

Hereupon Mentor faid, O Telemachus ! the dangers of the ifle of Cyprus were nothing in comparifon
of thofe which you do not apprehend at prefent.
Grofs vice excites horror, and brutish impudence, indignation ; but modeft beauty is much more dangerous. In loving it, we fancy we love nothing but
virtue, and yield infenfibly to the delufive charms
of a paffion, which we do not perceive 'till it is
almoft too late to extinguish it. Fly, my dear Telemachus, fly thefe nymphs, who are fo difcreet only
to enfnare you the better. Fly the dangers of your
youth ; but above all, fly this child whom you do
not know. It is Cupid, whom Venus has brought
into this ifland to revenge herfelf from the contempt
you fhewed of the worship which is paid her at
Cythera. He has wounded the heart of the
Goddefs Calypfo ; she has conceived a violent paffion for you ; he has enflamed all her attendant
nymphs,

nymphs, and you yourſelf, unhappy youth! burn, and hardly perceive it.

Telemachus often interrupted Mentor, ſaying, Why ſhould we not ſtay in this iſland? Ulyſſes is not living; he muſt long ſince have been buried in the waves. Penelope ſeeing neither him nor me return, has not been able to reſiſt ſo many ſuitors; her father Icarus has conſtrained her to accept of another husband. And ſhall I return to Ithaca to ſee her engaged in new bonds, and her plighted faith to my father broken? The Ithacans have forgotten Ulyſſes: To return were ruſhing on certain death, ſince Penelope's lovers have ſeized on all the avenues of the Port, to make our deſtruction at our return the ſurer.

Mentor replied, Lo the effects of a blind paſſion: We ſubtilly hunt after all the reaſons which favour it; we turn away our eyes that we may not ſee thoſe which condemn it, and are quick-ſighted only to deceive ourſelves and to ſtifle our remorſe. Have you forgot all that the Gods have done in order to bring you back to your own country? How did you get out of Sicily? Were not the evils you ſuffered in Egypt ſuddenly turned into bleſſing: What unſeen hand ſnatched you from all the dangers which hung over your head in the city of Tyre? After ſo many miracles, are you ſtill ignorant of what the Gods have in ſtore for you? But what am I ſaying! you are unworthy of it. As for me, I will depart; I ſhall eaſily find the means of eſcaping from this iſland. Degenerate ſon of ſo wiſe and ſo brave a father, lead here a ſoft inglorious life in the midſt of women, and do, in deſpite of the Gods, what your father thought unworthy of him.

Theſe diſdainful words pierced the very ſoul of Telemachus. He was moved at Mentor's reproaches; his grief was blended with shame; he dreaded the indignation and departure of his wiſe guide, to whom he was ſo much indebted; but a riſing paſſion, of which he himſelf was not conſcious,

had

had rendered him quite another man. What then, said he to Mentor, with tears in his eyes, do you esteem as nothing the immortality which the Goddess offers me; I esteem as nothing, replied Mentor, all that is repugnant to virtue and the commands of the Gods.   Virtue calls you back to your own country in order to see Ulysses and Penelope again; virtue forbids you to abandon yourself to an extravagant passion; the Gods, who have delivered you from so many perils that your glory may shine as bright as your father's, command you to quit this island. Love, the shameful tyrant, love alone, can detain you here.   Ah! what would you do with an immortal life without liberty, without virtue, without glory? Such a life would be the more miserable, in that it could never end.

To this Telemachus answered only by sighs. Sometimes he wished that Mentor had snatched him in spite of himself from this island, and sometimes that his rigid monitor were gone, that he might no longer be reproached with his weakness.   All these opposite thoughts racked his heart by turns, but none of them lasted long; his breast was like the sea which is the sport of all the adverse winds. He often lay extended and motionless on the sea-shore, and often in the midst of a gloomy wood, shedding bitter tears, and making loud laments like the roarings of a lion. He was grown lean; his hollow eyes were full of a consuming fire. His wan, dejected and disfigured face would have made one believe that he was not Telemachus.   His beauty, his sprightliness, his noble air had forsook him; he was dying away. As the flower which blows and diffuses its perfumes around the fields in the morning, decays gradually towards the evening, and loses its lively colours, and languishes and withers, and hangs down its lovely head, unable longer to support itself: So was the son of Ulysses at the very gates of death.

Mentor seeing that Telemachus could not resist the violence of his passion, formed an artful design to deliver him from so great a danger. He had observed that Calypso was passionately in love with Telemachus, and that Telemachus was not less in love with the young nymph Eucharis; for the cruel boy, to plague mankind, seldom makes them love the person by whom they are beloved. Mentor resolved to excite Calypso's jealousy. Eucharis being to go a hunting with Telemachus, Mentor said to Calypso, I have taken notice that Telemachus has a passion for hunting, which I never observed in him before; this diversion begins to give him a distaste to all others; he delights in nothing but the most savage woods and mountains. Is it you, O Goddess, who inspire him with this violent passion?

These words so cruelly stung Calypso, that she could not contain herself. This Telemachus, said she, who despised all the pleasures of the isle of Cyprus, cannot withstand the moderate beauty of one of my nymphs. How dares he vaunt of having performed so many wonderful actions, he whose heart is shamefully softened by effeminate pleasures, and who seems born to pass an obscure life among women? Mentor observing with pleasure how jealousy stung Calypso's heart, said no more, that he might not excite her suspicions; he expressed his concern only by a sad and dejected countenance. The Goddess discovered her uneasiness to him at every thing which she saw, and was continually making fresh complaints. This hunting-match, of which Mentor had informed her, compleated her fury; she knew that Telemachus had sought only to steal away from the other nymphs, in order to converse with Eucharis. A second chace was even already proposed, in which she foresaw that he would behave as he had in the first. To break Telemachus's measures, she declared that she would be one of their party; then all of a sudden, unable longer to moderate her resentment, she addrest him thus:

Is it for this, rash boy, that thou camest into my island, and escapedst the wreck with which Neptune
justly

juftly threatened thee, and the vengeance of the
Gods? Didft thou enter this ifland, which is open to
no mortal, but to defpife my power and the love
which I have fhewn thee? Ye Deities of Olympus
and Styx! hear a miferable Goddefs, make hafte to
confound this perfidious, this ungrateful, this impious wretch! Since thou art more obdurate and unjuft
than thy father, mayeft thou fuffer evils more lafting
and cruel than his? No, no, mayeft thou never fee
thy country more, the poor, the wretched Ithaca,
which thou haft not been afhamed to prefer to immortality: or rather, mayeft thou perifh in fight of
it amidft the billows; may thy body become the fports
of the waves, and be caft without hopes of fepulture
on this fandy fhore? May my eyes fee it devoured by
vultures! She whom thou loveft fhall fee it alfo: fhe
fhall fee it, her heart fhall break at the fight, and her
defpair prove a pleafure to me.

While Calypfo was fpeaking thus, her eyes were
red and fiery; they dwelt upon nothing, and had I
know not what of gloom and wildnefs. Her trem-
blings cheeks were chequered with black and livid
fpots; fhe changed colour every moment. A deadly
palenefs would frequently fpread itfelf over her face;
her tears flowed not as formerly in abundance; rage
and defpair feemed to have dried up their fource, and
they rarely trickled down her cheeks. Her voice was
hoarfe, trembling and broken. Mentor watched all
her motions, and fpoke no more to Telemachus. He
treated him as a patient who is given over, often
cafting looks of compaffion upon him.

Telemachus was confcious how culpable he was,
and how unworthy of Mentor's friendfhip; he dared
not lift up his eyes left they fhould meet thofe of his
friend, whofe very filence condemned him. Sometimes he longed to go and throw himfelf about his
neck, and to tell him how fenfible he was of his fault;
but he was with-held, fometimes by a falfe fenfe of
fhame, and fometimes by a fear of going farther than
he defired, in order to retreat from danger; for the
danger

danger feemed pleafing to him, and he could not yet
refolve to fubdue his fenfeleſs paffion.

The Gods and the Goddeffes of Olympus were affembled together, and obferving a profound filence,
kept their eyes fixt on Calypfo's ifland, to fee which
would be victorious, Minerva or Cupid. Cupid by
playing with the nymphs, had fet the whole ifland on
fire ; and Minerva, in the shape of Mentor, made ufe
of jealoufy, the infeparable companion of Love, againft
Love himfelf. Jupiter refolved to be a fpectator of the
combat, and to remain neuter.

Mean while Eucharis who was apprehenfive of
lofing Telemachus, practifed a thoufand arts to hold
him in her chains. She was now going a hunting with
him for the fecond time, and was attired like Diana.
Venus and Cupid had adorned her with new charms;
infomuch that her beauty on that day eclipfed the
beauty of the Goddefs Calypfo herfelf. Calypfo feeing her at a diftance, viewed herfelf at the fame time
in the cleareft of her fountains ; and being ashamed of
her own face, she hid herfelf in the moft fecret part of
her gotto, and fpoke thus all alone :

My endeavours then to difturb thefe two lovers, by
declaring that I would be at this chace, are, it feems,
in vain ! Shall I be there? What! aid her triumph,
and fuffer my beauty to be a foil to hers ! Muft
Telemachus by feeing me be ftill more enamoured
of his Eucharis? Wretch that I am ! what have I
done? No, I will not go, they shall not go themfelves ; I well know how to hinder them : I will
go and find Mentor, I will defire him to take Telemachus away, he shall carry him back to Ithaca.
But what do I fay? What will become of me, when
Telemachus is gone ? Where am I ? O cruel Venus,
what can I do? Venus, you have deceived me : Oh!
what a treacherous prefent you made me ! Pernicious boy! infectious Cupid! I opened my heart to
thee only in hopes of living happy with Telemachus,
and thou haft brought nothing into it but grief and
                                                        defpair.

defpair. My nymphs are revolted againft me, and my divinity ferves only to make my woes eternal. O! that I could put an end to my life and my pains! Thou, Telemachus, muft die, fince I cannot die. I will be revenged of thy ingratitude; thy nymph shall fee thee expire, I will kill thee before her eyes. But I rave! O wretched Calypfo! what wouldeft thou? Deftroy an innocent youth whom thou thyfelf haft plunged into this abyfs of miferies? It was I who applied the torch to the chafte Telemachus's bofom. What innocence! what virtue! what horror of vice! what refolution againft infamous pleafures! Should I have poifoned his heart? He would have left me. Well! muft he not leave me now, or I fee him full of contempt for me, and living but for my rival! Nay, nay, I fuffer no more than I have well deferved. Go, Telemachus, go, crofs the feas; leave the wretched Calypfo, unable to bear, or to lay down, the burden of life; leave her difconfolate, overwhelmed with shame, and defpairing with thy haughty Eucharis.

Thus fpoke Calypfo alone in her grotto: but rushing fuddenly out of it, Where are you, Mentor, faid she? is it thus that you fupport Telemachus againft vice, which he is now finking under? You fleep, while Love watches for opportunities againft you, I can no longer bear your shameful indifference. Will you always calmly fee the fon of Ulyffes difhonour his father, and neglect his high deftiny? Was it to you or me that his parents entrufted his conduct? I feek for remedies to cure his heart, and will you do nothing? There are lofty poplars, fit for building of a ship, in the remoteft part of this foreft; it was there Ulyffes built that in which he departed from this ifland. In the fame place you will find a deep cave wherein are all the tools which are neceffary for forming, and for joining together, the feveral parts of a veffel.

She had hardly fpoken thefe words, but she repented of them. Mentor loft not a moment; he
went

went to the cave, found the tools, felled the poplars, and in one day made and fitted out a veſſel for the ſea; for Minerva's power and skill require but little time to finish the greateſt works.

Calypſo was in a terrible agony of mind; longing on the one hand to ſee if Mentor's work went on, and not having reſolution enough on the other to quit the chace, and leave Eucharis and Telemachus to their liberty. Her jealouſy would not let her loſe ſight of the two lovers, but she endeavoured to turn the chace where she knew that Mentor was building a ship. She heard the ſtrokes of the axe and the hammer; she liſtened to them, and trembled at every one: But at the ſame time she apprehended that her attention to Mentor might prevent her obſerving ſome ſign, or glance, which Telemachus might make to the young nymph.

Mean while Eucharis ſaid to Telemachus in a jeering tone, Are you not afraid that Mentor will chide you for going a hunting without him? Oh! how are you to be pitied for living under ſo ſevere a maſter! Nothing can ſoften his auſterity; he affects an averſion to all ſorts of pleaſures, and cannot bear that you should taſte of any: nay, he imputes to you as a crime the moſt innocent things. You might indeed be governed by him, while you were incapable of governing yourſelf; but after ſo many proofs of your wiſdom, you should no longer ſuffer yourſelf to be uſed like a baby.

Theſe artful words pierced Telemachus's heart, and filled it with indignation againſt Mentor, whoſe yoke he wished to shake off. He was afraid to ſee him, and was ſo troubled that he made Eucharis no reply. At laſt towards the evening, the chace having paſt in a continual conſtraint on all ſides, they returned by a corner of the foreſt near the place where Mentor had been toiling all the day. Calypſo ſaw from afar that the bark was finished: her eyes were inſtantly overſpread with a thick cloud like that of death; her trembling knees failed beneath her; a cold ſweat ſeized

on

on all her limbs; she was forced to lean on the surrounding nymphs; and Eucharis holding out her hand to support her, Calypso gave her a terrible frown, and pushed it away.

Telemachus seeing the ship, and not seeing Mentor, who had finished his work and was already retired, asked the Goddess to whom the vessel belonged, and for what it was designed. At first she was at a loss for an answer, but at length she said, I ordered it to be built to send Mentor away; you shall no longer be troubled with this rigid friend, who opposes your happiness, and would be jealous if you should become immortal. Mentor leave me! I am ruined, cried Telemachus. O Eucharis! if Mentor forsakes me, I have none left but you. These words escaped him in the transport of his passion; he perceived his error in speaking them, but he had been in too much confusion to attend to their meaning. All the company was struck dumb with surprise. Eucharis blushed, and stood behind with down-cast eyes, quite confounded, and not daring to shew herself; but whilst shame appeared on her face, gladness dilated her heart. Telemachus was no longer himself, and could not believe that he had spoken so indiscreetly. What he had done appeared to him like a dream, but a dream which confounded and troubled him.

Calypso, more furious than a lioness robbed of her young, run at random up and down the forest, unknowing whither she went. At last she came to the entrance of her grotto, where Mentor was waiting for her. Begone from my island, said she, ye strangers, who came to trouble my repose; away with this young fool; and thou, rash dotard, thou shalt feel the effects of a Goddess's wrath, if thou dost not snatch him hence this instant. I will never see him more, nor will I suffer any of my nymphs to speak to him or to look upon him again: And this I swear by the Stygian lake, an oath at which the Gods themselves tremble. But know, Telemachus,
that

that thy miseries are not at an end: thou, ungrateful
wretch, shall not depart from my island but to be a
prey to new misfortunes; I shall be revenged, and
thou in vain shall regret Calypso. Neptune, still
incensed against thy father who offended him in Silicy,
and importuned by Venus whom thou despisedst in the
island of Cyprus, is preparing other tempests for thee.
Thou shalt see thy father who is not dead, but thou
shalt see him without knowing him; thou shalt not
meet him in Ithaca, 'till thou hast been the sport of
the most adverse fortune. Begone, I conjure the celestial powers to revenge me. Mayest thou in the midst
of the sea, suspended on the points of a rock and blasted
by thunder, vainly invoke Calypso, whom thy punishment will ravish with joy.

She had hardly spoken these words, but her troubled mind was ready to take contrary resolutions.
Love revived in her heart the desire of detaining Telemachus. Let him live, said she to herself, let him
stay here; perhaps he may at last be sensible of all my
good offices; Eucharis cannot like me confer immortality upon him. O blind Calypso! thou hast betrayed
thyself by thy oath; thou art bound, and the waves
of Styx, by which thou hast sworn, leave thee no
room for hope. Nobody heard these words, but one
might see the furies painted on her face; and all the
baleful venom of black Cocytus seemed to exhale from
her heart.

Telemachus was struck with horror, of which
Calypso perceived the cause: for what does not jealous love perceive? His terror redoubled the Goddefs's rage. Like a priestess of Bacchus, who fills the
air and makes the lofty mountains of Thrace ring with
her howlings, she runs across the woods with a dart
in her hand, calling her nymphs, and threatening to
kill all who refused to follow her. They, terrified at
this menace, run in crowds around her. Eucharis
herself advanced, with tearful eyes, looking from
afar at Telemachus, to whom she no longer durst to
speak. The Goddess trembled at the nymph's approach,

proach, and inſtead of being appeaſed by her ſubmiſſion, felt a new fury when ſhe obſerved that grief
brightened her beauty.

Mean while Telemachus remains alone with Mentor. He embraces his knees, for he durſt not look at,
nor embrace him in any other manner ; he ſheds a
flood of tears ; he attempts to ſpeak, but his voice
fails him, and his words ſtill more ; he knows neither what he is doing, or what he ought, nor what
he deſires to do. At laſt he cried out, O my real
father ! O Mentor ! deliver me from this train of
woes ; I can neither forſake nor follow you : Deliver
me from this train of woes ; deliver me from myſelf ;
take my life.

Mentor embraces him, comforts him, encourages
him, teaches him how to ſupport himſelf in his grief
without indulging his paſſion, and ſays : Son of wiſe
Ulyſſes, whom the Gods have ſo much loved and
whom they ſtill love, your ſuffering ſuch terrible miſeries is an effect of their kindneſs. Who has not experienced his own weakneſs and the ſtrength of his
paſſions, is not yet wiſe ; for he neither knows nor
is diffident of himſelf. The Gods have led you as it
were by the hand to the very brink of a precipice,
to ſhew you its depth, without ſuffering you to fall
into it. Now therefore learn what you would never
have known, had you not experienced it : You would
in vain have been told of the treaſons of Love, who
flatters to deſtroy, and under an appearance of ſweetneſs conceals the worſt of bitters. The boy, all-
over charming, came amidſt the ſmiles, the ſports and
the graces : You ſaw him ; he ſtole away your heart,
and you took a pleaſure in letting him ſteal it : You
ſought for pretences to continue ignorant of its
wounds, to deceive me and to flatter yourſelf, and
was apprehenſive of nothing. Lo the fruits of your
raſhneſs ; you now deſire death, and that is the only
hope which is left you. The diſtracted Goddeſs
reſembles an infernal Fury ; Eucharis burns with a
fire more tormenting than the bittereſt pangs of death,

and

and all the jealous nymphs are ready to tear each
other in pieces: Thefe are the doings of the traitor
Cupid, who appears fo fweet and gentle. Refume
your courage. How dear muft you be to the Gods,
fince they open you fo eafy a way to fly from Love,
and to fee your dear country again? Calypfo herfelf
is conftrained to drive you away; the ship is quite
ready; why do you delay to quit this ifland, where
virtue cannot dwell?

Mentor, as he fpoke thefe words, took him by
the hand, and dragged him towards the shore. Telemachus followed with reluctance, continually looking behind him, and gazing at Eucharis who was
going away from him. Not being able to fee her
face, he viewed her lovely plaited hair, her flowing
veftments and noble gait, and would gladly have
kiffed the very prints of her feet. Nay, when he had
loft fight of her, he ftill liftened, imagining that he
heard her voice; though abfent, he faw her; her
image was painted and living as it were before his
eyes; he even fancied that he talked to her, not knowing where he was, nor hearing Mentor.

At length awaking as it were out of a profound
fleep, he faid to Mentor, I am refolved to follow
you; but I have not yet taken my leave of Eucharis:
I had rather die than forfake her thus ungratefully.
Stay 'till I have feen her once again, and taken an
eternal farewell. Permit me at leaft to fay to her, O
nymph, the cruel Gods, the Gods jealous of my
happinefs, conftrain me to depart; but they shall
fooner put a period to my life, than blot you out of
my memory. O my father! grant me this laft, this
reafonable confolation, or rid me inftantly of life.
No, I will neither ftay in this ifland, nor abandon
myfelf to love; I have no fuch paffion in my breaft;
I feel no fentiments for Eucharis but thofe of friendship and gratitude; I shall be fatisfied with bidding
her once more farewell, and will then immediately
depart with you.

How

How I pity you, replied Mentor! your passion is so furious that you are not sensible of it. You think you are calm, and yet you beg for death ; you say that you are not vanquished by love, and yet you cannot leave the nymph you doat on. You see, you hear nothing but her ; you are blind and deaf to every thing else : A man raving in a fever says, I am not sick. O blind Telemachus! you were ready to renounce Penelope, who expects you ; Ulysses, whom you shall see again ; Ithaca, where you are to reign, and the glory and elevated fortune which the Gods have promised you by the many wonders which they have wrought in your favour : You were about to renounce all these blessings to lead an inglorious life with Eucharis. And will you pretend that love does not attach you to her? What troubles you? Why do you desire death? Why did you speak with such transport before the Goddess? I do not accuse you of insincerity, but I lament your blindness. Fly, Telemachus, fly ; love is not to be conquered but by flight. Against such an enemy, true courage consists in fear and flying; but in flying without deliberation, and without giving one's self time ever to look behind one. You have not forgotten the cares which you have cost me from your infancy, nor the dangers from which you have escaped by my counsels; be guided by me now, or suffer me to forsake you. Oh! did you but know my grief to see you run to your destruction! Did you but know what I endured when I durst not speak to you! your mother's pangs at your birth were less severe than mine. I was silent, I patiently bore my pains, I stifled my sighs to see if you would return to me again. O my son! my dear son! ease my heart ; restore me what is dearer to me than my life ; restore me the lost Telemachus, and restore yourself to yourself. If wisdom get the better of love in your breast, I live, and am happy ; but if love run away with you in spite of wisdom, Mentor can live no longer.

Whilst Mentor was speaking thus, he continued his way towards the sea; and Telemachus, who had

not

not yet refolution enough to follow him of his own accord, had enough however to fuffer himfelf to be led without refiftance. Minerva, all the while concealed under the form of Mentor, covering Telemachus with her invifible Ægis, and shedding divine rays around him, infpired him with a courage which he had never felt before, fince he had been in this ifland. Coming at length to a fteep rock on the fea-shore, which was perpetually buffeted by the foaming billows, and looking from this eminence to fee if the ship which Mentor had got ready were ftill in the fame place, they were fpectators of a melancholy fight.

Cupid was ftung to the quick when he faw that this unknown old man was not only infenfible of his arrows, but that he was taking Telemachus alfo away from him ; he wept for vexation, and went to find Calypfo, who was wandering up and down in her gloomy forefts. She could not fee him without fighing, and perceived that he opened all the wounds of her heart afresh. You a Goddefs, faid Cupid, and fuffer yourfelf to be conquered by a weak mortal, who is a prifoner in your ifland ! Why do you let him go ? O ! mifchievous Cupid, faid she, I will no longer liften to thy pernicious counfels; it was you drew me from my fweet and profound tranquillity, and plunged me into an abyfs of woes. There is no help for it; I have fworn by the waves of Styx that I will let Telemachus go, and Jupiter himfelf, the father of the Gods, dares not, with all his power, violate this dreadful oath. Begone, Telemachus, from my ifland; and thou, pernicious boy, begone; thou haft done me more mifchief than he.

Cupid, wiping away his tears, faid with a fneering malicious fmile, A mighty difficulty truly ! Leave this affair to me, keep your oath, and do not oppofe Telemachus's departure. Neither your nymphs nor I have fworn by the waves of Styx to let him depart. I will infpire them with the defign of burning the ship which Mentor has built with fo much expedition : his

furprifing

furprifing diligence shall be vain ; he himfelf shall be furprifed in his turn, and have no means left of taking Telemachus from you.

These foothing words filled Calipfo's heart with hope and joy. As a cooling zephir on the margin of a brook revives the languishing flocks, which the heat of the fummer confumes ; fo this fpeech allayed the Goddefs's defpair. Her face became ferene, her eyes grew mild, and the black cares which gnawed her heart, fled for a moment from her : she ftopped, she fmiled, she careffed the fportful boy, and by careffing him prepared new tortures for herfelf.

Cupid, pleafed with having prevailed on her not to oppofe the burning of the ship, went to perfuade the nymphs to do it. They were wandering and difperfed up and down on the mountains like a flock of sheep which the rage of ravenous wolves has caufed to fly from the shepherd. Cupid calls them together, and fays, Telemachus is, ftill in your power, haften to burn the bark which the rash Mentor has built for his flight. They immediately light their torches, they run to the shore, they quiver with fury, they howl and shake their dishevelled hair like Bacchanals. And now the flames afcend ; they confume the Veffel, which was built of dry wood and bedaubed with rofin ; whirlwinds of fmoaky flames afcend to the clouds.

Telemachus and Mentor feeing the blaze from the top of the rock, and hearing the shouts of the nymphs, the former was tempted to rejoice at it ; for his heart was not yet cured, and Mentor obferved that his paffion refembled an ill-extinguished fire, which from time to time breaks from under the ashes, and fends forth glittering fparks. Lo ! faid Telemachus, I am bound again in my fetters : we can no longer hope to quite this ifland.

Mentor plainly perceived that Telemachus was going to relapfe into all his weakneffes, and that he had not a moment to lofe ; he obferved at a diftance,

in

in the midft of the waves, a veffel riding at anchor, which durft not approach Calypfo's ifland, for all the pilots knew that it was inacceffible to mortals. Upon this, the fage Mentor fuddenly pufhing Telemachus, who was fitting on the edge of the rock, throws him headlong into the fea, and leaps into it himfelf. Telemachus, ftunned with the violence of the fall, drank in the briny waves, and became the fport of the billows; but coming to himfelf, and feeing Mentor holding out his hand to affift him in fwimming, he thought only of getting away from the fatal ifland.

The nymphs, who thought them their prifoners, fcreamed in a terrible manner, feeing that they could not prevent their flight. The difconfolate Calypfo returned to her grotto, which fhe filled with her fhrickings. Cupid finding his triumph changed into a fhameful defeat, fprung into the air, fhook his wings, and flew to the Idalian grove, where his cruel mother was waiting for him. The fon, ftill more cruel, comforted himfelf only by laughing together with her at all the mifchiefs he had done.

Telemachus perceived with pleafure that the farther he got from the ifland, the more his courage and his love of virtue revived. Now I experience, cried he to Mentor, what you told me, and what I could not believe for want of experience, that vice is conquered only by flight. O my father, how gracious were the Gods in giving me your affiftance! I deferved to have been deprived of it, and to have been left to myfelf. I now fear neither feas, nor winds, nor tempefts; I fear nothing but my paffions: Love alone is more to be dreaded than a thoufand fhipwrecks.

End of the Seventh Book.

THE

THE
ADVENTURES
OF
TELEMACHUS,
SON of ULYSSES.

BOOK the EIGHTH.

The ARGUMENT.

Adoam, the brother of Narbal, commands the Tyrian ship wherein Telemachus and Mentor are kindly received. The captain knowing Telemachus again, informs him of the tragical death of Pygmalion and Aſtarbe, and of Baleazar's advancement to the throne, whom the tyrant his father had diſgraced at Aſtarbe's inſtigation. During a repaſt which he gives to Telemachus and Mentor, Achitoas by the melody of his voice and lyre draws the Tritons, the Nereids, and the other Sea-Deities around the ship. Mentor taking a lyre, plays upon it much better than Achitoas. Adoam afterwards relates the wonders of Betica, and deſcribes the mildneſs of the air, and the other beauties of that country, whoſe inhabitants lead a quiet life with great ſimplicity of manners.

THE ship which was at anchor, and towards which they advanced, was a Tyrian bark that was bound to Epirus. Theſe Phœnicians had ſeen Telemachus in his voyage from Egypt, but did not know him again in the midſt of the waves. When Mentor was near enough to be heard, he cried out with a loud voice, raiſing his head above

the

the water, O Phœnicians, you who are so ready to
succour all nations, refuse not life to two men who
hope it from your humanity. If you have any reverence of the Gods, receive us into your vessel ; we
will go wherever you go. The commander answered,
We will gladly receive you ; we are not ignorant of
what we ought to do for strangers who seem in such
distress. Upon this they were immediately taken into
the ship.

They were scarcely on board, but they were unable
to breathe and motionless ; for they had swam a long
while, and struggled hard with the billows. By little
and little they recovered their strength, and other
cloaths were given them, because their own were heavy
with the water which had soaked into and poured from
every part of them. When they were in a condition
to speak, all the Phœnicians crowding about them,
desired to know their adventures. The commander
said, How did you get into the island, from whence
you came ; It is reported to be possessed by a cruel
Goddess, who never suffers any body to land in it.
Besides, it is surrounded by frightful rocks, against
which the sea vainly spends its rage, and none can
approach it without being wrecked.

Mentor answered, We were driven upon it ; we are
Greeks; our country is the island of Ithaca, which is
near Epirus whither you are bound. If you are unwilling to touch at Ithaca, which is in your way, we
shall be contented to be carried to Epirus, where we
shall find friends who will take care to supply us with
conveniencies for the short passage we shall have from
thence, and we shall for ever be obliged to you for
the joy of seeing again what is dearest to us in the
world.

Thus it was Mentor who spoke now, and Telemachus was silent, and suffered him to speak ; for
the errors he had committed in the island of Calypso,
had greatly increased his prudence. He was diffident
of himself; he perceived the necessity of always following the wise counsels of Mentor; and when he
could

could not fpeak to him to ask his advice, he at leaft confulted his eyes, and endeavoured to guefs at his thoughts.

The Phœnician captain fixing his eyes on Telemachus, thought that he remembered to have feen him before ; but his remembrance was confufed, and he could not render it clear. Give me leave, faid he, to ask you whether you remember that you have ever feen me before, as I methinks remember that I have feen you : your face is not unknown to me, it ftruck me at firft fight ; but I know not where I have feen you ; your memory perhaps may help mine.

Telemachus anfwered with furprife and joy, I am in the fame circumftances at the fight of you as you are with regard to me ; I have feen you, I know you again ; but I cannot to call to mind whether it was in Egypt or at Tyre. Hereupon the Phœnician, like a man who awakes in the morning, and recollects by little and little the fugitive dream which vanished as his waking, cried out on a fudden, You are Telemachus, with whom Narbal contracted a friendship in our return from Egypt : I am his brother, whom he undoubtedly often mentioned to you; I left you with him after our expedition to Egypt, being obliged to go beyond the remoteft feas into the famous Betica, near the pillars of Hercules. As I did therefore but juft fee you, it is no wonder that I had fo much difficulty in knowing you again at firft fight.

I plainly fee, replied Telemachus, that you are Adoam. I had but a glimpfe of you then, but I became acquainted with you by the converfation of Narbal. O how I rejoice at this opportunity of hearing news by you of a man who will ever be fo dear to me ! Is he ftill at Tyre ? Does he meet with no cruel treatment from the fufpicious and barbarous Pygmalion ? Adoam interrupting him, faid, Know, Telemachus, that fortune commits you to one who will take all imaginable care of you ; I will carry you back to the ifland of Ithaca before I go to Epirus, and Narbal's brother shall not have a lefs friend-

ship

ship for you than Narbal himſelf. This ſaid, he
obſerved that the wind which he waited for, began to
blow; he ordered the anchors to be weighed, the ſails
to be ſpread, and the ſea to be cleft by their oars. He
then took Telemachus and Mentor aſide, to diſcourſe
with them alone.

I will, ſaid he, looking upon Telemachus, ſatisfy
your curioſity. Pygmalion is no more; the juſt Gods
have rid the world of him. As he truſted nobody, ſo
nobody could truſt him. The good ſatisfied themſelves
with bewailing their miſeries and with flying from his
cruelties, without being able to reſolve to do him any
hurt; the wicked thought they could not ſecure their
own lives but by putting an end to his. There was
not a Tyrian who was not daily in danger of being
the object of his jealouſy. His guards themſelves were
more expoſed than others; for as his life was in their
hands, he feared them more than all the reſt of men,
and would on the leaſt ſuſpicion ſacrifice them to his
ſafety. Thus did his endeavours to render himſelf
ſafe, undermine his ſafety. Thoſe who had the care
of his life were in continual danger by his ſurmiſes,
and could not extricate themſelves from ſo terrible a
ſituation, but by preventing the tyrant's cruel ſuſpi-
cions by his death.

The impious Aſtarbe, of whom you have ſo often
heard, was the firſt who reſolved on the king's deſtruction. She was paſſionately in love with a rich
Tyrian youth, whoſe name was Joazar, and hoped
to place him on the throne. To ſucceed in this deſign
ſhe perſuaded the king that Phadaël, the elder of his
two ſons, was impatient to ſucceed his father, and
had conſpired againſt him; ſhe ſuborned falſe wit-
neſſes to prove the conſpiracy, and the unhappy king
put his innocent ſon to death. The ſecond ſon, whoſe
name was Baleazar, was ſent to Samos, under a pretence of learning the manners and ſciences of Greece:
but in reality becauſe Aſtarbe had ſuggeſted to the
king that it was neceſſary to ſend him away, that he
might not enter into a correſpondence with the male-
contents.

contents He was hardly failed, when thofe who had
the command of the ship, being corrupted by this
cruel woman, took their meafures to be wrecked in
the night, and faved themfelves by fwimming to fome
foreign barks that were waiting for them; having
thrown the young prince into the fea.

Mean while Aftarbe's amours were known to every
body but Pigmalion, who fancied that she would never love any one but him. Such an entire confidence
did that miftruftful prince repofe in that wicked woman, and fo exceffively was he blinded by his paffion
for her. His avarice at the fame time prompted him
to feek pretences to put Joazar to death, with whom
Aftarbe was fo paffionately in love; all his thoughts
were bent on feizing the riches of that young man.

But whilft Pygmalion was a prey to fufpicion,
love and avarice, Aftarbe was haftening to take away
his life. She apprehended that he had perhaps difcovered fomething of her infamous intrigues with this
youth. Befides, she knew that avarice alone would
be fufficient to induce the king, to commit an act of
cruelty with regard to Joazar, and concluded that
she had not a moment to lofe to prevent him. She
faw the chief officers of the court ready to dip their
hands in the king's blood, and daily heard of fome
new confpiracy; but she was afraid to entruft her defigns with any one who might betray her. At laft,
she concluded that it was fafeft to poifon Pigmalion.

He ufed moft commonly to eat in private with
her, and cooked himfelf all that he eat, not daring
to truft any hands but his own. He shut himfelf up in
the moft retired part of the palace, the better to conceal his fufpicions, and not to be obferved when he
was dreffing his victuals. He apprehended all delicacies, nor could he prevail upon himfelf to tafte any
thing which he knew not how to drefs himfelf. Not
only all forts of ragooes therefore which are prepared
by cooks, but even wine, bread, falt, oil, milk and
all the common aliments were not for his ufe. He eat

only

only the fruits which he gathered in his garden, or
the pulse which he had sowed and cooked himself.
And lastly, he never drank any water but what he
drew himself out of a fountain, which was locked
up in an apartment of his palace, and of which he
always kept the key. Though he seemed to have so
much confidence in Astarbe, yet he did not fail to take
precaution against her; he always obliged her to eat
and drink before him of every thing of which his repast was to consist, that he might not be poisoned
without her, and that she might have no hopes of
surviving him. But she took an antidote, with which
an old woman, still more wicked than herself, and
the confident of her amours, had furnished her; after
which she was no longer afraid to poison the king,
and she did it in this manner:

The moment they were about to begin their repast, the old woman I have mentioned, made a noise
all of a sudden at one of the doors. The king,
who continually fancied that he was going to be
murdered, is alarmed and runs to the door to see if
it was well secured. The old woman retires; the king
is confounded, not knowing what to think of the
noise he had heard, but afraid however to open the
door to see what was the matter. Astarbe encourages
him, caresses him and urges him to eat; she had put
poison into his golden cup, whilst he was gone to the
door. Pygmalion, according to his custom, made
her drink first, which she did without any apprehension, relying on her antidote. Pygmalion drank also,
and soon after fell into a swoon. Astarbe, who
knew that he was capable of killing her on the least
suspicion, began to rend her cloaths, to tear off her
hair, and to make bitter lamentations; she embraced
the dying king; she held him locked in her arms,
and bedewed him with floods of tears; for this artful
woman always had tears at command. At last,
seeing that the king's strength was exhausted and
that he was as it were in the agonies of death, and
being afraid that he should recover and cause her

to

to die with him, she passed from caresses and the tenderest marks of friendship to the most horrible fury; she rushed upon him and stifled him. She afterwards tore the royal signet from his finger, took the diadem from his head, and called in Joazar, to whom she gave them both; imagining that all those who had been attached to her, would espouse the interests of her, passion, and that her lover would be proclaimed king. But those who had been most assiduous to please her were groveling mercenary souls, who were incapable of a sincere affection. Besides they wanted courage, and were afraid of the enemies which Astarbe had drawn on herself; they were still more afraid of the haughtiness, dissimulation and cruelty of this impious woman, and every one for his own security wished for her destruction.

Mean while the whole palace is filled with a fearful tumult, and on all sides are heard cries of, The king is dead. Some are terrified, others run to arms, and all seem in pain for the consequences, but overjoyed at the news. Fame carries it from mouth to mouth throughout all the great city of Tyre, and there is not a single person who laments the king; his death is the deliverance and consolation of all his subjects.

Narbal, struck with so horrid a deed, bewailed like an honest man the wretched fate of Pygmalion, who had betrayed himself by his confidence in the impious Astarbe, and had chosen rather to be a monstrous tyrant, than to be, what a king ought to be, the father of his people. He applied his thoughts to the good of the state, and immediately assembled all men of probity to oppose Astarbe, under whom they would have seen a yet crueller reign than that which they now saw at an end.

Narbal knew that Baleazar was not drowned when he was thrown into the sea: They who assured Astarbe that he was dead, spoke as they thought; but favoured by the night, he escaped by swimming, and certain merchants of Crete, moved with compassion, took him into their ship. He durst not return to his

father's

father's kingdom, fufpecting that the wreck was a thing concerted for his deftruction, and dreading Pygmalion's cruel jealoufy as much as Aftarbe's artifices. He remained a long while wandering up and down in difguife, on the fea coaft of Syria, where the Cretan merchants had left him, and was even obliged to tend a flock to get his bread. At laft he found means to let Narbal know the condition he was in, not doubting but that he might fafely entruft his fecret and his life with one of fo tried a virtue. Narbal, though he was ill treated by the father, loved the fon, and was watchful of his intereft; but he took care of it only to hinder him from ever failing in his duty to his father, and he prevailed on him to bear his ill fortune with patience.

Baleazar had written thus to Narbal; If you think I may venture to come to you, fend me a gold ring, and I shall thereby immediately conclude that it is time for me to fet out for Tyre. Narbal did not think proper to fend for Baleazar while pygmalion was alive; he would thereby have hazarded the prince's life and his own, fo difficult was it to be fecure againft the rigorous inquifitions of Pygmalion. But as foon as that unhappy king had fuffered a fate fuitable to his crimes, Narbal immediately fent the gold ring to Baleazar. Baleazar inftantly fet out, and arrived at the gates of Tyre, when the whole city was in confufion about Pygmalion's fucceffor. He was readily acknow-ledged by the principal Tyrians and all the people; for they loved him, not out of any affection for the late king his father, who was univerfally hated, but on account of his own moderation and the fweetnefs of his temper. And then his long fufferings gave him a kind of luftre which brightened all his good quali-ties, and moved all the Tyrians in his favour.

Narbal convened the chief of the people, the old men who compofe the council, and the priefts of the great Goddefs of Phœnicia, who all faluted Baleazar as their king, and ordered him to be proclaimed by the heralds. The people anfwered by a thoufand shouts of
acclaim,

acclaim, which Aftarbe heard from the retired part
of the palace, where she was locked up with her bafe
and infamous Joazar. All the profligate wretches she
had employed during Pygmalion's life, had forfaken
her; for the wicked miftruft and are afraid of the
wicked, and do not defire to fee them in power, well
knowing how perfons like themfelves will abufe it,
and how great their oppreffion will be. But they are
more eafily reconciled to the good, becaufe they hope
to find them at leaft moderate and indulgent. Aftarbe
had none left about her but fuch as were acceffory to
her moft atrocious crimes, and could expect nothing
but punishment.

The palace was forced open; thofe wretches not
daring to make a long refiftance, nor thinking of ought
but flight. Aftarbe, difguifed like a flave, endeavoured to make her efcape; but a foldier knowing her, she
was taken, and with great difficulty faved from being
torn in pieces by the enraged populace, who were
dragging her along in the dirt, when Narbal refcued
her out of their hands. Upon this she begged to
fpeak to Baleazar, hoping to dazzle him with her
charms, and to make him believe that she could let
him into fecrets of importance. Baleazar could not
refufe to hear her. At firft she difcovered befides her
beauty fuch fweetnefs and modefty as were capable
of touching the moft irritated heart. She flattered the
prince by the moft delicate and infinuating praifes,
she reprefented to him how greatly Pygmalion had
loved her; she conjured him by his father's ashes to
pity her. she invoked the Gods as if she had fincerely
adored them; she shed floods of tears and threw herfelf at the new king's feet. But she afterwards ufed
all her arts to render his beft-affected fervants fufpected and odious to him. She accufed Narbal
of having entered into a confpiracy againft Pygmalion, and of having tampered with the people
to make himfelf king to Baleazar's prejudice; adding, that he defigned to poifon this young prince.
She invented the like calumnies of all other Tyrians
who

who were lovers of virtue, and hoped to find in Baleazar's heart the same diffidence and suspicions which she had seen in that of the king his father. But Baleazar, unable longer to endure her black malice, interrupted her, and called for a guard. She was conveyed to prison, and the wisest old men were commissioned to enquire into all her actions.

They discovered with horror that she had poisoned and strangled Pygmalion; the whole course of her life seemed to be a chain of monstrous crimes; and they were going to sentence her to be burnt in a slow fire, a punishment which is appointed for the greatest offences in Phœnicia. But when she perceived that she had no hopes left, she became like a fury come from hell, and swallowed poison, which she always carried about her to end her life, in case she should be doomed to suffer lingering tortures. Her guards perceived that she was in a violent agony, and endeavoured to comfort her : but she answered them only by signs, that she desired none of their comfort. She was put in mind of the righteous Gods whom she had offended; but instead of shewing the confusion and repentance due to her guilt, she lifted up her eyes to heaven with contempt and arrogance, as it were to insult the Gods.

Rage and impiety were stamped on her dying visage; one saw no remains of that beauty which had been fatal to so many men; all her charms were faded; her deaded eyes rolled in her head, and cast forth wild and savage glances; convulsions shook her lips, and kept her mouth gaping horribly wide; her shrunk and shrivelled face made hideous grimaces; a livid paleness and deadly cold had seized on all her limbs. Sometimes she seemed to recover her strength and spirits, but it was only to spend them in howling. At last she expired, leaving all who beheld her full of affright and horror. Her impious soul undoubtedly descended to those regions

gions of forrow, where the cruel Danaïds are eternally drawing water in leaky veffels ; where Ixion for ever turns his wheel ; where Tantalus, burning with thirft, cannot tafte the ftream which flies from his lips ; where Sifyphus in vain up-rolls an ever-falling ftone ; and where Tytius will eternally feel the gnawing vulture in his ever-growing bowels.

Baleazar being rid of this monfter, returned the Gods thanks by innumerable facrifices. He has begun his reign by a conduct directly oppofite to Pygmalion's ; he applies himfelf to the reviving of commerce, which daily languifhed more and more ; he follows Narbal's counfels in his moft momentous affairs, and yet is not governed by him ; for he infifts on feeing every thing with his own eyes. He hears all the different advices which are given him, and purfues that which feems to him the beft. He is beloved of the people, and in poffeffing their hearts, he poffeffes greater treafures than his father amaffed by his cruel avarice ; for there is no family which would not give him their all, were he in any preffing neceffity : What he leaves them therefore is more his own than if he took it from them. He has no need to take any precautions with regard to the fecurity of his life ; for he is always furrounded by the fureft of guards, the love of his people. There is not one of them who does not fear to lofe him, and would not hazard his own life to preferve that of fo good a king. He is happy, and all his fubjects are happy alfo ; he is fearful of over-burthening them, and they of not offering him a fufficient portion of their fubftance. He fuffers them to abound, and their abundance renders them neither intractable nor infolent ; for they are labourious , addicted to trade, and ftedfaft in preferving the purity of their ancient laws. Phœnicia is rifen again to her high pitch of grandeur and glory, and it is to her young king that fhe is indebted for fo much profperity. Narbal governs under him. O Telemachus ! were he to fee you now,

now, with what joy would he load you with prefents!
What a pleafure would it be to him to fend you back
in a magnificent manner to your own country! And
how happy am I in doing what he would rejoice to
do, in going to the ifland of Ithaca to place the fon
of Ulyffes on the throne, that he may reign there as
wifely as Balcazar reigns at Tyre!

When Adoam had fpoken thus, Telemachus,
charmed with the hiftory which the Phœnician had
recited, and ftill more fo with the marks of friendship
which he received from him in his diftrefs, embraced
him with great tendernefs. Adoam then asked him
by what accident he had entered Calypfo's ifland.
Telemachus in his turn related his departure from
Tyre; his paffage to the ifle of Cyprus; the manner of his finding Mentor again; their voyage to
Crete; the public games for the election of a king
after Idomeneus's flight; the refentment of Venus;
their shipwreck: the pleafure with which Calypfo received them; this Goddefs's jealoufy of one of her
nymphs; and how Mentor threw him into the fea, as
foon as he defcried the Phœnician ship.

After thefe relations, Adoam ordered a magnificent repaft, and to exprefs the greater joy, united
all the pleafures which were to be had. During the
repaft, which was brought in by young Phœnicians,
clad in white, with garlands of flowers on their heads,
the moft exquifite perfumes of the eaft were burnt;
and all the rowers benches were crowded with play-
ers on flutes, whom Architoas interrupted from
time to time by the fweet harmony of his voice and
lyre, which were worthy of being heard at the
table of the Gods, and of ravishing the ears of Apollo
himfelf. The Tritons, the Nereids, all the Deities
which are fubject to Neptune, and the fea-monfters
themfelves, allured by this melody, iffued from their
deep and humid grottoes, and fwam in shoals around
the ship. A company of young Phœnicians of an
uncommon beauty, clad in fine linnen whiter than
fnow, danced a long while the dances of their own
                                        country,

country, then thofe of Egypt, and laftly thofe of Greece. Trumpets from time to time made the waves refound to diftant shores.   The filence of the night, the calmnefs of the fea, the trembling light of the moon shed on the furface of the waters, and the dusky azure of the sky befpangled with glittering ftars, ferved to heighten the beauty of the fcene.

Telemachus being of a lively temper and eafily affected, relished all thefe pleafures ; but he was afraid to give a loofe to his inclinations. Since he had fo shamefully experienced in the ifle of Calypfo how apt youth is to be inflamed, he was apprehenfive even of the moft innocent pleafures, and fufpected every thing. He look'd on Mentor, to learn from his face and eyes what he ought to think of all thefe diverfions.

Mentor was very glad to fee him in this perplexity, and feemed to take no notice of it. At laft being moved with Telemachus's moderation, he faid to him with a fmile, I know what you are afraid of, and I commend you for your fear ; but you should not carry it too far. Nobody is more willing than I that you should tafte of pleafures, provided they are pleafures that do not take too firm a hold of you, nor enervate you.   Pleafures which refresh you, and which you may enjoy and yet continue to be mafter of yourfelf, are neceffary ; but not pleafures which run away with you.   I would recommend calm and moderate pleafures which do not deprive you of your reafon, nor ever degrade you into a furious brute.   It is now feafonable to unbend after all your toils. Be complaifant to Adoam, and tafte the pleafure which he offers you. Be merry, Telemachus, be merry. Wifdom has nothing of aufterity or affectation : it is she that beftows real pleafures ; she alone knows to feafon and to make them pure and lafting ; she knows to mix paftime and mirth with grave and ferious affairs ; she prepares pleafure by fatigue, and unbends from fatigue by· pleafure.   Wifdom is not ashamed of being gay when it is needful to be fo.

This

This said, Mentor took a lyre, and played on it with so much art, that Achitoas let his fall through envy and vexation. His eyes flamed, his troubled visage changed its colour, and every body would have observed his shame and confusion, had not Mentor's lyre ravished the souls of all who were present. They hardly dared to breathe left they should break the silence, and lose something of the heavenly song : they were all the while afraid that it would end too soon. Mentor's voice had no effeminate softness ; but it was various, strong, and humoured even the minutest things.

He sung first the praises of Jupiter, the father and king of Gods and men, who shakes the universe with his nod. Then he represented Minerva issuing out of his head, that is, wisdom, of which this God is the source, and which flows from him for the instruction of those who are willing to learn. Mentor sung these truths with so affecting a voice, and with such devotion, that the whole assembly thought themselves transported to the highest Olympus and the presence of Jupiter, whose looks are more piercing than his thunder. Afterwards he sung the unhappy fate of the youth Narcissus, who falling desperately in love with his own beauty, which he was continually viewing on the margin of a fountain, pined away with grief, and was changed into a flower which bears his name. And lastly he sung the tragical death of the lovely Adonis, whom a wild boar tore in pieces, and the enamoured Venus could not revive by all her bitter complaints to heaven.

None who heard him could retain their tears, and every one felt I know not what of pleasure in weeping. When he had done singing, the Phœnicians looked on each other with astonishment. One said, This is Orpheus ; it was thus that he tamed the savage beasts with his lyre, and removed the woods and the rocks ; it was thus that he enchanted Cerberus, that he suspended the torments of Ixion and the Danaïds, and moved the inexorable Pluto, to

permit

permit him to bring the fair Euridyce from hell. Another cried, No, it is Linus the fon of Apollo. You are miftaken, replied a third, it is Apollo himfelf. Telemachus was little lefs furprifed than the reft; for he did not know that Mentor could fing and play on the lyre in fo exquifite a manner. Achitoas having had leifure to hide his jealoufy, began to praife Mentor; but he blushed as he praifed him, and could not go through with his fpeech. Mentor obferving his confufion, took the word as it were with a defign to put a ftop to his encomiums, and endeavoured to make him eafy by giving him all the commendations he deferved. Achitoas however was difconfolate; for he perceived that Mentor excelled him ftill more by his modefty, than by the charms of his voice.

Mean time Telemachus faid to Adoam, I remember that you mentioned a voyage you made to Betica, after we left Egypt. Now Betica is a country of which fo many wonders are told, that one can hardly believe them. Pleafe to tell me if all that is reported of it be true. I shall with pleafure, faid Adoam, give you a defcription of this famous country, which is worthy of your curiofity, and furpaffes all that fame relates of it. Whereupon he began thus:

The river Betis glides through a fertile country, and under a temperate and ever-ferene sky. The country took its name from this river, which falls into the grand ocean near the pillars of Hercules, and the place where the raging fea, breaking down its mounds, formerly feparated the territories of Tarfis from thofe of Great Africa. This country feems to have preferved the pleafures of the golden age. The winters are mild, the bleak north-winds never blow there, and the heat of the fummer is always tempered by refreshing Zephirs, which cool the air towards the middle of the day. Thus the whole year is an happy union of the fpring and the autumn, which feem to shake hands together. The foil in the vallies and the plains yields two harvefts in a year. The high-ways
are

are bordered with lawrels, pomgranate, jeffamins, and other trees, which are always green and always in bloom. The mountains are covered with flocks which yield a fine wool that is fought after by all the known nations of the world. There are feveral gold and filver mines in this beautiful country ; but the inhabitants, plain and happy in their plainnefs, do not even deign to reckon gold and filver among their riches; they efteem nothing but what really fubferves the wants of man.

When we firft began to trade with thefe people, we found gold and filver applied amongft them to the fame ufes as iron, as in plough-shares. for inftance. As they had no foreign trade, they had no occafion for money. They are almoft all shepherds or hufbandmen. There are in this country but few artificers, for they tolerate no arts but thofe which fubferve the real neceffities of man : befides, moft of the men in this country, though addicted to agriculture and the tendance of their flocks, neglect not the exercife of fuch arts as are neceffary to their plain and frugal way of life.

The women fpin this wool, and make it into a fine and wonderful white cloth ; they make the bread, and drefs the victuals, which is but little trouble ; for they eat only fruits, or milk, and now and then a little flesh. The skins of their sheep they ufe in making a thin fort of covering for their legs and feet, and for thofe of their husbands and children. They make tents, of which fome are of waxed hides, and other of the bark of trees; they make and wash all the cloaths of the family, and keep their houfes in order and wonderfully neat. Their cloaths are eafily made ; for in this mild climate they wear only a fingle piece of fine light cloth, which is not cut at all, and which every one for the fake of decency, wraps in large folds about his body; giving it what form he pleafes.

The men exercife no arts, befides the culture of their lands and the tendance of their flocks, but that

of

of working in wood and in iron : And indeed they
feldom ufe iron, except for the tools which are neceffary to tillage. All the arts which relate to architecture are ufelefs to them, for they never build houfes.
It is, fay they, being too much attached to this world,
to erect a manfion in it, which is much more lafting
than we ; a fhelter from the injuries of the weather is
fufficient. As for all the other arts which are efteemed
among the Greeks, Egyptians, and all other civilized
nations, they deteft them as the inventions of vanity
and luxury.

When they are told of nations that have the art of
erecting ftately edifices, and of making gold and filver
furniture, ftuffs adorned with embroidery and precious
ftones, exquifite perfumes, delicate dishes, and inftruments whofe harmony is tranfporting ; they anfwer in thefe words, Thofe nations are very unhappy
in having employed fo much pains and induftry to
corrupt themfelves. Thofe unneceffary things enervate, intoxicate, and plague thofe who poffefs them,
and tempt thofe who are deftitute of them, to endeavour to acquire them by injuftice and violence. And
can one call a good, a fuperfluity which ferves only
to make men evil ? Are the inhabitants of thofe
countries more healthful and more robuft than we ?
Do they live longer ? Do they agree better among
themfelves ? Do they live a more free, a more quiet,
a more chearful life ? On the contrary, they muft needs
be jealous of each other, they muft feel the gnawings
of black and fhameful envy, they muft be always tortured by ambition, by fear, by avarice, and be incapable of pure fimple pleafures, fince they are the
flaves of fo many imaginary wants, on which they
make all their happinefs depend.

'Tis thus, continued Adoam, that thefe wife people reafon, who have learnt wifdom only by the ftudy
of fimple nature. They abhor our politenefs, and it
muft be owned that theirs is great in their amiable
fimplicity. They live all together without dividing
their lands ; every family is governed by its head, who

is

is indeed its king. The father has a right to punish his children or grand-children, who commit any evil action ; but before he punishes them, he confults the reft of the family. Thefe punishments hardly ever happen ; for innocence of manners, fincerity, obedience, and an horror of vice inhabit this happy region. It feems as if Aftrea, who is faid to have retired to heaven, were ftill concealed among thefe people here below. There is no need of judges among them ; for their own confcience is their judge. All their goods are in common ; the fruits of the trees, the product of the earth, and the milk of the flocks and herds are fuch abundant riches, that fo fober and abftemious a people have no occafion to divide them. Each family, wandering up and down in this beautiful country, removes its tents from one place to another, when it has confumed the fruits and eat up the paftures of that where it was fettled. They have therefore no private interefts to maintain among themfelves, and they love each other with a brotherly love which nothing interrupts. It is their abridging themfelves of vain riches and deceitful pleafures, which preferves this peace, union and liberty. They are all free, and all equal. There is no diftinction among them, but what is derived from the experience of the wife old men, or the extraordinary wifdom of fome young men, who equal the confummate virtue of the feniors. The cruel and peftilent voice of fraud, violence, perjury, law and war is never heard in a country fo dear to the Gods. Never did this climate blufh with human blood ; nay, that of lambs is hardly ever fhed there. When they are told of the bloody battles, the rapid conquefts, and revolutions which happen in other nations, they are at a lofs to exprefs their aftonifhment. What! fay they, do not men die faft enough, without deftroying each other? How fhort their fpan of life! and yet one would think that it feems too long to them. Are they fent into the world to tear each other in pieces, and to make themfelves mutually wretched ?

To

To conclude, the Beticans cannot conceive why conquerors who subdue vast empires are so much admired.   What madness is it, say they, to place one's happiness in governing other men, since it is so painful an office, if it be discharged with wisdom and justice ! But why should one take a pleasure in governing them whether they will or no ? All a wise man can do, is to submit to govern a willing people whom the Gods have committed to his care, or a people who entreat him to be as it were their father and their shepherd.   But to govern a people against their will, is to make oneself very miserable for the sake of the false honour of making them slaves.   A conqueror is one whom the Gods, incensed against mankind, have sent into the world in their wrath, to ravage kingdoms, to spread every where terror, misery and despair, and to make as many slaves as there are free men.   Does not a man who seeks for glory, abundantly find it, in wisely governing those whom the Gods have subjected to his power ? Does he think that he cannot merit praise but by being violent, unjust, haughty, an usurper and tyrannical to all his neighbours ? He should never think of war, but to defend his liberty.   Happy he, who not being the slave of another, has not the mad ambition of making another his slave ! The mighty conquerors, who are represented to us in such glorious colours, resemble overflowing rivers, which though they seem majestic, ravage all the fruitful fields which they ought only to water.

After Adoam had drawn this picture of Betica, Telemachus, who was charmed with it, asked him several curious questions. Pray do these people drink wine, said he ? They are so far from drinking it, replied Adoam, that they never make any. Not that they want grapes : no country yields more delicious, but they content themselves with eating them like other fruit, and dread wine as the corrupter of mankind.   It is a kind of poison, say they, which
inspires

infpires madnefs; it does not indeed kill a man but it degrades him into a brute. Men may preferve their health and ftrength without wine, and with it they run the risk of ruining both their health and their morals.

Telemachus then faid, I should be glad to know their laws relating to marriage. A man, replied Adoam, can have but one wife, and he is obliged to keep her as long as she lives. The honour of the men in this country depends as much on their fidelity to their wives, as the honour of women in others on their fidelity to their husbands. Never were people fo virtuous, nor fo jealous of their chaftity. The women are beautiful and engaging; but plain, modeft and laborious. Their marriages are peaceful, fertile and unfpotted. The husband and the wife feem to have but one foul in two different bodies, and they divide all their domeftic cares between them. The husband manages all affairs abroad, and the wife confines herfelf to thofe of the houfe. She comforts her husband; she feems born only to pleafe him; she wins his confidence; she charms him lefs by her beauty than her virtue, and the pleafure they take in each other's company lafts as long as they live. The fobriety of this people, their temperance and purity of manners, procure them a long life, and exempt them from difeafes. There are amongft them men of an hundred and of an hundred and twenty years old, who are ftill fprightly and vigorous.

I ftill want to know, added Telemachus, what they do to avoid war with their neighbours. Nature, faid Adoam, has feparated them from other nations, on one hand by the fea, and on the other, towards the north by high mountains. Befides, their neighbours refpect them for their virtue. Other nations not being able to agree together, have often made them the umpires of their differences, and pledged in their hands the lands and cities which were in difpute between them. As this wife people never committed any violence, nobody is miftruftful of them.

them. They smile when they hear of kings who
cannot settle the limits of their dominions among
themselves. Are they afraid, say they, that the earth
will not suffice mankind ? There will always be more
lands than they can cultivate. Whilst there are any
free and untilled tracts, we would not defend even our
own against neighbours who would seize upon them.
There is no such thing in any of the inhabitants of
Betica as pride, haughtiness, treachery, or a desire
of extending their dominion. As their neighbours
therefore have nothing to fear from such a people,
nor any hopes of making themselves feared by them,
they suffer them to be quiet. The Beticans would
forsake their country, or choose to die, rather than
submit to servitude. It is therefore as difficult to
subdue them, as they are incapable of desiring to
subdue others. This is the cause of the profound
peace between them and their neighbours.

Adoam concluded his account by relating in what
manner the Phœnicians carried on their trade in
Betica. These people, said he, were surprised when
they saw that strangers came so far through the waves
of the sea ; they suffered us to build a city in the
isle of Gades ; they received us kindly among themselves, and gave us a part of all that they had, without permitting us to pay for it. They offered likewise freely to give us all that remained of their
wool, after they had made a provision for their own
use : And indeed they sent us a rich present of it ;
it is a pleasure to them to bestow their superfluity on
strangers.

As for their mines, they abandoned them to us
without any difficulty : they were useless to them.
Men they thought were not over-wise in seeking
with so much labour in the bowels of the earth,
for what cannot make them happy, nor satisfy any
real want. Dig not, said they to us, so deep into
the earth ; be contented with ploughing it, and it
will yield you the substantial blessings of food ; you
will reap fruits from it which are of greater worth

than silver and gold, since men desire silver and gold
only to purchase aliments which are the support of
life.

We frequently offered to teach them navigation,
and to carry their young men into Phœnicia ; but
they would never consent that their children should
be taught to live like us. They would learn, said
they, to want all the things which are become necessary to you; nay, they would have them, for
they would relinquish virtue in order to obtain them
by fraud. They would become like a man that has
good legs, who by a disuse of walking, brings himself at last to the necessity of being always carried
like a person that is sick. As for navigation, they
admire the industry of that art ; but they think that
it is a pernicious art. If these men, say they, have
a sufficiency of the necessaries of life in their own
country, what do they go in quest of to another ? Is
not what suffices the calls of nature, sufficient for
them ? They deserve to be wrecked, since they seek
for death in the midst of tempest, to glut the avarice of merchants, and to humour the passions of
others.

Telemachus was charmed at hearing Adoam's
relation, and rejoiced that there was still in the
world a people, who followed uncorrupted nature,
and were at once so wise and happy. Oh ! how different, said he, are these manners from the vain and
ambitious manners of the nations who are esteemed
the wisest ! We are so depraved that we can hardly
believe that so natural a simplicity can be real. We
look on the manners of these people as a beautiful
fable, and they must needs look upon ours as a
monstrous dream.

End of the Eighth Book.

THE

THE
ADVENTURES
OF
TELEMACHUS,
SON of ULYSSES.

BOOK the NINTH.

The ARGUMENT.

Venus, still incensed against Telemachus, begs his des-
truction of Jupiter; but destiny not permitting him to
perish, the Goddess goes to concert with Neptune the
means to drive him from Ithaca, whither Adoam was
carrying him. They employ a deceitful Deity to impose
upon the pilot Athamas, who thinking that he was
arrived at Ithaca, enters full sail into the port of the
Salentines. Idomeneus, their king, receives Telema-
chus into his new city, where he was then preparing
a sacrifice to Jupiter for the success of a war against the
Mandurians. The priest consulting the entrails of the
victims, promises Idomeneus all he could hope for, and
gives him to understand that he would owe his good
fortune to his two new guests.

WHILE Telemachus and Adoam were thus
discoursing together, forgetful of sleep, and
not perceiving that the night was already in the middle of her course, an unfriendly and deceitful Deity
drove them from Ithaca, which their pilot Athamas
sought for in vain. Neptune, though propitious to the
Phœnicians, could no longer brook Telemachus's
escape from the tempest, which had thrown him on

H 2 the

the rocks of Calypso's island. Venus was still more provoked to see the youth triumphing after his victory over Love and all his charms. In a transport of grief she quitted Cithera, Paphos, Idalia, and all the honours which are paid her in the isle of Cyprus. She could no longer stay where Telemachus had despised her power. She ascends to bright Olympus, where the Gods were assembled around the throne of Jupiter. From hence they behold the stars rolling beneath their feet, and view the ball of earth like a little lump of dirt. The immense seas seem to them but as drops of water, with which this clod is a little diluted. The greatest kingdoms are in their eyes but a few grains of sand on the surface of this clod. Innumerable nations and the mightiest hosts are but like ants, quarrelling with each other for a blade of grass on this mole-hill. The Immortals laugh at the most serious affairs which disquiet feeble mortals, and look upon them only as the sports of children. What men style greatness, glory, power, deep policy seems to these supreme Deities but misery and weakness.

It is in this abode, so high above the earth, that Jupiter has fixed his immoveable throne. His eyes pierce the deepest abyss, and enlighten all the secret recesses of the heart. His mild and serene looks diffuse tranquillity and joy throughout the universe. On the contrary, when he moves his locks, he shakes the heavens and the earth. The Gods themselves, dazzled with the rays of glory which surrounded him, tremble as they approach him.

All the celestial Deities were at this instant around him. Venus presented herself in all her native charms. Her flowing robe was brighter than all the colours wherewith Iris decks herself amidst the dusky clouds, when she promises affrighted mortals an end of storms, and proclaims the return of fair weather. It was bound with the famous girdle on which the Graces are represented The
Goddess's

Goddess's tresses were tied negligently behind with a ribbon of gold. All the Gods were surprised at her beauty, as if they had never seen her before, and their eyes were dazzled with it, as those of mortals are, when Phœbus, after a long night, enlightens them with his rays. They looked on each other with amazement, and their eyes continually returned to Venus; but they perceived that those of the Goddess were bathed in tears, and that grief was painted on her face.

Mean while she moves towards the throne of Jupiter with a swift easy pace, like the rapid flight of a bird cleaving the immense spaces of air. He beheld her with complacency, gave her a gracious smile, and rose and embraced her. My dear daughter, said he, what grieves you? I cannot see your tears without concern; be not afraid to disclose your heart to me; you know my fondness and indulgence.

Venus replied with a sweet voice, interrupted by deep sighs, O father of Gods and men! can you who see all things, be ignorant of the cause of my grief? Minerva is not satisfied with erasing even the very foundations of the stately city of Troy which I protected, and with being revenged on Paris, who preferred my beauty to her's; she conducts through every land and sea the son of Ulysses, that cruel subverter of Troy. Telemachus is accompanied by Minerva, which is the cause of her not appearing here in her place with the other Deities. She hath led this rash boy to the island of Cyprus to affront me; he has despised my power; he has not so much as deigned to burn incense on my altars; he has expressed an abhorrence of the festivals which are celebrated in my honour; he has shut his heart against all my pleasures. In vain has Neptune, to punish him at my request, irritated the winds and the waves against him. Telemachus, thrown by a dreadful shipwreck on the island of

H 3   Calypso,

Calypso, has triumphed over Love himself whom I
sent into that island, to soften the heart of this
young Greek. Neither the youth, nor the charms of
Calypso and her nymphs, nor Cupid's burning shafts,
have been able to defeat the arts of Minerva. She has
snatched him from that island; I am confounded; a
boy is triumphant over me.

Jupiter, to comfort Venus, said, it is true, my
daughter, that Minerva protects the heart of this
young Greek against all the arrows of your son, and
that she is preparing him a glory which no youth ever
deserved. I am sorry that he has despised your altars,
but I cannot subject him to your power. I consent,
through my love of you, that he shall still wander by
land and sea, and that he shall live far from his native
country, exposed to all sorts of evils and dangers; but
destiny does not permit him to perish, nor his virtue
to yield to the pleasures with which you sooth mankind. Be comforted therefore, my daughter, and
content yourself with your dominion over so many
other heroes and Immortals.

As he spoke these words, he smiled on Venus with
the utmost grace and majesty. Rays, as bright as the
most piercing lightning, shot from his eyes. As he
fondly kissed the Goddess, he shed ambrosial odours
which perfumed Olympus. Venus could not but be
sensible to this salute of the greatest of the Gods.
Notwithstanding her tears and her grief, joy diffused
itself over her face, and she let down her veil to hide the
blush on her cheeks, and her confusion. All the af-
sembly of the Gods applauded the words of Jupiter;
and Venus, without losing a moment, went to find
Neptune, to concert with him the means of revenging
herself on Telemachus.

She related to Neptune, what Jupiter had said to
her. I knew before, answered Neptune, the unalterable decree of destiny; but if we cannot destroy
Telemachus in the billows, let us at least try all methods to make him miserable, and to retard his return

turn to Ithaca. I cannot confent to wreck the
Phœnician ship wherein he is embarked ; I love the
Phœnicians; they are my people ; no country cultivates my empire like them ; to them it is owing that
the fea is become the bond of the union of all the nations of the earth ; they honour me by continual facrifices on my altars ; they are juft, wife and induftrious in trade, and every where diffufe riches and
plenty. No, Goddefs, I cannot fuffer one of their ships
to be wrecked ; but I will caufe the pilot to lofe his
way, and to fteer far from Ithaca, whither he defigns
to go.   Venus, fatisfied with his promife, fmiled
malicioufly, and returned in her flying car to the
blooming meadows of Idalia, where the Graces, the
Sports and the Smiles exprefs their joy to fee her
again, dancing around her on the flowers which perfume this enchanting abode.

Neptune immediately difpatched a deceitful Deity
of the fame nature as dreams, fave only that dreams
do not deceive but during the time of fleep, whereas
this Deity inchants the fenfes of thofe who are awake.
This evil God, furrounded by an innumerable crowd
of winged illufions, that hovered around him, came
and shed a fubtle and inchanted liquor on the eyes
of the pilot Athamas, as he was attentively viewing
the brightnefs of the moon, the courfe of the ftars,
and the coaft of Ithaca, whofe fteep rocks he already
difcovered near him. The fame inftant the pilot's
eyes no longer faw any thing that was real. A falfe
heaven and a falfe earth were prefented to him. The
ftars feemed as if they had changed their courfe, and
were rolled back again. All Olympus appeared to
move by new laws, and the earth itfelf was changed.
A falfe Ithaca perpetually prefented itfelf to the
pilot to amufe him, whilft he was fteering from
the true. The nearer he approached to this illu-
five image of the coaft of the ifland, the farther
this image retired ; it perpetually fled before him,
and he knew not what to think of its flight. Sometimes he fancied that he already heard the noife ufual

in

in ports, and prepared, according to the orders he had received, to land privately in a little island which is near the great one, to conceal Telemachus's return from Penelope's suitors, who had formed a conspiracy against him. Sometimes he was afraid of the rocks, with which this coast of the sea is bordered, and fancied that he heard the terrible roaring of the billows breaking against them. Then all of a sudden he observed that the land seemed still a great way off. The mountains appeared to his eyes at this distance but like little clouds, which sometimes darken the horizon at the setting of the sun. Thus was Athamas astonished, and the impression of the delusive Deity which bewitched his eyes, sunk his spirits to a degree which he had never experienced before. He was even tempted to believe that he was not awake, but under the delusion of a dream. Mean while Neptune commanded the east-wind to blow, to drive the ship on the coast of Hesperia. The wind obeyed with so much violence, that the bark quickly reached the shore which Neptune had appointed.

Already was Aurora ushering in the day, and the stars which dread and are jealous of the rays of the sun, were going to hide their glimmering fires in the ocean, when the pilot cried out, I can at length no longer doubt it, we almost touch the island of Ithaca; rejoice, Telemachus; you in an hour will see Penelope again, and perhaps find Ulysses, re-seated on his throne.

At these words, Telemachus, who was motionless in the arms of sleep, awakes, starts up, goes to the helm, embraces the pilot, and with eyes yet hardly open surveys attentively the neighbouring coasts, and sighs when he finds not the shores of his native country. Alas! where are we, said he? This is not my dear Ithaca; you are mistaken, Athamas, and not well acquainted with a coast so remote from your own. No, no, replied Athamas, I cannot be mistaken when I view the

shores of this island. How many times have I entered your port? I know even its smallest rocks,
the coast of Tyre is hardly deeper imprinted on
my memory. Obſerve yon jutting mountain; ſee
that rock which riſes like a tower; do you not hear
the billows breaking againſt thoſe other rocks, which
ſeem to menace the ſea with their fall? But do you
not take notice of that temple of Minerva which
cleaves the clouds? Lo! there is the caſtle and houſe
of your father Ulyſſes. O Athamas! you are miſ-
taken, anſwered Telemachus; I ſee on the contrary
an high but level coaſt; I perceive a city which is not
Ithaca. Is it thus, ye Gods! that you ſport with
mankind!

Whilſt he was ſpeaking theſe words, the eyes of
Athamas were all of a ſudden reſtored; the charm
was broken; he ſaw the coaſt ſuch as it really was,
and acknowledged his error. I own, Telemachus,
cried he, that ſome malicious Deity had inchanted my
eyes: I thought that I beheld Ithaca, and a perfect
image of it was preſented to me; but now it vaniſhes
like a dream. I ſee another city, which is undoubtedly Salentum, that Idomeneus, a fugitive from
Crete, has lately founded in Heſperia. I perceive its
riſing and as yet unfiniſhed walls; I ſee a port that is
not entirely fortified.

Whilſt Athamas was obſerving the various buildings lately erected in this riſing city, and Telemachus was deploring his fate; the wind which Neptune cauſed to blow, drove them full ſail into a road,
where they were under ſhelter, and very near the
port.

Mentor, who was neither ignorant of Neptune's
revenge, nor of the cruel artifice of Venus, only
ſmiled at the miſtake of Athamas. When they were
in this road, he ſaid to Telemachus, Jupiter tries
you, but does not will your deſtruction; on the
contrary, he only tries you to open the path of glory
to you. Remember the labours of Hercules, and
let thoſe of your father be continually before your
H 5   eyes.

eyes. Who knows not to suffer, has not a noble soul. You must by your patience and fortitude weary out the cruel fortune, that delights to persecute you. I am less apprehensive for you of the most dreadful frowns of Neptune, than I was of the flattering caresses of the Goddess who detained you in her island. What do we wait for ? Let us enter the port; these people are friends ; we arrive among Greeks : Idomeneus, who has been ill used by fortune, will pity the unfortunate. Upon this they entered the port of Salentum, where the Phœnician ship was admitted without any difficulty, because the Phœnicians are at peace, and trade with all nations of the world.

Telemachus beheld this rising city with admiration. As a tender plant, which has been nourished by the sweet dews of the night, and feels in the morning the embellishing rays of the sun, thrives and opens its tender buds, and expands its verdant foliage, and discloses its odorous blossoms with a thousand new colours, and displays every moment one views it a fresh lustre ; so flourished Idomeneus's new city on the seashore : each day, each hour, it rose with magnificence, and presented strangers, who were afar off on the sea, with new ornaments of architecture which reached even to the heavens. The whole coast rung with the clamours of the workmen, and the strokes of the hammers. Stones were suspended in the air by corded cranes ; all the chiefs animated the people to labour, as soon as Aurora dawned ; and king Idomeneus, giving orders every where himself, caused the works to advance with incredible speed.

The phœnician ship was hardly arrived, but the Cretans gave Telemachus and Mentor all the marks of a sincere friendship, and made haste to inform Idomeneus of the arrival of the son of Ulysses. The son of Ulysses, cried he ! of Ulysses, that dear friend, that wise hero, by whom we at last subverted the city of Troy ! Conduct him hither, and let me con-

. vince

vince him how much I loved his father. Telemachus
was immediately prefented to him, and claims the
rites of hofpitality, by telling him his name. Idomeneus anfwered with a courteous fmiling countenance, Though I had not been told who you are, I
think that I should have known you. Lo! there is
Ulyffes himfelf. Lo his fparkling eyes, and fteady
looks.   Lo his air, at firft cold and referved, which
concealed fo much fprightlinefs and fuch numberlefs
graces. I perceive even that delicate fmile, that carelefs action, that fweetnefs, fimplicity and infinuation
of fpeech, which perfuaded before one had time to
fufpect it. Yes, you are the fon of Ulyffes, but you
shall be mine alfo. O my fon! my dear fon! what
adventure brings you to this shore ? Is it to feck your
father ? Alas! I have no tidings of him. We have
both been perfecuted by fortune; he has had the misfortune of not being able to find his country again,
and I that of finding mine filled with the wrath of the
Gods againft me.   While Idomeneus was fpeaking
thefe words, he looked fteadfaftly upon Mentor, as one
whofe face was not unknown to him, but whofe name
he could not recollect.

Telemachus anfwered with tears in his eyes :
O king! pardon a forrow which I cannot conceal
at a time when I ought only to exprefs my joy
and gratitude for your goodnefs. By your la-
menting the loft Ulyffes, you yourfelf teach me
to feel the misfortune of not finding my father.
I have long been feeking him in every fea ; but the
angry Gods neither permit me to fee him again,
nor to learn if he be wrecked, nor to return to Ithaca, where Penelope is pining away with the defire
of being delivered from her fuitors. I thought I
should have found you in the ifland of Crete ; I
was there informed of your hard fate, and little
imagined that I should ever have come near to
Hefperia, where you have founded a new kingdom. But fortune, who fports with mankind, and
continues me a vagrant in every land remote from

H. 6   Ithaca,

Ithaca, has at length thrown me on your coasts. And of all the wrongs she has done me, this is that which I bear the most willingly. Though she drives me far from my native country, she at least gives me to know the most generous of princes.

At these words Idomeneus tenderly embraced Telemachus, and leading him to his palace, said, Pray, who is this wise senior who accompanies you? I have, methinks, seen him before. It is Mentor, replied Telemachus, Mentor the friend of Ulysses, who entrusted him with the care of my infancy. What tongue can express my obligations to him!

Upon this Idomeneus advances and takes Mentor by the hand. We have, said he, seen one another before now. Do you remember the voyage you made to Crete, and the good counsels you gave me? But the warmth of youth at that time, and an appetite for vain pleasures, hurried me away; it was necessary for me to be instructed by my misfortunes, to learn what I was unwilling to believe. O wise old man, would to the Gods, that I had followed your advice. But I observe with astonishment, that you are hardly at all altered in so many years; you have the same freshness of countenance, the same upright stature, the same vigour; your hair only is a little whitened.

O mighty king, answered Mentor, were I a flatterer, I should tell you also that you still retain the same flower of youth which bloomed on your face before the siege of Troy; but I had rather displease you than wound the truth. Besides, I see by your wise discourse that you do not love flattery, and that one runs no risk in speaking to you with sincerity. You are very much altered; I should hardly have known you again. I plainly perceive the cause; it is your having laid your afflictions to heart. But you have gained by your sufferings, since you have acquired wisdom. A man should not be much concerned at the wrinkles which overspread his face, when his heart is exercised and strengthened in virtue.

And

And then you muſt know that kings always decay
ſooner than other men.   In adverſity, the troubles of
the mind and the toils of the body make them grow
old before their time ; in proſperity, the pleaſures of
a luxurious life wear them away ſtill faſter than all the
fatigues of war ; for nothing is ſo unhealthful as immoderate pleaſures.   Hence it is that princes, both in
peace and war, have always pains and pleaſures which
bring on old age before its natural ſeaſon.   Whereas
a life of ſobriety, temperance and ſimplicity, free
from diſquietudes and paſſions, regular and laborious, preſerves in the limbs of a wiſe man the ſpright-
ly vigour of youth, which without theſe precautions
is always ready to take its flight on the wings of time.
    Idomeneus, charmed with Mentor's diſcourſe,
would have heard him a long while, had he not been
put in mind of a ſacrifice which he was to offer to Jupiter.   Telemachus and Mentor followed him, ſurrounded by a great crowd of people, who gazed at the
two ſtrangers with great curioſity and eagerneſs.   The
Salentines ſaid one to another, Theſe two men are
very different.   The young one has ſomething wonderfully lively and amiable ; all the charms of youth
and beauty are diffuſed over his face and body ; but
this beauty has nothing ſoft nor effeminate : With
this tender bloom of youth he appears vigorous, robuſt
and hardened to labour.   The other, though much
older, has loſt nothing of his ſtrength.   His mien
ſeems at firſt ſight leſs majeſtic, and his countenance
leſs graceful ; but when one views him near, one finds
in his ſimplicity the marks of wiſdom and virtue,
with an aſtoniſhing elevation of ſoul.   When the
Gods deſcended to the earth to reveal themſelves to
mortals, they undoubtedly aſſumed ſuch forms of
ſtrangers and travellers.
    Mean time they arrive at the temple of Jupiter,
which Idomeneus, who was deſcended from that
God, had adorned with great magnificence.   It was
ſurrounded with a double row of green marble pillars.   The chapiters were ſilver.   The temple was all
                                                        incruſted

incrufted with marble with bas-reliefs, reprefenting
Jupiter's transformation into a bull, the rape of Eu-
ropa, and her paffage to Crete through the waves,
which feemed to reverence Jupiter, though he was
in a borrowed shape. Afterwards were feen the birth
and youthful age of Minos ; and then that wife king,
more advanced in years, giving laws to all his ifland
to make it flourish for ever. Here alfo Telemachus
obferved the principal events of the fiege of Troy, in
which Idomeneus had acquired the glory of a great
captain. Among the reprefentations of the battles,
he looked for his father ; he found him feizing the
horfes of Rhefus, whom Diomed had juft flain ; afterwards difputing with Ajax for the arms of Achilles
before an affembly of all the chiefs of the Grecian
army ; and laftly iffuing from the fatal horfe to shed
the blood of numberlefs Trojans.

Telemachus immediately knew him by thefe famous actions of which he had often heard, and which
Mentor had related to him. The tears flowed from
his eyes, his colour changed, and his countenance
was difordered. Idomeneus perceived it, though Telemachus turned afide to conceal his grief. Be not
ashamed, faid Idomeneus, to let us fee how much you
are affected with the glory and misfortunes of your
father.

Mean time the people affembled in crowds under
the vaft porticoes, formed by the double row of pillars which environed the temple. There were two
companies of boys and girls finging hymns in praife
of the God who holds the thunder in his hands.
Thefe children, who were felected for their extraordinary beauty, had long hair flowing over their
shoulders ; their heads were crowned with rofes and
perfumed, and they were all clad in white. Idomeneus
offered a facrifice of an hundred bulls to Jupiter, to
render him propitious in a war which he had undertaken againft his neighbours. The blood of the victims
fmoaked on all fides, and ftreamed like rivers into
deep vafes of gold and filver.

Old

Old Theophanes, beloved of the Gods, and the priest of the temple, kept his head during the sacrifice wrapped up in the lappet of his purple robe. He afterwards consulted the yet panting entrails of the victims, and then ascending the sacred tripod, Ye, Gods! cried he, who are these two strangers whom heaven sends hither? But for them, the war we have undertaken would be fatal to us, and Salentum would fall into ruins before its foundations were well finished. I see a young hero whom wisdom leads by the hand; it is not permitted to a mortal mouth to utter more.

As he spoke these words, his looks were wild, and his eyes sparkled; he seemed to gaze on other objects than those which were present before him; his face flamed; he was disordered and beside himself; his hair stood upright, his mouth foamed, his arms were raised and motionless, his loudened voice was more than human; he was out of breath, and could not contain within him the divine spirit which possessed him.

O happy Idomeneus, cried he again! What do I see! What evils avoided! What a sweet peace at home, but abroad what battles! What victories! O Telemachus; thy toils surpass those of thy father; the proud foe groans in the dust beneath thy sword; the brazen-gates, the inaccessible ramparts fall at thy feet. O mighty Goddess, let his father ——— O young man! thou at length again shalt see——— At these words his speech dies in his mouth, and he remains, as it were in spite of himself, amazingly silent.

All the people are frozen with fear; Idomeneus trembles, and dares not ask him to make an end of his speech. Telemachus himself is surprised, hardly understands what he hears, and can scarcely believe that he has heard those glorious predictions. Mentor was the only one whom the divine spirit did not terrify. You hear, said he to Idomeneus, the purpose of the Gods; Against whatever nation you fight,
the

the victory will be yours, and you will owe to the young son of your friend the success of your arms. Be not jealous of him, but make a right use of what the Gods give you by him.

Idomeneus not being yet recovered from his surprize, sought for words in vain; his tongue continued motionless. Telemachus coming sooner to himself, said to Mentor, The promise of so much glory affects me not; but, pray, to what can these last words refer, Thou again shalt see? To my father, or to Ithaca only? Why alas! did he not proceed? He has left me more doubtful than I was. O Ulysses! O my father! is it you yourself whom I am to see again? Can it be true? But I flatter myself; cruel oracle! thou delightest to sport with a miserable wretch; one word more, and I had been compleatly happy.

Mentor said to him, Revere what the Gods reveal, and do not attempt to pry into things which they are pleased to hide: rash curiosity deserves to be put to confusion. It is through wisdom and goodness that the Gods wrap up the fates of feeble mortals in an impenetrable night. It is useful to foresee what depends on us, that we may perform it well; but it is not less useful to be ignorant of what does not depend on our care, and of what the Gods design to do with us.

Telemachus, touched with these words, contained himself, though not without great difficulty. Idomeneus, who was recovered from his surprise, began on his part to give thanks to almighty Jupiter for sending him the young Telemachus and the wise Mentor, to make him victorious over his enemies. After a sumptuous repast, which followed the sacrifice, he thus addrest the two strangers:

I confess that I was not sufficiently versed in the art of government at my return to Crete, after the siege of Troy. You know, my dear friends, the misfortunes which robbed me of my crown in that great island, as you say that you have been there since I departed from it. And yet am I happy, abun-

dantly

dantly happy, if my moſt cruel diſaſters have inſtructed and made me wiſer.   I croſſed the ſeas like
a fugitive, purſued by the vengeance of Gods and
men.   All my former glory ſerved but to make my
fall the more ignominious and the more inſupportable.   I came to ſhelter my houſehold Gods on this
deſert coaſt, where I found nothing but lands uncultivated and over-run with thorns and brambles,
foreſts as old as the earth itſelf, and rocks which
were almoſt inacceſſible, and which ſerved for a
harbour to the ſavage beaſts.   And yet was I reduced to the neceſſity of being glad to poſſeſs, with
the handful of ſoldiers and companions, who were
ſo kind as to accompany me in my misfortunes,
this ſavage land, and to make it my country; deſ-
pairing of ever ſeeing that happy iſland again, where
the Gods gave me to be born and to reign.   Alas!
ſaid I to myſelf, what a change; What a fearful
example am I to princes! I ſhould be ſhewn to all
the rulers of the world as a leſſon of inſtruction to
them.   They fancy that they have nothing to fear,
becauſe of their elevation above the reſt of men:
Alas! their very elevation is the cauſe of their having every thing to fear.   I was formidable to my
enemies, and beloved by my ſubjects; I commanded a powerful and warlike people; fame had
founded my renown in the moſt diſtant nations; I
reigned in a fertile and delightful iſland; an hundred cities paid me an annual tribute of their
riches: my ſubjects acknowledged that I was deſcended from Jupiter, who was born in their country, and they loved me as the grandſon of the
wiſe Minos, whoſe laws make them ſo powerful
and happy.   What was wanting to my felicity,
except the knowing how to enjoy it with moderation? But my pride and the adulation I liſtened to, ſubverted my throne.   Thus will all kings
fall, who give themſelves up to their paſſions, and
to the counſels of flatterers.   I endeavoured all the
day to wear a face of chearfulneſs and hope, to
keep

keep up the spirits of my companions. Let us build, said I to them, a new city, which may make us amends for all our losses. We are surrounded by nations, who have set us a good example for such an enterprise. We see Tarentum rising near us, a new kingdom founded by Phalantus and his Lacedæmonians. Philoctetes gives the name of Petilia to a great city which he is building on the same coast. Metapontum is also a colony of the like kind. Shall we do less than all these strangers who are wanderers as well as we? Fortune is not more rigorous to us.

While I endeavoured by these words to sweeten the toils of my companions, I concealed a deadly anguish in the bottom of my heart. It was some comfort to me when the day-light forsook and night wrapped me in her shades, to be at liberty to bewail my wretched condition. Two floods of bitter tears would then stream from my eyes, and gentle slumber was a stranger to me. The next day I renewed my toils with fresh ardour. Lo the cause, Mentor, that you find me grown so old.

When Idomeneus had ended the relation of his miseries, he begged Telemachus and Mentor to assist him in the war wherein he was engaged. I will send you back, said he, to Ithaca as soon as the war is ended. Mean while I will send ships to all the most distant shores, to learn news of Ulysses. On what part soever of the known world storms or the anger of some Deity may have thrown him, I shall easily bring him from thence. The Gods grant that he be still alive! As for you, I will send you home with the best ships which were ever built in the island of Crete; they are built of timber felled on the true mount Ida, where Jupiter was born. This sacred wood is unperishable in the waves, and the winds and the rocks dread and severe it; nay, Neptune himself in his greatest rage is afraid to stir up the billows against it. Be assured therefore of returning happily and without

out any difficulty to Ithaca, and that no adverse Deity will again be able to make you wander over so many seas. The passage is short and easy. Send away the Phœnician ship which brought you hither, and think only of acquiring the glory of establishing the new kingdom of Idomeneus, to make him amends for all his misfortunes. 'Tis at this price, O son of Ulysses, that you will be deemed worthy of your father. Tho' rigorous Destiny should already have sent him down to Pluto's dreary realm, yet will all ravished Greece believe that it sees him again in you.

Here Telemachus interrupted Idomeneus. Let us send back the Phœnician ship, said he. Why do we delay to take arms and attack our enemies ? They are become ours. If we were victorious when we fought in Sicily for Ancestes, a Trojan and an enemy to Greece, shall we not be still more ardent and more favoured by the Gods, when we fight for one of the Grecian heroes, who subverted the unrighteous city of Priam ? The oracle we have just heard does not permit us to doubt it.

End of the Ninth Book.

THE

THE
ADVENTURES
OF
TELEMACHUS,
SON of ULYSSES.

BOOK the TENTH.

The ARGUMENT.

Idomeneus informs Mentor of the grounds of the war against the Mandurians. He relates that those people had at first yield to him the coast of Hesperia, where he had founded his city; that they retired to the neighbouring mountains, where some of their nation having been ill-treated by a party of his, they had deputed two old men to him, with whom he had settled articles of peace; and that after an infraction of this treaty by some of his subjects who were ignorant of it, these people were preparing to make war against him. During this relation of Idomeneus, the Mandurians, who had immediately taken arms, appear at the gates of Salentum. Nestor, Philoctetes and Phalantus, whom Idomeneus thought neuter, are against him in the army of the Mandurians. Mentor goes alone out of Salentum, to propose conditions of peace to the enemy.

MENTOR, looking with a mild and serene aspect on Telemachus, who was already fill'd with a noble ardour for battle, answered him thus. I am very glad, son of Ulysses, to see in you so laudable a passion for glory; but remember that your

father

father did not obtain fo much among the Greeks at
the fiege of Troy, but by showing himfelf to be the
wifeft and the moft moderate among them. Achilles,
tho' invincible and invulnerable, tho' fure of fpreading terror and death where-ever he fought, was not
able to take the city of Troy; he fell himfelf beneath
the walls of that city, which triumphed over the
vanquisher of Hector. But Ulyffes, whofe prudence
governed his courage, carried fire and fword amongft
the Trojans, and to him is owing the fall of thofe
high and haughty towers, which threatened for ten
years together, a confederacy of all Greece. As much
as Minerva is fuperior to Mars, fo much does a dif-
crete and forefeeing valour furpafs a hot and favage
courage. Let us therefore begin by informing ourfelves of the circumftances of this war which is to
be carried on. I shall not shun any dangers; but I
think, Idomeneus, that you should firft let us fee if
your war be juft; then againft whom you make it;
and laftly, on what forces you build your hopes of an
happy event.

Idomeneus replied, When we arrived upon this
coaft, we found here a favage people, who wandered
up and down the woods, and lived by hunting and on
the fruits which the trees fpontaneoufly produce.
Thefe people, who are called Mandurians, were affrighted at the fight of our ships and arms, and retired to the mountains; but as our foldiers were curious to fee the country, and defirous to chace the
ftags, they met with thefe fugitive favages: Whereupon their chiefs befpoke them thus. We abandoned the pleafant fea-shores, to yield them up to
you, and have nothing left but almoft inacceffible
mountains; it is certainly reafonable that you should
fuffer us here to enjoy peace and liberty. We find
you wandering, difperfed and weaker than we, and
have it in our power to kill you, and to conceal
even the very knowledge of your fate from your companions; but we would not dip our hands in the
blood of thofe who are men as well as we. Retire,
and

and remember that you owe your lives to our humanity; remember that it is from a people whom you style rude and savage, that you receive this lesson of moderation and generosity.

Those of our men who were thus sent back by those barbarians, returned to the camp, and related what had befallen them. The soldiers were enraged at it; being ashamed that Cretans should owe their lives to a band of fugitives, who seemed to them more like bears than men. They went to hunt in greater numbers than before, and with all sorts of arms, and quickly met with the savages, and attacked them. The combat was bloody; the arrows flying from each party as hail falls in a field during a storm. The savages were forced to retire to their steep mountains, where our men did not dare to pursue them.

A little while after, these people sent to me two of their wisest old men, who came to sue for peace, and brought me presents of the skins of some wild beasts which they had killed, and of the fruits of their country. After they had presented them to me, they spoke thus:

O king, we hold, as thou seest, the sword in one hand, and the olive branch in the other; (and indeed they held them both in their hands) there is peace or war; take thy choice; we should choose peace. It was for her sake that we were not ashamed to yield to thee the pleasant sea-coast, where the sun fertilizes the earth, and produces such a variety of delicious fruits; peace is sweeter than fruits. It was for her that we retired to those lofty mountains, eternally covered with ice and snow, where we never see the flowers of the spring, nor the rich product of autumn. We abhor that brutality, which under the specious names of ambition and glory madly ravages whole provinces, and sheds the blood of men who are all brothers. If thou art affected by this false glory, we are far from envying thee; we pity thee, and beseech the Gods to preserve us from the
like

like madnefs. If the fciences which the Greeks are
fo careful to learn, and the politenefs they boaft of,
infpire them only with this deteftable injuftice, we
think ourfelves very happy in not having thofe ac-
complishments ; we fhall always glory in being ignorant and barbarous, but juft, humane, faithful,
difintereſted, accuftomed to live on a little, and to
defpife the falfe delicacy which makes men want a
great deal. What we efteem, is health, frugality,
liberty, vigour of mind and body ; it is the love of
virtue, a reverence of the Gods, benevolence to our
neighbours, zeal for our friends, fidelity to all mankind, moderation in profperity, fortitude in adverfity, courage always to fpeak the truth boldly, an
abhorrence of flattery. Such are the people whom
we offer thee for neighbours and allies. If the angry Gods blind thee fo far as to make thee refufe
peace, thou wilt find, but too late, that the men
who through moderation love peace, are the moft
formidable in war.

While thefe old men were talking to me thus, I
was unwearied with looking upon them. Their
beards were long and uncouth, their hair fhorter
and hoary, their eye-brows bushy, their eyes lively,
their looks and countenance refolute, their fpeech
grave and full of authority, and their manners plain
and ingenuous. The furs, which ferved them for
cloaths, being tied in a knot on their shoulders, one
faw more nervous arms, and larger mufcles than
thofe of our wreftlers. My anfwer to thefe two
envoys was, that I defired peace. We with the
utmoft candour fettled feveral articles between us ;
we called all the Gods to witnefs them, and I fent
thefe two men back with prefents. But the Gods,
who drove me from the kingdom of my anceftors,
were not yet weary with perfecuting me. Our hunters, who could not fo foon be informed of the peace
we had concluded, meeting the fame day a large
body of thefe barbarians, who accompanied their
envoys in their return from our camp, attacked
them

them with fury, killed fome of them, and purfued the reft to the woods. Thus is the war kindled again. Thefe Barbarians believe that they can no longer rely on our promifes or oaths.

To ftrengthen themfelves againft us, they have called to their affiftance the Locrians, Apulians, Lucanians, Bruttians, and the people of Crotona, Neritum and Brundufium. The Lucanians come with chariots armed with fharp fcythes. Among the Apulians every one is covered with fome skin of a wild beaft which he has killed; they carry clubs full of great knots, and befet with fpikes of iron; they are almoft all of a gigantic ftature, and their bodies are rendered fo robuft by the hard exercifes to which they accuftom themfelves, that their very fight is frightful. The Locrians, who came from Greece, ftill favour of their origin, and are more humane than the others; but they have joined to the exact difcipline of the Grecian troops the ftrength of the Barbarians, and an habit of living hard, which makes them invincible. They have light wicker shields covered with skins, and long fwords. The Bruttians are as fwift in the race as the hart and the deer; one would think that even the tendereft grafs were not depreft under their feet; they hardly leave any footfteps in the fand. They rush fuddenly on the foe, and then difappear with equal rapidity. The people of Crotona are expert archers: A common man among the Greeks could not bend fuch a bow as one ufually fees amongft the Crotonians; and should they ever apply themfelves to our games, they will certainly obtain the prizes. Their arrows are dipped in the juice of certain venomous herbs, faid to be brought from the banks of Avernus, whofe poifon is mortal. As for thofe of Neritum, Meffapia and Brundufium, they are endued only with ftrength of body and valour without art. The out-cries which they fend even to the heavens, at the fight of the enemy, are terrible; they are pretty expert flingers, and darken the air
with

with showers of hurled ftones, but they fight without any order. This, Mentor, is what you defired to be informed of; you now know the rife of this war, and who are our enemies.

After this explanation, Telemachus, impatient to engage, thought nothing remained but to have recourfe to arms. Mentor checked him again, and thus befpoke Idomeneus. Whence comes it that even the Locrians, a people of Greek extraction, joined themfelves to Barbarians againft Greeks? Whence comes it that fo many colonies flourish on this coaft of the fea, without having the fame wars as you to maintain? O Idomeneus, you fay that the Gods are not yet weary of perfe-cuting you, and I fay that they have not yet tho-roughly inftructed you. The many evils you have fuffered have not yet taught you what ought to be done to prevent a war. What you your-felf relate of the integrity of thefe Barbarians, fuffices to shew that you might have lived in peace with them ; but haughtinefs and pride draw on the moft dangerous wars. You might have given them hoftages, and taken fome of them; it had been an eafy thing to have fent fome of your chiefs with their embaffadors to conduct them back in fafety. And fince this renewal of the war, you should have pacified them again, by reprefenting that your people had attacked them for want of knowing of the treaty which had juft been fworn to ; you should have offered them any fecurity they might have demanded, and should have decreed fevere punishments againft fuch of your fubjects as should break the alliance. But what has happened fince this beginning of the war?

I thought, replied Idomeneus, that it would be mean in us to fue to thefe Barbarians, who had pre-fently affembled all their fighting men, and had im-plored the affiftance of all the neighbouring nations, to whom they rendered us fufpected and odious. It

I   feemed

feemed to me that our fafeft courfe was immediately
to feize on certain defiles in the mountains, which
were ill-guarded. We feized them without any difficulty, and thereby put ourfelves in a condition to
harrafs the Barbarians. Here I have caufed towers
to be erected, from which our troops can with their
arrows opprefs all our enemies who may attempt to
come from the mountains into our country; and we
can enter into theirs, and ravage, whenever we pleafe,
their principal fettlements. By this means we are
able with unequal forces to refift the innumerable
multitude of enemies which furround us. In fine,
a peace between them and us is become very difficult; for we cannot give up thefe towers to them,
without expofing ourfelves to their incurfions, and
they look upon them as citadels, which we defign to
make ufe of to reduce them to flavery.

Mentor anfwered Idomeneus thus. You are a wife
king, and defire to be told the truth without any
foftenings. You are not like thofe weak men, who
are afraid to view it, and who, for want of refolution
and magnanimity to correct their errors, ufe their authority only to maintain thofe they have committed.
Know therefore that this barbarous people gave you
an admirable leffon, when they came to you to fue
for peace. Was it through weaknefs that they fued for
it ? Did they want courage or forces to oppofe you?
You fee that they did not, fince they are fo inured
to the hardships of war, and fupported by fo many
formidable neighbours. Why did you not imitate
their moderation ? Miftaken notions of shame and
honour have plunged you into thefe evils. You were
afraid of making your enemies too haughty, but you
were not afraid of making them too powerful, by
uniting fo many nations againft you by a haughty
unjuft conduct. Of what ufe are the towers you fo
much boaft of, but to lay all your neighbours under
a neceffity of perishing, or of caufing you to perish,
to fave themfelves from approaching flavery. You
erected

erected thefe towers only for your own fecurity, and
it is by thefe very towers that you are brought into
fuch imminent danger. The fafeft bulwark of a ftate
is juftice, moderation, integrity, and the affurance
your neighbours have of your being incapable of
ufurping their territories. The ftrongeft walls may
fall by divers unforefeen accidents, and fortune is capricious and fickle in war; but the love and confidence of your neighbours, when they have experienced your moderation, render your ftate invincible,
and almoft always prevent its being attacked : And
though an unjuft neighbour fhould attack it, all others
being interefted in its prefervation, immediately take
arms in its defence. This affiftance of fo many nations, who find their true intereft in fupporting yours,
would have made you much more powerful than thefe
towers, which render your evils incurable. Had you
at firft taken care to prevent the jealoufy of all your
neighbours, your rifing city would have flourifhed in
an happy peace, and you would have been the arbiter of all the nations of Hefperia. But let us confine
ourfelves at prefent to enquire how you may retrieve
the paft by the future. You began with telling me
that there are feveral Greek colonies on this coaft.
Now they muft be difpofed to affift you ; they have
not forgot either the great reputation of Minos the
fon of Jupiter, or your own labours at the fiege of
Troy, where you fo often fignalized yourfelf among
the Grecian princes in the common quarrel of all
Greece. Why do you not try to induce thefe colonies to efpoufe your caufe ?

They are all refolved, replied Idomeneus, to remain
neuter : Not but that they had fome inclination to
affift me ; but the too great luftre which this city had
from its birth, has alarmed them. Thefe Greeks, as
well as the other nations, were afraid that we had defigns on their liberty. They fancied, that after fubduing the Barbarians of the mountains, we fhould push
our ambition further. In a word, they are all againft

us: even they who do not openly engage in the war, wish to see us humbled; jealousy leaves us not a single ally.

Strange misfortune, replied Mentor! By endeavouring to appear too powerful, you ruin your power; and while you are abroad the object of the fear and hatred of your neighbours, you exhaust yourself at home by the efforts which are necessary to support such a war. O unhappy, thrice unhappy Idomeneus, whom even his misfortunes have instructed but by halves! Do you need a second fall, to learn to foresee the evils which threaten the greatest kings-? Come, leave this affair to me? do you only give me a particular account of these Greek cities that refuse to enter into an alliance with you.

The chief, replied Idomeneus, is the city of Tarentum, founded three years since by Phalantus. He collected together a great number of young men, born of women who forgot their husbands during the Trojan war. When the husbands returned, their wives endeavoured to pacify them, and disowned their crimes. These numerous youths, who were born out of wedlock, and knew neither father nor mother, lived in a boundless licentiousness; and the severity of the laws restraining their disorders, they united under Phalantus, a bold, intrepid and ambitious chief, who had won their hearts by his artifices. He came to this shore with these young Laconians, where they have made Tarentum a second Lacedæmon. On the other side, Philoctetes, who acquired such great renown at the siege of Troy by carrying the arrows of Hercules thither, has built in this neighbourhood the walls of Petilia, less powerful indeed, but more wisely governed than Tarentum. And lastly we have hard by us the city of Metapontum, founded by the sage Nestor and his Pylians.

How, replied Mentor, is Nestor in Hesperia, and have you not been able to engage him in your interest? Nestor! who has so often seen you combat against

the

the Trojans, and whose friend you was! I lost his friendship, answered Idomeneus, by the artifice of these people, who have nothing of barbarous but the name ; they have been artful enough to persuade him that I designed to make myself the tyrant of Hesperia.   We will undeceive him, said Mentor. Telemachus visited him at Pylos, before he came to settle his colony, and before we undertook our long voyages in quest of Ulysses. He cannot yet have forgot this hero, nor the marks of affection which he gave his son Telemachus. But the main thing is to cure him of his jealousy. It was by the umbrage given to all your neighbours, that this war was kindled, and it is by removing these vain surmises that it may be extinguished. Once more, I say, leave the management of this affair to me.

At these words Idomeneus embracing Mentor, dissolved into tears, and was not able to speak. At length he with difficulty uttered these words : O wise senior, sent by the Gods to repair all my errors, I confess that I should have been provoked at any other who should have spoken so freely to me as you have done ; I confess that you alone could induce me to sue for peace. I was resolved to perish, or to conquer all my enemies ; but it is fit to be guided by your counsels rather than by my passion. O happy Telemachus ! you can never go astray like me, since you have such a guide.   You, Mentor, may do what you please ; the wisdom of the Gods resides in you ; even Minerva herself could not give more salutary counsels.   Go, promise, conclude, yield up all that I have, Idomeneus will consent to all that you shall think proper to do.

While they were thus discoursing together, there was suddenly heard a confused noise of chariots, neighing of horses, terrible outcries of men and trumpets, which filled the air with their martial clangors. The general cry is, Lo ! the enemy has made a large circuit to avoid the guarded defiles ! Lo ! they come to besiege Salentum. The old men and

the women are in the utmoft confternation.   Alas!
faid they, did we forfake our dear country, the
fruitful Crete, and follow an unhappy prince through
fo many feas, to found a city which will be laid in
ashes like Troy ? They faw from the tops of their
new-erected walls, in the fpacious plain below, the
helmets, cuiraffes and shields of the enemy glitter
in the fun ; their eyes were dazzled with them.
They alfo beheld briftling pikes that covered the
earth, as it is cove ed by a plentiful harveft, which
Ceres prepares in the fields of Enna in Sicily, during
the eat of the fummer, to reward the husbandman
for all his toils. They already perceived the chariots armed with sharps fcythes, and could eafily dif-
tirguish every nation which was come to this war.

Mentor afcended an high tower to have a better
view of them. Idomeneus and Telemachus followed
clofe behind him. He was hardly arrived but he
perceived on one fide Philoctetes, and on the other
Neftor with his fon Pififtratus, Neftor was eafily
known by his venerable old age. How, cried Mentor ! You imagined, Idomeneus, that Philoctetes and
Neftor would be fatisfied with not affifting you : Lo!
they have taken arms againft you.   And if I am not
miftaken, thofe other troops which march fo flowly
and in fuch good order, are Lacedæmonians commanded by Phalantus. All are againft you : there is
not a fingle neighbour on this coaft, whom you have
not made your enemy without defigning it.

This faid, Mentor defcends in hafte from the
tower ; he goes to a gate in that part of the city towards which the enemy was advancing ; he orders it
to be opened, and Idomeneus furprifed at the majefty with which he does thefe things, does not dare
even to ask him his defign. Mentor makes a fign
with his hand that nobody should follow him, and
goes to meet the enemy, who were furprifed to fee
a fingle perfon prefenting himfelf before them. He
at a diftance shewed them an olive branch as a fign of
peace; and when he was near enough to be heard, he
                                                        defired

defired them to convene all their chiefs. The chiefs immediately affembled, and he befpoke them thus :

Generous affembly of fo many nations which flourish in rich Hefperia, I know that you are not come hither but for the common caufe of liberty. I commend your zeal : but give me leave to reprefent to you an eafy way to preferve the liberty and honour of all your people, without an effufion of human blood.

O Neftor ! O fage Neftor ! whom I fee in this affembly, you are not ignorant how fatal war is even to thofe who undertake it juftly, and under the protection of the Gods. War is the greateft of evils with which the Gods afflict mankind. You will never forget what the Greeks fuffered for ten years together before unhappy Troy. What divifions among their chiefs ! What ficklenefs of fortune ! What havock of the Greeks by the hands of Hector ! What diftrefs occafioned by this war in all the moft powerful cities, during the abfence of their kings ! At their return fome were shipwrecked at the promontory of Caphareus, and others met a dreadful death even in the bofom of their wives. Ye Gods ! it was therefore in your anger that you armed Greece for this celebrated expedition. O ye nations of Hefperia, may the Gods never give you fo fatal a victory ! Troy indeed lies in ashes ; but it had been better for the Greeks, were it ftill in all its glory, and the effeminate Paris in the enjoyment of his infamous amour with Helena. O Philoctetes ! fo long miferable and deferted in the ifle of Lemnos, are you not afraid of meeting the like calamities in a like war ? I know the Laconians have likewife experienced the troubles occafioned by the long abfence of the princes, captains and foldiers, who went againft the Trojans. O ye Greeks, who are come into Hefperia, your coming hither was only a continuation of the calamities, which fprung from the Trojan war.

I 4

Having

Having spoken thus, Mentor went towards the
Pylians ; and Neftor, who knew him again, advanced alfo to falute him. O Mentor, faid he, it is
with pleafure that I fee you again. It is many years
fince I faw you firft at Phocis ; you were but fifteen,
and yet I then forefaw that you would be as wife as
you have fince approved yourfelf to be. But what
adventure has brought you to thefe parts? Pray,
what is your expedient to put an end to this war?
Idomeneus has conftrained us to attack him. We
defire nothing but peace ; each of us had urgent
reafons to wish for it ; but we can no longer be fafe
with him. He has violated all his promifes with
regard to his neareft neighbours. Peace with him
would not be a peace ; it would only give him an
opportunity to break our league, which is our only
refource. He has difcovered to all other nations
his ambitious defign of enflaving them, and has left
us no means of defending our liberty, but by endeavouring to overturn his new kingdom. His
treachery has reduced us to the neceffity of deftroying him, or of receiving the yoke of bondage from
him. If you can find any expedient whereby we
may fafely confide in him, and be affured of a good
peace, all the nations you fee here will gladly lay
down theirs arms, and we shall own with joy that you
furpafs us in wifdom.

Mentor replied, You know, fage Neftor, that
Ulyffes entrufted his own Telemachus to my care.
The youth, impatient to learn the fortune of his
father, vifited you at Pylos, and you received him
with all the kindnefs he could expect from a faithful friend of his father ; you even gave him your own
fon to conduct him on his way. He afterwards undertook long voyages by fea, and has been in Sicily,
Egypt, the ifland of Cyprus, and that of Crete. The
winds, or rather the Gods have thrown him on this
coaft, as he was endeavouring to return to Ithaca.
We arrive in a happy minute to prevent the horror
of a cruel war. It is no longer Idomeneus, it is the
                                                    fon

son of the wise Ulysses, it is I who am answerable to you for every thing which shall be promised.

While Mentor was discoursing thus with Nestor in the midst of the confederate troops, Idomeneus and Telemachus, with all the Cretans in arms, were looking at him from the walls of Salentum; carefully observing how all that Mentor said was received, and wishing that they could hear the wise conversation of these two seniors. Nestor had always been reputed the most experienced and the most eloquent of all the kings of Greece. During the siege of Troy, it was he that restrained the boiling wrath of Achilles, the pride of Agamemnon, the fierceness of Ajax, and the impetuous courage of Diomed. Soft persuasions flow'd from his lips like a stream of honey; his voice alone was heard by all these heroes; all were silent as soon as he opened his mouth, and there was none but he who could appease the fierce dissentions of the camp. He began to feel the infirmities of chilly age; but his words were still full of strength and sweetness. He related things past to instruct the youth by his experiences, and though he was a little slow of speech, his relations were graceful.

This senior, who was the admiration of all Greece, seemed to have lost all his eloquence and majesty, as soon as Mentor was seen in his company. He looked withered and broken with age; whereas time seemed to have respected the strength and vigour of Mentor's constitution. Mentor's words, though grave and plain, had a vivacity and authority which began to be wanting in the other. All that he said was concise, exact and nervous. He never said the same thing twice, nor ever related any thing but what was necessary to the decision of the affair in debate. If he was obliged to speak several times of the same thing, to inculcate it, or to persuade, he did it by new turns and lively comparisons. He had also I know not what of complaisance and sprightliness, when he would accommodate himself to the wants of others, and insinuate any truth into them. These two ve-

I 5   nerable

nerable men were an affecting sight to this assembly of so many nations. Whilst all the allies, who were the enemies of Salentum, pressed one upon another to have a nearer view of them, and to hear their wise discourses ; Idomeneus and all his people endeavoured by their greedy eager looks to discover the meaning of their gestures and of the air of their faces.

End of the Tenth Book.

THE

THE
ADVENTURES
OF
TELEMACHUS,
SON of ULYSSES.

The ARGUMENT.

Telemachus, defirous of knowing what paffes between Mentor and the allies, caufes the gates of Salentum to be opened to him, and goes to Mentor. His prefence helps to induce the allies to accept of the conditions of peace which Mentor propofed to them. Idomeneus, whom Mentor fends for from the city to the army, confents to all that had been agreed upon. Hoftages are mutually given; a common facrifice is offered between the city and the camp to confirm this alliance and the kings enter as friends into Salentum.

ANd now Telemachus being grown impatient, fteals from the multitude that furrounds him, runs to the gate at which Mentor went out, and with authority commands it to be opened. Idomeneus, who thought him by his fide, is prefently furprifed to fee him running acrofs the plain, and already near to Neftor. Neftor knows him again, and advances, though with flow and heavy fteps, to meet him. Telemachus embraces and holds him locked in his arms without fpeaking. At length he cries, O my father, (I do not fcruple to call you fo) the misfortune of not finding my real father, and the benefits you have conferr'd upon me, give me a right to make use of so endearing a name. O my father, my dear father, do I see you again! O may I thus behold Ulysses! If any thing could make me amends for the loss of him, it would be the finding another Ulysses in you.

At these words Nestor could not retain his tears, and he felt a secret joy at seeing those which flowed with wonderful grace adown the cheeks of Telemachus. The beauty, sweetness and noble confidence of this young stranger, who without any precaution passed through so many troops of enemies, surprised the allies. Is he not, said they, the son of the old man who is come to speak to Nestor! They without doubt have both the same wisdom, though their ages are very different. In one, she as yet but blooms; in the other, she bears an abundance of the ripest fruits.

Mentor who was pleased to see the affection with which Nestor received Telemachus, made his advantage of this happy disposition. Lo the son of Ulysses, said he, so dear to all Greece, and so dear to you yourself, O sage Nestor! Lo! I deliver him up to you as an hostage, and as the most precious pledge which can be given you of the sincerity of Idomeneus's promises. You will easily suppose that I should not be willing that the son's destruction should follow that of the father, nor that the unhappy Penelope should reproach Mentor with sacrificing her son to the ambition of the new king of Salentum. With this pledge, who is come voluntarily to offer himself, and whom the Gods who are lovers of peace, send to you, I begin, O assembly of so many nations, to make you propositions for establishing a solid and everlasting peace.

At the word peace, a confused noise was heard from rank to rank. All these different nations murmured with rage, thinking that it was all lost time while the combat was delayed, and that all these speeches were made only to blunt their fury, and to let their prey escape. The Mandurians in particular were enraged that Idomeneus should hope to deceive them

again;

again; they often attempted to interrupt Mentor, through an apprehension that his wife discourses might draw off their allies, and began to be suspicious of all the Greeks in the assembly. Mentor perceiving this, immediately increased their jealousy, in order to sow discord in the minds of all these nations.

I confess, said he, that the Mandurians have cause to complain, and to demand some reparation of the wrongs they have suffered: but it is not just on the other hand that the Greeks, who settle colonies on this coast, should be suspected and hated by the old inhabitants of the country. On the contrary, the Greeks ought to be united together, in order to make themselves well treated by the other nations; their only business is to be moderate, and never to attempt to usurp the territories of their neighbours. I know that Idomeneus has had the misfortune to give you umbrage, but it is easy to cure you of all your suspicions. Telemachus and I offer ourselves as hostages, who will be answerable to you for Idomeneus's sincerity; we will remain in your hands 'till all the things which shall be promised you, be faithfully performed. What provokes you, ye Mandurians, cried he, is, that the Cretan troops have seized on the defiles of your mountains by surprise, and are thereby able to enter, as often as they please, into the territories to which you retired, in order to leave to them the flat country on the sea-shore. These defiles, which the Cretans have fortified with high towers that are full of soldiers, are therefore the true grounds of the war. Pray, tell me, is there any other?

Hereupon the chief of the Mandurians advanced, and spoke thus: What have we not done to avoid this war? The Gods are our witnesses that we did not renounce peace, 'till peace was irrecoverably banished from us by the restless ambition of the Cretans, and by their making it impossible for us to rely on their oaths. Infatuated nation! to reduce us against our will to the sad necessity of acting a desperate part against them, and of seeking our

safety

safety in their destruction! While they keep these defiles, we shall always think that they design to usurp our territories, and to reduce us to slavery. Were it true that they thought only to live in peace with their neighbours, they would be contented with what we readily gave up to them, and not persist in preserving the keys of a country, on whose liberty they had no ambitious designs. But you know them not, O wise senior; it is our great misfortune to know them. Forbear, O beloved of the Gods, to retard a just and necessary war, without which Hesperia could never hope for a lasting peace. Ungrateful, false and cruel nation, whom the angry Gods sent amongst us to trouble our repose, and to chastise us for our crimes! But having punished us, ye Gods! you will revenge us. You will not be less righteous with regard to our enemies than to us.

At these words the whole assembly was greatly agitated, and Mars and Bellona seemed to go from rank to rank, re-kindling in their hearts the rage of war, which Mentor endeavoured to extinguish. He thus resumed his discourse.

Had I nothing but promises to offer to you, you might refuse to rely upon them; but I offer you an undoubted and present security. If you are not satisfied with having Telemachus and me for hostages, you shall have twelve of the most eminent and valiant Cretans. But it is reasonable that you also should give hostages on your part; for Idomeneus, who sincerely desires peace, desires it without fear or cowardice; he desires it, as you yourselves say that you desire it, through wisdom and moderation; but not through the love of an effeminate life, or a want of resolution at the prospect of the dangers with which war threatens mankind. He is ready to die or to conquer, but he prefers peace to the most shining victory; he would be ashamed to be afraid of being vanquished, but he is afraid to be unjust, and is not ashamed to rectify what he has done amiss.

With

With fword in hand he offers peace, and does not defire imperioufly to prefcribe the condition of it ; for
he values not a forced peace.   He wishes for a peace
with which all parties may be fatisfied, which may
put an end to all jealoufies, allay all animofities, and
remove all diffidence.   In a word, Idomeneus enter-
tains fuch fentiments as I am fure you defire he should.
Nothing remains but to convince you of this, which
will be no difficult matter, if you will hear me with a
calm and unprejudiced mind.

Hear then, ye valiant people, and you, ye fage and
well-united chiefs, hear what I offer you on the part
of Idomeneus.   As it is not juft that he should have
it in his power to enter into the dominions of his
neighbours, nor that they should have it in their
power to enter into his ; he confents that the defiles
which he has fortified with high towers, shall be
guarded by neutral troops.   You, Neftor, and your
Philoctetes, are Greeks by birth ; but on this occafion
you have declared againft Idomeneus : You cannot
therefore be fufpected of being too favourable to his
intereft.   What animates you, is the common caufe
of the peace and liberty of Hefperia ; be then the
truftees and guardians of thefe paffes which are the
caufe of the war.   It is not lefs your intereft to hinder
the ancient inhabitants of Hefperia from deftroying
Salentum, a new colony of Greeks, like thofe which
you have founded, than to hinder Idomeneus from
ufurping the territories of his neighbours.   Hold the
balance between them, and inftead of carrying fire
and fword among a people whom you ought to love,
referve to yourfelves the glory of being their judges
and mediators.   You will tell me that you should
think thefe conditions admirable, if you could be
affured that Idomeneus would faithfully perform them :
I am going to fatisfy you as to that.

The hoftages I have mentioned will be a mutual
fecurity, 'till all the paffes are pledged in your hands.
When the fafety of all Hefperia, when that of Salentum itfelf and of Idomeneus, is in your power, will
you

you not be satisfied? Whom afterwards can you mistrust, except you mistrust yourselves? You are afraid to confide in Idomeneus, and Idomeneus is so far from designing to deceive you, that he desires to confide in you. Yes, to you will he intrust the repose, the lives and liberties of himself and all his subjects. If it be true that you only wished for a good peace, lo! she offers herself to you, and leaves you no pretence to draw back. Once again, imagine not that fear reduces Idomeneus to make you these offers; it is wisdom and justice which engage him to take this step, without being in any pain whether you impute to weakness what he does out of a regard to virtue. At first he committed some errors, and he glories in acknowledging them by these proposals, wherein he prevents you. It is weakness, it is vanity, it is gross ignorance of our own interest, to hope to conceal our faults, by endeavouring to maintain them with pride and haughtiness. Who owns his errors to his enemy, and offers to make satisfaction for them, thereby shows that he is become incapable of committing them, and that his adversary has every thing to apprehend from so wise and resolute a conduct, unless he concludes a peace. Take care left you in your turn give him cause to lay the blame upon you. If you reject peace and justice which court you now, peace and justice will be revenged. Idomeneus, who had reason to fear that he should find the Gods incensed against him, will now have them on his side against you. Telemachus and I will fight in his just cause. I call all the Gods of heaven and hell to be witnesses of the equitable proposals I make you.

This said, Mentor lifted up his arm to show these numerous nations the olive branch, which he held in his hand as a sign of peace. The chiefs, who viewed him near, were surprised and dazzled at the divine fire which sparkled in his eyes. He appeared with a certain majesty and authority superior to every thing that is seen in the greatest of mortals. The enchantment of his sweet and powerful words ravished
their

their hearts; they were like thofe fpells, which in the profound filence of the night, fuddenly arreft the moon and the ftars in the midft of Olympus, calm the enraged fea, filence the winds and the waves, and fufpend the courfe of the moft rapid rivers.

Mentor was in the midft of thefe furious nations, like Bacchus, when he was furrounded by tygers, which forgetting their fiercenefs, and drawn by the force of his enchanting voice, came to lick his feet, and to fawn upon him. At firft there was a profound filence through all the army. The commanders looked on one another, unable to withftand this man, or to conceive who he was. All the troops were motionlefs, and faftened their eyes upon him, not daring to fpeak left he should have fomething more to fay, and they should prevent his being heard Though they could think of nothing to add to what he had faid, they wished that he had fpoken longer. All that he had uttered was as it were engraved on every heart. As he fpoke, he gained their love, he gained their belief; every one was eager and waiting as it were to catch the leaft fyllabe that iffued from his mouth.

At length, after a pretty long filence, there was heard a hollow noife that fpread itfelf by degrees; it was no longer the confufed clamour of people raging with indignation, but on the contrary a gentle friendly murmur. There was already feen in every face I know not what of ferenity and mildnefs. The Mandurians, who were fo much irritated, felt that their arms were dropping out of their hands. The fierce Phalantus and his Lacedæmonians were furprifed to find their hearts fo foftened. The reft began to long for the happy peace which had been difplayed before them. Philoctetes, having a quicker fenfe than other by the experience of his own misfortunes, could not fupprefs his tears. Neftor, who was fo much tranfported with Mentor's difcourfe as not to be able to fpeak, tenderly embraced him; and all the people at once, as though it had been an appointed ed fignal, immediately cried out, O wife old man, you difarm us! peace! peace!

Neftor prefently attempted to fpeak; but all the impatient foldiers fearing that he was going to ftart fome difficulty or other, cried out once again, Peace! peace! Nor could they be filenced 'till all the chiefs of the army joined their cry of peace, peace.

Neftor feeing that he had not the liberty to make a fpeech in form, contented himfelf with faying, You fee, Mentor, the force of the words of a man of probity. When wifdom and virtue fpeak, they calm all the paffions. Our juft refentments are changed into friendfhip and defires of a lafting peace; we accept of the peace you offer us. At the fame time all the commanders held out their hands as a fign of confent.

Mentor run to the gate of Salentum to order it to be opened, and to let Idomeneus know that he might come out of the city without ufing any precautions. Neftor in the mean time embraced Telemachus, faying, Amiable fon of the wifeft of all the Greeks, may you be as wife and more happy than he. Have you difcovered nothing of his fortunes? The remembrance of your father, whom you refemble, has been a means of ftifling our indignation. Phalantus, though obdurate and favage, though he never faw Ulyffes, was moved by his misfortunes and by thofe of his fon. They were preffing Telemachus to relate his adventures, when Mentor returned with Idomeneus and a train of all the Cretan youth.

At the fight of Idomeneus, the allies felt that their refentment was kindling again; but the words of Mentor extinguished the fire when it was juft ready to break out. Why do we delay, faid he, to conclude this holy alliance, of which the Gods will be both witneffes and defenders? May they avenge it, if ever any impious wretch fhould dare to violate it, and may all the terrible evils of war, inftead of crushing the faithful and innocent people, fall on the perjured and execrable head of the ambitious man who shall
trample

trample under foot the sacred rights of this alliance !
May he be detested by Gods and men ! May he never enjoy the fruits of his perfidy ! May the infernal
Furies, in the most hideous forms, provoke his rage
and despair ! May he drop down dead without hopes
of sepulture ! May his body become a prey to dogs
and vultures, and may he in hell, in the deep gulph
of Tartarus, be for ever more cruelly tortured than
Tantalus, Ixion and the Danaids ! Or rather, may
this peace be as unshaken as the rocks of Atlas which
support the heavens ! May all these nations revere it,
and enjoy its fruits from generation to generation !
May the names of those who swear to it be mentioned
with love and veneration by our latest posterity !
May this peace, founded on justice and integrity, be
the model of every peace which shall hereafter be
made in all the countries of the world ; and may all
nations that desire to make themselves happy by uniting together, imitate the nations of Hesperia !

This said, Idomeneus and the other kings swore
to the peace, on the conditions that had been agreed
upon. Twelve hostages were given on each side.
Telemachus insists on being one of the number of
those given by Idomeneus ; but Mentor is not permitted to be one, because the allies desire that he
may remain with Idomeneus, in order to be answerable for his conduct and for that of his counsellors,
'till the entire execution of the things which were
promised. An hundred heifers as white as snow were
sacrificed between the city and the army, and as
many bulls of the same colour, whose horns were
gilt and adorned with garlands. The neighbouring
mountains rung with the frightful bellowings of the
victims, which fell beneath the sacred knife. The
smoaking blood streamed every where. Exquisite
wine was poured forth in abundance for the liba-
tions. The Haruspices consulted the yet-panting
entrails, and the priests burnt incense on the altar,
which formed a thick cloud, and perfumed the whole
country with its odours.

Mean

Mean while the foldiers on both fides, ceafing to view each other with hoftile eyes, began to difcourfe together of their adventures; they already refreshed themfelves after their toils, and had a foretafte of the fweets of peace. Several who had been with Idomeneus at the fiege of Troy, knowing thofe of Neftor again who had fought in the fame war, tenderly embraced each other, and mutually related what had befallen them, fince they had deftroyed the haughty city, which was the ornament of all Afia. They were already laid down on the grafs, were crowned with flowers, and drank the wine together which was brought in large veffels from the city, to celebrate fo happy a day.

Of a fudden Mentor faid, O princes, O affembled captains, you shall henceforth be but one people under different names and different chiefs: So the righteous Gods, who love mankind whom they made, are pleafed to be the bond of their perfect union. All the human kind is but one family, difperfed over the face of the whole earth; all men are brothers, and ought to love each other as fuch. Curfe on thofe impious wretches who feek a cruel glory in the blood of their brothers, which is their own blood! War indeed is fometimes neceffary; but it is the shame of the human race that it is unavoidable on fome occafions. Say not, princes, that it is defirable in order to acquire glory: true glory is not to be found beyond the limits of humanity. Who prefers his own glory to the feelings of humanity, is a monfter of pride, and not a man: he will not even obtain more than a falfe glory: for true glory is found only in moderation and goodnefs. Men may flatter him to gratify his foolish vanity; but they will always fay of him in private, when they will fpeak fincerely, He merited glory fo much the lefs, as his paffion for it was unreafonable. Mankind ought not to efteem him, fince he fo little efteemed mankind, and was prodigal of their blood through a brutal vanity. Happy the

the prince who loves his people and is loved by
them; who confides in his neighbours, and is confided in by them; who instead of making war against
them, prevents their having wars with each other,
and causes all foreign nations to envy the happiness
of his subjects in having him for their king! Be
mindful therefore to assemble together from time to
time, O you who govern the most powerful cities of
Hesperia; let there be a general meeting every three
years of all the kings here present to renew this
alliance by a fresh oath, to confirm your plighted
friendship, and to consult about your common interests. While you continue united, you will enjoy,
in this fine country, peace, glory and abundance:
abroad you will always be invincible. Nothing but
discord, which came from hell to plague mankind,
can disturb the felicity which the Gods are preparing
for you.

Nestor replied, You see by the readiness with
which we make peace, how far we are from desiring to make war through vain glory, or an unreasonable lust of aggrandizing ourselves at the expence of our neighbours. But what can we do
when we border on a violent prince, who knows
no law but his interest, and who loses no opportunity of invading the territories of other states?
Think not that I speak of Idomeneus; no, I no
longer entertain such a thought of him; it is Adrastus
king of the Daunians, from whom we have every
thing to fear. He despises the Gods, and imagines
that all men who are born into the world, are born
only to promote his glory by their servitude. He will
have no subjects, of whom he may be the king and
the father; he will have slaves and adorers. He
causes divine honours to be paid him. Hitherto blind
fortune has favoured his most injust enterprizes. We
made haste to attack Salentum, to get rid of the
weakest of our enemies, who had only begun to
establish himself on this coast, in order to turn our
arms afterwards against this more powerful foe. He
has

has already taken several cities from our allies. The
Crotonians have lost two battles against him. He
makes use of all sorts of means to gratify his ambition: Force and fraud, all is equal to him, provided he crushes his enemies.   He has amassed great
treasures; his troops are disciplined and inured to
war; his captains are experienced; he is well served;
he continually has his eyes himself on all who act
under him; he punishes the least faults severely,
and liberally recompenses the services which are
done him.   His own valour supports and animates
that of all his troops.   He would be a most accomplished prince, if justice and integrity were the rules
of his conduct; but he fears neither the Gods nor
the reproaches of his conscience; he even reckons
reputation as nothing; he looks upon it as a vain
phantom, which restrains only weak minds; he
deems nothing a real and solid good, but the possession of great riches, the being dreaded, and the
trampling all mankind under foot. His army will
soon appear upon our territories; and if the union
of so many nations does not put us in a condition to
oppose him, all hopes of liberty will be taken from
us.   It is Idomeneus's interest as well as ours, to
resist his neighbour who can suffer nothing in his
neighbourhood to be free.   Were we vanquished,
Salentum would be threatened with the same fate.
Let us all therefore make haste to prevent him.
While Nestor was speaking thus, they advanced
towards the city; for Idomeneus had invited all the
kings and principal commanders to go and pass the
night there.

End of the Eleventh Book.

THE

THE

ADVENTURES

OF

TELEMACHUS,

SON of ULYSSES.

BOOK the TWELFTH.

The ARGUMENT.

Nestor, in the name of the allies, asks assistance of Idomeneus against the Daunians their enemies. Mentor, who is desirous to regulate the polity of the city of Salentum, and to inure the people to agriculture, orders matters so that they are satisfied with having Telemachus at the head of an hundred noble Cretans. After his departure Mentor takes an exact survey of the city and the port, informs himself of every thing, and causes Idomeneus to make new regulations with regard to trade and government, to divide the people into seven classes, whose rank and birth he distinguishes by a diversity of habits, and to suppress luxury and useless arts, in order to employ the artificers in agriculture, which he renders honourable.

THE whole army of the allies had now erected their tents, and the plain was covered with rich pavilions of all sorts of colours, in which the weary Hesperians were waiting for sleep. When the kings with their retinue were come into the city, they seemed surprised that so many magnificent edifices had been raised in so short a time, and that the incumbrance of so considerable a war had not hindered

dered this infant city from rising and being embellished all at once.

They admired the wisdom and vigilance of Idomeneus, who had founded so fine a kingdom ; and every one conluded that peace being made with him, the allies would be very powerful, if he would enter into their league against the Daunians. This was proposed to.Idomeneus ; he could not reject so reasonable a proposition, and promised a supply of troops. But as Mentor was not ignorant of any thing which is neceffary to make a state flourish, he knew that the forces of Idomeneus could not be so considerable as they seemed to be ; he took him aside, and addreft him thus :

You see that our cares have not been useless to you. Salentum is preserved from the evils which threatened her : it will be your own fault if you do not raise her glory to the heavens, and equal the wisdom of your grandfather Minos in the government of your people. I continue to speak to you freely, supposing that you desire it, and that you abhor all flattery. While the kings were extolling your magnificence, I was thinking within myself of the rashness of your conduct. At the word rashness, Idomeneus's countenance changed, his eyes were disordered, he reddened, and could hardly help interrupting Mentor, to expres his refentment. Mentor said to him with a modest and respectful, but free and undaunted voice, I plainly see that the word rashness offends you : it would have been wrong in any body but me to have used it ; for kings ought to be treated with respect, and their delicacy tenderly handled even when we reprove them. Truth of itself shocks them enough without the addition of harsh terms ; but I imagined that you. could bear me to speak to you without any softenings, in order to show you your error. My defgn was to accustom you to hear things called by their name, and to perceive that when others give you advice about your conduct, they never dare to speak all that they think. It is neceffary, if you would not be deceived,

always

always to underſtand more than they ſay concerning things, which are not to your advantage. For my part, I will ſoften my words according to your neceſſities ; but it is uſeful to you, that a man of no intereſt or conſequence should ſpeak a rough language to you in private. Nobody elſe will ever preſume to do it : you will ſee the truth but by halves, and under fair diſguiſes.

At theſe words Idomeneus , who had already recovered his temper, ſeemed ashamed of his delicacy. You ſee, ſaid he to Mentor, the effects of an habit of being flattered. To you I owe the ſafety of my new kingdom, and there is no truth which I shall not think myſelf happy in hearing from your mouth : but pity a prince who has been poiſoned by flattery, and has not been able, even in his misfortunes, to find men generous enough to tell him the truth : No, I have never met with one who loved me enough to diſpleaſe me, by telling me the whole truth.

As he ſpoke theſe words, the tears came into his eyes, and he tenderly embraced Mentor : Upon which that wiſe old man ſaid, It is with pain that I force myſelf to ſay ſome harsh things to you ; but can I betray you by hiding the truth from you ? Put yourſelf in my place. If you have hitherto been deceived, it was becauſe you were willing to be ſo ; it was becauſe you were afraid of counſellors who were too ſincere. Have you ſought for men who were the moſt diſintereſted and the moſt likely to contradict you ? Have you been careful to chooſe ſuch as were the leaſt aſſiduous to pleaſe you, the leaſt ſelfish in their conduct, and the beſt qualified to cenſure your unreaſonable paſſions and opinions ? When you have met with flatterers, have you banished them from your preſence ? Were you miſtruſtful of them ? did you repoſe no confidence in them ? No , no, you have not done what they do who love truth, and deſerve to know it. Let us ſee if you will now have the courage to be humbled by the truth which condemns you.

I was ſaying then, that what draws ſo much applauſe upon you, deſerves to be cenſured. While you had so many enemies abroad, who threatened your not yet well established kingdom, you attended to nothing in your new city but the erecting of magnificent buildings. It was that, as you yourself have owned to me, which cost you so many restless nights. You have exhausted your riches; you have not turned your thoughts to the increase of your people, nor to the cultivation of the fertile lands of this coast. Are not these two things, a multitude of good subjects, and well-cultivated lands to maintain them, to be looked upon as the two essential bases of your power? A long peace was necessary at first, to favour the multiplication of your people. You should have applied your thoughts only to agriculture and to the enacting of the wisest laws. Vain ambition has pushed you to the very brink of the precipice. By endeavouring to appear great, you have well nigh ruined your true greatness. Make haste to retrieve these errors; put a stop to all your magnificent buildings? renounce this pomp, which would ruin your new city; let your people breathe in peace, and bend all your thoughts to make them abound, in order to facilitate marriages. Know that you are not a king but in proportion to the subjects which you have to govern; and that your power is to be measured not by the extent of the territories you possess, but by the number of men who inhabit them, and are zealous of obeying you. Possess a fertile though small tract of land ; stock it with multitude of laborious and well-disciplined inhabitants, and behave so as to win their affection ; and you are more powerful, more happy and more glorious, than all the conquerors who ravage so many kingdoms.

What shall I do then with regard to these kings, replied Idomeneus; Shall I confess my weakness to them? It is true that I have neglected agriculture, and even trade, which is so easy to me on this coast; I have thought only of erecting a magnificent city. Must I therefore my dear Mentor, disgrace myself in an assembly of so many princes, and discover my imprudence? If I must, I will; I will do it without hesitation,

tation, whatever pain it may cost me ; for you have taught me that a true king, who is born for his people, and owes himself entirely to them, ought to prefer the welfare of his kingdom to his own reputation.

This sentiment is worthy of the father of his people, replied Mentor ; it is by this goodness, and not by the vain magnificence of your city, that I perceive in you the soul of a true king. But your honour must be saved even for the interest of your kingdom. Leave this matter to me ; I will go and inform these kings that you are engaged to establish Ulysses, if he be still living, or at least his son, in the regal sway of Ithaca, and that you are resolved to expel from it by force all Penelope's suitors. They will easily conceive that this war will require a great number of troops, and will therefore consent to your furnishing them only with a small supply at first against the Daunians.

At these words Idomeneus looked like a man eased of an heavy burden. You, my dear friend, said he to Mentor, save my honour and the reputation of this rising city, by concealing my weakness from all my neighbours ; but what probability would there be in saying, that I will send troops to Ithaca to establish Ulysses there, or at least his son Telemachus, since Telemachus himself is engaged to go to the war against the Daunians ? Be not uneasy, replied Mentor ; I will say nothing but the truth. The ships which you will send to establish your trade, shall go to the coast of Epirus, and do two things at once ; they shall invite back to your coast the foreign merchants whom too high duties keep from Salentum, and endeavour to learn news of Ulysses. If he be still living, he cannot be far from the seas which divide Greece from Italy, and it is confidently reported that he has been seen among the Phœacians. And though there were no hopes of seeing him again, your vessels will do a signal piece of service to his son, by spreading in Ithaca and all the neighbouring countries the terror of the name of the young Telemachus, who is thought to be dead as well as his father. Penelope's wooers will be surprised to hear that he is

K 2   ready

ready to return with the fuccours of a powerful ally; the Ithacans will not dare to shake off the yoke; Penelope will be comforted, and perfevere in refufing to make choice of a new husband. Thus will you ferve Telemachus, while he fupplies your place among the confederates of this coaft of Italy againft the Daunians.

Hereupon Idomeneus cried out, Happy the prince who is fupported by wife counfels ! A prudent and faithful friend is of more worth to a king than victorious armies ! But doubly happy the king who is fenfible of his happinefs, and knows how to make his advantage of it by a right ufe of wife counfels ! For it often happens that he removes from his confidence men of wifdom and integrity who awe him by their virtue, in order to liften to flatterers whofe treachery he does not apprehend. I myfelf have fallen into this error, and I will tell you all the evils which were brought upon me by a falfe friend who flattered my paffions, in hopes that I in my turn would flatter his.

Mentor eafily convinced the confederate kings, that Idomeneus ought to charge himfelf with Telemachus's affairs, whilft he went with them. They were fatisfied with having the young fon of Ulyffes in their army, with an hundred Cretan youths, who were ordered by Idomeneus to accompany him, and were the flower of the young nobility whom the king had brought from Crete. Mentor had advifed him to fend them to this war. It is neceffary, faid he, to take care in times of peace to multiply the people; but left the whole nation should grow effeminate and ignorant of military affairs, the young nobility muft be fent to foreign wars: They will fuffice to keep up in the whole nation an emulation of glory, a love of arms, a contempt of fatigues and of death itfelf, and a knowledge of the art of war.

The confederate kings departed from Salentum well fatisfied with Idomeneus, charmed with the wifdom of Mentor, and overjoyed at taking Telemachus with them. But Telemachus could not moderate his grief when he was to part from his
friend.

friend. Whilft the allies were taking their leave, and fwearing to Idomeneus that they would maintain an eternal league with him; Mentor held Telemachus faft in his arms, and felt himfelf bedewed with his tears. I feel no joy, faid Telemachus, in going to acquire glory; I am fenfible of nothing but the grief of our parting. Methinks I fee that fatal time again, when the Egyptians fnatched me out of your arms, and fent me far from you, without leaving me any hopes of feeing you again.

Mentor made a kind reply to thefe words, in order to comfort him. This, faid he, is a very different feparation; it is voluntary, it will be fhort; you are going in purfuit of victory. You muft love me, my fon, with a lefs tender and more manly affection. Accuftom yourfelf to my abfence; you will not always have me with you. It muft be wifdom and virtue, rather than Mentor's prefence, which fuggeft to you what you ought to do.

As fhe fpoke thefe words, the Goddefs, concealed under the form of Mentor, covered Telemachus with her Ægis, and infufed into him a fpirit of wifdom and forefight, intrepid valour and gentle moderation, which are fo feldom found together. Go, faid Mentor, into the midft of the greateft dangers, as often as your going into them will be ufeful. A prince dif-honours himfelf more by fhunning dangers in battles, than by never going to the war. The courage of him who commands others, muft not be doubtful. If the prefervation of a chief or king be neceffary to a people, it is ftill more neceffary to them that his reputation, as to valour, be unqueftionable. Remember that he who commands, ought to be a pattern to all others; his example ought to ani-mate the whole army. Fear not, therefore, O Telemachus, any kind of danger, but perifh in battle rather than raife a doubt of your courage. Flatterers, who will be the moft eager to hinder you from expofing yourfelf to danger when it is neceffary, will be the firft to accufe you of cow-ardice in private, if they find you eafily with-held

K 3   on

on thefe occafions : but then do not go in queft of needlefs dangers. Valour cannot be a virtue, unlefs it be governed by prudence ; it is other-wife a fenfelefs contempt of life, and a brutal ar-dor ; rash valour is never fafe. Who is not mafter of himfelf in dangers, is rather fiery than brave ; he muft be befide himfelf in order to be raifed above fear, becaufe he cannot get the better of it by the natural temper of his heart. In this con-dition, if he does not run away, he is at leaft confounded ; he lofes that freedom of mind which is neceffary to give proper orders, to improve op-portunities, to rout the enemy, and to ferve his country. If he has all the heat of a foldier, he has not the difcretion of a commander : nay, he has not the real courage of a common foldier ; for the foldier is to preferve in battle that prefence of mind and temper which are neceffary to obey. Who rashly expofes himfelf, difturbs the order and difci-pline of the troops, fets an example of temerity, and often expofes the whole army to great difafters. They who prefer vain ambition to the fafety of the com-mon caufe, deferve to be punished, and not to be rewarded.

Take heed therefore, my dear fon, of purfuing glory with too much eagernefs. The true way to find it is calmly to wait for a favourable opportu-nity : virtue attracts fo much the more reverence, as she appears the more plain, the more modeft, the more averfe to all oftentation. As the neceffity of ex-pofing ourfelves to danger increafes, we need frefh fupplies of forecaft and courage, which continually become greater. For what remains, remember that you muft not draw upon yourfelf the envy of any man. On your part, be not jealous of the fuccefs of others ; praife them for all that merits praife, but praife them judicioufly ; and relate the good with plea-fure, conceal the ill, and do not even think of it with-out pain. Be not peremptory before the old com-manders, who have the experience which you want;

beca

hear them with deference, ask their advice, defire the
moft able of them to inftruct you, and be not
afhamed to attribute all your beft actions to their inftructions. Never liften to difcourfes which may be
defigned to excite your diffidence or jealoufy of the
other commanders. Converfe with them with confidence and franknefs. If you think they have been
wanting in refpect to you, unbofom yourfelf to them,
and lay all your reafons before them. If they are capable of perceiving the generofity of fuch a conduct,
you will charm and draw from them every thing which
you have any grounds to expect : if, on the contrary,
they are not reafonable enough to come into your
opinion, your own experience will teach you what
injuries may be expected from them ; you will take
your meafures fo as not to be again expofed to the
danger of having any more difputes with them as long
as the war lafts, and will have nothing to reproach
yourfelf withal. But above all, take care not to im-
part to certain flatterers, who are fowers of diffention,
the grounds of the uneafinefs which you may think
you have againft the chiefs of the army you are in.
I will ftay here, continued Mentor, to affift Idomeneus in the neceffity he is under of toiling for the welfare of his people, and to caufe him to put the finifh-
ing ftroke to his reparation of the errors, which ill
counfels and flatterers have induced him to commit in
this eftablifhment of his new kingdom.

Hereupon Telemachus could not forbear difcovering to Mentor fome furprife and even fome contempt
of Idomeneus's conduct ; but Mentor rebuked him
for it in a fevere tone. Are you furprifed, faid he, that
the worthieft men are but men, and betray fome remains of the weakneffes of humanity among the innumerable fnares and difficulties which are infeparable from royalty? Idomeneus indeed has been bred
up in notions of pomp and haughtinefs; but what
philofopher could have defended himfelf againft flattery, had he been in his place ? It is true that he
fuffered himfelf to be too much biaffed by thofe in
whom he confided ; but the wifeft princes are often

deceived,

deceived, whatever precautions they take to prevent
it. A king cannot do without ministers to lighten
his burden and to confide in, since he cannot do all
things himself. Besides, a king is much less acquainted than private men with those who are about
him; they are always masked in his presence, and
practice all kind of artifices to deceive him. Alas! my
dear Telemachus, you will experience this but too
much! We find in mankind neither the virtue nor
talents which we look for in them. In vain do we
study and found them, for we are daily mistaken in
them. Nay, we can never make the best of men, such
as we want to make them for the public good. They
have their prejudices, their inconsistencies, their jealousies; they are rarely to be persuaded or corrected.

The more people a prince has to govern, the more
ministers he will want, in order to do by them what
he cannot do himself; and the more men he is obliged to trust with authority, the more liable he is to
be deceived in the choice of them. The man who
to-day unmercifully censures kings, would to-morrow govern worse than they, and commit the same
faults, with others infinitely greater, were he entrusted with the same power. A private condition, when
it is attended with a little wit and a fluency of
speech, hides all natural defects, brightens dazzling
talents, and makes a man seem worthy of all the
posts to which he is not advanced; but authority
brings all qualifications to a severe test, and discovers great imperfections. Greatness is like certain
glasses which magnify all objects; all defects seem
to grow bigger in those elevated stations, where the
minutest things have important consequences, and
the slightest over-sights violent effects. The whole
world is hourly employed in observing a single man,
and in judging him with the utmost rigor. They who
judge him, have no experience of his condition;
they are not sensible of the difficulties of it, and require him to be so perfect, that they will not permit
him to be a man. And yet a king, however good and
wise he may be, is still a man; his genius has bounds,
                                                    and

and his virtue alfo ; he has humours, paffions, habits, of which he is not the abfolute mafter. He is befet with artful and interefted perfons ; he finds not the affiftance he feeks for, and falls daily into miftakes, fometimes through his own paffions, and fometimes through thofe of his minifters. Hardly has he repaired one fault, but he relapfes into another. Such is the condition of the wifeft and moft virtuous princes.

The longeft and beft reigns are too short and imperfect to rectify in the end the miftakes which have been inadvertently committed in their beginnings. All thefe miferies are inherent in a crown, human weaknefs finks under fo heavy a burden; we should pity and excufe kings. How are they to be pitied in having fo many men to govern, whofe wants are infinite, and who give fo much trouble to thofe who endeavour to govern them well. To fpeak freely, men are very much to be pitied in that they are to be governed by a king who is but a man like them ; for it would require Gods to reform men. But kings are not lefs to be pitied, fince being but men, that is weak and imperfect, they are to govern this innumerable multitude of corrupt and deceitful men.

Telemachus replied with fome warmth, Idomeneus by his own fault loft the kingdom of his anceftors in Crete, and but for your counfels he would have loft a fecond at Salentum. I own, anfwered Mentor, that he has been guilty of great faults ; but look in Greece, and in all the other beft governed countries, for a prince who has not committed inexcufable ones. The greateft men have in their temper, and in the turn of their mind, certain defects which give them a wrong bias, and the moft praife-whorty are they who have the courage to acknowledge and correct their errors. Do you think that Ulyffes, the great Ulyffes, your father, who is the pattern of all the kings of Greece, has not likewife his weakneffes and failings? Had not Minerva conducted him ftep by ftep, how often would he have funk under his dangers and difficulties, when

K 5.   fortune

fortune made him her sport? How often has Minerva restrained him or set him right, that she might continually lead him to glory by the path of virtue? Do not even expect, when you see him reigning in all his glory in Ithaca, to find him without imperfections; you will undoubtedly see some in him. Greece, Asia, and the islands of every sea, have admired him notwithstanding these failings; a thousand admirable qualities cause them to be forgotten. You will be very happy in having an opportunity to admire him also, and continually to study him as a pattern.

Accustom yourself, Telemachus, not to expect from the greatest men more than humanity is able to perform. Inexperienced youth gives a loose to presumptuous censures, which give it a disgust of all the examples which it ought to follow, and brings it into an incurable state of indocility. You ought not only to love, respect, and imitate your father, though he be not perfect, but you ought also to have an high esteem for Idomeneus. Notwithstanding all that I have blamed in him, he is naturally sincere, upright, equitable, liberal, beneficent; his valour is perfect; he detests fraud when he perceives it, and follows the real disposition of his heart. All his external qualifications are great and adequate to his station. His ingenuity in owning his mistakes, his good nature, his patience in suffering me to say the harshest things to him, his resolution to do himself the violence of a public reparation of his errors, and thereby to place himself above the censures of men, discover a truly great soul. Good luck, or the advice of others, may preserve a man of a very mean capacity from some particular faults; but an extraordinary virtue only can engage a king, so long seduced by flattery, to rectify his errors: it is much more glorious thus to rise again than never to have fallen. Idomeneus has committed the faults which almost all princes commit, but no prince does what he has done to correct himself. For my part I could not forbear admiring him, at the same time that he permitted me to contradict him. Do you admire him also, my
dear

dear Telemachus ; it is lefs for his reputation than your benefit, that I give you this advice.

By this difcourfe Mentor made Telemachus fen-fible, what danger there is of being unjuft, when we fuffer ourfelves to pafs fevere cenfures on others, ef-pecially on thofe who are charged with the cares and intricacies of government. He afterwards faid to him, It is time for you to depart ; farewell. I will wait for you here, my dear Telemachus ! Remember that they who fear the Gods, have nothing to fear from men. You will be in the greateft dangers, but know that Minerva will never forfake you.

At thefe words Telemachus thought that he felt the prefence of the Goddefs, and he would certainly have known that it was Minerva who was fpeaking in order to fill him with confidence, if the Goddefs had not recalled the idea of Mentor by faying ; For-get not, my fon, all the pains which I have taken in your infancy, to make you as wife and valiant as your father. Do nothing which is unworthy of his great example, and the virtuous maxims which I have en-deavoured to inftil into you.

The fun was rifing, and gilt the tops of the moun-tains, when the kings went out of Salentum and re-joined their troops, which had encamped about the city, and now began to march under their comman-ders. On all fides were feen the heads of briftling pikes ; the flashing of the shields dazzled the eye, and a cloud of duft afcended to the heavens. Idomeneus and Mentor conducted the confederate princes from the city to the plain. At length they parted, having interchanged the marks of a true friendship ; and the allies no longer doubted that the peace would be lafting, now they knew the good difpofition of Ido-meneus's heart, which had been reprefented to them very different from what it was, becaufe a judgment had been formed of him not from his natural temper, but from the flattering and unjuft counfels to which he had given himfelf up.

After the army was gone, Idomeneus led Mentor into every quarter of the city. Let us fee, faid Men-tor,

K 6

tor, how many men you have both in the city and in the country; let us number them, and examine how many husbandmen you have amongst them. Let us see how much corn, wine, oil, and other useful things your lands produce in the less fruitful years. By this means we shall know whether the country furnishes wherewithal to subsist all its inhabitants, and whether it yields a surplus besides to carry on a profitable trade with foreign nations. Let us enquire likewise into the number of your ships and seamen; it is by them that an estimate must be made of your power. He visited the port, went on board every particular ship, and informed himself to what country every vessel traded; what merchandise it carried out, what it took in return, and what was the expence of its voyage; what were the loans of merchants to each other; what companies they formed amongst themselves, to know if they were equitable and faithfully managed; and lastly what were the hazards of shipwreck and other mischances of trade, in order to prevent the ruin of merchants, who through a greediness of gain often undertake things which are above their abilities.

He appointed severe punishments for all bankruptcies, because those which are not fraudulent are almost always caused by rash undertakings. At the same time he laid down rules to make it easy to prevent them. He appointed magistrates to whom the merchants gave an account of their effects, profits, expences and enterprises. They were never permitted to risk the goods of others, nor could they risk more than a moiety even of their own. Again, what they could not undertake singly, they undertook in companies; and the laws of these companies were inviolable, by the severe punishment appointed for those who should not observe them. Moreover, trade was entirely free, and so far from being cramped by taxes, that rewards were promised to all merchants who could draw the commerce of any new nation to Salentum.

People therefore quickly flocking hither from all parts, the trade of this city resembled the flowing

and

and ebbing of the fea, and riches poured into it, as the waves roll one upon another.   Every thing here was imported and exported free of all duties.   All that came in was ufeful ; all that went out, left behind it other riches in its room.   Strict juftice prefided in the port in the midft of fo many nations.   Franknefs, integrity, candour, from the top of thefe lofty towers feemed to invite hither the merchants of the remoteft countries.   Every one of thefe merchants, whether he came from the eaftern shore, where the fun daily fprings from the bofom of the deep, or from the vaft ocean, where, tired with his courfe, he extinguishes his flames, lived in the fame peace and fafety at Salentum as in his own country.

As for the infide of the city, Mentor vifited all the magazines, all the tradefmens shops, and all public places.   He prohibited all foreign commodities which might introduce pomp and luxury.   He regulated the apparel, food, furniture, dimenfions and ornaments of the houfes for all the different conditions. He banished all ornaments of gold and filver, and faid to Idomeneus ; I know but one way to make your fubjects frugal in their expences, which is to fet them an example of it yourfelf.   It is neceffary for you to have a certain majefty in your appearance ; but your authority will be fufficiently denoted by your guards, and the attendance of your principal officers.   Be fatisfied therefore with a purple robe of fuperfine wool ; let the officers of ftate next to you be clad in the fame wool, and all the difference confift in the colour, and a fmall embroidery of gold on the border of your own robe.   Different colours will ferve to diftinguish the different conditions, without your having any need of gold, filver or precious ftones. Regulate the conditions by their birth.   Place in the firft rank thofe of the moft ancient and noble defcent. Such as have the merit and authority of places will be well fatisfied to come next to thefe ancient and illuftrious families, who have fo long been in the poffeffion of the firft honours.   Men who are not fo nobly born, will readily give place to them, provided you accuftom

custom them not to forget their former conditions in a too high and a too sudden elevation, and praise the moderation of those who are humble and modest in prosperity. The distinction which excites the least envy, is that which proceeds from a long series of ancestors.

As for virtue, it will be sufficiently excited, and men will be eager enough to serve the state, provided you bestow crowns and statues on illustrious actions, and make them the source of nobility to the children of those who perform them.

Persons of the first rank after you may be clad in white, with a gold fringe at the bottom of their garments. They may wear a gold ring on their finger, and a gold medal with your effigy on their neck. Those of the second rank may be clad in blue, and have a silver fringe and the ring, but no medal. The third in green, without the ring and fringe, but with the medal. The fourth in yellow. The fifth in a pale red or rose-colour. The sixth in a changeable white and red. The seventh, which will consist of the lowest of the people, in a mixture of white and yellow.

Let these be the habits of the seven different degrees of freemen; the slaves may be cloathed in a dark grey. Thus without any expence will every one be distinguished according to his rank, and all arts which only serve to cherish pride and vanity, will be banished from Salentum. All the artists who may be employed in these pernicious arts, will be useful in the necessary arts which are few in number, or in trade, or agriculture. No change must ever be suffered either in the sort of the cloth or fashion of the cloaths; for it is unworthy of men, destined to a serious and noble life, to amuse themselves with contriving affected attire, or to suffer their wives, in whom these amusements would be less scandalous, ever to be guilty of this extravagance.

Mentor, like a skilful gardener, who lops off the useless branches of fruit-trees, did thus endeavour to suppress pomp and vanity which corrupted their manners; he brought every thing back to a noble and fru-

gal

gal fimplicity. He likewife regulated the food of the
citizens and flaves.. What a shame, faid he; that men
of the higheft rank should make their greatnefs confift
in ragouts, whereby they enervate their minds, and
continually ruin the health of their bodies! They
ought to make their happinefs confift in their temperance, in their power to do good to others, and in
the reputation which their good actions will procure
them. Temperance renders the plaineft food very
agreeable; it is that which beftows the moft vigorous
health, and the pureft and moft lafting pleafures.
Your repafts therefore muft be confined to the beft
meats, but dreft without any fauces: the art of irri-
tating mens appetites beyond their real wants, is an
art of poifoning them. ‑

Idomeneus was very fenfible that he had been
wrong in fuffering the inhabitants of his new city to
foften and corrupt their manners, by violating all the
laws of Minos concerning fobriety : But the wife
Mentor let him know that the laws themfelves though
they were revived, would be ufelefs, if the example
of the king did not give them a fanction which they
could not derive from any thing elfe. Whereupon
Idomeneus regulated his table; admitting nothing to
it but excellent bread, a little wine of the growth of
the country, which is ftrong and pleafant, and fuch
plain food as he ufed to eat with the other Greeks at
the fiege of Troy. Nobody prefumed to complain
of a law which the king impofed upon himfelf; and
fo every one retrenched the fuperfluities and delicacies
in which they began to plunge themfelves at their repafts.

Mentor afterwards fuppreffed foft and effeminate
mufic which corrupted all the youth. Nor did he with
lefs feverity condemn the Bacchanalian mufic, which
is little lefs inebriating than wine, and is productive
of riots, debauchery, and lewdnefs. He confined all
mufic to the feftivals in the temples, there to celebrate the praifes of the Gods, and of heroes who had
left examples of the moft extraordinary virtues. Nor
did he but for the temples allow of the grand ornaments:

ments of architecture, such as columns, pediments, porticoes. He drew plain and beautiful plans for building an house, that was pleasant and commodious for a numerous family, on a small spot of ground; always taking care that the situation of it was healthful, that the apartments were independent on each other, that its œconomy and neatness might be easily preserved, and that it might be repaired at a small expence. He ordered that every house which was at all considerable, should have an hall and a little periftyle, with small rooms for all persons that were free; but he prohibited under severe penalties superfluous and magnificent apartments. These different models of houses, according to the largeness of each family, served to embellish one part of the city at a small expence, and to make it regular; whereas the other, already finished according to the caprice and vanity of private persons, was disposed, notwithstanding its magnificence, in a less agreeable and less commodious manner. This new city was built in a very short time; because the neighbouring coast of Greece furnished good architects, and a very great number of masons were sent for from Epirus, and several other countries, on condition that after they had finished their works, they should settle about Salentum, should take lands to clear there, and help to people the country.

Painting and sculpture appeared to Mentor to be arts which it was not right to lay aside; but he ordered that very few should be permitted to apply themselves to these arts at Salentum. He founded a school, wherein presided masters of an exquisite taste who examined the young students. There must, said he, be nothing low or lifeless in arts which are not absolutely necessary, and of consequence none ought to be admitted to study them but youths who have a promising genius, and who bid fair to arrive at perfection. Others who are born for less noble arts, may be usefully employed in the ordinary services of the republic. Sculptors and painters should never be made use of but to preserve the memory of great men and great actions; and it is in public edifices and places of burial,

rial, that the reprefentations ought to be preferved of what perfons of extraordinary virtue have performed for the fervice of their country. However Mentor's moderation and frugality did not hinder him from authorifing all thofe large ftructures which are deftined for horfe and chariot-races, wreftling, combats of the cæftus, and all other exercifes which improve the body, and render it more active and vigorous.

He fuppreft a prodigious number of tradefmen who fold wrought ftuffs of remote countries, embroideries of an exceffive price, gold and filver vafes embofled with figures of Gods, men and animals; and liquors and perfumes. He ordered alfo that the furniture of every houfe fhould be plain, and made fo as to laft a long while. So that the Salentines, who ufed to complain loudly of their poverty, began to be fenfible what a fuperfluity of riches they had. But they were falfe riches which made them poor, and they became really rich, in proportion to their refolution to ftrip themfelves of them. It is enriching ourfelves, faid they, to defpife fuch riches as drain the ftate, and to leffen our wants by reducing them to the real neceffities of our nature.

Mentor made hafte to vifit the arfenals and all the magazines, to fee if the arms, and all the other things which are neceffary to war, were in a good condition. For one muft, faid he, be always ready to make war, in order never to be reduced to the misfortune of making it. He found that feveral things were wanting every where. Whereupon he affembled artificers to work in iron, fteel and brafs. Burning forges were feen to rife, and whirlwinds of fmoke and flames, like the fiery eruptions of mount Etna. The hammer rung on the anvil that groaned beneath its reiterated ftrokes, which the neighbouring mountains and fea-fhores refounded. One would have thought one's felf in that ifland, where Vulcan, animating the Cyclops, forges thunder-bolts for the father of the Gods; and one faw all the preparations of war made by a wife forefight during a profound peace.

Mentor

Mentor afterwards went out of the city with Idomeneus, and found a great extent of fertile lands which remained uncultivated. Others were only half cultivated through the negligence or poverty of the husbandmen, who wanting hands and cattle, wanted resolution and the means of bringing agriculture to its perfection. Mentor seeing this desolate country, said to the king, The soil here is ready to enrich the inhabitants, but the inhabitants are not sufficient for the soil. Let us therefore take all the superfluous artificers in the city, whose trades would only corrupt good manners, and employ them to cultivate these plains and hills. It is a misfortune that these men, who have been trained up to professions which require a sedentary life, are not inured to labour; but here is a way to remedy this. The occupied lands must be divided amongst them, and the neighbouring people, who will do the hardest work under them, called to their assistance. And those people will do this, provided suitable rewards are promised them out of the produce of the lands they clear. They may afterwards possess a part of them, and so be incorporated with your own subjects, who are not numerous enough. If they are laborious and obedient to the laws, they will prove as good subjects as any you have, and increase your power. Your city artificers, being transplanted into the country, will train up their children to the toils and hardships of a country life. Besides, all the masons of foreign countries, who are at work in building your city, are engaged to clear part of your lands, and to become husbandmen; incorporate them with your own people as soon as they have finished their works in the city. These workmen will be overjoyed to pass their lives under a government which is now become so mild. As they are robust and laborious, their example will be a spur to the industry of the tradesmen, who will be transplanted from the city to the country, and with whom they will be intermixt. In process of time the whole country will be peopled with families that are vigorous, and addicted to agriculture.

For

For what remains, be not in pain with regard to the multiplication of these people ; they will soon become innumerable, provided you facilitate marriages. Now the way to facilitate them is very plain. Almost all men have an inclination to marry, and nothing but poverty hinders them from it. If you do not load them with taxes, they will easily live with their wives. and children ; for the earth is not ungrateful ; she always maintains with her fruits those who carefully cultivate her, and refuses them to none but such as are afraid to bestow their labour upon her. The more children husbandmen have, the richer they are, if the prince does not impoverish them ; for their children from their tenderest youth begin to assist them. The youngest tend the sheep in the pastures ; others who are more advanced in years, look after the herds, and the oldest go to plough with their fathers. Mean-time, the mother with the rest of the family prepares a plain repast for her husband and her dear children against they return, fatigued with the toils of the day ; she milks her cows and her sheep, which pour whole rivers into her pails ; she makes a good fire, about which the harmless peaceful family divert themselves with singing every evening till the time of soft repose ; she prepares cheeses, chesnuts, and preserved fruits as fresh as if they were just gathered.

The shepherd returns with his pipe, and sings to the assembled family the new songs which he has learnt in the neighbouring hamlets. The husbandman comes in with his plough, and his weary oxen advance, hanging down their heads, with a slow and tardy pace, notwithstanding the goad which urges them on. All the evils of labour end with the day. The poppies, which sleep by the command of the Gods sheds over the earth, sooth all gloomy cares by their charms, and hold all nature in a sweet enchantment ; every one sleeps without anticipating the cares of the morrow. Happy those unambitious, mistrustless, artless people, provided the Gods give them a good king who does not disturb their innocent joys ! But how horribly inhuman, to ravish from them,

them, through motives of pride and ambition, the
sweet fruits of the earth, for which they are indebted
only to the bounty of nature, and the sweat of their
brows! Nature alone out of her own fruitful bosom
would draw all that is necessary for an infinite number
of temperate and laborious men? but the pride and
luxury of particular persons reduce multitudes of
others to a frightful state of indigence.

What shall I do, said Idomeneus, if these people
whom I shall disperse over a fertile country, neglect
to cultivate it? Do, replied Mentor, quite the contrary of what is commonly done. Rapacious and un-
thinking princes make it their study to load those of
their subjects with taxes, who are most diligent and
industrious to improve their estates, because they
hope to be paid by them with the greatest ease; and
they at the same time lay lighter burdens on those
whom their own idleness renders more indigent. Invert this evil method, which oppresses the good, rewards vice, and introduces a supineness as fatal to
the king himself as to the whole state. Lay taxes,
mulcts, and even other severe penalties, if necessary,
on those who neglect their estates, just as you would
punish soldiers who should forsake their post in war.
On the contrary, grant favours and exemptions to
growing families, and increase them in proportion to
their diligence in cultivating their lands. Their families will quickly multiply, and they will all spirit up
each other to labour, which will even become honourable. The profession of an husbandman, being no
longer born down by its numerous pressures, will be
no longer despised. The plough will be again esteemed and held by victorious hands which have saved
their country. It will not be less glorious for a man
to cultivate the patrimony of his ancestors during an
happy peace, than to have bravely defended it in the
troubles of war. The whole country will bloom
again. Ceres will wear her crown of golden ears; Bacchus, pressing the grapes beneath his feet, will cause
rivers of wine, sweeter than Nectar, to stream down
the sides of the mountains; the hollow valleys will
echo

echo with the concerts of swains, who besides transparent brooks, will unite their pipes and their voices, while their skippings flocks, fearless of wolves, crop the flowery herbage.

Will you not be exceedingly happy, Idomeneus, in being the source of so many blessings, and in causing so many people to live under the shelter of your name in such a delightful tranquillity ? is not this glory more affecting than that of ravaging the earth, and spreading every where, almost as much at home, even in the midst of victories, as among vanquished foreigners, slaughter, confusion, dejection, horror, consternation, cruel famine and despair ?

Happy the king, who is so beloved of the Gods, and has a soul great enough to attempt thus to become the delight of his people, and to present to all ages so charming a prospect in his reign ! The whole earth, instead of fighting against his power, would throw itself at his feet, and beseech him to reign over it.

Idomeneus answered, But when the people shall thus live in peace and plenty, pleasures will corrupt them, and they will turn against me the very arms with which I had furnished them. Be not afraid, said Mentor, of this inconvenience ; it is only a pretence which is constantly alledged, to flatter prodigal princes who are desirous to load their people with taxes, and it may be easily remedied. The laws which we have just established relating to agriculture, will render the life of your subjects laborious ; and they will have necessaries only in the midst of their abundance, because we suppress all such arts as furnish superfluities : Nay, this very abundance will be lessened by facilitating marriages and by the great increase of families. Every family being numerous, and having but little land, will be obliged to cultivate it with incessant labour. It is luxury and idleness which make people insolent and rebellious. They will have bread indeed, and enough of it ; but they will have nothing but the bread and the fruits which their own lands produce, and they earn with the sweat of their brows.

To keep your people in this moderation, you must
forth-

forthwith settle the extent of ground which each family
shall possess. You know that we have divided all your
subjects into seven classes, according to their different
conditions. Now no family in any class must be allowed
to possess more land than is absolutely necessary to
maintain the persons of whom it is composed. This
rule being inviolable, the nobles will not be able to
make purchases from the poor : all will have lands;
but each will have but very little, and be thereby excited to cultivate it well. If in length of time lands
should be wanting at home, you may settle colonies
abroad, which would extend the limits of this state.

I think also that you ought to take care not to let
wine become too common in your kingdom. If too
many vines have been planted, they must be plucked
up. Wine is the source of the greatest evils among the
people; it is the cause of diseases, quarrels, seditions,
idleness, an aversion to labour, and family disorders.
Let wine therefore be preserved as a kind of cordial,
or very choice liquor that is used only in sacrifices and
on very extraordinary festivals ; but expect not to
make so important a rule to be observed, unless you
yourself set an example of it. Moreover, you must cause
the laws of Minos, relating to the education of children, to be inviolably observed. Public schools must
be established, in which they must be taught to fear
the Gods, to love their country, to reverence the laws,
and to prefer honour to pleasures and to life itself.

Magistrates must be appointed to have an eye upon
families and the manners of private persons. Have an
eye upon them yourself, for you are not the king, that
is the shepherd of your people, but to watch over your
flock both night and day. Thereby you will prevent
an infinite number of disorders and crimes. Those
which you cannot prevent, punish immediately with severity. It is clemency to make examples at first which
may stop the tide of iniquity. By a little blood shed in
due time, a great deal is afterwards saved, and it makes a
prince feared without being often severe. But how de-
testable a maxim is it for him to think to find his safety
only in the oppression of his people ? Not to instruct
them,

them, not to guide them to virtue, not to make himself beloved by them, to terrify them into defpair, to lay them under the dreadful neceffity either not to breathe with freedom, or to shake off the yoke of his tyrannical fway ; is this, I fay, the way to reign eafy ? Is this the path which leads to glory ?

Remember that the countries in which the power of the fovereign is moft abfolute, are thofe where the fovereigns are leaft powerful. They feize, they ruin every thing, they alone poffefs the whole ftate ; but then the whole ftate languishes. The fields are untilled and almoft defert, the cities dwindle away daily, the fprings of trade are dried up, and the king, who cannot be a king himfelf, and who is great but by means of his people, waftes away gradually by the infenfible wafting away of his fubjects, from whom he derives his riches and power. His kingdom is drained of money and men, and this laft lofs is the greateft and the moft irreparable. His abfolute power makes as many flaves as he has fubjects : they flatter him, they feem to adore him, they tremble at the leaft glance of his eyes : but when the leaft revolution happens, this monftrous power, which was carried to too violent an excefs, cannot continue. It has no refource in the hearts of the people : it has wearied out and provoked the whole body politick; it conftrains all the members of that body to pant after a change. At the firft blow that is given it, the idol is thrown down, dashed in pieces, and trampled under foot. Contempt, hatred, fear, refentment, fufpicion, in short, all the paffions unite againft fo odious a power. The king who in his vain profperity did not find a fingle man bold enough to tell him the truth, will not find in his misfortunes a fingle man who deigns to excufe him, or to defend him againft his enemies.

After this difcourfe, Idomeneus at Mentor's perfuafion made hafte to diftribute the wafte lands, to ftock them with the ufelefs artificers, and to execute every thing that had been refolved upon ; referving only for the mafons the lands which he had allotted to them, and which they could not cultivate 'till they had finished their works in the city.

End of the Twelfth Book.

THE
ADVENTURES
OF
TELEMACHUS,
SON of ULYSSES.

BOOK the THIRTEENTH.

The ARGUMENT.

*Idomeneus relates to Mentor his confidence in Protesi-
laus, and the artifices of this favourite, who had
conspired with Timocrates to destroy Philocles, and
to betray Idomeneus himself. He owns that being prejudiced by these two Men against Philocles, he had
ordered Timocrates to go and kill him in an expedition wherein he commanded his fleet ; that Timocrates having failed in his attempt, Philocles had spared
his life, and retired to the isle of Samos, after having
resigned the command of the fleet to Polymenes, whom
Idomeneus had appointed to succeed him by an order
under his own hand; and that notwithstanding
Protesilaus's treachery, he could not prevail on himself to part with him.*

AND now the fame of Idomeneus's mild and
gentle reign allures from all parts crowds of
people who come to incorporate themselves with
his, and to seek their happiness under so amiable a
government. Already the fields, which had been,
so long over-run with thorns and brambles, promise
rich harvests and fruits till then unknown ; the
earth opens her bosom to the plough-share, and

L   prepares

prepares her riches to recompenfe the husbandman; hope dawns every where. Flocks of sheep are feen bounding on the grafs in the valleys and on the hills, and herds likewife of bulls and heifers that make the lofty mountains echo with their lowings: Thefe cattle fattened the fields. Mentor found the means of procuring them; for he advifed Idomeneus to make with the Peucetes, a neighbouring nation, an exchange of all the fuperfluous things which were no longer fuffered in Salentum, for thefe flocks and herds which the Salentines wanted.

At the fame time the city and adjacent villages were full of lovely youths, who had long languished in want, and had not dared to marry for fear of increafing their miferies. When they faw that Idomeneus entertained fentiments of humanity, and was willing to be their father, they were no more apprehenfive of hunger, or any other plagues which heaven inflicts on the earth. Nothing was now heard but shouts of joy, and the fongs of fwains and husbandmen celebrating their nuptials: Infomuch that one would have thought one had feen the God Pan with multitudes of Satyrs and Fauns interfperfed among the Nymphs, and dancing to their tuneful flutes in the shade. All was ferene and fmiling: but their joys were moderate, and their pleafures only a refreshment after long fatigues, which quickened and made them the purer.

The old men, furprifed to fee what they durft not hope for in the whole courfe of their long lives, wept through an excefs of joy and love; and lifting up their trembling hands to heaven, O great Jupiter, faid they, blefs the king who refembles you, and is the choiceft prefent you ever beftowed upon us. He is born for the good of mankind; return him all the bleffings we receive from him. Our children's children, defcended from thefe marriages which he encourages, will owe every thing, even their very birth to him, and he will truly be the father of all his fubjects. The lads and laffes who married, expreffed
their

their raptures by finging the praifes of the author of their ravishing joys. Their mouths, and their hearts ftill more, were inceffantly filled with his name ; they thought themfelves happy in feeing, and were apprehenfive of lofing him ; for every family would bitterly have bewailed his lofs.

Upon this, Idomeneus owned to Mentor that he had never felt fo fenfible a pleafure as that of being beloved, and of making fo many people happy. I could not have believed it, faid he; I thought that all the grandeur of princes confifted in making themfelves feared ; that the reft of mankind were born for them ; and all I had heard of kings who were the darlings and delight of their people, feemed a meer fable to me : I am now convinced that it was truth. But I muft inform you how my heart was poifoned in my very infancy with regard to regal authority, which was the caufe of all the misfortunes of my life. Hereupon Idomeneus began the following narration :

Protefilaus, who is a little older than I, was of all the young men he whom I loved the moft : his fprightly daring temper hit my tafte. He entered into my pleafures, he flattered my paffions, and made me fufpicious of another young man, whofe name was Philocles, whom I likewife loved. The latter feared the Gods, had a great foul, and commanded his paffions ; he placed greatnefs not in raifing but in conquering himfelf, and in doing nothing mean. He often told me freely of my faults ; and even when he durft not fpeak, his filence and the grief of his countenance gave me fufficiently to underftand what he meant to reproach me with.

At firft his fincerity pleafed me. I often protefted to him, that I would hear and confide in him as long as I lived, in order to be preferved from flatterers. He told me all that I muft do to tread in the fteps of Minos, and to render my kingdom happy. He had not fo profound a wifdom as you, Mentor ; But I now perceive that his maxims were good. By

degrees

degrees the artifices of Protesilaus, who was jealous and very ambitious, gave me a disgust of Philocles. The latter not being forward or officious, suffered the other to get the ascendant, and was contented with always telling me the truth, when I was willing to hear it ; for it was my good, and not his own advancement that he sought.

Protesilaus insensibly persuaded me that he was a person of a morose and haughty temper, who censured all my actions, and asked nothing of me, because his pride would not let him stoop to be obliged, and made him aspire to the reputation of a man who is above all preferments. He added, that this young man, who told me so freely of my failings, spoke of them as freely to others; that he let people see that he had very little esteem for me ; and that by thus lessening my reputation, and by making a shew of an austere virtue, he sought to open himself a way to the throne.

At first I could not believe that Philocles had any such design; for there is in true virtue a certain candour and ingenuity which can neither be counterfeited nor mistaken, provided we consider it with attention. The perseverance however of Philocles in condemning my weaknesses began to tire me ; and Protesilaus's complaisance and unwearied diligence in finding me new pleasures, made me still more impatiently bear with the austerity of the other.

Mean time Protesilaus, unable to brook my not crediting all his insinuations against his rival, resolved to speak to me no more about him, but to convince me of their truth by something stronger than words. He accomplished his design of deceiving me in the following manner. He advised me to send Philocles to command a fleet which was to attack that of Carpathus. In order to induce me to it, You know, said he, that my commendations of him cannot be suspected; I own that he has courage, and a genius for war ; he will serve you better than any man, and I prefer your interest to all my resentment against him.

I was

I was extremely glad to find Protefilaus's heart, to whom I had intrusted the administration of my most important affairs, so upright and just. I embraced him in a transport of joy, and thought myself exceedingly happy in having reposed all my confidence in one who seemed so much above passion and self-interest. But alas ! how greatly are princes to be pitied ! This man knew me better than I knew myself : He knew that kings are usually suspicious and indolent ; suspicious through their continual experience of the artifices of the corrupt persons about them ; and indolent, because pleasure tyrannise over them, and they are habituated to have others to think for them, without taking the trouble of it themselves. He was sensible therefore that it would not be difficult for him to make me suspicious and jealous of a man who would not fail to perform great actions, especially as his absence would give him all opportunities of spreading snares for him.

Philocles at his departure foresaw what would befall him. Remember, said he, that I shall no longer have it in my power to defend myself; that my adversary only will have your ear; and that while I am serving you at the hazard of my life, I shall run the risk of having no recompense but your displeasure. You are mistaken, said I ; Protefilaus does not speak of you as you do of him ; He praises you, he esteems you, he thinks you worthy of the most important employments. Should he offer to say any thing against you, he would lose my confidence. Fear nothing, go your ways, and mind only to serve me well. He departed, and left me in a strange situation.

I must confess, Mentor, that I plainly saw how necessary it was for me to have several persons to consult, and that nothing was more prejudicial either to my reputation or the prosperity of my affairs, than to give myself up to one only. I had experienced that the wise counsels of Philocles had saved me from several dangerous errors, into which Protefilaus's haughtiness would have made me fall. I clearly per-

ceived

ceived that there was in Philocles a fund of probity and juſt principles, which was not ſo viſible in Proteſilaus; but I had ſuffered the latter to aſſume a certain peremptory air, which I now could hardly reſiſt. I was tired with being continually between two men whom I could not reconcile; and in this irkſome ſituation was ſo weak as to chooſe rather to run the risk of prejudicing my affairs, than not to enjoy my liberty. I durſt not even tell myſelf the ſhameful motive of this reſolution; and yet this ſhameful motive, which I dared not diſcover, operated ſecretly in the bottom of my heart, and was the true ſpring of all my actions.

Philocles ſurpriſed the enemy, obtained a compleat victory, and was haſtening to return, in order to prevent the ill offices of which he was apprehenſive. But Proteſilaus, who had not yet had time to deceive me, wrote him word that I ordered him to make a deſcent on the iſle of Carpathus, to reap the fruits of his victory. And indeed he had perſuaded me that I might eaſily make a conqueſt of that iſland; but then he managed matters ſo, that Philocles wanted ſeveral things which were neceſſary to ſuch an enterpriſe, and tied him down to certain orders which occaſioned various diſappointments in the execution of it.

Mean while he made uſe of a very corrupt domeſtic of mine, who took notice of the minuteſt things, to give him an account of them; though they appeared ſeldom to ſee each other, and never to agree in any thing. This domeſtic, whoſe name was Timocrates, came one day to tell me as an important ſecret, that he had diſcovered a very dangerous affair. Philocles, ſaid he, deſigns to make uſe of your naval forces to render himſelf king of the iſland of Carpathus. The commanders of the troops are his creatures; all the ſoldiers are won over by his profuſe liberalities, and yet more by the pernicious licentiouſneſs in which he permits them to live. He is puffed up with his victory. Here is a letter he wrote to one of his friends about his project of making
himſelf

himſelf king, which it is impoſſible to doubt of after
ſo evident a proof.

I read the letter, and it ſeemed to me to be Philocles's hand, which Proteſilaus and Timocrates had
counterfeited with great exactneſs. This letter threw
me into a ſtrange ſurpriſe. I read it again and again ;
and could not perſuade myſelf that it was written by
Philocles, when I recalled to my troubled mind all the
ſtrong proofs he had given me of his diſintereſtedneſs
and integrity. And yet what could I do? how could
I not credit a letter, in which I thought I certainly
knew the hand-writing of Philocles?

When Timocrates ſaw that I could no longer with-
ſtand his artifice, he puſhed it yet further. May I
preſume, ſaid he, with ſome heſitation, to deſire you
to take notice of one particular in this letter? Philocles tells his friend that he may talk in confidence
with Proteſilaus concerning ſomething which he ex-
preſſes only in a Cypher: Proteſilaus is certainly engaged in the deſign of Philocles, and they are reconciled at your expence. You know that it was Proteſilaus who urged you to ſend Philocles againſt the
Carpathians. He has lately ceaſed to ſpeak againſt
him as he often did heretofore. On the contrary, he
extolls him, he excuſes him on all occaſions : They
for ſome time viſited each other with great civility.
Without doubt Proteſilaus has concerted meaſures
with Philocles to ſhare the conqueſt of Carpathus
with him. You yourſelf know how he preſſed the
undertaking of this enterpriſe contrary to all rules,
and that he expoſes your naval forces to deſtruction,
to gratify his ambition. Do you believe that he
would be thus ſubſervient to that of Philocles, if
there were ſtill a miſunderſtanding between them?
No, no, there is no doubt but that they are cloſely
united together to raiſe themſelves to an high pitch
of power, and perhaps to ſubvert the very throne
on which you yourſelf reign. In ſpeaking to you in
this manner, I know that I expoſe myſelf to their
reſentment, if, notwithſtanding my ſincere advice,

you

you ftill leave your authority in their hands. But no matter, provided I tell you the truth.

Thefe laft words of Timocrates made a deep impreffion upon me. I no longer doubted of the treafon of Philocles, and miftrufted Protefilaus as his friend. Timocrates in the mean while was inceffantly faying, If you wait till Philocles has conquered the ifle of Carpathus, it will be too late to put a ftop to his defigns. Haften therefore to make fure of him while you can. I was fhocked at the deep diffimulation of men, and knew no longer in whom to confide; for having difcovered Philocles's treachery, there was not a man on the earth whofe virtue could cure me of my fufpicions. I refolved to put the perfidious wretch to death as foon as poffible; but I dreaded Protefilaus, and knew not what to do with regard to him: I was afraid to find him guilty, and afraid likewife to truft him.

At length I could not help telling him, in my confufion, that I was grown jealous of Philocles. He feemed furprifed at it; he reprefented to me his upright and moderate conduct; he magnified his fervices; in a word, he did all that was neceffary to convince me that he had too good an underftanding with him. On the other fide, Timocrates loft no opportunity to make me take notice of their friendfhip, and to induce me to deftroy Philocles, while it was in my power to do it. See, my deareft Mentor, how unhappy kings are, and how liable to be made the tools even of thofe who feem to tremble at their feet.

I thought I fhould act a mafter-piece of policy, and difconcert the meafures of Protefilaus, by privately fending Timocrates to the fleet to put Philocles to death. Protefilaus played the hypocrite to the laft, and deceived me the more effectually, the more naturally he acted the part of one who is deceived himfelf. Timocrates departed, and found Philocles under great difficulties in his defcent. He was in want of every thing; for Protefilaus, not

knowing

knowing whether his forged letter would effect the
ruin of his enemy, was willing to have another expedient ready at the same time, the miscarriage of
an enterprise of which he had given me very raised
expectations, and could not fail to irritate me against
Philocles. The latter sustained this difficult war by his
courage, capacity, and the love which the soldiers
had for him. Though the whole army knew that this
descent was rash, and would be fatal to the Cretans,
yet every one laboured as much to make it succeed,
as if his life and happiness depended on his success:
Every one was contented hourly to hazard his life
under a leader so wise and so intent on making himself beloved.

Timocrates had every thing to apprehend in at-
tempting to dispatch a general in the midst of an
army who so passionately loved him; but mad ambition is blind. Timocrates thought nothing difficult
to gratify Protesilaus, with whom he imagined he
should share an absolute dominion over me after the
death of Philocles; and Protesilaus could not bear
a man of probity, whose very sight was a secret reproach of his crimes, and who by opening my eyes
might ruin all his projects.

Timocrates seduced two captains who were continually with Philocles; he promised them great rewards in my name, and then told Philocles that he
came by my order to acquaint him with some secret
affairs, which he was to communicate to him in the
presence of these two captains only. Whereupon Philocles having shut himself up with them, Timocrates
stabbed him with a poniard, but it slipt aside, and
did not penetrate far. Philocles, with great composure
of mind, wrested it from him, and made use of it
against him and the other two; and calling out at the
same time, some soldiers ran to the door, broke it
open, and disengaged Philocles from the hands of the
three assassins; who being confused, had made but a
faint attack upon him. They were seized, and would
have been torn in pieces by the enraged army, had

L 5   not

not Philocles with-held them. He then took Timocrates
aside, and asked him who had put him upon committing so black a deed. Timocrates, terrified with the apprehension of death, immediately shewed him the order I had given him under my own hand to kill Philocles: and, as traitors are always cowards, endeavoured
to save his life by discovering Protesilaus's treachery.

Philocles, though he was shocked at finding so
much malice in mankind, acted a very moderate
part. He declared to the whole army that Timocrates was innocent; he provided for his safety, and
sent him back to Crete. He then resigned the charge
of the army to Polymenes, whom I had appointed
by an order written with my own hand, to command
when Philocles should be slain. And lastly, having
exhorted the soldiers to continue faithful in their allegiance to me, he went by night on board a small
bark, which carried him to the isle of Samos, where
he now lives in peace, poverty and solitude; making
statues to get his bread, and not caring to hear of
false and unjust men, but especially of kings, whom
of all men he deems the blindest and most unhappy.

Here Mentor interrupted Idomeneus. Well, said
he, were you long in discovering the truth ? No, replied Idomeneus : I perceived by degrees the artifices
of Protesilaus and Timocrates : They quarrelled with
each other, (for the wicked find it very difficult to
continue united) and their dissention plainly shewed
me the deep abyss into which they had plunged me.
Well, answered Mentor, did you not resolve to get
rid of them both ? Alas ! replied Idomeneus, are
you ignorant of the weaknesses and difficulties which
princes labour under ? When they have once delivered
themselves up to corrupt and presumptuous men, who
have art enough to make themselves necessary, they
can no longer hope for the least freedom. Those
whom they despise the most, are the very persons
whom they treat the best, and on whom they heap
their favours. I abhorred Protesilaus, and yet I continued him in his power. Strange illusion : I was
overjoyed

overjoyed that I knew him, and yet had not refolution enough to refume the authority I had given him. Befides, I found him good natured, complaifant, induftrious in flattering my paffions, zealous for my intereft; in short, I found reafons to excufe my weaknefs to myfelf, becaufe I was a ftranger to true virtue, for want of choofing men of probity to conduct my affairs. I thought that there were none on the earth, and that integrity was only a beautiful phantom. What fignifies it, faid I, to make a great ftir to get out of the hands of one corrupt man, only to fall into thofe of another, who will not be more difinterefted nor more fincere than he. Mean time the fleet under the command of Polymenes returned: I thought no more of the conqueft of the ifle of Carpathius, and Protefilaus could not diffemble fo deeply, but that I difcovered how vexed he was to hear that Philocles was fafe in Samos.

Mentor interrupted Idomeneus in order to ask him, if he continued, after fo black a piece of treachery, to entruft all his affairs to Protefilaus. I was, replied Idomeneus, too averfe to bufinefs, and too fupine to be able to get out of his hands; for I then muft have difconcerted the fcheme I had laid down for my own cafe, and have been at the trouble of inftructing fomebody elfe, which I had not refolution enough to undertake: I rather chofe to fhut my eyes, that I might not fee Protefilaus's artifices; and only eafed my mind by letting fome of my particular confidents know, that I was not a ftranger to his villanies. Thus did I fancy that I was but half deceived, fince I knew that I was deceived. Sometimes, however, I made Protefilaus himfelf fenfible that I bore his yoke with impatience; and often took a pleafure in contradicting him, in publickly cenfuring fome of his actions, and in determining contrary to his opinion; but as he knew my floth and fupinenefs, he gave himfelf no concern about any difcontent of mine. He obftinately returned to the attack; fometimes in an importunate, and fome-

times in a cringing and infinuating way. And when
he perceived that I was exafperated againft him, he
then particularly doubled his diligence to furnish new
amufements which were likely to mollify or embark
me in fome affair, wherein he might have an opportunity to render himfelf neceffary, and to make the
moft of his zeal for my honour.

Though I was upon my guard againft him, yet
this way of foothing my paffions always got the better of me. He knew my fecrets; he cafed me under
my difficulties; he made every body tremble at my
power. In short, I could not refolve to part with
him; and, by maintaining him in his poft, I put it
out of the power of all honeft men to fhow me my
true intereft. From this time there was no freedom
of fpeech in my counfels; truth fled far from me;
and error, which paves the way to the downfall of
princes, was a judgment upon me for having facri-
ficed Philocles to Protefilaus's cruel ambition. Even
they who had moft zeal for my perfon and the good
of the ftate, thought themfelves under no obligation
to undeceive me, after fo dreadful an example. I
myfelf, dear Mentor, was afraid left truth should
break through the cloud, and reach even to me, in
fpite of all my flatterers; for not having the refolution to follow it, its light was troublefome to me:
And then I was confcious that it would have occafioned me the bittereft compunction, and not have refcued me from fo unhappy a fituation. My effeminacy,
and the afcendant which Protefilaus had infenfibly
gained over me, plunged me into a kind of defpair
of ever recovering my liberty. I was unwilling to
view my fhameful condition myfelf, or to fuffer others
to do it. You know, my dear Mentor, the vain pride
and falfe glory in which kings are bred up; they will
never be in the wrong. To hide one fault they commit a hundred. Rather than own that they are miftaken, and give themfelves the trouble of rectifying
their errors, they fuffer themfelves to be deluded all
their lives long. Such is the condition of weak and
                                    indolent

indolent princes, and such was mine precisely, when I was obliged to go to the siege of Troy.

At my departure I left the management of my affairs to Protesilaus, and he governed in my absence with pride and inhumanity. The whole kingdom of Crete groaned under his tyranny; but nobody durst send me word of the oppression of my people; knowing that I was afraid of seeing the truth, and that I gave up to Protesilaus's cruelty all who ventured to speak against him. But the more fearful people were of discovering the evil, the more violent it grew. He afterwards constrained me to dismiss the valiant Merion, who had attended me with great glory to the siege of Troy. He was grown jealous of him, as he was of all whom I loved, and who gave any proofs of virtue.

You must know, my dear Mentor, that this is the source of all my misfortunes. It was not so much my son's death that occasioned the revolt of the Cretans, as the vengeance of the Gods, who were incensed at my crimes, and the hatred of the people, which Protesilaus had drawn upon me. When I shed my son's blood, the Cretans, tired of my rigorous government, had lost all patience; and the horror of this last action only induced them to make a public discovery of what long since had been concealed in their hearts.

Timocrates attended me to the siege of Troy, and gave an account privately in his letters to Protesilaus of all the discoveries he could make. I plainly perceived my thraldom, but endeavoured not to think of it, despairing of a remedy. When the Cretans revolted at my arrival, Protesilaus and Timocrates were the first who fled. They would without doubt have deserted me, had I not been constrained to fly almost as soon as they. Be assured, my dear Mentor, that men who are insolent in prosperity, are always the most abject cowards in adversity. Their heads turn as soon as absolute power forsakes them; they

become

become as cringing as they were proud, and pafs in
a moment from one extreme to the other.

Mentor faid to Idomeneus, But whence comes it,
as you fo thoroughly know thefe two wicked men,
that you ftill keep them about you, as I fee you
do ? I am not furprifed at their following you, as they
could do nothing better for their own intereft, and I
think that you have done a generous action in affording them an afylum in your new fettlement ; but
why do you deliver yourfelf up to them again after
fo many fatal trials ?

You know not, anfwered Idomeneus, how ufelefs
all experience is to effeminate, fupine, and unthink-
ing princes. They are diffatisfied with all things, and
have not courage to redrefs any thing. So many years
of familiarity were chains of iron which linked me to
thefe two men, who befet me every hour. Since I have
been here, they have put me upon the exceffive expences which you have feen ; they have exhaufted
this rifing ftate ; they have drawn this war upon me
which but for you I should have funk under. I should
foon have experienced at Salentum the fame misfortunes which I fuffered in Crete ; but you at length
have opened my eyes, and infpired me with the courage I wanted, to deliver myfelf from bondage. I
know not what you have done to me ; but fince you
have been here I find myfelf quite another man.

Mentor then asked Idomeneus, how Protefilaus be-
haved in the prefent change of affairs. Nothing is
more artful, replied Idomeneus, than his conduct
fince your arrival. At firft he ufed all indirect methods
to make me fufpicious. He himfelf, indeed, faid nothing againft you, but feveral perfons came and told
me that thefe two ftrangers were much to be feared.
One, faid they, is the fon of the deceitful Ulyffes ;
the other wears a difguife, and has a deep head : they
are ufed to wander from kingdom to kingdom ; and
who knows that they have not formed fome defign
upon this ? Thefe adventurers themfelves relate that
they have caufed great confufions in the countries
through

through which they have paffed. Ours is an infant unfettled ftate, and the leaft commotions might overturn it.

Protefilaus faid nothing, but he endeavoured to make me fee the danger and extravagance of all the reformations which you made me undertake. My own intereft was the argument he made ufe of: If you let your fubjects abound, faid he, they will work no longer, but grow proud, intractable, and be always ready to revolt. Nothing but weaknefs and poverty makes them pliable, and hinders them from refifting authority. He has often endeavoured to refume his former afcendant over me, covering it with a pretended zeal for my fervice. By eafing the people, faid he, you debafe the royal power, and thereby do the people themfelves an irreparable injury; for it is neceffary for your own quiet that they fhould be kept humble.

To all this I anfwered, that I fhould eafily keep the people firm in their allegiance to me by making myfelf beloved by them; by remitting nothing of my authority, though I lightened their burden; by refolutely punifhing all offenders; by giving children a good education, and by being ftrict in keeping all my fubjects up to a plain, fober and laborious life. How! faid I, is it not poffible to make people obedient without ftarving them to death? What inhumanity! what brutal policy! How many nations do we fee mildly governed and yet loyal to their princes! that which caufes rebellions, is the reftlefs ambition of the grandees of a ftate, when they are entrufted with too much power, and their paffions fuffered to ftretch beyond bounds; it is the neglecting to punish the licentioufnefs of other orders in the ftate; it is the multitude of the great and the vulgar who live in luxury, in pomp and idlenefs; it is the too great number of military men, who have neglected all the employments which are ufeful in time of peace; in fhort, it is the defpair of the injured people; it is the cruelty and pride of princes, and their luxury, which makes them

them incapable of watching over the members of the
state, in order to prevent disturbances: These are the
causes of rebellions, and not the permitting the la-
bourer to eat the bread in peace, which he has earned
by the sweat of his brows.

When Protesilaus saw that I was immoveable in
these maxims, he took a course quite contrary to his
former, and began to act agreeable to principles which
he could not destroy; pretending to relish them, to be
convinced of their truth, and to be obliged to me for
having enlightened his understanding in these matters. He anticipates all my desires to ease the poor,
and is the first to represent their wants to me, and to
cry out against extravagance. You yourself know
that he praises you, that he pretends to repose a confidence in you, and does every thing to please you.
As for Timocrates, he begins to lose the good graces
of Protesilaus, having had thoughts of rendering
himself independent. Protesilaus is jealous of him,
and it was partly by their differences that I discovered
their perfidy.

Have you then, said Mentor to Idomeneus with
a smile, been so weak as to suffer yourself to be ty-
rannised over for so many years by two traytors,
whose treasons you knew! Ah! you know not, replied Idomeneus, the ascendant which artful men
have over a weak and indolent prince, who gives up
the management of his affairs to them. Besides, I
have told you already, that Protesilaus now enters
into all your schemes for the public good.

Mentor with a grave air proceeded thus: I but too
plainly see how much the wicked prevail over the
good in the courts of kings: You are a sad example
of it. But you say that I have opened your eyes
as to Protesilaus, and yet they are still so far closed,
as to leave the administration of your affairs to him,
though he is not worthy to live. Know that the
wicked are not incapable of doing good: They do
that, or evil, indifferently, when it subserves their
ambition. They do themselves no violence in com-

mitting

mitting evil, becaufe no fentiment of goodnefs, nor no principle of virtue with-holds them; neither is it any pain to them to do good, becaufe their depravity inclines them to do it in order to feem good, and thereby impofe upon the reft of mankind. Properly fpeaking, they are incapable of virtue, though they appear to practife it; but to the reft of their vices they are capable of adding hypocrify, the moft deteftable of all. As long as you are abfolutely determined to do good, Protefilaus will be ready to do it alfo, in order to preferve his authority; but if he finds you ever fo little inclined to flacken, he will ufe all arts to make you relapfe into your errors, that he may be at liberty to refume his fraudful and cruel difpofition. Can you live with honour and in peace, while fuch an one is hourly about you, and you know that the wife the faithful Philocles lives in poverty and difgrace in the ifland of Samos?

You ingenuoufly acknowledge, Idomeneus, that bold and wily men who are prefent, have an abfolute afcendant over weak princes; but you ought to add, that princes labour under another and no lefs an unhappinefs, the eafily forgetting the virtue and fervices of the abfent. The multitudes who furround princes, are the caufe that no one makes a deep impreffion upon them: They are ftruck only with what is prefent and flatters them: every thing elfe is foon effaced. Virtue efpecially but flightly affects them, becaufe virtue, inftead of flattering them, contradicts and condemns them for their follies. And is it any wonder that they are not beloved, fince they love nothing but their grandeur and their pleafures?

End of the Thirteenth Book.

THE

THE
ADVENTURES
OF
TELEMACHUS,
SON of ULYSSES.

BOOK the FOURTEENTH.

The ARGUMENT.

*Mentor prevails on Idomeneus to send Protesilaus and
Timocrates to the isle of Samos ; and to recall Philocles, in order to replace him with honour near his
person. Hegesippus , who is charged with this commission , executes it with joy. He arrives with these
two men at Samos, where he finds his friend Philocles contentedly leading an indigent and solitary
life. Philocles does not consent without much reluctance to return to his countrymen ; but when he
knows that it is the pleasure of the Gods , he embarks with Hegesippus , and arrives at Salentum,
where Idomeneus , who is no longer the same man,
receives him in a friendly manner.*

HAVING spoken these words , Mentor convinced Idomeneus that it was necessary to put
away Protesilaus and Timocrates, as soon as possible,
and to recall Philocles. The only difficulty which
with-held the king from it , was his apprehension of
the severity of Philocles. I own , said he , that I cannot help being a little apprehensive of his return,
though I love and esteem him. I have from my
earliest youth been accustomed to praises, to an of-
ficiousness

ficioufnefs and complaifance which I cannot hope to find in Philocles. Whenever I did any thing which he difliked, his gloomy looks fufficiently shewed that he condemned me; and when he was in private with me, his manners, though refpectful and decent, were rough and auftere.

Do you not obferve, anfwered Mentor, that princes who are corrupted by flattery, think every thing rough and auftere which is free and ingenuous? Nay, they go fo far as to imagine that a man is not zealous for their fervice, and is an enemy to their authority, who has not a flavish foul, and is not apt to flatter them in an unrighteous ufe of their power. All freedom and generofity of fpeech appears to them infolent, cenforious, and feditious. They are fo delicate, that every thing which is not flattery, galls and provokes them. But let us go farther: Suppofing that Philocles is rough and auftere, is not his aufterity more valuable than the pernicious adulation of your counfellors? Where will you find a man without failings? And is not the failing of telling you the truth too freely, that which you ought to apprehend the leaft? Or rather, is it not a failing which is neceffary to correct yours, and to overcome that antipathy to the truth which flattery has given you? You ftand in need of a man who loves nothing but truth; who loves you more than you love yourfelf; who will tell you the truth whether you will or not, and force your intrenchments; and Philocles is this neceffary man. Remember that a prince is exceedingly happy, if one fuch generous perfon, who is the moft precious treafure of his kingdom, be born in his reign; and that the greateft punishment which he has to apprehend from the Gods, is the lofing fuch an one, if he renders himfelf unworthy of him for want of knowing how to make a proper ufe of him. As for the failings of men of virtue, you should contrive means to know them, but should not let them deprive you of their fervice. Rectify them, but never give yourfelf blindly up to their indifcreet zeal. Give them

- a fa-

a favourable hearing, honour their virtue, let the
public fee that you know how to diftinguish it; and
above all, take care to be no longer what you have
hitherto been. Princes who have been fpoiled as you
were, contenting themfelves with defpifing corrupt
men, make no fcruple to employ them, and to heap
benefits upon them. On the other hand, they boaft
that they can diftinguish men of virtue, but they give
them only empty praifes; not daring to truft them
with employments, nor to admit them into their familiarity, nor to beftow favours upon them.

Hereupon Idomeneus faid, that he was ashamed of
having fo long delayed to deliver oppreft innocence,
and to punish thofe who had impofed upon him. And
Mentor had now no difficulty at all to determine the
king to difcard his favourite; for as foon as favourites
are rendered fufpected and troublefome to their mafter,
the weary and embarraffed prince feeks only to get rid
of them. His friendship vanishes, fervices are forgotten, and the fall of favourites gives him no pain
at all, provided he fees them no more.

The king immediately gave fecret orders to Hegefippus, who was one of the principal of his houf-
hold, to arreft Protefilaus and Timocrates, and to convey them in fafety to the ifland of Samos; to leave
them there, and to bring back Philocles from this
place of his exile. Hegefippus, furprifed at this commiffion, could not help weeping for joy. Now, faid
he to the king, you are going to wish the hearts of
your fubjects. Thefe two men have been the caufe of
all your misfortunes and of all thofe of your people.
For thefe twenty years have all men of virtue groaned
under them, and their tyranny was fo cruel, that they
hardly durft to do that: They bear down all who attempt to come at you by any canal but theirs.

Hegefippus then difcovered to the king a great
number of perfidious and inhuman actions committed
by thefe two men, which had never come to Idomeneus's ear, becaufe nobody durft to accufe them. He
gave him an account likewife of his difcovery of a

                                                    fecret

fecret confpiracy to deftroy Mentor. The king shivered with horror at what he heard.

Hegefippus haftened to feize Protefilaus in his houfe. It was not fo large, but more commodious and pleafanter than the king's. The architecture was in a better tafte, and Protefilaus had embellished it with the riches he had extracted out of the blood of the unfortunate. He happened at that time to be in a marble faloon near his baths, negligently lying on a purple couch embroidered with gold; he feemed weary and fpent with his toils, and his eyes and brows difcovered I know not what of trouble, of melancholy and wildnefs. The great officers of ftate were ranged around him on carpets, adjufting their faces to his, and obfervant even of the minuteft glance of his eyes. His mouth was hardly open, when every body cried out with admiration of what he was going to fay. One of the principal perfons of the company repeated to him with ridiculous exaggerations, what Protefilaus himfelf had done for the king. Another affured him that Jupiter having deceived his mother had begotten him, and that he was the fon of the father of the Gods. A poet came and fung verfes to him, wherein he affirmed that Protefilaus, being taught by the mufes, had equalled Apollo himfelf in all the various works of wit. Another poet, yet more bafe and impudent, ftyled him in his verfes the inventor of the polite arts, and the father of the people whom he rendered happy, and defcribed him with the horn of plenty in his hand.

Protefilaus heard all thefe praifes with a cold, heedlefs, and fcornful air, like a man who is very confcious that he merits yet greater, and that he is too condefcending in fuffering himfelf to be praifed. There was a flatterer who took the liberty to whifper in his ear a farcafm againft the policy which Mentor was endeavouring to eftablish. Protefilaus fmiled, and the whole affembly burft out into a laugh, though it was impoffible for the greater part of them to know what had been faid; but Protefilaus refuming his fevere

and

and haughty air, every one was awed and silent again. Several of the nobles waited for the happy moment when Protesilaus might condescend to come and hear them, and seemed anxious and confounded because they had some favours to ask of him. Their suppliant posture spoke for them. They appeared as submissive as a mother at the foot of the altar, imploring the Gods to restore her only son to health. All seemed pleased, and to love and admire Protesilaus, though they harboured in their hearts an implacable enmity against him.

At this very instant Hegesippus enters, seizes Protesilaus's sword, and tells him that he was going by the king's command to carry him to the island of Samos. At these words all Protesilaus's arrogance fell like a loosened rock from the top of a steep mountain. Lo! he now throws himself quaking with fear at Hegesippus's feet, he weeps, he faulters, he stammers, he trembles, he embraces the knees of a man whom an hour before he did not deign to honour with a look. All his flatterers seeing him ruined past redemption, changed their adulations into merciless insults.

Hegesippus would not allow him time either to take a last farewel of his family, or to fetch some private papers. Every thing was seized, and carried to the king. Timocrates being arrested at the same time, was extremely surprised; for he imagined, as he had quarrelled with Protesilaus, that he could not be involved in his ruin. They depart in a bark which was got ready for them, and arrive at Samos, where Hegesippus leaves these two wretches; and to fill up the measure of their misfortunes, he leaves them together Here they furiously reproach each other with the crimes they had committed, and which were the cause of their fall; despairing of ever seeing Salentum again, and condemned to live far from their wives and their children; I do not say far from their friends, for they had none. The very men who had spent so many years in pomp and pleasure, being now

left

left in an unknown country, where they had no
means of getting their bread but by their labour,
were, like two wild beasts, continually ready to tear
each other in pieces.

Hegesippus in the mean time inquired in what
part of the island Philocles lived, and was told that it
was on a mountain at a good distance from the city,
where a cave served him to dwell in. Every body
spoke with admiration of this stranger. Since he has
been in this Island, said they, he has offended nobody. Every one admires his patience, his labour,
and tranquillity of mind. Though he has nothing,
he always seems satisfied; and though he lives here
quite out of the way of business, destitute of money
and without authority, yet he obliges all who deserve it, and has a thousand ingenious ways of doing
good offices to all his neighbours.

Hegesippus goes towards the cave, and finds it
open and empty ; for Philocles's poverty and simplicity of manners were so great that he had no occasion to shut the door when he went out. A coarse
bulrush-mat served him for a bed. He seldom kindled a fire, because he eat nothing dressed ; living all the summer on fresh-gathered fruits, and on
dates and dried figs in the winter ; and slaking his
thirst at a fountain which poured in crystal sheets
from a rock. He had nothing in his cave but carv-
ing tools, and a few books which he read at set
hours, not to embellish his wit or gratify his curiosity, but to inform his mind when he unbent it from
labour, and to learn to be good. As for sculpture,
he applied himself to it only for the sake of exercise,
to avoid idleness, and to get his bread without being
obliged to any body.

Hegesippus, as he entered the cave, admired the
statues which Philocles had begun ; particularly a
Jupiter, whose serene countenance was so full of majesty, that he was easily known to be the father of
Gods and men. In another part was a Mars with a
rugged, fierce and threatning aspect. But what was
                                                    most

moſt ſtriking, was a Minerva encouraging the arts; her countenance was ſoft and noble; her ſtature tall and eaſy, and her attitude ſo lively, that one would have thought she was going to walk. Hegeſippus having viewed the ſtatues with pleaſure, went out of the grotto, and at a diſtance, under a large tree, beheld Philocles reading on the graſs; he goes towards him; Philocles ſees him, and knows not what to think. Is not that Hegeſippus, ſaid he to himſelf, with whom I ſo long lived in Crete? But what probability is there that he should come to ſo remote an iſland? Or is it not rather his ghoſt returned ſince his death from the Stygian shore?

While he was thus doubting, Hegeſippus came ſo near him, that he could not but know and embrace him. Is it then you, ſaid he, my dear old friend? What chance, what tempeſt has thrown you on this shore? Why have you left the iſland of Crete? Is it ſuch a misfortune as mine, that tears you from our native country?

Hegeſippus anſwered, It is not a misfortune, but on the contrary the goodneſs of the Gods which brings me hither. He then related to him Proteſilaus's long tyranny, his intrigues with Timocrates, the evils into which he had plunged Idomeneus, the fall of that prince, his flight to the coaſts of Heſperia, the building of Salentum, the arrival of Mentor and Telemachus, the wiſe maxims which Mentor had inſtilled into the king's mind, and the diſgrace of the two traitors: he added, that he had brought them to Samos to ſuffer the baniſhment which they had cauſed Philocles to ſuffer; and concluded with ſaying, that he had orders to conduct him to Salentum, where the king, who was ſenſible of his innocence, would intruſt him with his affairs, and load him with riches.

Lo that cave, replied Philocles, properer to harbour wild beaſts than to be inhabited by men. I have there for many years taſte more comfort and peace of mind, than I ever did in the gilded palaces of the

Iſland

island of Crete. Men no longer deceive me ; for I neither see them, nor hear their flattering and poisonous discourse. I have no further need of them ; for my hands hardened to labour, easily furnish me with the simple food which is necessary for me. A slight cloth, as you see, suffices to cover me. Having now no wants, and enjoying the utmost tranquillity and all the sweets of liberty, which my books teach me how to make a good use of, what should I go in quest of among jealous, fraudful, and inconstant men ? No, no, my dear Hegesippus, do not envy me my happiness. Protesilaus, by endeavouring to betray the king and to destroy me, has betrayed himself, and done me no harm at all : On the contrary, he has done me the greatest good ; he has delivered me from the hurry and slavery of public affairs, and to him I am indebted for my dear solitude, and all the innocent pleasures I here enjoy. Return, Hegesippus, return to the king ; help him to support the miseries of his greatness, and what you desire me to do for him, do yourself, since his eyes, so long shut against the truth, have at last been opened by the wise person you call Mentor, let him be retained in his service. As for me, it is not proper after my shipwreck that I should quit the haven into which the storm has so happily thrown me, and commit myself again to the mercy of the winds. O how greatly are kings to be pitied ! how worthy those who serve them, of compassion ! If they are wicked, how miserable do they render mankind, and what tortures are prepared for them in the black gulf of Tartarus ! If they are good, what difficulties have they to overcome ! What snares to avoid ! What evils to suffer ! Once again, my dear Hegesippus, leave me, I say, in my happy poverty.

While Philocles was talking thus with great vehemence, Hegesippus beheld him with wonder. He had formerly seen him in Crete, during his administration of the most important affairs, meagre, languishing, exhausted; for his ardent and austere temper made him wear himself away in fatigues ; he

M   could

could not without indignation fee vice unpunished ; he required a certain exactnefs which is never found in bufinefs ; his employments therefore ruined his tender health ; but at Samos Hegefippus beheld him plump and vigorous. The bloom of youth in fpite of his years was renewed on his countenance. A fober, quiet and laborious life had given him as it were a new conftitution.

You are furprifed, faid Philocles with a fmile, to fee me fo altered. I owe this freshnefs and perfect health to my folitude. My enemies have given me what I could never hope to find in the moft elevated ftation. Would you have me quit fubftantial bleffings to purfue imaginary ones, and to plunge myfelf again in my former miferies ? Be not more cruel than Protefilaus ; at leaft do not envy me the happinefs I derive from him.

Hegefippus then reprefented to him, but in vain, every thing which he thought proper to move him. Are you then, faid he, infenfible of the pleafure of feeing your friends and relations again, who long for your return, and whom the bare expectation of embracing you overwhelms with joy ? But can you who fear the Gods, and love to do your duty, efteem as nothing the ferving your king, the affifting him in all his good defigns, and the rendering fo many people happy ? Is it allowable for a man to abandon himfelf to a favage philofophy, to prefer himfelf to all the reft of mankind, and to love his own eafe more than the happinefs of his fellow-citizens ? Befides, it will be thought that it is out of refentment that you refufe to fee the king ; if he defigned to do you an injury, it was becaufe he did not know you : It was not the true, the good, the juft Philocles whom he defigned to deftroy; it was a very different perfon whom he defigned to punish. But now he knows you, and does not miftake you for another, he feels all his former friendship revive in his heart ; he expects you ; he already ftretches out his arms to embrace you, and impatiently numbers the days, the hours, till he fees you

you. Is your heart so hardened as to be inexorable to
your king and to all your dearest friends?

Philocles, who was moved when he first perceived
Hegesippus, resumed his austere air on hearing this
discourse. Like a rock against which the winds rage,
and all the groaning billows break in vain, he remained immoveable; nor intreaties nor arguments
could find any passage to his heart. But the moment
Hegesippus began to despair of prevailing upon him,
Philocles, having consulted the Gods, discovered
by the flight of birds, the entrails of victims, and
divers other omens, that he was to go with Hegesippus.

Hereupon he opposed it no longer, but prepared
for his departure; though not without regretting the
desert where he so many years had lived. Alas! said
he, must I leave you, my delightful grotto, where
peaceful slumbers nightly came to refresh me after the
toils of the day! Here the fatal sisters, in the midst
of my poverty, spun my days of a gold and silken
thread. He fell on the earth, and weeping adored
the naiad who had so long slaked his thirst with her
limpid wave, and the nymphs that dwelt on all the
neighbouring mountains. Echo heard his wailings,
and with a plaintive voice repeated them to all the
rural deities.

Philocles then went to the city with Hegesippus, in
order to embark. He imagined that the unhappy
Protesilaus, overwhelmed with shame and indignation, would avoid seeing him; but he was mistaken:
For corrupt men have no shame, and are always
ready to stoop to any kind of meanness. Philocles
modestly kept out of the way, that he might not be
seen by this wretch; being apprehensive that the
sight of a prosperous rival, who was going to be
raised on his ruin, would increase his misery. But
Protesilaus eagerly sought after Philocles, and endeavoured to move his pity, and to engage him to
solicit the king that he might return to Salentum.
Philocles was too sincere to promise, that he would

M 2   try

try to get him recalled; for he knew better than any one how pernicious his return would have been. He talked to him however with great mildness; he pitied him, endeavoured to comfort him, and exhorted him to appeafe the Gods by the purity of his manners, and an exemplary patience under his fufferings. And as he had heard that the king had ftript Protefilaus of all his ill-gotten wealth, he promifed him two things which he afterwards faithfully performed: One was, to take care of his wife and children, who remained at Salentum, in a frightful ftate of poverty, expofed to public indignation; the other was, to fend Protefilaus in this remote ifland, fome fupplies of money to alleviate his mifery.

Mean while the fails fwelling with a favourable gale, Hegefippus grows impatient, and haftens the departure of Philocles. Protefilaus fees them embark; his eyes are motionlefs and fixed on the fhore; they then purfue the bark as it cleaves the waves, and is continually driven farther off by the winds: And even when he could fee it no longer, its image remains in his mind. At length diftracted, furious, defpairing, he tears off his hair, rolls himfelf on the fand, upbraids the Gods with their rigour, and calls relentlefs death to his aid, but calls in vain; for death, regardlefs of his prayers, deigns not to deliver him from his numerous woes, nor has he the courage to deliver himfelf.

Mean time the bark, favoured by Neptune and the winds, quickly arrives at Salentum. The king being told that it was entering the port, immediately ran with Mentor to meet Philocles. He tenderly embraced him, and expreffed a great concern for having fo unjuftly perfecuted him. This confeffion, inftead of feeming a weaknefs in a prince, was looked upon by all the Salentines as the effort of a great foul, which rifes above its errors by owning and refolving to repair them. Every body wept with joy to fee this virtuous lover of the people, and to hear the king talk with fo much wifdom and goodnefs.

Philocles

Philocles received the king's careffes, with a refpectful modeft air; he was impatient to fteal away
from the acclamations of the people, and followed
Idomeneus to the palace. Mentor and he quickly
repofed as much confidence in each other, as if they
had paffed their lives together, though they never
faw one another before; for the Gods, who have not
given eyes to the wicked to know the good, have
given eyes to the good to know one another. They
who relish virtue, cannot be together without con-
tracting a friendship, by means of the virtue they
love. Philocles foon asked the king's leave to retire
to a folitary place near Salentum, where he continued
to live in poverty as he had done at Samos.   The
king and Mentor went almoft every day to vifit him
in his retirement, where they concerted the means
of ftrengthening the laws, and of giving a folid form
to the government for the good of the public.

The two principal things which they confidered,
were the education of children, and the manner of
living in time of peace. As to children, faid Mentor,
they are lefs the property of their parents than of the
public; they are the children of the people, and are
their hope and ftrength; it is too late to correct
them, when they are corrupted; it avails little to
exclude them from employments, when they have
rendered themfelves unworthy of them; it is better
to prevent the evil than to be obliged to punish it.
The king, added he, who is the father of all his
people, is ftill more particularly the father of all the
youth; they are the bloffom of the whole nation,
and the fruits muft be prepared in the bloffom. Let
not the king therefore difdain to be watchful, and
to caufe others to be watchful, of the education of
children. Let him be fteady in caufing the laws of
Minos to be obferved, which ordain that children
be educated in a contempt of pain and death; that
honour be placed in flighting pleafures and riches;
that injuftice, lying, ingratitude, and luxury be ac-
counted infamous vices; that they be taught from

M 3   their

their tenderest infancy to sing the praises of heroes who were beloved of the Gods, who have done generous actions for their country, and have distinguished their courage in battle ; that the charms of music strike their souls in order to soften and purify their manners ; that they be taught to be kind to their friends, faithful to their allies, just to all mankind, even to their most cruel enemies ; and that they be less apprehensive of death and tortures, than of the least upbraiding of their conscience. If children are early imbued with these important maxims, and the melody of music insinuate them into their hearts, there will be few who will not burn with a love of glory and virtue.

Mentor added, That it was of great importance to institute public schools, in order to habituate the youth to the hardest bodily exercises, and to prevent effeminacy and idleness, which ruin the best constitutions. He was likewise for having a great variety of games and shows, that might be a spur to the people, but especially such as would exercise and render their bodies active, pliant and vigorous ; and to these he annexed rewards in order to excite a generous emulation. But what he was most zealous for, as being most conducive to purity of manners, was, that young men should marry betimes, and that their parents, without any views of interest, should leave them to choose wives of agreeable tempers and persons, to whom they might be constant in their love.

But while they were thus concerting means to keep the youth chaste and innocent, and to make them laborious, tractable, and fond of glory, Philocles, who delighted in war, thus addrest himself to Mentor : In vain will you employ our youth in all these exercises, if you let them languish in a perpetual peace, wherein they will have no experience of war, nor no need to give proofs of their valour. You will thereby enfeeble the nation ; its courage will insensibly be unnerved, its manners corrupted by plea-

sures,

fures, and other warlike nations will find no difficulty in making a conqueft of it. And thus, by endeavouring to avoid the evils of war, they will fall into the miferies of flavery.

Mentor anfwered, The evils of war are more terrible than you imagine. War exhaufts a people, and continually expofes them to the danger of being ruined, even when they obtain the greateft victories. With whatever advantages a man enters into a war, he is never fure of ending it without being liable to the moft tragical reverfes of fortune. With whatever fuperiority of forces he engages in battle, the leaft miftake, a panick, a nothing fnatches the victory out of his hands, and transfers it to his enemies. And though he held victory as it were in chains in his camp, yet he deftroys himfelf in deftroying his foes. For he depopulates his own country; he leaves the lands almoft uncultivated; he interrupts trade; and what is much worfe, he weakens the beft laws and winks at a depravity of manners. The youth no longer addict themfelves to letters. The neceffity of the time obliges him to tolerate a pernicious licentioufnefs in the army. Juftice, government, every thing fuffers in the confufion. A king who sheds the blood of fuch multitudes, and caufes fo many calamities in order to acquire a little glory, or to extend the bounds of his kingdom, is unworthy of the glory he purfues, and deferves to lofe what he poffeffes for having endeavoured to ufurp what he has no right to.

But the courage of a nation may be exercifed in time of peace. You already know what bodily exercifes we inftitute; the prizes to excite emulation, and the maxims of glory and virtue, with which the fongs of the great actions of heroes will fill the fouls of children almoft from their very cradles: Add to thefe helps, that of a fober and laborious life. But this is not all: As foon as any nation in alliance with yours, is engaged in a war, the flower of your youth muft be fent thither, efpecially thofe who have difcovered a genius for war, and are the beft qualified

to profit by experience. You will thereby maintain
an high reputation among your neighbours, who will
court your alliance, and be afraid of losing it. And
thus without having a war at home and at your own
expence, you will always have a warlike and intrepid
body of youth. Notwithstanding you have peace in
your own kingdom, you must not fail to treat those
with great honour who have a talent for war ; for
the true way to avoid war and to maintain a lasting
peace, is to cultivate arms, to honour men who ex-
cell in the profession of them, always to have some
who have been trained up in foreign countries, and
who know the strength and discipline of neighbouring nations, and their manner of making war ; and
to be equally incapable of making it through ambition, and of dreading it through effeminacy. By being thus always prepared for it on occasion, one is
hardly ever reduced to the necessity of making it at all.

As for your allies, when they are ready to engage
in a war with each other, it is your part to become
their mediator. You thereby acquire a more solid and
unquestionable glory than that of conquerors ; you
win the love and esteem of strangers ; they all stand
in need of you, and you reign over them by the confidence they repose in you, as you reign over your
subject by your authority. You are the repository
of their secrets, the arbiter of their treaties, the master of their hearts. Your fame flies to the most distant countries, and your name is like a sweet perfume which diffuses itself from country to country
even to the remotest nations. If a neighbouring people attack you in these circumstances contrary to the
rules of justice, it finds you warlike, prepared, and,
what is a much greater security, beloved and suc-
coured : All your neighbours are alarmed for you,
and persuaded that the public safety depends on your
preservation. This is a much stronger rampart than
all the walls of cities, or the most regular fortifica-
tions : this is substantial glory. But how few princes
are there who are wise enough to pursue it, or rather,

ther, who do not fly from it! They pursue a delusive phantom, and leave true honour behind them for want of knowing it.

When Mentor had spoken thus, Philocles looked upon him with astonishment; and then turning his eyes on the king, was charmed to see how greedily Idomeneus stored up in his heart all the words which poured like a torrent of wisdom from the mouth of this stranger.

Thus did Minerva, in the form of Mentor, establish all the best laws and most useful maxims of government at Salentum; not so much to make the kingdom of Idomeneus flourish, as to show Telemachus, when he should return, a striking example of the effects of a wise administration with regard to the happiness of the people, and the lasting glory of the prince.

End of the Fourteenth Book.

THE

THE
ADVENTURES
OF
TELEMACHUS,
SON of ULYSSES.

BOOK the FIFTEENTH.

The ARGUMENT.

Telemachus in the camp of the allies wins the affection of Philoctetes, who was at first prejudiced against him on account of his father Ulysses. Philoctetes relates to him his adventures, with which he interweaves the particulars of the death of Hercules, occasioned by the poisoned tunic which the centaur Nessus had given to Dejanira. He informs him how he obtained of this hero his fatal arrows, without which the city of Troy could not have been taken; how he was punished for betraying his secret, by all the miseries he suffered in the isle of Lemnos; and how Ulysses employed Neoptolemus to engage him to go to the siege of Troy, where he was cured of his wound by the sons of Esculapius.

IN the mean time Telemachus was signalising his courage amidst the dangers of war. When he departed from Salentum, he was very assiduous to win the affection of the old captains, whose reputation and experience were the most consummate. Nestor, who had seen him before at Pylos, and who always loved Ulysses, treated him as if he had been his own son; giving him instructions which he enforced by
various

various examples, and relating to him all the adventures of his youth, and all the moſt remarkable things which he had ſeen performed by the heroes of the laſt age.   The memoıy of this wiſe ſenior, who had lived thrice the age of man, was as it were an hiſtory of ancient times engraved on braſs and marble.

Philoctetes had not at firſt the ſame affection for Telemachus as Neſtor had.   The hatred which he had ſo long harboured in his heart againſt Ulyſſes, prejudiced him againſt his ſon ; and he could not without uneaſineſs ſee all that he thought the Gods were doing in favour of this youth, in order to render him equal to the heroes who had ſubverted the city of Troy.   But at length the prudent deportment of Telemachus entirely overcame the reſentment of Philoctetes, who could not help loving his engaging and modeſt virtue.   He often took him aſide, and ſaid, my ſon, (for I no longer ſcruple to call you ſo) your father and I were, I own, a long while enemies to each other.   I own alſo that my heart was not appeaſed after we had ſubverted the haughty city of Troy ; and that I found it difficult when I ſaw you, to love virtue in the ſon of Ulyſſes : With this I often reproached myſelf.   But virtue, when it is gentle, unaffected, ingenious and modeſt, at length overcomes every thing.   Philoctetes was afterwards inſenſibly engaged to tell him what had kindled in his heart ſo much enmity againſt Ulyſſes.

I muſt, ſaid he, begin my hiſtory higher.   I every where attended the great Hercules, who freed the earth from ſo many monſters, and in whoſe ſight the other heroes were but as feeble reeds near a large oak, or little birds in the preſence of the eagle.   His misfortunes and mine proceeded from love, the ſource of all the moſt terrible diſaſters.   Hercules, who had conquered ſo many monſters, could not conquer this ſhameful paſſion : Cupid, the cruel boy made him his ſport.   Nor could he recollect without bluſhing with ſhame, that he had formerly been ſo

M 6   forgetful

forgetful of his glory, as to spin with Omphale queen
of Lydia, like the most abject and effeminate of mankind; so far was he hurried away by his blind paffion. An hundred times has he confessed to me, that
this part of his life had tarnished his virtue, and almost effaced the glory of all his labours. How great,
ye Gods! is the weakness and inconstancy of men!
they think themselves all sufficient, though they can
withstand nothing. Alas the great Hercules was
entangled again in the snares of love, which he had
so often detested. He conceived a passion for Dejanira: She was his wife, and happy had he been had
he been constant to her; but Iole's youth, on whose
face the graces were pictured, quickly ravished his
heart. Dejanira, burning with jealousy, bethought
her of the fatal tunic, which the centaur Neffus had
bequeathed her at his death, as a certain means to
awaken the love of Hercules, as often as he should
seem to neglect her and to be fond of another. This
tunic, imbrued with the venomous blood of the centaur, contained the poison of the arrows with which
that monster was slain. You know that the arrows
with which Hercules killed this perfidious centaur,
had been dipt in the blood of the Lemæan Hydra,
and that this blood poisoned those arrows to such a
degree, that all their wounds were incurable.

Hercules having put on this tunic, presently felt the
devouring fire, which infinuated itself even into the
marrow of his bones. He roared in a horrible manner, making mount Œta and all the deep valleys ring
with his cries: nay, the sea, itself seemed to be moved;
the most furious bulls in their conflicts could not
have made a more terrible bellowing. The ill-fated
Lychas, who had brought him this tunic from Dejanira, presuming to approach him, Hercules seized
him in the transports of his anguish, and as a slinger
whirls a stone in his sling, in order to cast it the farther,
whirled him swiftly round, and then with his potent
hands hurled him from the top of the mountain into
the billows of the sea, where he was immediately
transformed

transformed into a rock, which still retains an human shape, and being continually beaten by the angry waves, alarms the wary pilot at a distance.

After this misfortune of Lychas, believing I should no longer be safe with Hercules, I thought of hiding myself in the deepest caverns of the earth. With one hand I beheld him easily up-root the lofty firs and ancient oaks, which for several ages had braved the winds and the tempests; with the other, he vainly endeavoured to tear the fatal tunic from his back; it was glued to his skin, and as it were incorporated with his limbs: as he tore that, he tore off his skin and his flesh, and drenched the earth with torrents of blood. At length his virtue getting the better of his anguish, he cried out, You see! my dearest Philoctetes! the evils which the Gods inflict upon me; they are righteous; I have offended them; I have violated conjugal love; having vanquished so many enemies, I meanly suffered myself to be vanquished by a beautiful stranger; I perish, and I am willing to perish to appease the Gods. But alas! my dear friend, whither do you fly? My excessive tortures have indeed made me commit an act of cruelty on the wretched Lychas, for which my conscience upbraids me; he knew not that he presented me poison, nor deserved to suffer. But do you think that I can forget my friendship for you, and that I would rob you of your life? No, no, I shall never cease to love Philoctetes. Philoctetes shall receive my fleeting soul in his bosom; he shall collect my ashes together. Where are you then, my dear Philoctetes! Philoctetes! the only hope which is left me here below.

This said, I immediately ran towards him; he stretches out his arms to embrace me, but draws them back again, for fear of kindling in my bosom the cruel fire with which he himself was consumed. Alas! said he, even this consolation is no longer allowed me. As he speaks thus, he collects together the trees he had torn up by the roots; he makes a funeral pile of them on the top of the mountain; he ascends it with

with tranquillity; he overspreads it with the skin of the Nemean lion, which he had so long worn on his shoulders, when he travelled from one end of the earth to the other to destroy monsters, and deliver the distressed; he leans on his club, and bids me light the pyre.

My hands trembling with horror could not deny him this cruel office; for his life was so racked with tortures, that it was no longer a gift of the Gods. I was moreover apprehensive lest the violence of his pangs should transport him to act something unworthy of the virtue which had astonished the universe. Perceiving the flames begin to catch the pyre, Now, cried he, my dear Philoctetes, I am convinced of the sincerity of your friendship; for you love my honour more than my life: may the Gods reward you for it! I bequeath you what I have of the most valuable in the world, these arrows dipt in the blood of the Lernæan Hydra. You know that their wounds are incurable; they will render you as invincible as I have been, and no mortal will dare to contend with you. Remember that I die your faithful friend, and never forget how dear you have been to me. And if you are really touched with my sufferings, you will afford me the last consolation in your power, a promise never to discover to any mortal either my death, or the place where you conceal my ashes. Alas! I promised, nay I swore it as I bedewed his pyre with my tears; a beam of gladness darted from his eyes. But he was suddenly involved in curling flames, which stifled his voice, and almost snatched him from my sight. However, I beheld him again through the fire with a countenance as serene as if it had been crowned with flowers, perfumed and encircled by his friends, amidst the merriments of a sumptuous banquet.

Soon did the fire consume all his earthly and mortal part; soon was there nothing left of what he had received from his mother Alcmena at his birth: But he preserved by Jupiter's decree that subtle and immortal substance, that celestial flame, the true principle
ciple

ciple of life, which he had received from the father
of the Gods. He afcended therefore to drink nectar
with them under the gilded roofs of shining Olympus; where the immortals gave him for his wife the
lovely Hebe, the Goddefs of youth; who ufed to
pour the nectar into Jupiter's cup, before Ganymede.
was preferred to that honour.

For my part, I found an inexhauftible fource of forrows, in the very arrows he bequeathed me in order
to raife me above the heroes. The confederate kings
quickly undertook to revenge Menelaus on the infamous Paris, the ravifher of Helen, and to fubvert the
empire of Priam. The oracle of Apollo gave them to
underftand that they muft not hope for an happy iffue
of that war, unlefs they had the arrows of Hercules.

Your father Ulyffes, who in all their councils conftantly difcovered the greateft wifdom and art, undertook to perfuade me to accompany them to the
fiege of Troy, and to carry the arrows thither, which
were he thought in my poffeffion. Hercules had not
been feen for a long while; there was no talk of any
new exploit of his; monfters and wicked men began
to appear again with impunity. The Greeks knew
not what to think concerning him; fome faid that
he was dead, and others that he was gone as far as
the frozen bear in order to tame the Scythians; but
Ulyffes maintained that he was dead, and undertook
to make me confefs it. As he came to me while I
was yet inconfolable for the lofs of the great Alcides,
he found it very difficult to accoft me; for I could
not bear the fight of men, nor the thoughts of being
torn from the deferts of mount Œta, where I had
feen my friend die: I heeded but to recall the image
of that hero to my mind, and to weep at the fight of
thofe fcenes of horror. But foft and powerful perfuafion hung on your father's lips; he feemed almoft
as much afflicted as I; he poured forth floods of
tears; he infenfibly won my heart and my confidence, and moved me with pity for the kings of
Greece, who were going to fight in a juft caufe,
and

and could not fucceed without me. He could not
however extort from me the fecret of Hercules's
death, which I had fworn never to reveal; but he
no longer doubted of it, and preffed me to show him
where I had concealed his ashes.

Though I had, alas! an abhorrence of being guilty
of perjury, by revealing a fecret which I had promifed the Gods never to reveal; yet was I fo weak
as to evade the oath which I durft not violate : the
Gods have punished me for it : I ftamped with my
foot on the earth where I had depofited the ashes of
Hercules. I then went and joined the confederate
kings, who received me with the fame joy as they
would have received Hercules himfelf. As I was
paffing through the ifland of Lemnos, I had a mind
to show all the Greeks the efficacy of my arrows,
and going to shoot a deer which was rushing into a
wood, I heedlefsly let the arrow fall from my bow
on my foot, where it made a wound which I ftill feel.
I was immediately racked with the fame tortures
which Hercules himfelf had fuffered, and filled the
ifland both night and day with my wailings ; black
corrupted blood iffuing from my wound, infected
the air, and diffufed a ftench through the whole
Grecian camp, which was enough to fuffocate men
of the moft robuft conftitutions. The whole army
was ftruck with horror at my diftrefs ; every one
concluding that it was a judgment which the righteous Gods had inflicted upon me.

Ulyffes, who had engaged me in this war, was the
firft to forfake me. I have fince been convinced that
he did it, becaufe he preferred victory and the common intereft of Greece to all motives of friendship
and decency with regard to any particular perfon. It
was no longer poffible to facrifice in the camp, fo
much did the horror and infection of my wound, and
the violence of my shrieks difturb the whole army.
But as foon as I faw myfelf deferted by all the
Greeks at the inftigation of Ulyffes, his conduct
feemed to me to be full of the moft shocking inhu-
                                                        manity

manity and the blackeft treachery. Alas! I was
blind, and did not fee that it was juft that the wifeft
men fhould be my enemies, as well as the Gods
whom I had offended.

I remained, during almoft the whole fiege of Troy,
all alone, without fuccour, without hope, without
comfort, a prey to the moft terrible tortures in this
defert and favage ifland, where I heard but the roaring of the billows that dashed againft the rocks. In
the midft of this folitude I found an empty cave, in
a rock that lifted its two points like two heads to the
heavens, and poured forth a limpid fpring. This
cave was a harbour for wild beafts, to whofe fury I
was expofed both night and day. I heaped fome
leaves together for a bed : My whole furniture was a
wooden bowl rudely wrought, and fome tattered
cloaths, with which I bound up my wound to ftop
its bleeding, and with which I likewife ufed to cleanfe
it. Here, abandoned by men, the object of the wrath
of the Gods, I fpent my time in shooting doves and
other birds which flew around the rock, with my
arrows. And when I had killed any for my fuftenance, I was forced with extreme pain to crawl along
the earth to pick up my prey. In this manner did my
hands provide me wherewithal to fubfift on.

The Greeks indeed, when they went away, left
me fome provifions, but they did not laft long. I
ufed to kindle my fire with flints. This life, dreadful
as it was, as it was remote from falfe ungrateful
men, would have feemed pleafant to me, had I not
been borne down by my pains, and inceffantly ru-
minating on my dire mifchance. What! faid I; en-
tice a man from his native country, under pretence
of his being the only one who could avenge Greece,
and then leave him in this defert ifland while he was
afleep ! For I was afleep when the Greeks departed.
Judge how great was my furprife, and how many
tears I shed, when I awaked and faw their veffels
ploughing through the waves. I fearched every corner of this favage and frigthful ifland, but alas ! I
                                        found

found in it nothing but forrow. In fact, there is neither harbour, nor trade, nor hofpitality, nor does any man willingly land there. One fees but wretches who have been driven upon it by ftorms, and one cannot hope for fociety but from shipwrecks ; and even thofe durft not take me along with them : they dreaded the wrath of the Gods and that of the Greeks. Here for ten long years did I fuffer pain and hunger ; here I fed my devouring wound, and even hope itfelf was extinguished in my heart.

Returning one day from feeking fome medicinal herbs for my wound, I faw in my cave a handfome graceful youth, but of an haughty air and heroic ftature. Methought I beheld Achilles himfelf, fo much had he of his features, looks and gait ; his age only convinced me that it could not be he. I obferved both pity and confufion blended together in his face ; he was moved at feeing with what pain and how flowly I crawled along ; my piercing and doleful cries, which the echoes of every shore refounded, melted his very heart.

O ftranger ! faid I, while I was yet a good way off, what difafter has brought you to this uninhabited ifland ? I know the Grecian habit, that habit which is ftill fo dear to me. Oh ! how I long to hear thy voice, and to find on thy lips the language which I learnt in my infancy, and which I have fpoke to nobody for fo long a time in this folitude. Be not ftartled at the fight of fo wretched a creature ; you ought rather to pity him.

Neoptolemus had hardly told me that he was a Greek, when I cried out. O inchanting words after fo many years of filence and never-ceafing pain ! O my fon ! what misfortune, what ftorms, or rather what propitious winds have brought you hither to end my woes ! He replied, I am of the ifland of Scyros ; I am returning thither, and am faid to be the fon of Achilles : You know the whole.

So short an anfwer not fatisfying my curiofity, I faid, O fon of a father whom I greatly loved, thou
darling

darling of thy grandfire Lycomedes, what brings you hither? whence come you? He replied, that he came from the siege of Troy. You were not, said I, in the first expedition. Why, said he, were you? I plainly see, answered I, that you are a stranger to Philoctetes's name and misfortunes. Alas! wretch that I am, my persecutors insult me in my miseries! Greece is ignorant of my sufferings; my sorrows increase; the Atridæ have brought me to this; may the Gods requite them for it!

I then told him how the Greeks had deserted me. As soon as he heard my complaints, he made his. After the death of Achilles, said he—I immediately interrupted him, saying, How! Achilles dead! O my son! excuse my breaking in upon your narration by the tears I owe your father. You comfort me, replied Neoptolemus, by your interruption. How delightful is it to me to see Philoctetes bewail my father!

Neoptolemus resuming his discourse, said, After the death of Achilles, Ulysses and Phænix came to me, assuring me that they could not subvert the city of Troy without me. They had no difficulty to persuade me to go with them; for my grief for the death of Achilles, and my desire of inheriting his glory in that famous war, were sufficient motives to induce me to do it. I arrive at the siege, the army gathers around me, and every one swears that he beholds Achilles again; but he, alas! was no more. Young and unexperienced, I thought I might expect every thing from persons that bestowed such praises upon me. I immediately ask the Atridæ for my father's armour; they cruelly reply, you shall have every thing else that belonged to him; but as for his armour it is designed for Ulysses.

Upon this I am troubled, I weep, I rave: But Ulysses without the least emotion said, Young man, you have not borne your part with us in the perils of this long siege; you have not merited such arms, and already talk too haughtily; you shall never have them:

them. Unjuftly robbed by Ulyffes, I am now returning to the ifle of Scyros, lefs incenfed againft him than againft the Atridæ. May all who are their enemies, be beloved of the Gods! O Philoctetes! I have told you all.

I then asked Neoptolemus why Ajax Telamon did not prevent fuch a piece of injuftice. He is dead, anfwered he. Dead, cried I! and Ulyffes not dead ; he on the contrary profpers in the army! I then inquired after Antilochus the fon of the wife Neftor, and Patrochus fo dear to Achilles. They are dead alfo, faid he. Hereupon I once again cried out, How! dead! What, alas! do you tell me! Thus cruel war mows down the good and fpares the wicked. Ulyffes then is living ; and fo, no doubt, is Therfites? Thefe are the doings of the Gods, and yet we celebrate their praifes !

While I was in this rage againft your father, Neoptolemus went on to deceive me, adding thefe melancholy words. Far from the army of the Greeks, where evil prevails over good, I am going to live contented in the rude ifland of Scyros. Farewell, I go ; may the Gods heal your wound.

I inftantly faid, O my fon, I conjure you by the manes of your father, by your mother, by all that is deareft to you in the world, not to leave me alone in this miferable condition. I am not ignorant how burdenfome I shall be to you, but it would be dishonourable in you to forfake me ; throw me into the prow, the ftern, the fink itfelf, or wherever I may incommode you the leaft. None but great fouls know how much glory there is in being good. Leave me nor in a defert, where there is no human footftep; take me into your own country, or into Eubœa, which is not far from mount Œta, Trachinium, and the pleafant banks of the river Sperchius : fend me back to my father. Alas! I fear he is dead : I defired him to fend me a ship : either he is dead, or thofe who promifed to tell him my diftrefs, did not do it. O my fon, I fly to you for fuccour. Remember

ber the inftability of all human things: Who is in profperity, fhould apprehend the abufing it, and relieve the diftreffed.

This is what the excefs of my anguifh prompted me to fay to Neoptolemus; he promifed to take me with him. I then burft into exclamations again. O happy day ! O lovely Neoptolemus, worthy of thy father's glory. Ye dear companions of this voyage, permit me to bid this difmal manfion adieu. Lo ! where I have lived ; imagine what I have fuffered ; nobody elfe could have borne it : But neceffity was my tutor, and fhe teaches men what they would never otherwife know : They who have never fuffered, know nothing ; they know neither good nor evil, they are ftrangers to mankind, they are ftrangers to themfelves. This faid, I took my bow and my arrows.

Neoptolemus defired me to let him kifs thofe celebrated arms which had been confecrated by the invincible Hercules. I replied, you may do what you pleafe, I can deny thee nothing ; it is thou, my fon, who now reftoreft me the light, my country, my aged father, my friends, myfelf ; you may touch thefe arms, and boaft of being the only Greek that has deferved to touch them. Hereupon Neoptolemus enters my grotto to admire my arms.

Mean while I am feized with exquifite pains ; I rave ; I no longer know what I do ; I afk for a fharp fword to cut off my foot, and cry out, O much defired death, why comeft thou not ? O young man ! burn me this inftant as I burnt the fon of Jupiter. O earth, earth, receive a dying wretch that can rife no more ! In this agony I fell fuddenly, as ufual, into a found fleep ; a copious difcharge of fweat began to relieve me ; black corrupted blood iffued from my wound. During my fleep it had been eafy for Neoptolemus to have taken my arms and gone away ; but he was the fon of Achilles, and was not born to deceive.

When I awaked I perceived his confufion : he fighed like one who knows not to diffemble, and

acts

acts contrary to his inclination. Wilt thou deceive me, said I? What's the matter? You must go with me, said he, to the siege of Troy. I instantly replied, Ah, what said you, my son? give me back the bow; I am betrayed; rob me not of my life. Alas! he answers not; he looks calmly upon me; nothing moves him. O ye shores! ye promontories of this island! ye savage beasts! ye steepy rocks! 'tis to you I make my complaints; for I have but you to whom I can complain: my groans are familiar to you. Must I be betrayed by the son of Achilles? He robs me of the sacred bow of Hercules; he would drag me in triumph to the Grecian camp; not perceiving that this were triumphing over a corps, a shadow, a phantom. Oh! had he attacked me in my vigour! Nay, even now he does it unawares. What shall I do? O my son! restore my arms; be like thy father, be like thyself. What sayest thou? Nothing! Thou savage rock, to thee I return naked, miserable, abandoned, destitute of food. In this den shall I die all alone; having my bow no longer to kill the wild beasts, they will devour me: no matter. But, my son, you seem not a bad man; ill advice prompts you to this; return me my arms, and be gone.

Neoptolemus with tears in his eyes and a low voice said, Would to the Gods that I had never departed from Scyros! Mean time I cry out, Ah! what do I see? Is not that Ulysses? I instantly hear his voice; he replies, Yes, it is Ulysses. Had Pluto's sable realm yawned, and shown me dismal Tartarus, which the Gods themselves dread to see, I should not, I own, have been seized with greater horror. I then exclaimed again, witness thou Lemnian earth! and thou, O sun! can'st thou behold and suffer this? Ulysses, perfectly calm, replied, Jupiter commands, and I obey. Darest thou name Jupiter, said I? See'st thou this youth who was not born for fraud, and hurts himself in doing what you force him to do? We come not, said Ulysses, to injure or deceive you;

we

we come to deliver you, to cure you, to give you the
glory of subverting Troy, and to carry you back to
your own country; 'tis you, and not Ulysses, who
are Philoctetes's enemy.

I then said to your father every thing which rage
could dictate. Since thou deserted'st me on this
shore, said I, why do you not leave me here in peace?
Go, seek renown in battle and every kind of pleasure; share your happiness with the Atridæ, and
leave me my misery and pain. And why would you
force me away? I am nothing now, I am already
dead. Why do you not think at present, as you did
heretofore, that I am not able to go; that my wailings and the stench of my wound would interrupt
the sacrifices? O Ulysses, author of my woes, may
the Gods — but the Gods hear me not: nay, they
stir up my enemy against me. O my native country! never shall I see thee more! Punish, ye Gods!
if there be one just enough to pity me, punish Ulysses, and I shall think myself cured.

While I was speaking thus, your father, quite
composed, beheld me with an air of compassion, like
a man who instead of being provoked at, bears with
and excuses the distraction of a wretch soured by
misfortunes. Like a rock on the top of a mountain
which derides the fury of the winds, and lets them
waste their rage while it remains immoveable; your
father silently waited 'till my anger had spent itself.
For he knew that the way to reduce mens passions to
reason is not to attack them 'till they begin to grow
languid through a kind of weariness. He afterwards
addrest me thus. O Philoctetes! what have you
done with your reason and your courage? This is
the time to use them. If you refuse to go with us
in order to fulfill the glorious designs of Jupiter with
regard to you, farewell; you are unworthy of being
the deliverer of Greece and the subverter of Troy.
Remain at Lemnos; these arms I bear away shall
give me the glory which was destined to you. Let
us be gone, Neoptolemus; it is in vain to talk to
him;

him; pity for a single perfon ought not to make us neglect the common fafety of Greece.

Upon this I was like a lionefs robbed of her young, that fills the woods with her roarings. Thou cave, faid I, I'll never forfake thee, thou shalt be my grave; O manfion of my woes! Nothing now to fubfift on, no remains of hope! O lend me a fword to flay myfelf! O that the birds of prey were able to bear me hence! I shall no longer shoot them with my arrows. O precious bow, confecrated by the hands of the fon of Jupiter! Dear Hercules! if thou ftill retaineft the leaft compaffion, art thou not filled with indignation? Thy bow is no longer in the hands of thy faithful friend; it is in the impure the fraudful hands of Ulyffes. Ye birds of prey, ye favage brutes, no longer fly this cave, my hands are no longer armed with arrows; I, wretch that I am, can do you no harm; come, devour me; or rather may mercilefs Jupiter's thunder ftrike me dead!

Your father having tried all other means of per-fuading me, at laft thought that it would be beft to return me my arms. He accordingly made a fign to Neoptolemus, who immediately reftored them. Hereupon I faid, O worthy fon of Achilles, you prove yourfelf to be fo; but fuffer me to difpatch my enemy. I was going to shoot an arrow at your father; but Neoptolemus with-held me, faying, re-fentment difturbs your reafon, and hinders you from feeing the bafenefs of the action you are going to commit.

As for Ulyffes, he feemed as unconcerned at my arrows as at my reproaches. I was ftruck with his in-trepidity and patience, and ashamed of having endea-voured in the firft tranfports of my rage to make ufe of my arms to kill him who had caufed them to be reftored to me; but as my refentment was not yet appeafed, I could not bear to be obliged for them to one I fo greatly hated. Neoptolemus in the mean while faid, Know that the divine Helenus, the fon of Priam, coming out of the city of Troy by the com-

mand

mand and infpiration of the Gods, unveiled futurity
to us. Ill fated Troy shall fall, faid he; but it cannot fall till it is attacked by him who has Hercules's
arrows; neither can that man be cured 'till he comes
before the walls of Troy, where the fons of Æfculapius will cure him.

I now felt a conflict in my bofom; being affected
with Neoptolemus's franknefs and juftice in reftoring
me my bow, but unable to prevail with myfelf to
live if I muft fubmit to go with Ulyfles : a faulty
shame held me in fufpenfe. Shall I be feen, faid I
to myfelf, in the company of Ulyfles and the Atridæ?
What would the world think of me!

While I was in this uncertainty, I all of a fudden
hear a voice more than human, and fee Hercules
in a bright cloud encircled with rays of glory. I
eafily recollected his manly features, his robuft body,
and plain manner; but he had a loftinefs and majefty
which were never fo confpicuous in him while he was
fubduing of monfters. He befpoke me thus:

You hear, you fee Hercules. I have left lofty
Olympus to tell you the commands of Jupiter. You
know by what labours I obtained immortality. You
muft go with the fon of Achilles to tread in my fteps
in the paths of glory. You shall be cured, and shall
kill Paris, the author of fo many woes, with my arrows. After the taking of Troy, fend rich fpoils to
your father Pæan on mount Œta, and let them be
placed on my grave as a monument of the victory
owing to my arrows. And you, fon of Achilles, I
tell you that you cannot be victorious without Philoctetes, nor Philoctetes without you. Go therefore
like two lions in queft of prey together. I will fend
Æfculapius to Troy to cure Philoctetes. Above all,
ye Greeks, love and practife religion; every thing
elfe dies, but that lives for ever.

Having heard thefe words, I cried out, O happy
day! O pleafing light! that after fo many years doft
manifeft thyfelf at laft? I obey thee, I'll depart
the moment I have bid thefe fcenes adieu. Farewell.

well, dear cave! Thou nymph of thefe humid meads, farewell; I no more fhall hear thefe murmuring billows. Farewell, thou fhore, where the bleak winds fo oft have pierced me. Farewell, ye promontories, where echo fo often repeated my groans. Farewell, ye fweet fprings, that were fo bitter to me. Farewell, thou Lemnian land; let my departure be happy, fince I am going whither the will of the Gods and my friends call me.

We then departed, and arrived at the fiege of Troy. Machaon and Podalirius by the divine fcience of their father Æfculapius cured me, or at leaft put me in the condition wherein you now fee me. I have no pain; I have recovered all my ftrength, but am a little lame. I killed Paris, as the huntfman fhoots a timorous fawn with his arrows. Ilion was foon reduced to afhes; you know the reft. The remembrance however of my fufferings made me retain fome averfion to Ulyffes, and his virtue could not appeafe my refentment; but the fight of a fon that refembles him, and whom I cannot forbear loving, begets a tendernefs in my heart for the father himfelf.

End of the Fifteenth Book.

THE

THE
ADVENTURES
OF
TELEMACHUS,
SON of ULYSSES.

BOOK the SIXTEENTH.

The ARGUMENT.

*Telemachus quarrels with Phalantus about some pri-
soners whom they both claim; he fights with and
overcomes Hippias, who despising his youth, had
forcibly carried away those prisoners for his brother
Phalantus. But Telemachus, little satisfied with his
victory, privately laments his rashness and error,
which he would be glad to repair. At the same time
Adrastus, king of the Daunians, being informed that
the confederate kings were solely intent on making
up the breach between Telemachus and Hippias, goes
and attacks them unawares. Having surprised an
hundred of their ships to transport his troops to their
camp, he immediately sets it on fire, begins the attack
on Phalantus's quarters, kills his brother Hippias,
and very much wounds Phalantus himself.*

WHILE Philoctetes was thus relating his adventures, Telemachus remained as it were
suspended and motionless, and fixed his eyes on the
great man that was speaking. All the different passions
which had agitated Hercules, Philoctetes, Ulysses
and N:optolemus, were seen as they were represented
in their turns on the artless countenance of Tele-

machus.

machus. During the courfe of this narration he fometimes cried out and interrupted Philoctetes, without
thinking on what he did ; fometimes he appeared
thoughtful, like one who is maturely weighing the
confequences of things : And when Philoctetes was
defcribing the confufion of Neoptolemus who knew
not to diffemble, Telemachus feemed to be in the
fame confufion ; one would at that inftant have taken
him for Neoptolemus himfelf.

Mean while the confederate army was marching
in good order againft Adraftus king of the Daunians, who defpifed the Gods, and fought only to deceive men. Telemachus found it very difficult to
behave with prudence among fo many princes who
were jealous of each other. He was to render himfelf odious to none, and to make himfelf beloved of
all. Now though he was naturally frank and good-
natured, yet he was not over-complaifant ; he feldom confidered what might oblige others ; he was
not fond of money, but then he knew not the art of
giving. Thus with a noble and well-difpofed heart,
he feemed neither obliging, nor friendly, nor liberal,
nor grateful for the care which was taken of him,
nor attentive to diftinguifh merit. He followed his
own inclination without reflection. His mother Penelope had bred him up, in fpite of Mentor, in an
haughtinefs and pride, which fullied all his amiable
qualities. He looked upon himfelf to be of a
different nature from the reft of mankind ; others
feemed to him to be fent into the world by the Gods
only to pleafe him, to ferve him, to prevent all his
wishes, and to make him their fole arbiter in all
things, as though he were a God. The happinefs of
ferving him was in this opinion a fufficient recompenfe
for thofe who did it. Nothing muft ever be impoffible
in which his fatisfaction was concerned, and the leaft
delays moved his hafty temper.

Had any one feen him thus in his natural difpofition, he would have thought him incapable of loving
any thing but himfelf, and that he was affected with
nothing

nothing but his own glory and pleasure. This indifference however as to others, and perpetual regard for himself proceeded only from the ferment he was continually thrown into by the violence of his passions. He had been fondled and humoured by his mother from his cradle, and was a signal instance of the misfortunes of a high birth. The calamities he suffered even from his greenest years had not been capable to qualify this haughtiness and vehemence of his temper. Though he had been destitute of all things, forsaken and exposed to numerous evils, yet he had lost nothing of his pride : That continually rose up again, as the pliant palm incessantly rises of itself, whatever efforts are made to depress it.

While Telemachus was with Mentor, these failings did not appear, and were daily decreasing. Like a fiery courser that bounds over the spacious meadows, that stops neither at steepy rocks, nor precipices, nor torrents, and that obeys but the voice and hand of a single person who knows to manage him; Telemachus, full of a noble ardor, could not be restrained but by Mentor alone : But then a look of his would instantly stop him in his swiftest career; he immediately comprehended its meaning ; he recalled every sentiment of virtue to his heart, and his reason in a moment rendered his countenance calm and serene : Neptune, when he lifts his trident, and threatens the swelling billows, does not more suddenly still the lowering tempests.

When Telemachus was alone, all his passions that had been restrained like a torrent by a strong dike, took their natural course ; he could not brook the arrogance of the Lacedæmonians and of Phalantus who was at their head. This colony, which had founded Tarentum, was composed of young men who were born during the siege of Troy, and had never had any education. Their illegitimate birth, the dissolute lives of their mothers, and the licentiousness in which they had been bred up, gave them

something

something of wildness and barbarity ; they refembled a band of robbers more than a colony of Greeks.

Phalantus fought all opportunities of contradicting Telemachus. He often interrupted him in council, defpifing his advice as that of an unexperienced youth ; he bantered and treated him as an effeminate ftripling ; he made all the chiefs of the army take notice of his flighteft failings ; he endeavoured to fow jealoufies every where, and to render Telemachus's high fpirit odious to all the allies.

One day Telemachus having taken fome Daunians prifoners, Phalantus pretended a right to them, alledging that he, at the head of his Lacedæmonians, had defeated that part of the army, and that Telemachus, finding the Daunians already vanquished and put to flight, had no trouble but the giving them quarter, and the conducting them to the camp. Telemachus on the contrary maintained, that he had hindered Phalantus from being defeated, and had gained the victory over the Daunians. They both pleaded their caufe in an affembly of the confederate princes ; where Telemachus being fo far tranfported as to threaten Phalantus, they would inftantly have fought, had they not been with-held.

Phalantus had a brother, whofe name was Hippias, famous through the whole army for his valour, ftrength and dexterity. Pollux, faid the Tarentines, did not wield the ceftus better, nor could Caftor have excelled him in the management of an horfe: He was almoft equal to Hercules in ftature and ftrength. The whole army was afraid of him ; for he was ftill more quarrelfome and brutal than ftrong and valiant.

Hippias feeing with what haughtinefs Telemachus menaced his brother, goes immediately to feize the prifoners, in order to convey them to Tarentum, without waiting for the decifion of the affembly. Telemachus being privately told of this, went out trembling with rage. Like a foaming boar in purfuit of the hunter that wounded him, did Telemachus rove up and down the camp, looking with eager eyes

eyes for his enemy, and brandishing the dart with which he defigned to kill him. At length he meets him, and his rage redoubles at the fight.

He was no longer the wife Telemachus, inftructed by Minerva in the form of Mentor; he was a madman, or a furious lion. He immediately cries out to Hippias, Stay, thou bafeft of men, ftay; we will foon fee if thou art able to rob me of the fpoils of thofe I have vanquished: Thou shalt not lead them to Tarentum; go, inftantly defcend to the gloomy banks of Styx. He faid, and threw his javelin; but throwing it with fo much fury that he could take no aim, it miffed Hippias. Hereupon Telemachus draws the golden-hilted fword, which Laertes had given him at his departure from Ithaca as a pledge of his love. Laertes himfelf had ufed it with great glory in his youth, and dyed it in the blood of feveral famous leaders of the Epirots, in a war wherein he was victorious. Telemachus had hardly drawn his fword, when Hippias, refolving to make an advantage of his ftrength, rushed upon him in order to wreft it out of his hands. The fword is broken between them; they feize and clofe with each other. Lo! they now refemble two fierce brutes, that ftrive to tear one another in pieces; fire fparkles in their eyes, they shrink up, they ftretch out, they ftoop down, they rife again, they fpring forwards, they thirft for blood. Lo! They are engaged hand to hand and foot to foot, twifting their two bodies together, fo that they feemed to be but one. But Hippias being of a maturer age, feemed as if he would overpower Telemachus, whofe tender youth was not fo nervous. And now Telemachus being out of breath, feels his knees tremble: and Hippias feeing him ftagger, redoubles his efforts. The fon of Ulyffes had been flain, and fuffered the punishment due to his temerity and paffion, had not Minerva, who was watchful of him at a diftance, and had let him fall into this extremity of danger only for his inftruction, determined the victory in his favour.

' The Goddefs herfelf did not quit the palace of Salentum, but fent Iris the fwift meffenger of the Gods. Iris flying with nimble wings cleaves the immenfe fpaces of the air, leaving behind her a long track of light which looked like a cloud of a thoufand different colours : she did not reft herfelf till she came to the fea-shore, where the numberlefs army of the allies was encamped. She fees at a diftance the ftrife, the ardor and efforts of the two combatants; she trembles at the fight of the danger the young Telemachus is in; she approaches involved in a bright cloud which she formed of fubtle vapours, the inftant Hippias, confcious of his ftrength, thought himfelf victorious; she covered Minerva's youthful pupil with the Ægis which the wife Goddefs had entrufted to her. Telemachus, whofe ftrength was exhaufted, immediately begins to feel fresh vigour. As he revives, Hippias is difpirited, and finds himfelf terrified and oppreffed by fomething divine. Telemachus preffes hard upon him, attacking him fometimes in one pofture and fometimes in another; he makes him reel; he gives him no time to recover himfelf; at laft he throws him on the ground and falls upon him. A huge Idæan oak, felled by a thoufand ftrokes of the hatchet with which the whole foreft refounded, does not make a more terrible noife in its fall; the earth groans; all things around it are shaken.

. Mean while Telemachus recovered his reafon as well as his ftrength. Hippias was fcarcely fallen beneath him, when the fon of Ulyffes was fenfible of the fault he had been guilty of in thus affaulting the brother of one of the confederate kings whom he came to affift. He called to mind with confufion the wife counfels of Mentor; he was ashamed of his victory, and perceived that he deferved to have been overcome. Mean time Phalantus tranfported with fury, ran to his brother's affiftance; and would have transfixed Telemachus with his javelin, had he not been afraid of transfixing Hippias alfo, whom Telemachus

machus held under him on the ground. The son of Ulysses could easily have taken his antagonist's life; but his anger was appeased, and he thought only of repairing his fault by shewing his moderation. He rises, saying, O Hippias! I am satisfied with having taught you not to despise my youth. Take your life; I admire your strength and courage; the Gods have preserved me; yield to their power, and let us for the future only fight together against the Daunians. While Telemachus was speaking, Hippias got up, besmeared with dust and blood, and full of shame and rage. Phalantus not daring to take the life of him who had so generously given it to his brother, was doubtful and disordered. All the confederate kings ran to them, and led Telemachus one way, and Phalantus and Hippias another. Hippias had lost his fierce and haughty air, and was ashamed to lift up his eyes. The whole army was greatly astonished that Telemachus had been able at so tender an age, when men are not arrived at their full strength, to vanquish Hippias, who in might and bulk resembled the giants, those sons of earth, that formerly attempted to drive the Immortals from Olympus.

But the son of Ulysses was far from receiving any pleasure from this victory. While the army thought they could not sufficiently admire him, he retired to his tent ashamed of his fault, unable to support himself, and bewailing his hastiness of temper. He was sensible how unjust and unreasonable he was in his transports; he found great vanity, weakness and meanness in his unbounded haughtiness, and perceived that true greatness is inseparable from moderation, justice, modesty and humanity: He perceived this; but not presuming to hope that he should amend after so many relapses, he was at war with himself, and was heard to roar like a lion in his fury.

He remained two days shut up all alone in his tent, punishing and unable to prevail on himself to go into company. Alas! said he, shall I dare to see

Mentor

Mentor again? Am I the fon of Ulyffes, the wifeft and moft patient of men? Did I come to bring diffention and diforder into the army of the allies? Is it their blood, or that of Daunians their enemies, which I ought to shed? I have acted rashly; I knew not even to throw my javelin; I expofed myfelf in combat againft Hippias with ftrength unequal, and should have expected nothing but death and the shame of being vanquished. And what of that? I should have been no more: no, the rash Telemachus, the fenfelefs youth who does not profit by any advice, would have been no more: my shame would have ended with my life. Could I alas! fo much as hope never to do again what I am now fo grieved for having done, I should be happy, abundantly happy; but perhaps before the clofe of this very day I shall commit, nay wilfully commit, the very faults of which I am at prefent fo much ashamed and have fo great an abhorrence. O fatal victory! O praifes which I cannot bear! praifes which are bitter reproaches of my folly!

While he was thus folitary and difconfolate, Neftor, and Philoctetes came to fee him. Neftor defigned to convince him how much he had been in the wrong; but the wife fenior prefently perceiving the youth's affliction, changed his grave remonftrances into expreffions of kindnefs, in order to allay his grief.

This quarrel retarded the progrefs of the confederate princes, who could not march towards the enemy 'till they had reconciled Telemachus with Phalantus and Hippias; being hourly apprehenfive left the Tarentine troops should fall upon the hundred young Cretans that came with Telemachus to this war. All was in confufion through the fault of Telemachus only; and he perceiving the many prefent evils and future dangers of which he was the author, abandoned himfelf to the bitterest grief. All the princes were in a great perplexity: They durft not order the army to march, left Telemachus's Cretans and Phalantus's Tarentines should fight with each
other

other as they went along ; they had great difficulty to keep them from it even in the camp, where they were narrowly watched. Neftor and Philoctetes were inceffantly going backwards and forwards from Telemachus's tent to that of the implacable Phalantus, who breathed nothing but revenge. Neither Neftor's fweet eloquence nor the great Philoctetes's authority could pacify his favage heart, which was moreover continually irritated by the inflaming difcourfe of his brother Hippias. Telemachus was much calmer, but dejected by a forrow which nothing could alleviate.

While the princes were in this commotion, all the troops were under great confternation : The whole camp looked like a houfe of mourning that had juft loft the father of the family, the fupport of all his relations, and the fweet hope of his little children.

During this diforder and confternation of the army; there was fuddenly heard a frightful noife of chariots and arms, of neighing fteeds and outcries of men, fome victorious and fpurred on to carnage, others running away, dying, or wounded. A black cloud of whirling duft overfpreads the heavens and covers the whole camp. The duft is prefently followed by a thick fmoke which condenfes the air, and hinders refpiration. There was likewife heard an hollow noife like that of the curling flames which mount Ætna belches from the bottom of its burning bowels, when Vulcan with his Cyclops is forging thunderbolts there for the father of the Gods. Terror feized on every heart.

The vigilant and indefatigable Adraftus had furprifed the allies ; having concealed his route from them, and procured intelligence of theirs. He had marched with incredible expedition round an almoft inacceffible mountain, whofe paffes had almoft all been feized by the allies. Now the allies being in poffeffion of thefe paffes thought themfelves perfectly fafe, and even fancied that they should be able by their means to fall upon the enemy on the other fide of the mountain, when fome troops which they expected,

N. 6.

pected, were arrived. Adraſtus, who was very lavish
of his money in order to get intelligence of his enemies, had been informed of their reſolution ; for
Neſtor and Philoctetes, though otherwiſe very wiſe
and experienced commanders, were not ſufficiently
ſecret in their enterpriſes. Neſtor, now in the decline
of life, was too fond of relating things which tended to
his own praiſe. Philoctetes was naturally leſs talka-
tive, but then he was ſo paſſionate, that if one moved
his haſty temper ever ſo little, one might make him
diſcover things which he had reſolved to conceal.
Artful men had found the key to his heart, and drew
from it the moſt important ſecrets. They needed only to provoke him ; being then tranſported and beſide
himſelf, he would burſt out into menaces, and vaunt
of having infallible means to accompliſh his deſigns :
And if they ſeemed ever ſo little doubtful of his
means, he would immediately be ſo inconſiderate as
to explain them, and let the cloſeſt ſecrets ſlip from
his boſom. Like a fine but cracked veſſel through
which leak all the moſt delicious liquors, the heart of
this great commander could retain nothing.

Traitors, corrupted by Adraſtus's money, did not
fail to make their advantage of the foibles of theſe
two princes. They were continually flattering Neſtor
with empty praiſes ; they reminded him of his paſt
exploits, admired his foreſight, and were never weary
of applauding him. On the other ſide, they were perpetually laying ſnares for the fiery temper of Philoctetes, and talked to him of nothing but difficulties,
accidents, dangers, inconveniencies, irretrievable over-
ſights ; for as ſoon as his warm diſpoſition took fire,
his wiſdom forſook him, and he was no longer the
ſame man.

Telemachus, notwithſtanding the failings we have
taken notice of, was much more prudent as to the
keeping of a ſecret. He had been habituated to it by
his misfortunes, and the neceſſity he had been under
from his infancy of concealing his thoughts from Penelope's ſuitors. He knew to keep a ſecret without
                                              telling

telling an untruth. And then he had not that reserved
and mysterious air, which is usual to close men ;
he never seemed burdened with the secret he was to
keep, but was always free, easy, open, like a person that bears his heart on his lips. But though he
said every thing that could be said without any ill
consequences, yet he knew to stop precisely, and
without affectation, at the things which might create
suspicions, or furnish a hint to discover his secret.
Hereby his heart was impenetrable and inaccessible ;
even his best friends knew nothing but what he
judged proper to lay before them for their advice,
and there was but Mentor alone for whom he had no
reserve. He did indeed confide in others, but in different degrees, and in proportion to the proofs they
had given him of their friendship and discretion.

Telemachus had often observed that the resolutions of the council were a little too much known in
the camp, and had advised Nestor and Philoctetes of
it ; but they, though men of great experience, did not
sufficiently attend to so useful an hint. Old age is not
at all pliable ; inveterate habits bind it as it were in
chains, and its failings become incurable. Like trees
whose rough and knotty trunks are hardened by
length of time and cannot be straightened, men hardly
have it in their power at a certain age to bend themselves contrary to customs which have grown old
with them, and are entered into the very marrow of
their bones. They often indeed are conscious of
them when it is too late ; they bewail them in vain,
for tender youth is the only age wherein it is in a
man's power to correct his errors.

There was in the army a certain Dolopian, whose
name was Eurimachus, who was fawning, insinuating, had the art of adapting himself to all the tastes
and inclinations of the princes, and was ingenious
and industrious in finding out new ways of pleasing
them. When one heard him, one would think there
was no difficulty in any thing, and when his advice
was asked, he was sure to hit upon that which was
most

most agreeable. He was an entertaining fellow : he
bantered the weak, he cringed to those of whom he
stood in awe, and so skilfully seasoned his flattery,
that it was grateful to the most modest ear; he was
grave with the grave, and merry with those who were
merrily-inclined ; for it was no pain to him to assume
any form whatever. Sincere and virtuous men, who
are always the same, and who subject themselves to
the rules of virtue, can never be so agreeable to
princes as those who flatter their prevailing passions.
Eurimachus understood war ; he was capable of business, and had, in order to make his fortune, attached himself to Nestor, whose confidence he had won,
and from whose heart, which was a little vain and
sensible to flattery, he drew every thing which he
desired to know.

Though Philoctetes did not make him his confident, yet the fire and impatience of his temper had
the same effects as Nestor's confidence. For Eurimachus needed only to contradict and provoke him,
and he discovered all. This fellow had received
large sums of Adrastus, to send him intelligence of
all the designs of the allies. The Daunian king had
several deserters in their army, who were to make
their escape one after another from the confederate
camp, and to return to his. When there was any
thing of importance to be communicated to Adrastus,
Eurymachus used to dispatch one of these deserters:
The treachery could not easily be discovered ; because as they never carried any letters, nothing was
found upon them, if they were taken, that could render Eurimachus suspected.

Adrastus therefore constantly prevented all the enterprises of the allies : a resolution was hardly taken
in the council, but the Daunians did precisely what
was necessary to hinder its success. Telemachus
was indefatigable in his endeavours to find out the
cause of this, and to excite the suspicions of Nestor
and Philoctetes ; but his cares were vain, for their
eyes were not to be opened.

Ir

It had been resolved in council to wait for a large number of troops which were to arrive, and an hundred ships had been sent privately by night to transport them the more expeditiously from a very rugged sea-coast to which they were to come, to where the army was encamped. Mean time the confederates thought themselves secure, because their troops were in possession of the straits of the neighbouring mountain, which was an almost inaccessible side of the Appennines. The army was encamped on the banks of the river Galesus, near the sea. This delightful country abounds in pasturage, and in all things necessary to the subsistence of an army. Adrastus was on the other side of the mountain, which the allies believed it was impossible for him to pass. But as he knew they were yet but weak, that a great re-inforcement was coming, that ships were waiting for the troops which were to arrive, and that the army was divided by Telemachus's quarrel with Phalantus, he immediately made a large circuit, marching night and day along the sea-shore, and going through ways which had always been deemed absolutely impassable. Thus do resolution and labour surmount the greatest obstacles ; thus is there hardly any thing impossible to the daring and the patient of fatigues : and thus do those who sleep and magnify difficulties into impossibilities, deserve to be surprised and opprest.

Adrastus early in the morning surprised the hundred ships which belonged to the allies. As these ships were ill guarded and apprehensive of nothing, he took them without resistance, and made use of them to transport his troops with incredible dispatch to the mouth of the Galesus ; he then sailed very expeditiously up the river. The advanced guards of the confederate camp that were stationed towards the river, imagined that these barks had brought them the troops which were expected, and immediately shouted aloud for joy. Adrastus and his soldiers landed before they could be known, and fall upon the

the allies, who apprehend nothing, as they are scattered up and down in an open camp, unarmed, and without a commander.

The part of the camp which Adrastus first attacked, was that of the Tarentines, where Phalantus commanded. The Daunians entered it with such vigour, that the Lacedæmonians youth being in a surprise, could not resist them. While they are looking for their arms, and hinder each other in their confusion, Adrastus orders the camp to be fired. The flames instantly ascend from the tents, and reach the very clouds; roaring like a deluge that pours over a whole country, and up-roots, and bears away by its rapidity the largest oaks, the corn, barns, stables, flocks and herds. The wind impetuously drives the fire from tent to tent, and the whole camp instantly resembles an old dry forest, which a single spark has kindled into a blaze.

Phalantus, though he has the nearest view of the danger, can apply no remedy to it. He perceives that his troops will all perish in the flames, if they do not immediately abandon the camp; but he perceives also how much the confusion of such a retreat is to be dreaded before a victorious enemy. He begins however to draw off his half-armed Lacedæmonian youth, but Adrastus allows them no time to breathe. On one side a band of skilful archers gall Phalantus's soldiers with innumerable arrows, and slingers on the other pour a flinty shower. Adrastus himself, marching sword in hand at the head of a chosen band of the most intrepid Daunians, pursues the fugitives by the light of the flames; he mows down all who escape them with his keen steel; he swims in blood; he cannot slake his thirst of slaughter: lions and tigers equal not his fury when they rend the shepherds and their flocks. Phalantus's troops sink before him: their courage forsakes them; pale death, led on by an infernal fury whose head bristles with snakes, freezes the blood in their veins;

their

their benumbed limbs ſtiffen, and their ſhivering knees rob them even of the hopes of flight.

Phalantus, whom ſhame and deſpair ſtill ſupply with ſome remains of ſtrength and vigour, lifting up his hands and eyes to heaven, ſees his brother Hippias fall at his feet, beneath the blows of Adraſtus's thundering hand. Hippias is ſtretched on the earth, and rolls in the duſt; black bubbling gore ſpouts like a torrent from the deep wounds in his ſide; his eyes exclude the light, and his furious ſoul iſſues out with his blood. Phalantus himſelf, all beſmeared with his brother's gore, and unable to aſſiſt him, finds himſelf beſet with a crowd of enemies who ſtrive to fell him to the earth. His ſhield is pierced with a thouſand darts; he is wounded in ſeveral parts of his body, and cannot rally his flying troops: The Gods ſee, but do not vouchſafe him their pity.

End of the Sixteenth Book.

THE
ADVENTURES
OF
TELEMACHUS,
SON of ULYSSES.

BOOK the SEVENTEENTH.

The ARGUMENT.

Telemachus, clad in his divine armour, runs to Phalantus's assistance, kills Iphicles the son of Adrastus, repulses the victorious enemy, and would have obtained a compleat victory over them, if a sudden storm had not put an end to the battle. He afterwards orders the wounded to be carried off, and takes care of them himself, particularly of Phalantus. He celebrates the funeral rites of his brother Hippias, and presents him with his ashes which he had collected together in a golden urn.

JUPITER in the midst of all the celestial Deities beheld the slaughter of the allies from the top of Olympus ; and at the same time consulting the immutable Destinies, saw all the chiefs whose thread of life was that day to be cut by the fatal scissars. All the Immortals looking earnestly upon him to read his pleasure in his countenance, the father of Gods and men, with a sweet but majestic voice, said : You see to what an extremity the confederates are reduced, you see Adrastus overthrowing his enemies ; but this is a deceitful spectacle. The glory and prosperity of the wicked is short ;

the

the impious Adraftus, deteftable for his perfidy, shall not obtain a compleat victory. This calamity befalls the allies only to teach them to correct their errors, and to keep their enterprifes more fecret. The wife Minerva is now preparing fresh glory for her darling, the young Telemachus. He faid; and all the Gods continued to view the combat in filence.

Mean time Neftor and Philoctetes are informed that part of the camp is already burnt; that the flames, driven by the winds, were continually fpreading; that the troops were in diforder, and that Phalantus could no longer fuftain the efforts of the enemy. Thefe dreadful words no fooner ftrike their ears but they run to arms, affemble the officers, and order them to haften out of the camp to efcape the flames.

Telemachus, who was dejected and inconfolable, now forgets his grief, and takes his arms, the ineftimable prefent of the wife Minerva, who appearing in the shape of Mentor, pretended that she had received them of an excellent artift of Salentum, though she had in reality prevailed on Vulcan to make them in the fmoaky caverns of mount Ætna.

Thefe arms were fmooth as glafs, and glittered like the rays of the fun. On the shield were feen Neptune and Pallas contending which of them should have the honour of giving their name to an infant city. Neptune ftruck the earth with his trident, and one beheld a furious fteed fpringing from it. Fire darted from his eyes, and foam iffued from his mouth. His mane waved with the wind; his pliant and nervous legs moved with vigour and fwiftnefs. He did not walk; he bounded by the mere ftrength of his loins, but with fuch rapidity that he left no footfteps behind him: And one thought one heard him neigh.

In another part was Minerva prefenting olives, the fruit of the tree of her own planting, to the inhabitants of her new city. The bough on which the fruit hung, was an emblem of gentle peace and plenty,
                                                preferable

preferable to the troubles of war, of which the horse was a symbol. The Goddess obtained the victory by her plain and useful gifts, and stately Athens bore her name.

Minerva was also seen assembling around her all the polite arts, which were represented by little children with wings. Terrified at the brutal fury of all-destroying Mars, they fled to her for shelter, as bleating lambkins fly for refuge to their dams at the sight of a ravenous wolf, that darts with extended flaming jaws to devour them. Minerva, with a disdainful and angry countenance was also confounding by the excellence of her works, the foolish temerity of Arachne, who presumed to vie with her as to the perfection of her tapestry. One saw the wretch's lessening limbs losing their form, and changing into those of a spider.

Near this part Minerva appeared again, giving advice to Jupiter himself in the war of the giants, and sustaining all the other affrighted Deities. She was also represented with her lance and Ægis on the banks of Xanthus and Simois, leading Ulysses by the hand, reviving the courage of the flying Greeks, and withstanding the efforts of the most valiant Trojan commanders and of the formidable Hector himself; and lastly, introducing Ulysses into the fatal machine which was in a single night to subvert the empire of Priam.

Another part of the shield represented Ceres in the fruitful fields of Enna, in the midst of Sicily. The Goddess was assembling the inhabitants together, who were scattered up and down, and lived by hunting, or picking up the wild fruits that dropped from the trees. She taught these rude mortals the art of manuring the earth, and of extracting their food out of her fertile bosom; she presented them with a plough, and taught them to yoke the oxen to it. One might see the earth parting into furrows by means of the sharp-edged share; and then one beheld the golden harvests which hid the fruitful fields.

The

The reaper with his fickle was cutting down the kindly fruits of the earth, and paying himfelf for all his toils. Iron, elfewhere an inftrument to deftroy, was here ufed but to procure a plenty, and to give birth to every kind of pleafure.

The nymphs, with wreaths of flowers on their heads, were dancing together, near a grove in a meadow, on the banks of a river. Pan was playing on his pipe, and the Fauns and wanton Satyrs were frisking together in a corner. Bacchus, crowned with ivy, was likewife there, leaning one hand on his Thyrfus, and holding in the other a vine adorned with leafy branches and cluftering grapes. His beauty was effeminate, but blended with I know not what of noble, of amorous and languishing. He looked as when he appeared to the unhappy Ariadne, when he found her folitary, forfaken, overwhelmed with forrow on an unknown shore.

To conclude, in all parts were feen multitudes of people; old men bearing their firft fruit to the temples; young men tired with the toils of the day, returning home to their wives; their wives going to meet them, fondling their little children, and leading them by the hand. There were alfo shepherds that feemed to fing, and others to dance to the found of their reeds. Every thing was an image of peace, plenty, and pleafure; every thing feemed fmiling and happy: Nay, the very wolves were fporting among the sheep in their paftures, and the lion and the tyger having quitted their fiercenefs, were feeding with tender lambkins: A child was their shepherd, and he governed them all with his crook. This delightful picture put one in mind of all the charms of the golden age.

Telemachus being clad in this celeftial armour, inftead of taking his own shield, takes the terrible Ægis, which Minerva had fent him by Iris, the fwift meffenger of the Gods. Iris had taken away his own shield without his perceiving it, and had
given

given him the Ægis, dreadful even to the Gods themfelves, inftead of it.

Thus armed he runs out of the camp to avoid the flames, and calls all the chiefs of the army to him with a ftrong voice, which inftantly revives all the terrified allies. Celeftial fire fparkles in the eyes of the youthful warrior. He all the while feems as calm, as free and compofed, as diligent in iffuing out his orders, as a wife fenior could who is intent on the regulation of his family, and the inftruction of his children; but then he is as rapid and violent in the execution, as an impetuous river, which not only rolls its foamy waves with rapidity, but alfo bears away with its torrent the heavieft veffels with which it is loaded.

Philoctetes, Neftor, and the chiefs of the Man-durians and of the other nations perceived that the fon of Ulyffes had I know not what of authority, to which they were forced to fubmit. The experience of the feniors fails them; counfel and wifdom forfake all the commanders; nay, jealoufy itfelf, fo natural to man, is extinguished in every heart; all are filent, all admire Telemachus, all wait for his commands without reflecting on what they do, and as if they had been ufed to do it. He advances and afcends an eminence; and from thence obferving the pofture of the enemy, he inftantly judges that it is neceffary to ufe the utmoft difpatch to furprife them in the diforder into which they had put themfelves by burning the confederate camp. He fetches a compafs with great expedition, followed by all the moft experienced commanders, and falls upon the Daunians in the rear, at a time when they thought that the army of the allies was involved in the flames. The Daunians are difordered by this fudden attack, and fall beneath Telemachus's hands, as leaves in the clofe of autumn in the forefts, when the boifterous north-wind, bringing back the winter, makes the trunks of the old trees groan, and violently shakes all the branches. The earth is
strewed

ſtrewed with men ſlain by Telemachus. With his
javelin he pierces the heart of Iphicles, the youngeſt
of Adraſtus's children, who preſumed to, engage
him, in order to ſave his father's life, who was in
danger of being killed by Telemachus. The ſon of
Ulyſſes and Iphicles were both handſome, vigorous,
expert and brave, of the ſame ſtature, of the ſame
ſweet diſpoſition, of the ſame age, and both alike
dear to their parents ; but Iphicles reſembled a
flower in the fields, which blooms and is cut down
by the ſcythe of the mower. Telemachus then kills
Euphorion, the moſt renowned of all the Lydians
that came into Hetruria. His ſword afterwards ſlays
Cleomenes, who was lately married, and had pro-
miſed his bride to bring her the rich ſpoils of the
enemy ; but he was never to ſee her again.

Adraſtus quivers with rage when he ſees that his
ſon and ſeveral of his commanders are dead, and
that victory is ſlipping out of his hands. Phalantus,
juſt ready to ſink at his feet, looks like a half-ſlain
victim, that ſtarts from the ſacred knife, and flies
away from the altar. A moment more had been
ſufficient for Adraſtus to have compleated the Lacedæmonian's deſtruction.

Phalantus drowned in his own blood and in that
of thoſe who fought around him, hears the ſhouts of
Telemachus coming to his relief. The ſame inſtant
life returns, and the cloud which had already overſpread his eyes, diſperſes. The Daunians perceiving this unexpected attack, leave Phalantus to re-
pulſe a more dangerous enemy. Adraſtus reſembles
a tiger, from whom a company of ſhepherds ſnatch
the prey he was going to devour. Telemachus
ſeeks him in the throng, being deſirous to end the
war at once by delivering the allies from their implacable enemy ; but Jupiter would not grant the
ſon of Ulyſſes ſo quick and eaſy a victory. Nay,
Minerva herſelf was willing that he ſhould ſuffer
more hardſhips, that he might be the better qualified
to govern.

The

The impious Adraftus was preferved therefore by the father of the Gods, that Telemachus might have time to acquire more glory and virtue. A thick cloud which Jupiter formed in the air, faved the Daunians; dreadful thunders fpoke the will of the Gods. One would have thought that the eternal vaults of high Olympus were going to break down on the heads of feeble mortals; lightnings cleft the clouds from pole to pole, and the eye was fcarcely dazzled by their piercing fires, but all was wrapt again in the moft hideous midnight darknefs. A fluicy shower which fell at the fame time, contributed likewife to part the two armies.

Adraftus made his advantage of the fuccour of the Gods without being duly fenfible of their power, and by this ingratitude merited to be referved for a feverer vengeance. He immediately marched his army between the half-burnt camp, and a morafs which reached quite to the river; and this he did with fuch dexterity and difpatch, that his retreat was a proof of his readinefs at expedients and of his prefence of mind. The allies fpurred on by Telemachus, were eager to purfue him; but by the favour of the ftorm he efcaped from them, as a fwift-winged bird efcapes from the nets of the fowler.

The allies now return to their camp, and think only of repairing their lofs. As they entered it, they beheld the moft lamentable effects of war; the fick and the wounded, wanting ftrength to crawl out of their tents, had not been able to fave themfelves from the flames: They feemed half-burnt, and with a doleful dying voice fent up bitter cries to heaven, which pierced the very foul of Telemachus. He could not retain his tears; he often turned away his eyes through horror and compaffion, nor could without shuddering behold their bodies, though ftill alive, devored to a lingering and painful death, and looking like the flefh of victims that has been burnt on the altars, and diffufes a fmell all around.

Alas!

Alas! cried Telemachus, lo! the evils which
war draws after it! How blind a fury poffeffes
wretched mortals! They have but a few days to
live on the earth, and thofe are days of forrow;
why then will they quicken the pace of death which
is already fo near? Why will they add fo many
shockings evils to the bitternefs with which the Gods
have crouded their fpan of life? Men are all brothers, and yet they tear each other in pieces. Savage brutes are lefs cruel than they: Lions make
not war upon Lions, nor tygers upon tygers; they
attack but animals of a different fpecies. Man only,
notwithftanding his reafon, does what creatures
void of reafon never did. And then, why thefe
wars? Are there not lands enough in the world to
fupply all men with more than they can cultivate?
What a wafte of defolate tracts which mankind can
never ftock with inhabitants! What then! does
ambition, a prince's aiming at the vain title of a
conqueror, kindle wars in countries fufficiently
large? Yes, a fingle perfon, fent into the world by
the Gods in their wrath, brutally facrifices millions
to his vanity. Every thing muft be deftroyed;
every thing muft fwim in blood; every thing muft
be involved in flames, that what efcapes the fword
and fire, may perish by famine ftill more cruel than
they; and all this, that a fingle man who mocks
at human nature, may gratify his humour and ambition in this general devaftation. What a monftrous kind of vanity! Can one too much deteft
and defpife men who have thus far forgotten humanity? No, no, inftead of being demi-Gods,
they are not fo much as men, and ought to be had
in execration in all the ages by which they hoped
to be admired. Oh! how cautious ought kings to
be with refpect to the wars they undertake! Their
wars ought to be juft; nay more, they ought to be
neceffary for the public weal. The blood of the
people ought not to be shed but to fave the people

them-

themſelves in caſes of extremity. But flattering
counſels, falſe notions of glory, groundleſs jealouſies, unbounded avarice, hid under fair diſguiſes,
in short imperceptible motives, almoſt always hurry
kings into wars which render them miſerable, which
tempt them needleſsly to risk their all, and prove as
fatal to their own ſubjects as their enemies. Thus
reaſoned Telemachus.

But he did not ſatisfy himſelf with deploring the
evils of war; he endeavoured to ſoften them. He
went himſelf into the tents, to relieve the ſick and
the dying ; he gave them money and medicines ;
he comforted and encouraged them by friendly diſcourſes, and ſent others to viſit thoſe he could not
viſit himſelf.

There were among the Cretans that accompanied
him, two old men whoſe names were Traumaphilus
and Nozophugus. Traumaphilus had been at the
ſiege of Troy with Idomeneus, and had learnt the
divine art of healing wounds, of Æſculapius's ſons.
He uſed to pour into the deepeſt and moſt enve-
nomed a certain odorous liquid which eat away the
dead and mortified fleſh ſo that there was no need
of inciſion, and quickly formed new fleſh, which
was ſounder and of a better colour than the former.
As for Nozophugus, he had never ſeen the ſons of
Æſculapius, but had by means of Merion been poſ-
ſeſſed of a ſacred and myſterious book which Æſculapius had given his ſons. Beſides, Nozophugus
was beloved of the Gods ; he had compoſed hymns
in honour of Latona's children, and daily ſacrificed
a white ſheep without blemish to Apollo, by whom
he was often inſpired ; he no ſooner ſaw a ſick perſon but he knew the cauſe of his malady by his
eyes, his complection, the conformation of his body,
and his manner of breathing. Sometimes he ad-
miniſtered ſudorifics, and ſhewed by the ſucceſs of
ſweating, how much the opening or ſhutting of the
pores contributes to the diſorder or reſtoration of
the whole bodily machine. Sometimes in lingering
diſtempers

diftempers he gave certain draughts, which gradually ftrengthened the noble parts, and renewed men's
vigour by fweetning their blood. But he ufed to
declare that it was through a want of virtue and refolution, that men fo often needed phyfic. It is a
fhame to mankind, faid he, that they fhould have
fuch a multitude of maladies; for found morals are
productive of health. Their intemperance converts
into deadly poifons the aliments which are defigned
to preferve their lives. Immoderate pleafures fhor-
ten men's days more than medicines can lenghten
them. The poor are feldomer fick for want of
food, than the rich are by eating too much. Aliments which are too grateful to the palate, and
caufe men to eat more than is needful, poifon inftead of nourifhing. Medicines themfelves are real
evils which ruin the conftitution, and fhould never
be ufed but on urgent occafions. The grand me-
dicine, which is always innocent and always ufeful,
is fobriety, moderation in all forts of pleafures,
tranquillity of mind, and bodily exercife. Thereby
is generated a fweet and well tempered blood, and
redundant humours are diffipated. Thus was the
wife Nozophugus lefs admirable on account of his
cures, than on account of the regimen he prefcrib-
ed to prevent difeafes, and to render medicines ufelefs.

These two men being fent by Telemachus to vifit
all the fick in the army, cured many by their medicines, but more by the care they took to have
them well looked after; for they made it their bufinefs to keep them clean, in order to prevent any
unwholefome air, and to make them obferve a fober
and regular diet during their recovery.

All the foldiers moved by thefe benefits, rendered
thanks to the Gods for having fent Telemachus
into the confederate army. He is not a man, faid
they; he is undoubtedly fome beneficent Deity in
an human fhape: At leaft if he be a man, he re-
femblels the reft of mankind lefs than he does the

Gods; he is come into the world only to do good, and is more amiable for the sweetness of his temper and his humanity than for his valour. Oh! that we could have him for our king! but the Gods reserve him for some happier people whom they love, and among whom they design to renew the golden age.

Telemachus as he went in the night to visit the several quarters of the camp by way of precaution against any stratagems of Adrastus, heard these praises, which could not be suspected of adulation, like those which flatterers often bestow on princes to their faces, supposing that they have neither modesty nor delicacy, and that nothing is necessary to gain their favour but to praise them beyond measure. The son of Ulysses could relish nothing but truth; he could bear no commendations but those which were privately given him in his absence, and he had really deserved. To such his heart was not insensible; he felt that sweet, that pure delight which the Gods have annexed to virtue only, and which ill men, for want of having experienced it, can neither comprehend nor believe; but he did not indulge himself in this pleasure. All the faults he had committed would presently crowd into his mind; he forgot not his natural haughtiness, and indifference for mankind; he was secretly ashamed of being born with so hard a heart, and of appearing so inhuman; he referred to the wise Minerva all the glory which was given him, thinking that he himself did not deserve it.

It was you, great Goddess, said he, who gave me Mentor to instruct me, and to rectify my evil disposition; it is you who give me the wisdom to improve by my faults, and to be diffident of myself; it is you who check my impetuous passions; it is you who make me sensible of the pleasure of relieving the distrest; but for you I should be hated, and deserve to be so; but for you, I should commit irreparable errors, and be like a child, that unconſcious of its weakneſs, quits its mother, and falls the very firſt ſtep it takes.

Neſtor and Philoctetes were ſurpriſed to ſee Telemachus become ſo humane, ſo careful to oblige, ſo officious, ſo ready to relieve the wants of all, and ſo skilful and induſtrious to prevent them; they perceived him to be quite another man, but knew not how to account for it. What ſurpriſed them yet more, was the care he took of Hippias's funeral. He went himſelf to fetch his bloody and disfigured body from the place where it was buried under an heap of dead; he ſhed pious tears over it, and ſaid, O mighty ſhade, thou now knoweſt how much I eſteem thy valour. Thy haughtineſs indeed provoked me, but thy failings proceeded only from the warmth of youth. I well know how much need that age has of pardon. We ſhould hereafter have been ſincere friends. I alſo was in the wrong. Why, ye Gods! have you raviſhed him from me, before it was in my power to force him to love me?

Telemachus afterwards cauſed his body to be waſhed with odorous liquors, and then ordered a funeral pyre to be prepared. Lofty pines groaning beneath the ſtrokes of the axe, roll from the tops of the mountains. Oaks, thoſe aged ſons of earth, that ſeemed to menace heaven, tall poplars, elms with verdant heads and thick leaved branches, and beeches, the honour of the woods, are brought and laid upon the banks of the river Galeſus. There a pile, reſembling a regular building, is erected; the flame begins to appear, and curling clouds of ſmoke aſcend to the skies. The Lacedæmonians advanced with ſlow and mournful ſteps, with downcaſt eyes and pikes inverted; the deepeſt ſadneſs is imprinted on their wild faces, and floods of tears ſtream from their eyes. Next them came the aged Pherecides, leſs bowed down by his numerous years than by the grief of ſurviving Hippias, whom he had brought up from his infancy. He lifted up his hands and his tearful eyes to heaven. Since Hippias's death he had refufed all manner of fuftenance; gentle fleep had not been able to weigh down his eye lids, nor to fufpend his anguish a moment : he walked with tottering fteps behind the crowd, unknowing whither he went. Not a fingle word proceeded from his mouth, for his heart was too much oppreft; he was fpeechlefs through grief and defpair. But when he faw the kindling pyre, he was inftantly tranfported and cried out,

O Hippias, Hippias! I shall never fee thee more! Hippias is no more, and yet I ftill live! O my deareft Hippias! It was I, a cruel and mercilefs wretch! it was I taught thee to defpife death. I hoped thy hands would have clofed my eyes, and that thou wouldeft have catched my lateft breath. Ye cruel Gods! to lenghten out my life that I might fee the death of Hippias! O my dear child! whofe education has coft me fo many cares, I shall fee thee no more; but I shall fee thy mother die of grief, reproaching me with thy death; I shall fee thy youthful wife beat her bofom and tear off her hair, and I shall be the caufe. O beloved shade! fummon me to the ftygian shore; the light is hateful to me; it is thou alone, my dear Hippias, I wish to fee again. Hippias! Hippias! O my deareft Hippias! I live but to pay my laft duty to thy ashes.

Mean time the corps of youthful Hippias appeared, ftretched out at its length, and borne on a bier adorned with purple, gold and filver. Death, which had extinguished his eyes, had not been able to efface all his beauty, for there ftill remained on his pallid vifage a faint picture of the graces. Around his neck, whiter than fnow, but reclined on his shoulder, waved his long black hair, which, more beautiful than that of Atys or Ganymede, was now to be reduced to ashes. In his fide was feen the deep wound which let out all his blood, and fent him down to Pluto's gloomy realm.

Telemachus

Telemachus, forrowful and dejected, came next to the corps, and ftrewed flowers upon it. When it arrived at the pyre, the fon of Ulyffes could not fee the flames catch the linnen it was wrapt in, without weeping afresh. Farewell, brave Hippias, faid he; for I dare not call thee my friend; be appeafed, thou shade, who haft merited fo much glory! Did I not love thee, I should envy thy happinefs: thou art delivered from the miferies we ftill fuffer, and haft retreated from them in the path of glory. Ah! how happy should I be in making a like end! May Styx not ftop thy ghoft! may the Elyfian fields be open to it! may fame preferve thy renown throughout all ages, and may thy ashes reft in peace!

He had fcarcely fpoken thefe words which were intermingled with fighs, but the whole army made a loud lamentation; they were moved for Hippias, whofe gallant actions they recited, and their forrow for his death recalling all his good qualities to their minds, made them forget the failings which were owing to the impetuofity of youth and a bad education: But they were ftill more moved with the tender fentiments of Telemachus. Is this then, faid they, the proud, the haughty, the fcornful, the ftubborn young Greek? Lo! how gentle, how humane, how kind he is. Without doubt Minerva, who fo greatly loved his father, loves him alfo; she without doubt has made him the choiceft prefent which the Gods can make to men, by giving him a heart fufceptible of friendship, as well as wifdom.

And now the body was confumed by the flames. Telemachus himfelf befprinkled the yet fmoaking ashes with perfumed liquors; he then inclofed them in a golden urn, which he crowned with flowers, and carried it to Phalantus; who was ftretched at his length, pierced with various wounds, and fo extremely weak that he had a near profpect of the gloomy gates of hell.

Already had Traumaphilus and Nozophugus, whom the fon of Ulyffes had fent to him, admi-

niftered

niftered all the affiftance of their art ; they had gradually recalled his foul, which was ready to take its
flight ; new fpirits infenfibly revived him ; an agreeable penetrating vigour, the balm of life, infinuated
itfelf from vein to vein even to the inmoft receffes of
his heart, and a pleafing warmth fnatched him from
the icy hands of death. The moment his fwooning
was over, grief fucceeded : He began to be fenfible
of the lofs of his brother, which he had not before
been in a condition of feeling. Alas! faid he, why
all thefe pains to fave my life ? Were it not better
for me to die, and follow my deareft Hippias ? I faw
him perish by my fide. O Hippias, the joy of my
life, my brother, my dear brother, thou art no more!
I then no more shall fee thee, nor hear thee, nor embrace thee, nor tell thee my pains, nor comfort thee
under thine ! Ye Gods ! ye enemies of mankind !
there is no Hippias for me! Is it poffible ? Is it not
a dream ? No, it is but too true. O Hippias, I have
loft thee, I faw thee die, and muft live till I have revenged thy death : I will facrifice the cruel Adraftus,
befmeared with thy blood, to thy manes.

Whilft Phalantus was fpeaking thus, Traumaphilus
and Nozophugus endeavoured to appeafe his grief,
that it might not increafe his diforders, and prevent
the effect of their medicines. Perceiving of a fudden that Telemachus was coming to him, his heart
was at firft agitated by two contrary paffions ; on
one hand, he retained a refentment of all that had
paft between Telemachus and Hippias, which was
quickened by his grief for Hippias's death ; and on
the other he could not be ignorant that he owed
the prefervation of his own life to Telemachus, who
had fnatched him, quite covered with blood and
half dead, out of Adraftus's hands. But when he
faw the golden urn in which the dear ashes of his
brother Hippias were inclofed, he shed a torrent of
tears ; he immediately embraced Telemachus without being able to fpeak, and at length with a feeble
voice, interrupted with fobbings, he faid :

Worthy

Worthy fon of Ulyffes, your virtue compels me to love you; to you I am indebted for this remainder of life which draws towards its end; but I am indebted to you for fomething much dearer to me. But for you, my brother's body had been the prey of vultures; but for you, his shade, deprived of fepulture, had miferably wandered on the Stygian banks, and been continually repulfed by the inexorable Charon. Muft I be fo much obliged to one I have fo much hated? Reward him, ye Gods! and rid me of fo wretched a life. As for you, Telemachus, perform for me the laft duties which you performed for my brother, that nothing may be wanting to your glory.

This faid, Phalantus was quite fpent and overwhelmed with an excefs of grief. Telemachus ftood by him, not daring to fpeak to him, and waiting till he should recover his ftrength. Phalantus foon returning from his fwoon, took the urn out of Telemachus's hands, kiffed it feveral times, bedewed it with his tears, and faid; Ye dear, ye precious afhes! when shall mine be inclofed in this urn with you! O thou ghoft of Hippias, I follow thee to the shades below; Telemachus will revenge us both.

And now Phalantus's diforder daily decreafed by the care of the two men who were skilled in the fcience of Æfculapius. Telemachus conftantly attended them when they vifited their patient, to make them the more diligent to haften his cure; and the whole army admired the goodnefs of his heart in thus relieving his greateft enemy, more than the valour and wifdom he had difcovered in faving the confederate army in battle. Telemachus at the fame time was indefatigable in the hardeft toils of war. He flept little, and his flumbers were often interrupted either by advices; which he received at all hours of the night as well as of the day, or by his vifiting the feveral quarters of the camp, which he never did twice together at the fame hour, that he might the more eafily furprife thofe that were not fufficiently vigilant; he used often to return to his tent besmeared with sweat and dust; his food was plain; he lived like the common soldiers, to set them an example of sobriety and patience. The army having but little provisions in this incampment, he thought fit to stop the murmurs of the soldiers by voluntarily bearing himself the same inconveniencies as they. His body, instead of being weakened by so laborious a life, was strengthened and hardened daily; he began to lose the soft graces which are as it were the bloom of youth; his complection grew browner and less delicate, and his limbs more robust and nervous.

End of the Seventeenth Book.

THE

THE
ADVENTURES
OF
TELEMACHUS,
SON of ULYSSES.

BOOK the EIGHTEENTH.

The ARGUMENT.

Telemachus, perſuaded by various dreams that his fa-
ther Ulyſſes is not on the earth, executes his deſign of
going to ſeek him in hell. He goes privately out of
the camp, attended by two Cretans as far as a temple
near the famous cavern of Acherontia ; he there
plunges through a dark dreary paſſage, arrives on the
banks of Styx, and is taken by Charon into his bark
He goes and preſents himſelf before Pluto, whom he
finds prepared to permit him to ſeek for his father.
He croſſes Tartarus, where he ſees the tortures of
the ungrateful, the perjured, the hypocrite, and par-
ticularly of bad kings.

ADRASTUS, whoſe troops had been conſi-
derably weakened in this engagement, retired
behind mount Aulon, to wait for various re-inforce-
ments, and to endeavour once more to ſurpriſe his
enemies : So an hungry lion, driven back from the
sheep-fold, returns to the gloomy wood, and re-en-
ters his den, where he whets his teeth and claws, and
waits for a favourable opportunity to deſtroy the
whole flock.

Tele-

Telemachus having taken care to eftablish a ftrict difcipline through all the camp, thought only of executing a defign which he had formed and concealed from all the chiefs of the army. He had long been difturbed every night with dreams, which shewed him his father Ulyffes. His dear image ufed conftantly to return towards the end of the night, before Aurora came with her dawning fires to chace the wandering ftars from heaven, and gentle flumbers with all their trains of fluttering dreams from the earth. Sometimes he thought he faw Ulyffes in a delightful ifland on the bank of a river in a flowery meadow, quite naked, and furrounded by nymphs who were throwing him garments that he might cover himfelf with them. Sometimes he thought he heard him talking in a palace all glittering with gold and ivory, where men with wreaths of flowers on their heads were liftening to him with pleafure and admiration. And Ulyffes would often appear to him of a fudden amidft the merriments and pleafures, of feftivals, wherein the fweet harmony of a voice was heard in concert with a lyre more ravishing than that of Apollo, and than the voices of all the Mufes.

When Telemachus awaked, he was troubled at thefe agreeable dreams. O my father! my dear father Ulyffes! cried he, the moft frightful dreams would be more pleafing to me. Thefe images of felicity convince me that you are already defcended to the manfion of happy fouls, whofe virtue the Gods reward with an eternal peace. Methinks I fee the Elyfian fields. Oh! how dreadful it is to hope no more! O my much-loved father! Shall I never fee thee? Shall I never embrace him who fo dearly loved me, and in queft of whom I undergo fo many toils? Shall I never hear that mouth fpeak which ufed to utter wifdom? Shall I never kifs thofe hands, thofe dear victorious hands, which have vanquished fo many enemies? Will they not punish Penelope's frantic fuitors, nor Ithaca ever rife again from its ruin? You, ye Gods, who hate my father, you fend me

me thefe fearful dreams to rob my heart of every
hope, to rob me of my life. No, I will live no longer in this uncertainty. What fay I! Alas! I am but
too certain that my father is no more; I'll go even
to hell to feek his ghoft. Thefeus, the impious Thefeus, who prefumed to offer violence to the infernal
deities, defcended thither; but piety is my motive
for going. Hercules defcended thither: I indeed
am not Hercules; but an attempt to imitate him is
glory. Orpheus, by the recital of his misfortunes,
moved the heart of that God who is reprefented as
inexorable, and obtained his leave for Eurydice's return to the living. I am more worthy of compaffion
than Orpheus, for my lofs is greater. Who would
compare a young girl, who was no more than multitudes of others, with Ulyffes the admiration of all
Greece? We will go, we will die, if it muft be fo.
And why should I, whofe life is fo miferable, be
afraid of death? O Pluto! Proferpine! I will quickly try if you are fo inexorable as you are faid to be.
O my father, having vainly compaffed earth and feas
to find you, I will now go and fee if you are not in
the gloomy manfions of the dead. Though the Gods
refufe to let me fee you on earth, and in the enjoyment of the light of the fun, perhaps they will
not refufe to let me fee at leaft your ghoft in the fable
realm of night.

Telemachus, as he fpoke thefe words, bedewed his
bed with his tears. He immediately rofe, and endeavoured by means of the light to footh the fmarting grief thefe dreams had occafioned; but the arrow having pierced his heart, he carried it every
where with him. During his anguish he refolved to
defcend to hell at a famous place, which was not
far from the camp; it is called Acherontia, becaufe
there is a hideous cavern there, which leads down
to the banks of Acheron, a river whereby the Gods
themfelves are cautious how they fwear. The city
was built on the top of a rock, like a neft on the top
of a tree. At the foot of the rock was the cavern,
which

which fearful mortals durft not approach. The shepherds were careful to turn their flocks from it. The fulphurous vapours of the Stygian lake which inceffantly exhaled through this opening, infected all the air. Nor herbs nor flowers grew around it; there no gentle Zephirs ever breathed, no vernal bloom was feen, nor autumn's precious gifts. The earth was parched and languid, and one faw but a few fatal cypreffes and leaflefs shrubs. Even at a diftance Ceres all around denied the husbandmen her golden harvefts, and Bacchus feemed in vain to promife his delicious fruits, for the cluftering grapes withered inftead of ripening. The mournful Naiads poured no limpid ftream; their waves were always bitter and muddy. In this fpot over-run with thorns and brambles, no birds did ever warble, nor find a grove to retreat to; they went and fung their loves under a milder sky. Here nothing was heard but the croaking of ravens, and the difmal fcreams of the owl. The grafs itfelf was bitter, and the flock, which fed on it, felt not the pleafing joy which makes them bound along. The bull fled from the heifer, and the difconfolate fwain forgot his pipe and his flute.

Out of this cavern iffued from time to time a black thick fmoke, which formed a kind of night at the mid of day. The neighbouring people then redoubled their facrifices to appeafe the infernal Divinities; but men in the flower of their age and earlieft bloom of youth, were often the only victims which thefe cruel Deities took a pleafure in facrificing by a fatal contagion.

It was here Telemachus refolved to find a way to Pluto's gloomy manfion. Minerva, who inceffantly watched over him and covered him with her Ægis, had rendered Pluto propitious to him; Jupiter himfelf, at her requeft, having commanded Mercury, who daily defcends to hell to deliver up to Charon a certain number of dead, to bid the king of the shades permit the fon of Ulyffes to enter into his empire.

Telemachus

Telemachus steals out of the camp by night; he travels by the light of the moon, and invokes that powerful Deity, who being in the heavens the bright planet of the night, and on earth the chaste Diana, is in hell the formidable Hecate. This Goddess kindly heard his vows; because his heart was pure, and he was led by the pious affection which a son owes to his father.

He was scarcely arrived at the mouth of the cavern, when he heard the subterraneous empire roar; the ground trembled beneath his feet, and the heavens were armed with lightnings and flashes of fire, which seemed to fall on the earth. The young son of Ulysses felt his heart moved, and his whole body covered with a cold sweat; but his courage supported him. Lifting up his hands and eyes to heaven, Ye mighty Gods, cried he, these omens, which I deem propitious, I accept with pleasure; compleat your work. He said, and redoubling his pace, rushed boldly forward.

Whereupon the thick smoke which rendered the mouth of the cavern fatal to all animals that approached it, was dispersed, and the poisonous stench ceased for a while. Telemachus entered alone; for what mortal durst attend him? Two Cretans, who came with him to a certain distance from the cave, and to whom he had communicated his design, waited in a temple at a distance, trembling, half dead, offering up their vows, and despairing of ever seeing Telemachus again.

Mean time the son of Ulysses rushed sword in hand into this horrible darkness. He presently perceives a faint glimmering light, like that which is seen in the night-time on the earth; he observes the airy ghosts fluttering around him, and drives them away with his sword. He afterwards sees the dolesome banks of the boggy river, whose foul and sluggish waters are continually whirling round. On the shore he discovers an innumerable crowd of unburied dead, vainly presenting themselves to the inexorable Charon.

ron. This God, whose everlasting age is eternally surly and morose but full of vigour, threatens them, drives them away, and immediately admits the young Greek into his bark. Telemachus, as he enters it, hears the groans of a disconsolate ghost.

What occasions your distress, said he? Who were you on the earth? I was, replied the shade, Nabopharzan king of haughty Babylon. All the nations of the east trembled at the very sound of my name; I caused myself to be worshipped by the Babylonians in a marble temple, where I was represented by a golden statue, before which were burnt both night and day the most precious perfumes of Æthiopia. Whoever presumed to contradict me, was immediately chastised for it. New pleasures were daily invented to make my life more delightful, and I was still young and robust. Oh! what joys had I to taste on a throne! But a woman whom I loved, and who did not love me, made me very sensible that I was not a God. She poisoned me. I now am nothing. My ashes were yesterday deposited in a pompous manner in a golden urn. My people wept for me; they tore off their hair; they seemed as if they would throw themselves into my flaming pyre to die with me, and they still go and pour forth their groans at the foot of the stately tomb in which my ashes are laid: But nobody really laments me; my memory is abhorred even in my own family, and I already suffer here below an horrible kind of treatment.

Telemachus moved by this sight, said, Were you really happy while you reigned? Did you feel that sweet peace of mind, without which the heart is always opprest and withers in the midst of pleasures? No, replied the Babylonian, I do not even know what you mean. The sages indeed vaunt of this peace as the only good; but for me, I never experienced it. My heart was continually agitated by new desires, by fear and by hope. I endeavoured to make myself giddy by the rapid motions of my passions, and I took care to maintain the intoxicating career, and to make

it

it lasting. The shortest interval of calm reason had been very irksome to me. This is the peace which I enjoyed; all other seemed to me but a fable and a dream. These are the blessings which I regret.

The Babylonian, as he spoke thus, wept like a mean-spirited wretch, that had been enervated by prosperity, and had not been used to bear adversity with fortitude. There were several slaves about him who had been put to death to honour his funeral. Mercury had delivered them up to Charon with their king, and had given them an absolute power over him whom they had served on the earth. The shades of these slaves were no longer afraid of Nabopharzan's shade; they held it in chains, and offered it the most cruel indignities. One said to him, Were we not men as well as thee? What made thee so frantic as to think thyself a God? Shouldest thou not have remembered that thou wert of the same race as others? Another, to insult him, said, Thou wert in the right in being unwilling to be taken for a man; for thou wert a monster void of humanity. A third cried out, Well! where are thy flatterers now? Wretch, thou hast no longer any thing to give; thou hast not the power to do any more mischief; thou art become the slave even of thy own slaves. The Gods are slow to do justice, but they do it at last.

At these grating words Nabopharzan threw himself prostrate on the earth, tearing off his hair in a fit of rage and despair. But Charon said to the slaves: Haul him up by his chain, raise him whether he will or no; he shall not have even the consolation of hiding his confusion; all the ghosts of Styx must be witnesses of it, to justify the Gods, who have so long suffered this impious wretch to reign on the earth. This, Babylonian, is but the beginning of thy sorrows; prepare thyself to be tried by Minos, the inflexible judge of hell.

During this speech of the terrible Charon, the bark reached the shore of Pluto's realm. All the ghosts ran to view the living mortal that appeared in the

the boat in the midst of the dead; but the moment Telemachus set his foot on the shore, they fled like the shades of night, which the least glimpse of day disperses. Charon with a brow less wrinkled, and eyes less fierce than usual, said to the young Greek, Thou mortal beloved of the Gods, since it is given thee to enter the kingdom of night, which is inaccessible to the living, make haste and go where the Destinies call thee; go along this gloomy path to the palace of Pluto, whom you will find on his throne; he will permit you to enter regions whose secrets I am forbidden to discover to you.

Hereupon Telemachus advances with hasty steps. He sees on all sides fluttering shades more numerous than the grains of sand on the sea-shore; and observing the confusion and hurry of this infinite multitude, and the profound silence of these spacious regions, he is struck with an holy fear. His hair rises upright on his head, on his arrival at the inexorable Pluto's drear abode; his knees tremble, his voice fails him, and it is with difficulty that he is able to address these words to the God: You behold, O tremendous Deity, the son of the unhappy Ulysses; I am come to enquire if my father be descended into your empire, or if he be still wandering on the earth.

Pluto was seated on a throne of ebony. His countenance was pale and severe, his eyes hollow and sparkling, his brows wrinkled and threatening. The sight of a living man was hateful to him, as the light is offensive to the eyes of animals that are used to go out of their retreats only by night. By his side appeared Proserpine, who alone attracted his looks, and seemed a little to mollify his heart. She enjoyed an ever-blooming beauty; but she seemed to have joined to her divine charms I know not what of the obduracy and cruelty of her husband.

At the foot of the throne was pale devouring death, with his keen scythe, which he was continually whetting. Around him hovered gloomy cares, cruel jealousy, revenge all dropping with blood and covered with wounds;

wounds; groundless hate; avarice gnawing her own
flesh; despair rending herself with her own hands;
mad ambition overthrowing every thing; treason
thirsting for blood, and unable to enjoy the evils she
had occasioned; envy pouring her deadly venom
around her, and raging at her want of power to injure; impiety digging a bottomless pit, and flinging
herself in despair into it; ghastly spectres; phantoms which assume the form of the dead to terrify
the living; frightful dreams, and want of sleep as
tormenting as they: All these dreadful images environed the haughty Pluto, and crowded his palace.
He answered Telemachus in a voice which made the
bottom of Erebus roar.

Young mortal, destiny has given thee to violate
this sacred asylum of shades; pursue thy glorious
fortune; I shall not tell thee where thy father is;
it suffices that thou art free to look for him. As he
was a king upon the earth, you need only run
through, on one hand, that part of dreary Tartarus
where wicked kings are punished, and the Elysian
fields, on the other, where good kings are rewarded.
But you cannot go from hence to the Elysian fields,
without passing through Tartarus. Hasten thither,
and quit my dominions.

Telemachus instantly seems to fly through those
empty and immense spaces, so much did he long to
know if he should see his father, and to get out of
the dreadful presence of the tyrant who awes both
the living and the dead. Near him he presently perceives the dismal Tartarus, from which issued a
black thick smoke, whose poisonous steam would
have been mortal, had it been diffused in the mansions of the living. This smoke hovered over a
river of fire and whirlwinds of flames, whose roaring like that of the most impetuous torrents falling
from the highest rocks into the deepest abysses, prevented ones hearing any thing distinctly in these regions of sorrow.

Telemachus

Telemachus being secretly encouraged by Miner-va, enters this gulf undaunted. He immediately perceived a great number of men who had lived in the lowest stations, and were punished for having sought riches by fraud, treachery and cruelty. He observed many impious hypocrites, who pretending to love religion, had used it only as a specious pretence to gratify their ambition, and to impose upon the credulous. These wretches, who had abused virtue itself, though it is the most precious gift of the Gods, were punished as the most wicked of all mankind. Children who had killed their fathers and their mothers, wives who had dipt their hands in their husband's blood, and traytors who had violated all the most solemn oaths, and sacrificed their country, suffered less cruel tortures than these hypocrites : Such is the pleasure of the three judges of hell, and their reason for it, is because hypocrites are not satisfied with being wicked like other impious wretches ; they endeavour to be thought good, and make men by their counterfeit virtue, afraid of relying on true. The Gods whom they mocked, and rendered contemptible to men, take a pleasure in exerting their whole power to revenge themselves of their insults.

Near these appeared others, who, though not esteemed culpable by the vulgar, are persecuted by the divine vengeance without mercy : These are the ungrateful, the liar, the flatterer who applauded vice, malignant censurers who endeavoured to sully the purest virtue, and those who rashly judged of things without knowing them thoroughly, and thereby injured the reputation of the innocent.

But of all kinds of ingratitude, that which is committed with regard to the Gods, was punished as the blackest. What ! said Minos, is a man reputed a monster, who is ungrateful to his father, or his friend, of whom he has received some favours, and does he glory in being ungrateful to the Gods, of whom he holds his life, and all the blessings it includes ! Does

he

be not owe his birth to them more than to the father
and mother of whom he was born? The more
crimes are winked at and excused on the earth, the
more are they the objects of an implacable vengeance,
which nothing escapes, in hell.

Telemachus seeing the three judges sitting, and
passing sentence on a person before them, was so
free as to ask them what his crimes were. Upon
which the criminal took the word, and cried, I never did any harm; I placed all my delight in doing
good; I was generous, liberal, just, compassionate;
with what then can I be charged? Whereupon Minos said, Thou art charged with nothing as to men;
but didst thou not owe them less than the Gods?
What is this justice thou vauntest of? Thou hast
failed in no duty towards men, who are nothing:
thou hast been virtuous, but thou didst ascribe all
thy virtue to thyself, and not to the Gods who gave
it thee; for thou wouldest needs enjoy the fruits of
thy own virtue and make that the only spring of
thy happiness. Thou hast been thy own Deity; but
the Gods who made all things, and made nothing
but for themselves, cannot give up their right. Thou
hast forgotten them; they will forget thee, and deliver thee up to thyself, since thou resolved'st to be
thy own and not theirs. Now therefore find thy
consolation, if thou canst, in thy own bosom. Lo!
thou art now for ever separated from men whom thou
soughtest to please. Lo! thou, who wast thy own
idol, art now alone with thyself. Be assured that
there is no true virtue without a reverence and love
of the Gods, to whom all things are due. Thy false
virtue, which long dazzled the eyes of men who are
easily imposed upon, will now be put to confusion.
Men judging of virtue and vice by what thwarts or
suits with their interest, are blind both as to good
and evil. Here a divine light overthrows all their
superficial opinions, and often condemns what they
admire, and justifies what they condemn.

At thefe words the Philofopher, as if he had been thunderftruck, could not fupport himfelf. The complacency with which he had formerly contemplated his moderation, his courage and generous inclinations, was changed into defpair. A furvey of his own heart, which had been an enemy to the Gods, became his punishment. He views himfelf, and cannot ceafe to view himfelf. He fees the vanity of the opinions of men, whom in all his actions he fought to pleafe. There is an univerfal change of every thing within him, as if all his bowels had been turned up-fide down; he no longer finds himfelf the fame man, and every prop in his heart fails him. His confcience whofe teftimony ufed to pleafe him fo highly, rifes up againft him, and bitterly reproaches him with his miftaken and chimerical virtues, which had not the worship of the Deity for their principle and end; he is troubled, aftonished, overwhelmed with shame, remorfe and defpair. The Furies indeed do not torment, becaufe they are fatisfied with giving him up to himfelf, as his own heart abundantly revenges the derided Gods. He feeks the blackeft corners to hide himfelf from the reft of the dead, unable to hide himfelf from himfelf; he feeks for darknefs, but he cannot find it. A troublefome light follows him every where; every where the piercing rays of truth purfue him, in order to avenge the truth he neglected to follow. Every thing which he loved, becomes hateful to him, as being the fource of his miferies, which are to be eternal. O fool, fays he to himfelf, I have known neither Gods, nor men, nor myfelf. No, I have known nothing, fince I never loved the only true good. All my fteps have been erroneous; my wifdom was but folly; my virtue was only a blind and impious pride; I was my own idol.

At laft Telemachus beheld the kings who had been condemned for abufing their power. On one hand a vengeful Fury prefented a mirror which shewed them all the deformity of their vices. There
they

they saw, and could not avoid seeing, their grofs vanity and greediness of the moft ridiculous encomiums : their barbarity to mankind, whom they ought to have rendered happy ; their infenfibility to virtue : their fears to hear the truth ; their affection for bafe flatterers ; their fupinenefs, their luxury, their indolence, their mifplaced jealoufies, their pomp ; their exceffive magnificence, founded on the ruin of the people ; their ambition to purchafe a little empty glory with the blood of their citizens ; and laftly their inhumanity, in daily feeking for new delights, in the tears and defpair of the miferable multitude. In this mirror they continually viewed themfelves, and found that they were more frightful and monftrous than the Chimera which Bellerophon vanquished, than the Lernæan Hydra which was fubdued by Hercules, and even than Cerberus himfelf, though he difgorges from his three yawning mouths, a black venomous gore, which is enough to poifon the whole race of mankind.

At the fame time, on the other hand, another Fury repeated to them in an infulting manner all the praifes which their flatterers had beftowed upon them while they were living, and held up another mirror in which they faw themfelves fuch as adulation had defcribed them ; the contraft of thefe two portraits was the punishment of their vanity. It was remarkable that the wickedeft of thefe princes were thofe to whom the moft fulfome commendations had been given in their life-time ; becaufe the wicked are more dreaded than the good, and are not ashamed to require the bafe incenfe of the poets and orators of their time.

They are heard to groan in this profound darknefs, where they can fee nothing but the infults and derifions which they are doomed to fuffer, and have nothing about them that does not repulfe them, that does not thwart them, that does not confound them. Whereas on the earth they fported with the lives of men, and pretended that all things were made for

their

their ufe; in Tartarus they are delivered up to all
the caprices of certain flaves, who make them in
their turn feel all the rigours of fervitude. They
ferve with reluctance, and defpair of ever being able
to foften their captivity. Under the lashes of thefe
flaves, now become their mercilefs tyrants, they are
like the anvil under the ftrokes of the hammers of
the Cyclops, when Vulcan urges them to work in
the burning forges of mount Ætna.

There Telemachus faw pale, ghaftly, difmayed
countenances; for gloomy grief preys on thefe guilty
wretches. They are terrified at themfelves, and can
no more shake off this terror than their nature itfelf.
They need no other punishment of their crimes than
their crimes themfelves, which they continually fee,
in all their enormity, ftaring them in the face and
haunting them like hideous fpectres. To avoid thefe,
they feek for a more powerful death than that which
feparated them from their bodies; they call in their
defpair for a death which will extinguish all fenfe
and confcioufnefs; they implore the abyffes to fwal-
low them up, and to fcreen them from the vengeful
and perfecuting rays of truth. But they are referved
for a vengeance which diftils upon them drop by
drop, and is inexhauftible. The truth which they
dreaded to fee, becomes their punishment; they fee
it, and have eyes only to fee it rife up againft them.
The fight of it pierces them, rends them, tears them.
It refembles lightning; without hurting the out-fide,
it penetrates to the inmoft bowels. The foul, like
metal in a flaming furnace, is as it were melted by
this vindictive fire, which deftroys its whole texture,
but confumes nothing; which diffolves even the firft
principles of life, and yet makes it impoffible to die.
They are racked with inconceivable tortures; they
can find no comfort nor reft for a fingle moment;
they exift only by their fury againft themfelves, and
a defpair which makes them outrageous.

Among thefe objects, which made Telemachus's
hair rife upright on his head, he faw feveral of the
ancient

ancient kings of Lydia, who were punished for having preferred the pleasures of an effeminate life to the toils of making their people happy, which ought to be inseparable from royalty.

These princes reproached each other with their blindness. one said to another, who had been his son, Did I not often, during my old age and before my death, recommend to you the redressing the evils which I had occasioned by my negligence? Ah unhappy father! replied the son, it was you who ruined me; it was your example that inspired me with a love of pomp, with pride, voluptuousness and cruelty. Seeing you reign in such luxury and with a crowd of flatterers about you, I was habituated to love flattery and pleasure; I thought that the rest of men were with respect to kings, what horses and other beasts of burden are with respect to men; animals which we value only for their service, and as they contribute to our convenience. This I believed; it was you that made me believe it, and I now suffer these numberless miseries for imitating you. To these reproaches they added the most shocking imprecations, and seemed in a rage to tear each other in pieces.

Around these kings still hovered, like owls in the night, cruel jealousies, groundless alarms, diffidence which revenges the people of the cruelty of their princes, an insatiable thirst of riches, false glory which is always tyrannical, and shameful luxury which doubles all the miseries of men, and has it not in her power to yield them substantial pleasures.

Several of these kings were severely punished, not for the evil which they had done, but for the omission of the good which they ought to have done. All the crimes of the people that proceed from a negligent execution of the laws, were imputed to their kings, who ought to reign only that the laws may reign by their ministry. To them also were imputed all the disorders which arise from pomp, luxury and all other excesses which reduce men to extremity, and tempt them to violate the laws for the sake of money.

P   Those

Those kings especially were treated with the greatest rigour, who instead of being good and watchful shepherds of the people, had studied only to worry the flock like ravenous wolves.

But what astonished Telemachus yet more, was to see in this abyss of darkness and misery, a great number of kings, who having past on the earth for tolerable good kings, had been condemned to the pains of Tartarus for submitting to be governed by wicked and crafty men. They were punished for the evils which they had suffered to be committed by their authority. Most of these had been so weak, that they had been neither good nor bad; they had never been afraid of knowing the truth, but they had not relished virtue, nor placed their delight in doing good.

End of the Eighteenth Book.

THE

THE

ADVENTURES

OF

TELEMACHUS,

SON of ULYSSES.

BOOK the NINETEENTH.

The ARGUMENT.

*Telemachus enters into the Elyfian fields, where he is
known by Arcefius his great grandfather, who affures
him that Ulyffes is living, that he will fee him again
in Ithaca, and reign there after him. Arcefius gives
him a defcription of the felicity which good men enjoy, and efpecially good kings, who in their life-time
ferved the Gods, and were a bleffing to the people they
governed. He makes him obferve, that the heroes
who had excelled only in the art of war, are much
lefs happy in a place by themfelves. He gives Telemachus fome inftruétions, who then returns with
fpeed to the confederate camp.*

WHEN Telemachus came out of this place, he
found himfelf relieved, as if a mountain had
been removed from his breaft; he was fenfible by this
relief, of the mifery of thofe who are confined there
without hopes of ever being releafed, and was terrified to fee how much more rigoroufly kings were tormented than other offenders. What! faid he, fo
many duties, fo many dangers, fo many fnares, fo
many difficulties in getting at the truth in order to

guard

guard againſt others and againſt one's ſelf alſo ! and
at laſt ſo many tortures in hell, after one has been ſo
envied, ſo diſquieted, ſo thwarted during a ſhort life !
O how ſenſeleſs is he that is ambitious of reigning :
Happy the man who confines himſelf to a private
and peaceful ſtation, in which he may with leſs difficulty be virtuous !

As he made theſe reflections, his ſoul was diſordered, he trembled, and fell into a conſternation, which
made him feel ſomething of the deſpair of the wretches he had juſt ſeen ; but as he went away from
this doleſome manſion of darkneſs, horror and deſpair, his courage began inſenſibly to revive : He
already felt, and had a glimpſe of the pure and ſweet
light of the abode of heroes.

Here reſided, ſeparated from the reſt of the juſt,
all the good kings that had ever ruled over mankind.
As wicked princes ſuffered puniſhments in Tartarus,
infinitely more ſevere than private offenders ; ſo good
kings enjoyed in the Elyſian fields an happineſs infinitely greater than that of other men who had loved
virtue on the earth.

Telemachus advanced towards theſe princes, who
were in fragrant groves on an ever-ſpringing and
flowery turf. A thouſand limpid rills watered, and
diffuſed a delicious freſhneſs over theſe enchanting
ſcenes. An infinite number of birds made the groves
ring with their tuneful chantings. One beheld the
vernal flowers ſpringing beneath one's feet, at the ſame
time that the richeſt autumnal fruits were hanging on
the trees. There were never felt the raging dog-
ſtar's heats : there the lowering boreal winds never
durſt to breathe the ſeverities of winter. Neither
blood thirſty war, nor cruel envy that bites with an
invenomed tooth, and bears writhen adders in her
boſom and around her arms, nor jealouſy, nor diffidence, nor fear, nor vain deſires, do ever approach
this happy manſion of peace. Here the day never
ends, and night with her ſable veil is a ſtranger. A
pure and grateful light is diffuſed around the bodies
of

of these righteous men, and invests them with its rays as with a garment. This light does not resemble the glimmering light, which enlightens the eyes of wretched mortals, and is nothing but darkness; it is rather a celestial glory than a light. It more thoroughly penetrates the grossest bodies than the rays of the sun penetrate the purest crystal. It never dazzles: on the contrary, it strengthens the eyes, and conveys an inexpressible serenity through all the recesses of the soul. This is the only food of the blessed. It proceeds from and enters into them; it penetrates and is incorporated with them, as aliments are incorporated with us. They see it, they feel it, they breathe it; it causes an inexhaustible fountain of tranquility and joy to spring up in them. They are immersed in this abyss of delights as fishes in the sea. They covet nothing more; they have all things without having any thing, for the taste of this pure light appeases the hunger of their hearts. All their desires are satisfied, and their plenitude raises them above every thing that empty greedy mortals pursue on the earth. All the surrounding delights are nothing to them, because the consummate happiness which comes from within, leaves them no cravings for any thing they see of delightful without. They are like the Gods, who replenished with nectar and ambrosia, would not deign to feed on any gross aliments which might be set before them at the most sumptuous tables of mortals. All evils fly far from these serene abodes; death, sickness, want, pain, sorrow, remorse, fear, hope itself which often gives us as much trouble as fear, divisions, hatred, quarrels, can have no admission here.

Should the lofty mountains of Thrace, whose brows, covered with ice and snow from the beginning of the world, cleave the clouds, should they I say be thrown from their foundations that are fixed in the center of the earth, the souls of these righteous men would not even be moved: They only pity the miseries which depress those who live in the world; but it is a sweet

and

and peaceful pity, that does not in the least lessen their unchangeable felicity. Eternal youth, endless happiness, a glory wholly divine, is painted on their faces; but their joy has nothing of wanton or indecent. It is a sweet, a noble, a majestic joy; it is a sublime, a ravishing taste of truth and virtue. They every moment experience without interruption that extacy of soul which a mother feels at the sight of a beloved son whom she thought dead: but the rapture which quickly forsakes the mother, never flies from their souls. It never languishes a moment; it is always new: they taste the transports of inebriating joys without their disorder and stupefaction. They discourse together of what they see and of what they taste. They despise and deplore the soft pleasures, and the vain grandeur of their former condition; they review with pleasure the few but sorrowful years, in which they were under a necessity of combating against themselves, and against a torrent of corrupt men, in order to be virtuous; they admire the assistance of the Gods who led them, as it were by the hand, through innumerous dangers to virtue. Something inconceivably divine flows incessantly through their souls, like a flood of the Divine nature itself which is united to them. They see, they taste that they are happy, and are conscious that they shall always be so; they sing the praises of the Gods, and make all together but one voice, one mind, one heart: The same tide of felicity ebbs and flows as it were in their united souls.

In these heavenly raptures ages roll away more swiftly than hours among mortals; and yet a thousand and a thousand ages subtract nothing from their happiness, which is always new and always perfect. They all reign together, not on thrones which the hand of man can subvert, but in themselves and with an unalterable power; for they no longer need to make themselves formidable by a power borrowed of a vile and wretched people. They no longer wear those vain diadems, whose lustre conceals numberless

fears

fears and anxious cares; the Gods themfelves having
crowned them, with their own hands, with crowns
which nothing can tarnish.

Telemachus, who was feeking his father, and expected to find him in thefe enchanting regions, was
fo ravished with this tafte of peace and happinefs, that
he would have been glad to have found him there, and
was forry that he himfelf was obliged to return to the
fociety of mortals. Here, faid he, is life indeed,
whereas ours is but death. But he was aftonished as
he had feen fo many kings in the tortures of Tartarus, that he faw fo few happy in the Elyfian fields;
he was thereby convinced that there are very few
princes refolute and courageous enough to refift their
own power, and to repulfe the numerous flatterers
who are ufed to ftir up all their paffions. Good kings
therefore are very rare, and moft are fo wicked that
the Gods would not be juft, if having fuffered them
to abufe their power in their life-time, they did not
chaftife them after their death.

Telemachus not feeing his father Ulyffes among
all thefe kings, looked for the divine Laërtes his
grandfire. While he was feeking him in vain, a
venerable majeftic old man came towards him, whofe
age did not refemble that of mortals, who are bowed
down with the weight of years on the earth. One
perceived only that he had been old before his death;
for all the gravity of age was now blended with all
the graces of youth, which revive in the moft decre-
pid the moment they are introduced into the Elyfian
fields. This fenior advanced haftily, and viewed
Telemachus with complacency, as one who was
very dear to him. Telemachus, who did not know
him, was in pain and fufpenfe.

I excufe my dear fon, faid this fenior, your not
knowing me; I am Arcefius, the father of Laërtes.
I finished my courfe a little before my grandfon U-
lyffes departed for the fiege of Troy. Though thou
wert then but an infant in thy nurfe's arms, I conceived great hopes of thee, and they have not deceived

P 4.

ceived me ; since I see that thou art descended into
Pluto's kingdom in quest of thy father, and that the
Gods support thee in this enterprise. O my happy
child ! the Gods love thee, and are preparing a glory
for thee which will equal that of thy father. And
happy I to see thee again ! Cease to search for Ulysses
here ; he is still alive, and is reserved to be the re-
storer of our house in the island of Ithaca. Laërtes
himself, though bowing under a weight of years, still
enjoys the light, and waits for his son's coming to
close his eyes. Thus mortals pass away like flowers
which bloom in the morning, and wither and are
trodden under foot in the evening. The generations
of men roll away like the waves of a rapid river ;
nothing can stop the tide of time, which draws after
it every thing that seems the most immoveable.
Thou thyself, my son, my dear son, thou who now
enjoyest such a sprightly pleasurable youth, do thou
remember that this gay season is but a flower which
will wither almost as soon as it is blown. Thou wilt
perceive thyself insensibly alter : The smiling graces,
the sweet pleasures which attend thee, strength, health,
joy, will vanish like a pleasing dream ; nothing but a
regretful remembrance will be left thee. Languid old
age, that enemy to pleasure, will come and wrinkle
thy brows, bow down thy body, weaken thy limbs,
dry up the source of joy in thy heart, and make thee
loath the present, and apprehensive of the future,
and insensible to all things but pain. This time appears to you at a distance. Alas ! thou deceivest thyself, my son ; it comes with hasty wings : Lo : It is
here. What advances with such rapidity is not far
from thee, and the present fleeting moment is already
at a distance, since it ceases to be the instant we speak,
and can approach us no more. Never rely therefore,
my son, on the present ; but support thyself in the
rugged thorny path of virtue by viewing the future.
Prepare thyself a mansion, by purity of manners and
a love of justice, in this blissful abode of peace. Thou
shalt quickly see thy father resume his authority in
                                          Ithaca ;

Ithaca; thou wert born to reign after him; but alas!
my son, how deceitful is a crown! When one views
it at a diftance, one fees nothing but grandeur, luftre
and pleafures; but when near, it is all befet with
thorns. A private perfon may without reproach lead
a life of eafe and obfcurity; but a king cannot, without dishonouring himfelf, prefer a life of pleafure and
indolence to the painful duties of government. He
owes himfelf to his fubjects; he is never permitted
to be his own mafter, and his leaft over-fights are of
the greateft confequence, becaufe they make his people wretched, and that fometimes for ages. He ought
to curb the audacioufnefs of the wicked, to fupport
innocence, to fupprefs calumny. It is not enough
for him not to do any evil; he muft do all the poffible good of which the ftate ftands in need. Nay, it
is not enough that he does good himfelf; he muft
likewife prevent all the evil which others would do,
were they not reftrained. Be apprehenfive therefore,
my fon, be apprehenfive of fo dangerous a fituation;
arm thyfelf with refolution againft thyfelf, againft
thy paffions, and againft flatterers.

Arcefius, as he fpoke thefe words, feemed animated
by a divine fire, and let Telemachus fee by his countenance that he greatly pitied kings on account of
the miferies which are infeparable from a crown.
When it is affumed, faid he, to gratify one's felf, it
is a monftrous tyranny: and when it is affumed to
difcharge the duties of it, and to govern a numerous
people, as a father governs his children, it is a grievous thraldom, which requires an heroic fortitude and
patience: And it is accordingly certain, that they
who have really reigned virtuoufly, here enjoy every
thing which the power of the Gods can beftow in
order to render their happinefs compleat.

While Arcefius was fpeaking in this manner, his
words funk deep into Telemachus's heart, and were
engraved upon it, like the figures which a fkilful artift
engraves on brafs, and defigns to tranfmit to the view
of the lateft pofterity. This fage difcourfe was like a

subtle flame that penetrated into the bowels of the young Telemachus; he found himself moved and on fire; something divine seemed to melt his heart within him. What he had in his inmost parts secretly consumed him; he could neither contain it nor support it, nor resist so violent an impression: It was a lively pleasing sensation, immixed with pains capable of depriving one of life.

Telemachus beginning at length to breathe more freely, perceived in the countenance of Arcesius a great resemblance of Laërtes; nay, he fancied that he had a confused idea of having seen the like features in his father Ulysses, when he departed for the siege of Troy.

This remembrance melted his very heart; sweet and joyful tears streamed from his eyes. He was desirous of embracing so dear a person and several times attempted it in vain. The empty shade eluded his arms, as flattering objects slip from a man in a dream when he thinks himself sure of them: One while the thirsty mouth of the sleeper pursues a fugitive stream; another while his lips move to form words which his stiffened tongue cannot utter; then his hands are eagerly extended, and catch nothing. So Telemachus was unable to gratify his fondness: He sees Arcesius, he hears him, he talks to him, he cannot feel him. At length he asks him who the persons are whom he sees around him.

You see, my son, replied the sage senior, men who were the ornament of their times, and the glory and happiness of the human race; you see the small number of kings who were worthy to be so, and who faithfully discharge the office of Gods on the earth. The others whom you see near, but separated from them by that little cloud, enjoy a much lower degree of glory. Those indeed are heroes; but the reward of their valour and military expeditions cannot be compared with that of wise, just and beneficent princes.

Among

Among thefe heroes you fee Thefeus, whofe face is fomewhat melancholy. He had the misfortune to be too credulous with regard to an artful wife, and is ftill grieved for having requefted of Neptune the cruel death of his fon Hippolitus. O how happy! had he not been fo paffionate and fo eafily provoked! You likewife behold Achilles leaning on his fpear, by rea-fon of the wound he received in his heel by the hand of the effeminate Paris, which put an end to his life. Had he been as juft, wife, and moderate as he was intrepid, the Gods would have granted him a long reign; but they pitied the Phthians and Dolopians, over whom, according to the courfe of nature, he would have reigned after Peleus, and determined not to deliver fo many people to the mercy of a fiery man, who was more eafily enraged than the moft ftormy fea. The fatal fifters fhortened the thread of his days, and he refembled a flower, which when hardly blown is cut down by the plough-fhare, and falls be-fore the clofe of the day which gave it birth. The Gods made ufe of him, as of floods and tempefts, to punish the crimes of men; they made Achilles their engine to throw down the walls of Troy, in order to revenge Laomedon's perjury, and Paris's unlawful love. Having made this ufe of the inftrument of their vengeance, they were appeafed, and refufed, not-withftanding the tears of Thetis, to fuffer this young hero to continue longer in the world, who was fit only to difturb mankind, and to overturn cities and kingdoms.

But doft thou fee that other perfonnage there with that fierce countenance? It is Ajax, the fon of Tela-mon, and the coufin of Achilles. You undoubtedly are not ignorant of his glory in battle. After the death of Achilles he pretended that his armour could be given to none but himfelf; your father did not think that he ought to yield it to him; the Greeks adjudged it in favour of Ulyffes. Ajax killed himfelf through rage and vexation, and indignation and fury are ftill vifible in his face. Do not approach him, my

P 6.   fon;

son ; for he would think that you intended to insult him in his misfortunes, though he really merits pity. Do you not perceive that he looks upon us with uneasiness, and is entering abruptly into that gloomy grove, because we are odious to him ? On the other side you see Hector, who had been invincible, if the son of Thetis had not lived at the same time. But lo! there goes Agamemnon, who still bears the marks of Clytemnestra's perfidy. O my son, I tremble when I think of the calamities of the impious Tantalus's family. The enmity of the two brothers, Atreus and Thyestes, filled that house with horror and blood. Alas ! what a multitude of others does a single crime draw after it ? Agamemnon returning at the head of the Greeks from the siege of Troy, had not time to enjoy in peace the glory he had acquired : Such is the fate of almost all conquerors. All the persons you see there were formidable in war ; but they were not amiable and virtuous. Accordingly they are admitted only into the second mansion of the Elysian fields.

As for these, they reigned with justice, they loved their subjects, and are the favourites of the Gods. While Achilles and Agamemnon, who were so prone to dissention and war, do still even here retain their pains and natural failings, while they vainly regret the loss of their lives, and are grieved at their being now but empty and impotent shadows ; these righteous princes, being purified by the divine light, on which they feed, have nothing more to wish for the completion of their happiness. They view the anxious cares of mortals with pity ; and the greatest affairs which disquiet the ambitious, appear to them like the sports of children. Their souls are replenished with truth and virtue, which they draw at the fountain head. They have nothing more to suffer from themselves or others, no more desires, no more wants, no more fears. All is at an end as to them, except their felicity, which cannot end.

Take notice, my son, of old king Inachus, who founded the kingdom of Argos. What sweetness !

What

What majesty in his old age; Flowers spring beneath his steps. His easy gait resembles the flight of a bird. He holds an ivory lyre in his hand, and sings in an eternal transport the marvellous works of the Gods. His heart and mouth breathe an exquisite perfume. The harmony of his voice and lyre would ravish both Gods and men. Thus is he rewarded for loving the people whom he assembled within his new walls, and whose legislator he was.

On the other side, thou mayest see among those myrtles, Cecrops the Egyptian, who was the first king of Athens, a city sacred to the Goddess of wisdom, whose name it bears. Cecrops bringing useful laws from Egypt, which was the source of letters and morality, to Greece, softened the savage nature of the Attic towns, and united them in the bands of society. He was just, humane, compassionate; he left his subjects in affluence, and his own family in moderate circumstances, being unwilling that his power should descend to his children, because he thought that others were more worthy of it.

In that little valley I must likewise shew you Ericthon, who invented the art of making money of silver. He did it with a view of facilitating commerce between the islands of Greece; but he foresaw the inconveniencies which would attend this invention. Apply yourselves, said he to the people, to multiply the riches of nature among you, which are the true riches: Manure the earth, that you may have plenty of corn, wine, oil and fruits; take care to have innumerable flocks and herds, which may feed you with their milk and cloath you with their wool, and you will thereby place yourselves in circumstances of never being afraid of poverty. The more children you have, the richer you will be, provided you inure them to labour; for the earth is inexhaustible, and increases her fertility in proportion to the number of inhabitants that cultivate her with care; she liberally rewards all such for their toils, whereas she is sparing, and ungrateful to those who cultivate her in a negligent

gent manner. Confine yourselves therefore chiefly to the true riches which suffice the wants of man. As for money, it must be esteemed only as it is necessary either in the wars which we are inevitably forced to maintain abroad, or for the trading in some necessary commodities which are wanting in our own country: And it is accordingly to be wished, that men would cease to trade in all things which serve only to maintain extravagance, pomp and luxury.

The sage Erichthon would often say, I greatly fear, my children, that I have made you a fatal present, in communicating to you the invention of money. I foresee that it will excite avarice, ambition, pomp; that it will cherish an infinite number of pernicious arts, which tend only to the softening and to the corruption of manners; that it will give you a disgust of the happy simplicity in which all the repose and all the security of life consists; that it will in short make you despise agriculture, which is the foundation of the life of man, and the source of all real blessings: But the Gods are witnesses to the integrity of my heart, in imparting this invention to you, which is in itself useful. At last when Erichthon perceived that money corrupted the people as he had foreseen, he retired through grief to a savage mountain, where he lived poor and sequestered from mankind to an extreme old age, and would not concern himself in the government of cities.

A little while after him the famous Triptolemus appeared in Greece, whom Ceres taught the art of tilling the earth, and of covering it every year with a golden harvest. Not that men before him were strangers to corn or to the manner of multiplying it by sowing, but they were not perfect in the art of tillage, till Triptolemus, sent by Ceres, came with a plough in his hand, to offer the Goddess's gifts to all who should have resolution enough to conquer their natural sloth, and addict themselves to constant labour. Quickly did Triptolemus teach the Greeks to furrow the earth, and to make her fruitful by

rending

rending her bosom; quickly did the ardent and indefatigable reapers cause the yellow ears which covered the fields, to fall beneath their sharp-edged sickles. Even wild and savage people, who wandered up and down the woods of Epirus and Ætolia, in quest of acorns for their food, softened their manners, and became subject to laws, when they had learnt how to make the harvests rise, and to live on bread. Triptolemus made the Greeks relish the pleasure of owing their riches only to their labour, and of finding in one's own field all that is necessary to render life easy and happy. This simple, this innocent plenty, which is inseparable from agriculture, made them recollect the wise counsels of Erichthon; they contemned money and all artificial riches, which are riches only in the imagination of men, which tempt them to pursue dangerous pleasures, and divert them from labour, wherein they would find all real blessings, together with purity of manners and perfect freedom. The Greeks therefore knew that a fertile and well-cultivated field is the real treasure of a family, which is wise enough to chuse to live frugally as their fathers lived. And happy had they been had they remained steady in maxims so proper to make them powerful, free, happy, and worthy of being so by a solid virtue! But alas! they begin to admire false riches; they by little and little neglect the true, and degenerate from this admirable simplicity. O my son, you will one day reign; then remember to bring men back to the practice of agriculture, to honour that art, to encourage those who apply themselves to it, and not to suffer men to live idle, or to be employed in arts which nourish pomp and luxury. These two men, who were so wise on the earth, are here beloved of the Gods. Take notice, my son, that their glory as much surpasses that of Achilles and other heroes who excelled only in battle, as the delightful spring is pleasanter than the icy winter, or as the light of the sun is brighter than that of the moon.

W hile

While Arcefius was talking in this manner, he
perceived that Telemachus's eyes were fixed on a
little laurel grove, and a river bordered with violets,
rofes, lillies and feveral other fragrant flowers, whofe
lively colours refembled thofe of Iris, when she defcends from heaven to the earth, to declare the commands of the Gods to mortals.   The great king Sefoftris was in this beautiful grove, and Telemachus
knew him again, though he was a thoufand times
more majeftic than he had ever been on the throne
of Egypt.   Rays of benign light shot from his eyes,
and dazzled thofe of Telemachus.   When one faw
him, one would have thought that he was inebriated
with nectar; fo much had the divine fpirit raifed
him above the reach of human reafon as a reward of
his virtues.

Telemachus faid to Arcefius, O my father, I perceive Sefoftris, the wife king of Egypt, whom I
faw not long fince.   That indeed is Sefoftris, replied
Arcefius; and you fee by him how bountifully the
Gods reward good princes.   But you muft know
that all this happinefs is nothing in comparifon of
that which was defigned him, if too great a profperity had not made him forget the rules of moderation
and juftice.   His paffion to lower the pride and info-
lence of the Tyrians, engaged him to take their city.
This conqueft infpired him with a defire of making
others; and fuffering himfelf to be feduced by the
vanity of conquerors, he fubdued, or to fpeak more
juftly, he ravaged all Afia.   At his return to Egypt
he found that his brother had feized upon the crown,
and had by an unrighteous adminiftration changed
the beft laws of the country.   Thus did his great
conquefts only ferve to imbroil his own kingdom.
But what made him more inexcufable, was his being fo
intoxicated with vain glory, as to caufe his chariot to be
drawn by the proudeft of the kings he had conquered.
He was afterwards fenfible of his error, and ashamed of
having been fo inhuman. Such was the fruit of his victories, and fuch are the mifchiefs which conquerors bring
upon

upon themselves and their kingdoms, by endeavouring to usurp those of their neighbours. This was what sullied the reputation of a prince who was otherwise so just and beneficent, and it is this which diminishes the happiness which the Gods had prepared for him.

Dost thou not see him, my son, whose wound appears so glorious? He was a king of Caria, Dioclides by name, who sacrificed himself for his people in battle, because the oracle had declared that the nation whose king should perish, would be victorious in the war between the Carians and the Lycians.

Take notice of that other personage also : He was a wise legislator, who having enacted laws which were adapted to make his subjects virtuous and happy, made them swear that they would never violate any of them in his absence. This done, he departed, became a voluntary exile from his country, and died poor in a foreign land, in order to oblige his people by this oath for ever to observe such salutary laws.

The other whom you see, is Eunesimus, king of the Pylians, and one of the ancestors of the sage Nestor. During a pestilence which ravaged the whole earth and covered the banks of Acheron with new ghosts, he laying down his life for so many millions of innocent persons, besought the Gods to lay aside their wrath. The Gods heard him, and here bestowed a real crown upon him, of which all earthly crowns are but empty shadows.

The old man whom you see with a wreath of flowers on his head, is the famous Belus: He reigned in Egypt, and married Anchynoe the daughter of the God Nilus, who conceals the source of his waters, and enriches the country by his inundations. He had two sons; Danaüs, whose history you know, and Egyptus who gave his name to this beautiful kingdom. Belus thought himself richer by the plenty he procured his subjects, and by their affection for him, than by all the taxes which he could have imposed upon them. These men, my son, whom you look upon as dead, are alive; and the wretched life which men drag

on

on the earth is death: The names only are changed.
May the Gods render thee virtuous enough to merit
this blessed life, which nothing can put a period to,
nor disquiet! But hasten hence; it is time to go and
seek thy father.   Alas! what blood wilt thou see
shed before thou findest him! But then what glory
awaits thee in the fields of Hesperia! Be mindful of
the wise Mentor's counsels: if thou followest them,
thy name will be glorious among all nations and in
all ages.

He said; and immediately conducted Telemachus
to the ivory door which leads out of Pluto's darksome
realm.   Telemachus departed, with tears in his eyes,
without being able to embrace him; and ascending
from these gloomy regions, hastened back to the confederate camp; having in his way rejoined the two
young Cretans, who had accompanied him as far as
the cavern, and expected to see him no more.

End of the Nineteenth Book.

THE.

THE
ADVENTURES
OF
TELEMACHUS,
SON of ULYSSES.

BOOK the TWENTIETH.

The ARGUMENT.

In an assembly of the chiefs, Telemachus prevails on them not to surprise the city of Venusium, which had been left by both parties in trust in the hands of the Lucanians. He shews his wisdom with regard to two deserters; one of them, whose name was Acanthus, had undertaken to poison him, and the other, named Dioscorus offered the allies the head of Adrastus. In the ensuing battle Telemachus carries death wherever he goes in quest of Adrastus; and that king, who seeks him also, meets with and kills Pisistratus, the son of Nestor. Philottetes comes to his assistance, and as he is about to kill Adrastus, is wounded and obliged to retire from the battle. Telemachus follows the cries of the confederates, of whom Adrastus makes a terrible havock; he engages this enemy, and gives him his life, on conditions which he imposes upon him. Adrastus getting up again, attempts to surprise Telemachus, who seizes him a second time, and takes away his life.

IN the mean time the chiefs of the army assembled to deliberate whether they should seize on Venusium, a strong city, which Adrastus had formerly usurped.

uſurped from his neighbours the Peucetæ of Apulia; who had entered into the league againſt Adraſtus, in order to demand juſtice for that invaſion. Adraſtus, to ſatisfy them, had delivered the city by way of truſt into the hands of the Lucanians; But he had corrupted the Lucanian garriſon and its commander by his money; ſo that the Lucanians had in reality leſs authority than he in Venuſium; and the Apulians, who had conſented that the Lucanians garriſon ſhould keep Venuſium, had been over-reached in this negotiation.

A citizen of Venuſium, named Demophantes had privately offered the allies to deliver up one of the gates of the city to them by night. This propoſal was ſo much the more advantageous, as Adraſtus had laid up all his proviſions and military ſtores in a caſtle, near Venuſium, which could not defend itſelf if that city were taken. Philoctetes and Neſtor had already declared that they ought to embrace ſo favourable an opportunity; and all the other commanders being ſwayed by their authority, and dazzled by the advantages which would ariſe from ſo eaſy an enterpriſe, approved their opinion: But Telemachus at his return did all he could to diſſuade them from it.

I am not ignorant, ſaid he, that if ever a man deſerved to be circumvented and deceived, it is Adraſtus, who has ſo often deceived all others. I plainly ſee that in ſurpriſing Venuſium you will only take poſſeſſion of a city which belong to you, ſince it belongs to the Apulians, a nation who have entered into your league. I own that you may do this with a greater ſhow of reaſon, as Adraſtus who put this city as a pledge into the hands of the Lucanians, has corrupted the governor and the garriſon, in order to enter it whenever he ſhall think proper. And then I am ſenſible as well as you, that if you take Venuſium, you will the next day become maſters of the caſtle in which Adraſtus has lodged all his ſtores; and that you would thus in two days put an end to this formidable war. But is it not better to periſh than to conquer by ſuch means? Muſt fraud be

repelled

repelled by fraud? Shall it be said that so many
princes having entered into a league to chastise the
impious Adrastus for his treacheries, are become
treacherous like him? If it is lawful for us to act
like Adrastus, he is not guilty, and our endeavours
to punish him are wrong. What! has all Hesperia,
supported by so many Greek colonies, and heroes
returned from the siege of Troy, no other arms
against the perfidy and perjury of Adrastus, but perfidy and perjury? You have sworn by things the
most sacred to leave Venusium as a pledge in the
hands of the Lucanians. But their garrison, say you,
is corrupted by Adrastus's money; I perceive that as
well as you. But this garrison is still in the pay of
the Lucanians; it has not refused to obey them, and
has, at least in appearance, observed the neutrality.
Neither Adrastus nor any of his soldiers have ever entered Venusium; the treaty subsists, and your oath is
not forgotten by the Gods. Shall we keep our promises, only when we want plausible pretences to break
them? Shall we be faithful and religious observers of
oaths, only when we can get nothing by violating
them? If the love of virtue and the fear of the Gods
have no influence upon you, have at least some concern for your reputation and interest. If you give
mankind this pernicious instance of breaking your
word and of violating your oath to terminate a war,
what wars will you not kindle by this impious conduct? What neighbour will not be constrained to apprehend every thing from and to detest you? Who for
the future in the most pressing exigencies will confide
in you? What security will you be able to give when
you design to be sincere, and when it is of consequence to you to persuade your neighbours that you
are so? Will a solemn treaty do it? You will have
trampled one under your feet. Will an oath do it?
Ah! will it not be known that you look upon
the Gods as cyphers, when you expect to draw any
advantage from perjury? You will not therefore
be safer in peace than in war. Every thing which
comes

comes from you, will be received as a difguifed or open war. You will perpetually be the enemies of all who shall have the misfortune to be your neighbours. All tranfactions which require reputation, probity and confidence, will become impoffible to you; you will have no means of making people believe what you promife.

There is, added Telemachus, a yet nearer concern which muft needs affect you, if you have any fenfe of probity, or any forefight with regard to your own intereft, viz, that fo treacherous a conduct would be an internal attack upon your whole league, and quickly ruin it; your perjury would caufe Adraftus to triumph.

The whole affembly, murmuring at thefe words, asked him how he could take upon him to fay, that an action which would infallibly make the confederates victorious, would ruin the confederacy? How, replied he, will you be able to confide in each other, if you once violate your fincerity, the only band of fociety and confidence? When you have laid it down as a maxim, that the laws of probity and fidelity may be difpenfed with for the fake of fome fignal advantage, which of you will truft another, fince another may find it very advantageous to falfify his word and to deceive you? Where will you be then? Which of you will not endeavour by his own artifices to prevent thofe of his neighbour? What will be the fate of a confederacy of fo many nations, when they have agreed among themfelves after a general difcuffion of the matter, that it is lawful to over-reach one's neighbour and to violate one's plighted faith? How great will your mutual jealoufies be, your diffentions, your zeal to deftroy each other? Adraftus will have no occafion to attack you; you will fufficiently worry one another, and juftify his perfidies. Ye fage, ye magnanimous princes, you who fo wifely govern innumerable multitudes, difdain not to hearken to the counfels of a young man. Should you ever fall into the moft terrible extremities into which war fometimes
times

times precipitates men, you may rife again by your
vigilance and the ftruggles of your virtue; for true
courage never defpairs: But if you have once broken
down the barrier of honour and probity, your ruin is
inevitable: you can never revive the confidence which
is neceffary to make all important affairs fuccefsful,
nor reclaim men to the principles of virtue which you
have taught them to defpife. And what do you apprehend? Are you not brave enough to conquer
without treachery? Is not your valour, together with
the forces of fo many nations, fufficient for this? Let
us fight, let us die, if it muft be fo, rather than conquer by fuch vile means. Adraftus, the impious
Adraftus, is in our power, provided we abhor imitating his bafenefs and perfidy.

When Telemachus concluded his fpeech, he perceived that foft perfuafion had flowed from his lips,
and funk deep into their hearts. He obferved that
there was a profound filence throughout the whole
affembly; every one's thoughts being employed, not
on him or the graces of his words, but on the force
of truth, which was fo ftriking in the whole courfe
of his reafoning. Amazement was painted on their
faces. At length an hollow murmur was heard fpreading itfelf by little and little through the whole affembly. They all looked one upon another, being
afraid to fpeak firft, and waiting till the principal
commanders fhould declare themfelves, though every
one found it difficult to retain his fentiments. At laft
the grave Neftor pronounced thefe words:

Worthy fon of Ulyffes, the Gods prompted you to
fpeak, and Minerva, who fo often infpired your father, fuggefted to you the wife and generous counfel
which you have given us. I do not regard your youth,
I fee Minerva in all you have faid. You have pleaded
the caufe of virtue. Without virtue the greateft advantages are real loffes; without virtue men foon
draw on themfelves the vengeance of their enemies,
the jealoufy of their allies, the hatred of all good men,
and the juft wrath of the Gods. Let us therefore
leave

leave Venufium in the hands of the Lucanians, and
think of conquering Adraftus only by our courage.

He faid; and the whole affembly applauded the
wifdom of his words. But every one, as he gave his
applaufe, turned his eyes with amazement towards
the fon of Ulyffes, and imagined that he faw the wifdom of Minerva, his infpirer, shine forth in him.

There foon arofe another queftion in the council of
the kings, by which he did not acquire lefs glory.
Adraftus, ever bloody and perfidious, fent into the
camp one Acanthus a deferter, who was to poifon the
moft illuftrious chiefs of the army. He was particularly ordered to fpare no pains to effect the death of
the young Telemachus, who was already become the
terror of the Daunians. Telemachus, who had too
much courage and candour to be miftruftful, readily
and kindly received this wretch, who had feen Ulyffes in Sicily, and who related to him the adventures
of that hero. He fubfifted him, and endeavoured to
comfort him in his misfortunes; for Acanthus complained of having been deceived and unworthily
treated by Adraftus. But this was cherishing and
warming a venomous viper in his bofom, which was
ready to fting him to death. Another deferter was
taken whofe name was Arion, whom Acanthus was
fending back to Adraftus, to inform him of the ftate
of the confederate camp, and to affure him that he
would the next day poifon the principal kings and
Telemachus at an entertainment which the latter
was to give him. Arion being apprehended, con-
feffed his treafon, and it was fufpected that Acanthus
was concerned with him, becaufe they were intimate
friends; but Acanthus, who was a deep diffembler
and not to be daunted, defended himfelf fo artfully
that he could not be convicted, nor the bottom of the
confpiracy difcovered.

Several of the kings were of opinion that they
ought in this uncertainty to facrifice Acanthus to the
public fafety. He muft, faid they, be put to death;
the life of a fingle perfon is nothing, when the fafety

of

of so many princes is concerned. What if an innocent person perish, when the point in debate is the preservation of those who represent the Gods among men?

What an inhuman maxim! what barbarous policy, replied Telemachus; How! are you so lavish of human blood! O you who are appointed the shepherds of men, and who govern them only to take care of them as a shepherd takes care of his flock, you are it seems ravenous wolves and not shepherds; at most you are shepherds only to fleece and flay the flock, instead of leading it into good pastures. According to you a man is guilty the moment he is accused; to be suspected merits death; the innocent are at the mercy of the envious and the slanderer; and the more your tyrannical jealousy increases in your bosom, the greater number of victims must be slain.

Telemachus spoke these words with an authority and vehemence that carried an irresistible conviction with it, and overwhelmed the authors of such base advice with shame. He afterwards said in a milder tone: As for me I am not so fond of life as to pay so dear for it; I had rather that Acanthus should be a villain than be one myself, and that he should rob me of my life by treachery than that I should be so unjust as to put him to death on suspicion only. But have a little patience, ye princes, who as you are appointed kings, that is judges, of the people, should know how to try men with justice, wisdom and moderation; have patience I say, and give me leave to examine Acanthus in your presence.

Hereupon he questions Acanthus concerning his correspondence with Arion; he presses him with a thousand circumstances, and several times makes as if he would send him back to Adrastus, as a deserter that deserved to be punished, to see whether he was afraid of being sent back or not. But Acanthus's voice and countenance continued calm and composed, and from thence Telemachus concluded that he could not be innocent. Not being able however to draw

Q him

him into a confeſſion, Telemachus at laſt ſaid, Give
me your ring, I will ſend it to Adraſtus. At this demand of his ring Acanthus grew pale, and was in
confuſion. Telemachus, whoſe eyes were continually fixed upon him, perceived it and took the ring.
I will immediately ſend it, ſaid he, to Adraſtus by
the hands of your acquaintance Polytropas the Lucanian, and he ſhall pretend that he is ſent ſecretly by
you. If by this means we diſcover your correſpondence with Adraſtus, you ſhall die without mercy in
the moſt racking tortures; but if on the contrary you
now confeſs your guilt, you ſhall be pardoned, and
we will content ourſelves with ſending you to an
iſland where you ſhall want for nothing. Upon this
Acanthus made a full diſcovery ; and Telemachus
prevailing on the kings to give him his life according
to his promiſe, he was ſent to one of the Echinadian
iſlands, where he lived unmoleſted.

A little while after, one Dioſcorus, a Daunian of
an obſcure birth, but of a violent and daring ſpirit,
came by night to the camp of the allies, and made
them an offer of aſſaſſinating king Adraſtus in his
tent. This he was able to effect : for a man is maſter
of the lives of others, when he does not value his own.
This Dioſcorus breathed nothing but revenge, becauſe Adraſtus had taken from him his wife whom
he paſſionately loved, and who was equal in beauty
to Venus herſelf. He had privately concerted meaſures to enter the king's tent by night, and to be favoured in this attempt by ſeveral Daunian captains ;
but he thought it neceſſary that the confederate princes ſhould attack Adraſtus's camp at the ſame time,
that he might in the confuſion more eaſily eſcape,
and carry off his wife. If he could not carry her off,
he was content to periſh, after he had killed the king.

As ſoon as Dioſcorus had explained his deſign to
the kings, every body turned towards Telemachus,
as it were to ask his deciſion of the matter. The Gods,
ſaid he, who have preſerved us from traitors, forbid
us to employ them. And though we were not virtuous
enough

enough to abhor treason, yet our own interest would be sufficient to induce us to reject it; for when we have given a sanction to it by our example, we shall deserve to have it turned against us; and from that moment which of us would be safe? Adrastus may possibly avoid the blow which threatens him, and make it fall on the confederate kings. Besides, war would cease to be war; wisdom and virtue would be of no use, and we should see nothing but perfidy, treason and assassinations. We ourselves should feel, and should deserve to feel, their fatal effects, since we should authorise the greatest of evils. I think therefore that this traitor ought to be sent back to Adrastus. I own indeed that this prince does not deserve it; but all Hesperia and all Greece, which have their eyes upon us, deserve such a conduct from us as the price of their esteem. Besides, we owe to ourselves, we owe to the righteous Gods, this abhorrence of treachery.

Upon this Dioscorus was sent to Adrastus, who trembled at the danger he had been in, and could not enough wonder at the generosity of his enemies; for the wicked have no idea of pure and disinterested virtue. Adrastus could not but admire what he saw, though he had not resolution enough to commend it. This noble action of the allies recalled to his mind an odious remembrance of all his treacheries and cruelties. He sought to lessen the generosity of his enemies, and was ashamed to appear ungrateful to those to whom he owed his life; but corrupt men soon harden themselves against every thing which might give them the least compunction. Adrastus perceiving that the reputation of the allies daily increased, thought himself under a necessity of performing some signal action against them; and as it was not in his nature to do a virtuous one, he resolved at least to endeavour to obtain so eminent advantage over them by arms, and hastened to engage them.

The day of battle being come, Aurora in her rosy progress scarcely began to open the gates of the east to the sun, when the young Telemachus out-stripping

Q 2

the

the vigilance of the oldeft commanders, broke from
the arms of balmy fleep, and put all the officers in
motion. His helmet, crowned with waving hair, already glittered on his head, and the cuirafs he wore
dazzled the eyes of the whole army. The work of
Vulcan had, befides its native beauty, the fplendor of
the Ægis which was concealed in it. He held a fpear
in one hand, and pointed with the other to the feveral
pofts which it was neceffary to fecure. Minerva had
filled his eyes with a divine fire, and his countenance
with a noble majefty, which already promifed victory.
He marched ; and all the princes, forgetting their age
and dignity, found themfelves hurried along by a fuperior power, which compelled them to follow his
fteps. Impotent jealoufy could no longer find admif-
fion to their hearts. Every thing yields to him whom
Minerva invifibly leads by the hand. His behaviour
had nothing of impetuoufity or rashnefs : he was affable, calm, patient, always ready to hear others and
to profit by their counfels ; but active, cautious, extending his views to the remoteft exigencies, difpofing
every thing in the beft manner, never confounding
himfelf nor others, excufing errors, rectifying mifcarriages, obviating difficulties, never exacting too
much of any one, and every where infpiring freedom
and confidence. If he gave an order, it was in the
plaineft and moft perfpicuous terms ; he repeated it,
to give the perfon who was to execute it, a clearer
idea of it ; he faw by his eyes whether he apprehended
it right, and then made him explain in a familiar
manner, how he underftood his words, and what was
the principal end of his enterprife. When he had
thus founded the capacity of the perfon he employed,
and made him thoroughly underftand his defigns, he
did not fend him away till he had given him fome
mark of his efteem and confidence by way of encou-
ragement. Thus all whom he employed were full of
zeal to pleafe him and to fucceed in their commiffi-
ons, without being cramped by any apprehenfion of
his imputing their ill fuccefs to them ; for he excufed

all

all mifcarriages which did not proceed from the want of good will.

The horizon looked red and enflamed by the dawning rays of the fun, and the fea blazed with the fires of the new-born day. All the coaft was over-fpread with men, arms, horfes, rolling chariots; and a confufed uproar was heard, like that of the angry billows when Neptune in the deep abyfs ftirs up the lowering tempefts. Thus Mars began by the din of arms, and the horrid equipage of war, to fire every heart with fury. The plain was thick fet with briftling pikes, like ears of corn which hide the fertile furrows in the times of harveft. Already had a cloud of rifing duft gradually ftolen the heavens and the earth from the eyes of men, and confufion, horror, flaughter, ruthlefs death advanced.

The arrows hardly began to fly, when Telemachus lifting up his hands and eyes to heaven, uttered thefe words: O Jupiter, father of Gods and men, thou feeft the juftice of our caufe, and that we have not been ashamed to fue for peace. We engage with reluctance; we would fpare the blood of man, and do not hate even this cruel, this perfidious, this facrilegious foe. Behold thou and determine between him and us. If we muft die, our lives are in thy hands; if Hefperia is to be delivered, and the tyrant overthrown, it will be thy power and the wifdom of thy daughter Minerva which will give us the victory; the glory of it will be due to thee. Thou holdeft the balance, and decideft the fate of battles. For thee we fight; and as thou art righteous, Adraftus is more thy enemy than ours. If thy caufe is victorious, before the clofe of the day, the blood of a whole hecatomb fhall ftream on thy altars.

He faid, and inftantly drives his fiery foaming courfers into the thickeft ranks of the enemy. The firft he met was Periander the Locrian, clad in the skin of a lion which he had killed in his travels in Cilicia. He was armed like Hercules with an enormous club, and refembled the giants in ftrength and ftature. As foon

as he saw Telemachus, he despised his youth
and beautiful countenance. It well befits thee, said
he, effeminate boy, to dispute the glory of combat,
with us! Go, child, go to hell, and seek thy father.
As he spoke these words, he raised his knotty, ponderous and iron-spiky club, which looks like the
mast of a ship, which makes every one apprehensive
of its fall, and threatens the head of the son of
Ulysses. But he eludes the blow, and rushes upon
Periander as rapidly as an eagle cleaves the air. The
descending club dashes in pieces the wheel of a chariot which was near that of Telemachus.   Mean
while the young Greek wounds Periander in the
throat with a dart; the bubbling blood spouts from
the gaping wound, and stops his voice ; his fiery
steeds no longer feeling his fainting hand, and the
reins flowing on their necks, carry him here and there;
he falls from his chariot; his eyes are closed against
the light, and pallid death is already stamped on his
ghastly visage. Telemachus pitied him, and immediately gave his body to his domestics ; keeping the
club and lion's skin as a token of his victory.
   He then seeks Adrastus in the throng, and in
seeking him sends a croud of warriors to hell : Hileus,
whose car was drawn by a pair of steeds, which resembled those of the Sun, and were bred in the spacious
meadows which the Aufidus waters : Demoleon, who
in Sicily did heretofore almost equal Eryx in the
combat of the cæstus : Crantor, who was the host and
friend of Hercules, when that son of Jupiter, in his
way through Hesperia, deprived the infamous Cacus
of his life : Menecrates, who was said to resemble
Pollux in wrestling : Hypocoon the Salapian, who
imitated Castor's address and graceful manner in the
management of a steed : Eurymenides the famous
hunter, who was always besmeared with the blood of
bears and wild boars, which he killed on the snowy
tops of the cold Appennine, and who was said to be so
dear to Diana that she herself taught him the art of
shooting with arrows : Nicostratus, the vanquisher of
the

the giant, vho ufed to vomit fire on the rocks of mount
Garganus : Eleanthus, who was to marry young Pholoe, daughter of the river Liris. She had been promifed
by her father to him that should deliver her from a winged ferpent, which was engendered on the banks of the
river, and was to devour her in a few days, according
to the prediction of an oracle. This youth, through
an excefs of love, made a vow to kill the monfter or
to perish in the attempt ; he fucceeded but did not
tafte the fruits of his victory. For while Pholoe was
preparing for her happy nuptials, and impatiently expected Eleanthus, she heard that he had followed
Adraftus to the war, and that the fatal fifters had cruelly cut the thread of his life. She filled the woods
and the mountains near the river with her wailings ;
her eyes fwam in tears ; she tore off her lovely trefles;
she neglected the flowery garlands she ufed to gather,
and taxed the heavens with injuftice.   As she wept
inceffantly both night and day, the Gods moved by
her forrows, and by the prayers of the river, put an
end to her grief: For she poured forth fuch floods of
tears, that she was fuddenly changed into a fountain,
which gliding into the bofom of the river, mingles her
ftream with that of the God her father.   But the
water of this fountain is ftill bitter ; nor fprings the
grafs on its banks ; nor is there any shade but that of
the cyprefs on its melancholy borders.

Adraftus in the mean time hearing that Telemachus
fpread terror all around him, fought him with great
eagernefs; he expected that he should eafily conquer
fo young an adverfary, being furrounded by thirty
Daunians of extraordinary ftrength, dexterity and
courage, to whom he had promifed great rewards, if
they could by any means whatever deftroy Telemachus in the battle. Had they then met him, thefe
thirty men, by environing Telemachus's chariot,
while Adraftus attacked him in the front, would undoubtedly have flain him without any difficulty, but
Minerva mifled them.

Adraftus thought that he faw and heard Telemachus in a valley at the foot of a hill, where there was

Q 4   a crowd

a crowd of combatants; he runs, he flies, he longs
to sate himself with blood; but instead of Telemachus he finds the aged Nestor, who with a trembling
hand was throwing some random unavailing darts.
Adrastus in his rage attempts to kill him, but a band
of Pylians poured around their king.

Hereupon a cloud of arrows darkened the air, and
hid all the combatants; nothing was heard but the
doleful cries of the dying; and the clattering of the
arms of those who fell in the conflict; the earth groaned beneath an heap of dead, and rivers of blood
streamed every where. Bellona and Mars, with the
infernal Furies, clad in robes all dropping with gore
feasted their cruel eyes on the fight, and incessantly
renewed the rage of every heart. These Deities, the
deadly foes of mankind, chased far away from both
parties generous compassion, sedate valour, and soft
humanity; there was nothing in this confused and
enraged throng but slaughter, revenge, despair and
brutal fury. The sage and invincible Pallas herself
shivered, and started back with horror at the sight.

Mean time Philoctetes marching slowly, and holding the arrows of Hercules in his hands, advanced
to Nestor's assistance. Adrastus not being able to
reach the divine senior, had hurled his darts at several Pylians, and made them bite the ground. He
had already slain Eusilas, so swift of foot that he
hardly imprinted his footsteps in the sand, and who
in his own country out-run the most rapid currents
of the Eurotas and Alpheus. At his feet were fallen
Entiphron more lovely than Hylas, and as keen a
hunter as Hippolytus; Pterelas, who accompanied
Nestor to the siege of Troy, and was dear to Achilles himself for his strength and courage; Aristogi-
ton, who bathing in the waves of the river Acheloüs,
is said to have privately received of that God the
power of assuming all kind of forms: And indeed
he was so pliant and nimble in all his motions, that
he slipt out of the strongest hands. But Adrastus with
a thrust

a thrust of his spear rendered him motionless, and his soul immediately took its flight with his blood.

Nestor seeing his most valiant captains fall beneath the hands of the cruel Adrastus, like the golden ears in harvest beneath the keen sickle of the indefatigable reaper, forgot the danger to which he vainly exposed his age. His wisdom forsook him, and he thought only of pursuing with his eyes his son Pisistratus, who on his part ardently maintained the fight, to drive the danger from his father; but the fatal moment was come, when Pisistratus was to convince Nestor, how wretched men often are by living too long.

Pisistratus pushed so violently at Adrastus with his spear, that the Daunian would have fallen, had he not avoided it; but while Pisistratus, staggered with the false thrust he had made, was recovering his spear, Adrastus run his javelin into the midst of his belly. His bowels came out with a torrent of blood; his colour faded like a flower cropt by the hands of a nymph in the meadows; his eyes were almost extinguished, and his voice began to fail him. Alceus his governor, who was near him, caught him as he was ready to fall, and had only time to convey him into his father's arms, where he endeavoured to speak and give the last marks of his fondness; but as he opened his mouth he expired.

While Philoctetes was spreading slaughter and horror around him, to repel the efforts of Adrastus, Nestor clasped the body of his son in his arms, rending the heavens with his cries, and unable to bear the light. Wretch that I am, said he, in being a father and in living so long! Ah! why, ye cruel Fates! why did ye not cut the thread of my life when I chased the Calydonian boar; or in my expedition to Colchos, or at the first siege of Troy? I should not then have died inglorious, nor with anguish. I now drag a painful, despicable, impotent old age; I live but to suffer; I have no sense but of sorrow. O my son! my dear son Pisistratus! When I lost thy brother Antilochus, I had thee to comfort me; I have thee

Q 5

thee:

thee no more; nothing will comfort me now; all is over as to me. Hope, the only sweetner of human woes, is a blessing which concerns me not.   Antilochus! Pisistratus! O my dear children, I lost you both methinks to-day; the death of the one opens again the wound which the other had made in my heart. Never shall I behold thee more. Who shall close my eyes? Who collect my ashes? O my dear Pisistratus! thou as well as thy brother didst die like a man of courage; I alone cannot die.

This said, he attempted to kill himself with a dart which he had in his hand; but he was with-held. And the body of his son being wrested from him, the unhappy old man fell into a swoon, and was carried to his tent, where having a little recovered his strength he would have returned to the battle, had he not been detained by force.

Mean time Adrastus and Philoctetes were in quest of each other. Their eyes sparkled, like those of a lion and a leopard striving to tear each other in pieces, in the fields which the Cayster waters. Menaces, the rage of war, and bloody revenge appeared in their savage looks. They carry certain death wherever their hurl their darts, and all the combatants behold them with terror. They are now within sight of each other, and Philoctetes takes one of those dreadful arrows, which in his hands never mist their aim, and whose wounds were incurable; but Mars, who favoured the cruel and intrepid Adrastus, would not suffer him to perish so soon, being desirous of making him his instrument of prolonging the horrors of war, and of heightening the carnage. The Gods as yet forbore to make Adrastus an example of their justice, in order to chastise mankind and to shed their blood.

The moment Philoctetes designs to attack him, he himself is wounded by the spear of Amphimachus, a young Lucanian, who was more lovely than the famous Nireus, whose beauty was only inferior to that of Achilles of all the Greeks that fought at the fiege of Troy. Philoctetes was hardly wounded, when he aimed the arrows at Amphimachus which pierced him to the heart. His fine black eyes immediately loft their luftre, and were overfpread with the shades of death. The rofes of his lips, more ruddy than thofe with which the rifing Aurora ftrews the horizon, faded : a ghaftly palenefs deadened his cheeks : his foft, his delicate face was inftantly deformed. Philoctetes himfelf was moved with pity, and all the combatants made loud laments, feing the youth weltering in his blood, and his locks, as lovely as thofe of Apollo, trailing in the duft.

Philoctetes having flain Amphimachus was obliged to retire from the battle ; having loft a great deal of his blood and his ftrength. Befides, his old wound in the heat of the action feemed ready to bleed afresh and to renew his pains ; for the fon of Æfculapius by their divine skill had not been able to cure him entirely. Lo! he is ready to fall on an heap of bloody bodies which furround him ; but Archidamus, the moft bold and expert foldier of all the Œbalians, whom he had brought with him to found Petelia, forces him from the fight the moment Adraltus would eafily have felled him at his feet. Adraftus now finds nothing which prefumes to refift him, or to retard his victory : Every thing falls, every thing flies before him ; he refembles a rapid ftream, which having over-fwelled its mounds, fweeps away, with its furious torrent, the corn, the flocks, the shepherds and villages.

Telemachus heard at a diftance the shouts of the victors, and beheld the diforder of the confederates flying before Adraftus, like an herd of timorous deer crofling the fpacious plains, the woods, the mountains, and even the moft rapid rivers, when they are purfued by the hunters. He deeply fighs ; indignation is manifeft in his eyes ; he quits the place where he had long fought with great danger and glory ; he runs to fuftain the fugitives ; he advances all befmeared with the blood of a multitude of enemies

Q vj   whom

—whom he had ſtretched on the duſt ; and at a diſtance ſhouts loud enough to be heard by both armies.

Minerva had infuſed ſomething terrible into his voice, which made the neighbouring mountains ring : that of the cruel Mars ſounds not louder in Thrace, when he calls the infernal Furies, war and death. This ſhouting of Telemachus inſpires his own party with courage and intrepidity, and chills the enemy with fear. Even Adraſtus is aſhamed to find himſelf diſordered ; being terrified with I know not how many fatal preſages, and animated rather by deſpair than a ſedate valour. Thrice were his trembling knees going to ſink beneath him, and thrice he drew back without thinking on what he did. A ſwooning paleneſs and a cold ſweat ſpread over all his limbs ; his hoarſe and faultering voice could ſound no word diſtinct ; his eyes ſparkling with a gloomy fire, ſeem ready to ſtart out of his head : he looks like Oreſtes tortured by the Furies ; all his motions are convulſive. Now he begins to believe that there are Gods ; he fancies that he ſees them incenſed againſt him, and that he hears a hollow voice ariſing from the deepeſt hell, and citing him to dreary Tartarus. Every thing made him ſenſible of an heavenly and inviſible hand ſtretched over his head, and ready to fall heavy upon him. Hope was extinguiſhed in his heart, and his courage vaniſhed, like the day-light when the ſun ſinks into the boſom of the waves, and the earth is wrapt in the ſhades of night.

The impious Adraſtus, who had already been ſuffered to live too long, if mankind had not wanted ſuch a ſcourge ; the impious Adraſtus, I ſay, draws near his lateſt hour. He madly runs to meet his inevitable fate ; horror, ſtinging remorſe, conſternation, fury, rage, deſpair attend his ſteps. He ſcarcely ſee Telemachus, but he fancies that he ſees Avernus yawn, and whirlwinds of flames, iſſuing from dreary Phlegeton, ready to ſwallow him up. He cries out, and his mouth remains open without being able to utter a word. So a perſon aſleep in a frightful

ful dream open his lips, and ſtrives to ſpeak; but his ſpeech continually fails him, and he ſeeks it in vain. Adraſtus with a trembling haſty hand hurls his javelin at Telemachus. The latter is undaunted, like one favoured of the Gods, and defends himſelf with his shield. Victory already ſeems to cover him with her wings, and to hold a crown over his head. A calm and compoſed courage glittered in his eyes, and one would have taken him for Minerva herſelf, ſo wiſe and diſcreet he appears in the greateſt dangers. Adraſtus's javelin is repelled by the shield. Upon which the Daunian inſtantly draws his ſword, to deprive the ſon of Ulyſſes of the advantage of throwing his javelin in his turn. Telemachus ſeeing Adraſtus with his ſword in his hand, immediately draws his alſo, and drops his uſeleſs javelin.

When they were thus cloſely engaged, all the other combatants ſilently laid down their arms to gaze upon them, and from this ſingle combat expected the iſſue of the war. Their ſwords, bright as the flashes whence the bolts are hurled, frequently croſs each other, and deal their fruitleſs blows upon their burnished and reſounding armour. The two combatants ſtretch themſelves out, shrink themſelves up, ſtoop down, riſe again in an inſtant, and at length grapple with each other. The ivy growing at the foot of an elm, does not more cloſely embrace its hard and knotty trunk, with its entwining arms, even to its higheſt branches, than theſe two combatants graſp each other. Adraſtus having loſt nothing of his ſtrength, and that of Telemachus not being yet at its height; the former makes ſeveral efforts to ſtagger and throw his antagoniſt by ſurpriſe. At laſt he endeavours to ſeize the ſword of the young Greek, but in vain; for the moment he attempts it, Telemachus lifts him from the ground, and throws him on the ſand. And now this wretch, who had always deſpiſed the Gods, betrays an unmanly apprehenſion of death; he is ashamed to ask his life, and yet cannot help manifeſting his deſire of it. He endeavours to move Telemachus's compaſſion.

Son

Son of Ulysses, said he, I at length acknowledge the righteous Gods; they punish me as I have deserved; nothing but distress opens mens eyes, and shews them the truth; I see it, it condemns me; but let an unfortunate prince put you in mind of your father, who wanders far from Ithaca, and let him excite your pity.

Telemachus, who kneeled upon him, and had already raised his sword to plunge it into his throat, immediately replied; I sought nothing but victory and the peace of the nations I came to assist; I do not delight in blooshed. Live therefore, Adrastus; but live to repair your faults; restore every thing which you have usurped; re-establish peace and justice on the coast of great Hesperia, which you have stained by numberless massacres and treacheries; live and become another man. Learn by your fall that the Gods are righteous, that the wicked are miserable, that they deceive themselves by seeking for happiness in violence, inhumanity and falshood, and in short that nothing is so delightful and happy as a plain and steady virtue. Give us as hostages your son Metrodorus, with twelve of the principal persons of your nation.

This said, Telemachus suffers Adrastus to rise, and holds out his hands to him without suspecting his treachery. But Adrastus immediately darts another javelin at him, which was very short and he had kept concealed. It was so sharp, and so artfully thrown, that it would have pierced Telemachus's armour, had it not been divine. Adrastus at the same time runs behind a tree to avoid the pursuit of the young Greek. Whereupon Telemachus cries out, Lo! Daunians, the victory is ours; the impious wretch saves himself only by his treachery. Who fears not the Gods, is afraid of death; on the contrary, who fears the Gods, fears nothing but them. In speaking these words, he advances towards the Daunians, and makes a sign to those of his own party who were on the other side of the tree, to intercept the perfidious Adrastus. Adrastus

rus is ready to be taken, makes as if he would go
back again, and attempts to break through the Cretans who obftruct his paffage. But Telemachus, fwift
as a thunderbolt hurled by the hand of the father of
the Gods from the top of Olympus on the heads of
the guilty, flies inftantly on his enemy; he feizes him
with his victorious hands, he throws him on the
earth, as the cruel north-wind beats down the tender
harvefts which gild the fields; he hears him no more,
though the impious wretch makes a fecond attempt to
abufe his goodnefs; he plunges his fword into him,
and hurls him headlong into the flames of dreary
Tartarus, a punishment worthy of his crimes.

End of the Twentieth Book.

THE

THE
ADVENTURES
OF
TELEMACHUS,
SON of ULYSSES.

BOOK the TWENTY-FIRST.

The ARGUMENT.

Adraſtus being dead, the Daunians hold out their hands to the allies as a ſign of peace, and deſire a king of their own nation. Neſtor being inconſolable for the loſs of his ſon, abſents himſelf from the aſſembly of the chiefs, where ſeveral are of opinion that they ought to divide the countries of the conquered, and to yield the territory of Arpi to Telemachus. Far from accepting of this offer, Telemachus ſhews it to be the common intereſt of the allies to make Polyda-mas king of the Daunians, and to leave them in poſ-ſeſſion of their lands. He afterwards perſuades thoſe people to give the country of Arpy to Diomedes, who happened at that time to arrive in Heſperia. The troubles being thus ended, they all ſeparate, in order to return every one to his reſpective country.

ADRASTUS was hardly dead but all the Dau-nians, inſtead of bewailing their defeat and the loſs of their chief, rejoiced at their deliverance, and held out their hands to the allies in token of peace and reconciliation. Metrodorus, the ſon of Adraſtus, whom his father had bred up in maxims of diſſimu-lation, injuſtice and inhumanity, was coward enough

to fly; but a flave, an accomplice in all his infamous
and cruel actions, whom he had made free and loaded with riches, and to whom he had committed
himfelf in his flight, thought only of betraying him
for his own intereft; he flew him as he fled by a
wound in the back; he cut off his head, and carried to the camp of the confederates, expecting a
great reward for a crime which put an end to the
war. But they abhorred the villain, and ordered him
to be put to death.

Telemachus feeing the head of Metrodorus, who
was a youth of wonderful beauty, and naturally of
an excellent difpofition, which had been corrupted by
pleafures and ill examples, could not retain his tears.
Alas! cried he, lo the effects of the poifon of profperity in a young prince; the more elevated his
condition and the more fprightly his temper, the further he ftrays from every fentiment of virtue. I
fhould now perhaps have been like him, had not the
misfortunes in which, I thank the Gods, I was born,
and the inftructions of Mentor, taught me to govern
my paffions.

The affembled Daunians defired, as the only condition of peace, that they might have a king of their
own nation, who might by his virtues wipe off the
reproach with which the impious Adraftus had ftained
the crown. They thanked the Gods for deftroying the
tyrant; they crouded to kifs Telemachus's hand
which had been dipt in the monfter's blood, and
their defeat was as it were a triumph to them. Thus
in a moment irrecoverably fell the power which
threatened all others in Hefperia, and made fo many
nations tremble. As in platforms which feem firm
and immoveable, but are by little and little under-
mined, the feeble toils which attack their foundations are a long while derided, nothing appears to
be weakened, all is fmooth, nothing fhakes; while
all the props are gradually deftroyed, till the moment the earth finks, and leaves a chafm behind it:
So an unjuft and fraudful power, whatever fuccefs

it

it may procure by its violence, digs a pit beneath its
own feet. Treachery and cruelty by degrees fap all
the moft folid foundations of unlawful authority.
Men admire it, and dread it, and tremble before it,
till the inftant it is no more. It finks beneath its
own weight, and nothing can raife it up again;
becaufe it hath with its own hands deftroyed the
true fupports of probity and juftice, which beget love
and confidence.

The leaders of the army affembled the next day to
grant the Daunians a king, and every one was delighted to fee the two camps blended together by fo
unexpected a friendfhip, and the two armies which
were now become but one. The fage Neftor was not
in a condition to be prefent at this council, becaufe
his grief and age had withered his heart, as a fhower
beats down and caufes a flower to languifh in the
evening, which in the morning, while Aurora was
rifing, was the glory and ornament of the verdant
fields.   His eyes were become inexhauftible fountains of tears. Balmy fleep, which fooths the acuteft
pains, fled far away from them; and hope, the
food of the human heart, was extinguifhed in him.
All aliments were bitter to this unfortunate old man.
The light was odious to him; his foul defired only
to quit his body, and to plunge into the eternal night
of Pluto's empire.   In vain was all the difcourfe of
his friends; his drooping heart loathed their friendfhip, as a fick man loaths the moft delicate food:
To all the moft affecting things which could be faid
to him, he only replied by groans and fighs. He
now and then was heard to fay, O Pififtratus! Pififtratus! Pififtratus! my fon! thou calleft me, I come.
Thou, Pififtratus, wilt render death a pleafure to me.
O my dear fon! the only bleffing I crave, is to fee
thee again on the Stygian fhore. And then would he
pafs whole hours without fpeaking a word, fighing, and
lifting up his hands and tearful eyes to heaven.

Mean while the affembled princes were waiting
for Telemachus, who remained with Pififtratus's
body,

body, ſtrewing a profuſion of flowers, and the moſt
exquiſite perfumes upon it, and shedding the bittereſt
tears. My dear companion! ſaid he, I shall never
forget my ſeeing thee at Pylos, my going with thee
to Sparta, and my finding thee again on the coaſt of
the great Heſperia. I am thy debtor for a thouſand
and a thouſand good offices; I loved thee, thou
lovedſt me alſo : I knew thy valour; it would have
ſurpaſt that of ſeveral famous Greeks. Alas! it has
occaſioned thee a glorious death; but then it has
robbed the world of a blooming virtue which would
have equalled that of thy father. Yes, thy wiſdom
and eloquence would, when matured by age, have
been, like that ſenior's, the admiration of all Greece.
Thou didſt already poſſeſs that ſweet inſinuation, which
whenever he ſpeaks, is irreſiſtible ; that ſimple manner of narration; that ſage moderation, which is a
charm to ſooth the irritated mind; that authority,
which ariſes from wiſdom and the force of good
counſels. When thou ſpokeſt, every one lent an ear,
every one was prepoſſeſſed in thy favour, every one
wished to find thee in the right; thy plain, thy un-
adorned words ſtole as gently into the heart as dews
deſcend on the ſpringing graſs. Alas! how many
bleſſings which we enjoyed a few hours ſince, are
ravished from us for ever! Piſiſtratus, whom I embraced in the morning, is now no more, nothing
but a ſad remembrance of him is left us. Ah! hadſt
thou cloſed Neſtor's eyes, and not we thine, he
would not then have ſeen what he now ſees, nor have
been the moſt wretched of fathers.

This ſaid, Telemachus ordered the gory wound in
Piſiſtratus's ſide to be washed, and cauſed him to be
laid on a purple bed : Where with his head reclined
and pale as death, he reſembles a young tree, which
having covered the earth with its shade, and shot its
flourishing branches to heaven, is wounded by the
keen axe of the woodman ; and having no longer any
hold of its roots, or the earth, that fruitful mother
which nourishes her plants in her boſom, it droops
and

and loses its verdure; it can no longer support itself, it falls; its branches, which used to hide the heavens, are faded, withered, dragged in the dust; it is now but a mere trunk, cut down and despoiled of all its honours. Thus Pisistratus, a prey to death, was now borne away by those who were to lay him on the fatal pyre. The flames already mount to heaven. A band of Pylians with downcast streaming eyes, with arms reversed, and gentle steps attended. The body is quickly burnt, and the ashes are put into a golden urn, which Telemachus, who takes care of the whole ceremony, commits as a great treasure to Callimachus, who had ben Pisistratus's governor. Keep these ashes, said he, the sad but precious remains of him whom you loved, keep them for his father; but do not present them unto him till he has fortitude enough to ask for them: What provokes sorrow at one time, alleviates it at another.

Telemachus afterwards went into the assembly of the confederate kings, where every one, as soon as he saw him, was silent in order to hear him. He blushed, and could not be prevailed on to speak. The praises which were bestowed upon him by publick acclamations, on account of his late actions, increased his confusion, and he wished that it had been in his power to hide himself. This was the first time he ever appeared confounded and dubious. At length he asked it as a favour, that they would not commend him any more. Not, said he, that I do not love praise, especially when it is bestowed by such good judges of virtue; but because I am apprehensive of being too fond of it; its corrupts mankind, it makes them full of themselves, and renders them vain and presumptuous: We should deserve and shun it. There is a resemblance between the justest and most groundless praises; and tyrants, the most wicked of all men, are those who cause themselves to be praised the most by flatterers. What pleasure is there in being commended like them? Valuable praise is that which you will give men in my absence, If I am happy enough

enough to deferve it. If you think me really virtuous, you mult alfo think me modeft and apprehenfive of vanity. Spare me therefore if you efteem me, and do not praife as if I were enamoured of applaufe.

Telemachus having fpoken thus, made no reply to thofe who continued to extol him to the skies, and by an air of indifference quickly put a ftop to the encomiums they beftowed upon him. They began to apprehend that their praifes were offenfive; but their admiration increafed, every one knowing the tendernefs he had shewed for Pififtratus, and the care he had taken to pay him the laft offices of friendship. The whole army was more affected with thefe marks of the goodnefs of his heart, than with the amazing proofs he had given of his wifdom and valour. He is wife, he is valiant, faid they in private to each other; he is beloved of the Gods, and the true hero of our age; he is more than human. But all this is only marvellous and matter of aftonishment. He is humane, he is good, he his a faithful and affectionate friend; he is compaffionate, liberal, beneficent, and wholly theirs whom he ought to love; he is the delight of thofe who live with him; he has divefted himfelf of his haughtinefs, indifference and pride. This is what is ufeful, this is what touches the heart, this is what endears him to us, and makes us affected with all his virtues: This is what makes us all ready to lay down our lives for him.

As foon as thefe difcourfes were ended, the council confidered the neceffity of giving the Daunians a king. Moft of the princes who were prefent, were of opinion that they ought to divide Daunia, as a conquered country, among themfelves; and they offered Telemachus for his share the fertile territory of Arpi, which twice in a year yields the rich prefents of Ceres, the delicious gifts of Bacchus, and the ever-verdant fruits of the olive, a tree facred to Minerva. This country, faid they, ought to make you forget the barren Ithaca and its cottages, the frightful rocks of Dulichium, and the favage woods of Zacynthus. Go no longer in queft of your father, who without
                                                           doubt

doubt perished in the waves at the promontory of Caphareus, through the vengeance of Nauplius and the wrath of Neptune; nor of your mother, who has yielded to her suitors since your departure; nor of your country, whose soil is not so favoured of heaven as that which we offer you. He heard these discourses with patience; but the rocks of Thrace and Thessaly are not more deaf and insensible to the plaints of despairing lovers, than Telemachus was to all these offers.

For my part, replied he, I am not affected with riches and pleasures. What profits it to possess a greater extent of land, and to govern a greater number of men? The prince thereby but increases his troubles and lessens his liberty. Even the wisest and most moderate persons find misery enough in life, without adding to it the toils of governing intractable, restless, unjust, false and ungrateful men. When a man seeks to be the master of others for his own sake, and regards nothing but his own authority, pleasures and glory; he is impious, and a tyrant, and the scourge of the human race. When on the contrary he endeavours to govern them according to right maxims, and only for their own good, he is not so much their master as their guardian; he gets nothing by it but infinite trouble, and is far from desiring to stretch his authority farther. The shepherd who does not prey upon his flock, who defends it against wolves at the hazard of his life, and watches both night and day to lead it into rich pastures, has no desire to increase the number of his sheep, nor to seize on those of his neighbour; this were to increase his toils. Though I have never governed, added Telemachus, yet have I learnt from laws and wise legislators, how painful an office it is to rule cities and kingdoms. I am therefore contented with my barren Ithaca. Though it be small and barren, I shall acquire sufficient glory, if I reign over it with justice, piety and courage. My reign will even commence but too soon. The Gods grant that my father,

escaping

escaping the fury of the billows, may reign over it to the extremest old age, and that I may long learn under him how to subdue my passions, in order to know how to govern those of a whole nation!

Telemachus then said, Hear, ye assembled princes, what I think myself obliged to say to you for your own interest. If you give the Daunians a just king, he will govern them with justice and teach them how beneficial it is to preserve their sincerity, and never to usurp the dominions of their neighbours; which they could never learn under the impious A-drastus. While they are swayed by a wise and moderate prince, you will have nothing to apprehend from them. They will be indebted to you for the good king that you will have given them; they will be indebted to you for the peace and prosperity they will enjoy. Instead of attacking, they will continually bless you, and both the prince and the people will be the work of your hands. If on the contrary you divide their country among yourselves, the evils which will ensue, and of which I tell you beforehand, are these : The Daunians driven to despair will begin the war again; they will justly fight for their liberty, and the Gods, who are enemies to tyranny, will fight for them. And if the Gods interfere, you will sooner or later be confounded, and your prosperity will vanish like smoke. Counsel and wisdom will be taken from your commanders, courage from your armies, and fertility from your lands. You will deceive yourselves with false hopes, you will be rash in your enterprizes, you will silence men of probity who tell you the truth, you will fall of a sudden, and it will be said of you, Are these the flourishing nations who were to give law to the whole earth ? Lo ! they fly before their enemies ; they are the sport of nations who trample them under their feet. These are the doings of the Gods : this is what unjust, haughty and inhuman nations deserve.

Again,

Again, confider that if you attempt to divide this conqueft among you, you will unite all the neighbouring nations againft you.   Your confederacy, formed to defend the common liberty of Hefperia againft Adraftus, will become odious ; and you yourfelves will be juftly accufed by all the world of aiming at univerfal tyranny.   But fuppofing that you are victorious over the Daunians and all other nations, this victory will prove your deftruction, and I will tell you in what manner.   Confider that this enterprife will diffolve your union. As it is not founded on juftice, you will have no rule to fettle every claimant's pretenfions among yourfelves ; every one will infift that his fhare of the conqueft be proportioned to his power ; not one of you will have authority enough over the reft to make a peaceable partition.   Lo ! the fource of a war, of which your grandchildren will not fee the end.   Is it not better to be juft and moderate, than to follow one's ambition through fuch a multitude of dangers and inevitable calamities ? Are not a profound peace, its train of fweet and innocent pleafures, a happy plenty, the friendship of one's neighbours, the glory which is infeparable from juftice, the authority which is acquired in rendering ourfelves by our integrity the arbiter of all foreign nations ; are not thefe, I fay, more defirable bleffings than the foolish vanity of an unjuft conqueft ? O kings ! O princes ! you fee that I have no intereft in what I fay ; have regard therefore to one who loves you enough to contradict and difpleafe you, by fetting the truth before you.

While Telemachus was difcourfing in this manner with an authority which they had never feen in any other, and all the aftonished and fufpenceful princes were admiring the wifdom of his counfels, there was heard a confufed noife which fpread itfelf through the camp, and reached even to the place where the affembly was held. A ftranger, it was faid, is juft landed on this coaft with a band of foldiers. This unknown perfon is of a lofty mien ; every thing in him looks
heroic ;

heroic; one eafily perceives that he has fuffered a long while, and that his great courage has rendered him fuperior to all his fufferings. The people of the country, who guard the coaft, at firft refolved to repel him as an enemy that was come to invade them: But drawing his fword with an intrepid air, he told them that he knew how to defend himfelf in cafe he were attacked, but that he defired nothing but peace and hofpitality. Upon which he held out an olive branch as a fuppliant; he was heard; he defired to be brought before thofe who rule in this part of Hef--peria, and is conducted hither to be examined by the affembled kings.

This was hardly faid, but the ftranger entered with a majefty which furprifed the whole affembly. He might eafily have been taken for the God of war, when he affembles his blood-thirfty troops in the mountains of Thrace. He began thus:

O ye shepherds of the people, who are undoubtedly affembled here to defend your country againft its enemies, or to give life to the moft righteous laws, hear a man whom fortune has perfecuted. May the Gods grant that you may never tafte the like diftrefs! I am Diomed, king of Ætolia, who wounded Venus at the fiege of Troy. The vengeance of that Goddefs purfues me through the whole world. Neptune, who can refufe nothing to the divine daughter of the fea, gave me up to the rage of the winds and the billows, which have often dashed my ships in pieces againft the rocks. Inexorable Venus has robbed me of all hopes of ever feeing again my kingdom, my family, and that grateful light of the country where I firft beheld the day. No, I shall never fee more what was deareft in the world to me. I come, after various shipwrecks, to feek on thefe unknown shores a little repofe and a fafe retreat. If you fear the Gods, and efpecially Jupiter who takes care of ftrangers; if you have any fenfe of pity, refufe me not fome barren corner of thefe fpacious regions, fome defert, fome fandy fpot, or fteepy rocks,

R   where

where I and my companions may found a city which may at least be a melancholy image of our lost country. We only desire some small tract which is useless to you. We will live in peace and strict friendship with you; your enemies shall be ours; we will espouse all your interests, and desire nothing but to live according to our own laws.

While Diomed was speaking thus, Telemachus keeping his eyes fixed upon him, discovered all the different passions in his countenance. When Diomed began to mention his long sufferings, he hoped that this majestic person would prove to be his father. As soon as he had declared that he was Diomed, Telemachus's countenance withered like a beautiful flower, blasted by the cruel breath of the bitter north-winds. And at last Diomed's complaint of the implacable wrath of a Goddess melted his soul, by reviving his idea of the like calamities which his father and he had suffered; tears of grief and joy run down his cheeks, and he immediately fell upon Diomed's neck and embraced him.

I am, said he, the son of Ulysses whom you formerly knew, and who was not unuseful to you when you seized the famous horses of Rhesus. The Gods have treated him as well as you without mercy. If there is truth in the oracles of Erebus, he is still alive; but alas! he lives not for me. I have abandoned Ithaca in quest of him, but I cannot find him, nor my way back to Ithaca. Judge by my distress of my pity for yours. The benefit of afflictions is to learn to sympathize with others in their troubles. Though I am but a stranger here, yet have I the power, O mighty Diomed, (for notwithstanding the miseries which overwhelmed my country in my infancy, I have not been so ill educated as to be ignorant of your glory in battle;) I have the power, I say, O most invincible of all the Greeks next to Achilles, to procure you some relief. The princes here present are humane; they are sensible that there is no virtue, no true courage, no solid glory without humanity.

nity. Misfortune adds a new luftre to the glory of the great. They are not perfect, till they have tafted of adverfity ; their lives not affording examples of patience and fortitude. Virtue in diftrefs melts every heart which has any relifh for virtue. Leave the care therefore of your confolation to us ; fince the Gods, in fending you hither, confer a favour upon us, and we ought to think ourfelves happy in being able to foften your miferies.

While he was fpeaking, Diomed looked ftedfaftly and with aftonishment upon him, and found his heart greatly affected. They embraced as if they had been long bound in the bands of a ftrict friendship. O worthy fon of the wife Ulyffes, faid Diomed, I per- ceive in you the fweetnefs of his countenance, the grace of his fpeech, the ftrength of his eloquence, the noblenefs of his fentiments, and the wifdom of his thoughts.

Philoctetes then embraced the great fon of Tydeus, and they related to each other their difaftrous adven- tures. Philoctetes afterwards faid, You will without doubt be very glad to fee the fage Neftor ; he has juft loft Pififtratus the laft of his children, and all that is now left him in life is a tearful path which leads him to the grave. Come and footh his grief ; an unfortunate friend is fitter than any other to allay the anguish of his heart.

Hereupon they repaired to Neftor's tent, whofe mind and fenfes were fo depreft by grief, that he hardly knew Diomed again. At firft Diomed wept with him, and their interview redoubled the old man's forrow ; but by degrees the prefence of this friend relieved his heart, and one might eafily per- ceive that his woes were a little fufpended by the pleafure of reciting his fufferings, and of hearing in his turn what had happened to Diomed.

While they were difcourfing together, the affem- bled kings and Telemachus were confidering what they were to do. Telemachus advifed them to give Diomed the country of Arpi, and to choofe Polyda-

R 2   mas,

mas, who was of their nation, king of the Daunians. This Polydamas was a famous general whom Adraſtus, through jealouſy would never employ, leſt the ſucceſs of his arms, of which he hoped alone to have all the glory, should be attributed to this able commander. Polydamas had often told him in private, that he expoſed his life and the ſafety of the ſtate too much in this war againſt ſo many confederate nations, and had endeavoured to prevail on him to obſerve a more upright and moderate conduct towards his neighbours; but men who hate the truth, hate thoſe alſo who are bold enough to ſpeak it, and are not affected with their ſincerity, their zeal, or diſintereſtedneſs. The ſeducements of proſperity hardened Adraſtus's heart againſt the moſt wholeſome counſels. By not following them, he daily triumphed over his enemies; for haughtineſs, breach of faith and violence, continually made him victorious. The evils with which Polydamas had ſo long threatened him, did not happen. Adraſtus laughed at an apprehenſive wiſdom, which was perpetually foreſeeing inconveniencies. Polydamas became inſupportable to him; he was removed from all his poſts, and left to languiſh in ſolitude and poverty.

Polydamas was at firſt greatly dejected at this diſgrace; but it gave him what he wanted, by showing him the vanity of exalted ſtations. He became wiſe at his own expence; he rejoiced that he had been unfortunate; he learned by degrees to ſuffer, to live upon a little, calmly to nouriſh his ſoul with the truth, to cultivate ſecret virtues, which are of much greater worth than the glaring; in fine, to live without mankind. He dwelt in a deſert at the foot of mount Garganus, where an half-arched rock ſerved him for a houſe; a brook which fell from a mountain, ſlaked his thirſt, and ſome trees preſented him their fruits. He had two ſlaves, who tilled a little field, with whom he himſelf toiled with his own hands. The earth liberally rewarded him for his pains, and ſuffered him to want for nothing; he had

not

not only fruits and pulſe in abundance, but all ſorts
or fragrant flowers alſo. . There he deplored the mi-
ſery of nations, which the mad ambition of a prince
hurries on to their ruin.   There he daily expected
that the righteous Gods, notwithſtanding their for-
bearance, would cruſh the impious Adraſtus.   The
more his proſperity encreaſed, the nearer he thought
he ſaw his inevitable fall ; for imprudent meaſures
attended with ſucceſs, and power ſcrewed up to the
higheſt pitch of abſolute authority, are the forerun-
ners of the downfall of kings and kingdoms.   When
he heard of Adraſtus's defeat and death, he diſcovered
no joy that he had foreſeen it, nor that he was rid
of the tyrant ; he only grieved leſt he ſhould. ſee the
Daunians in ſervitude.

This was the man whom Telemachus propoſed
to be advanced to the throne.   He had for ſome time
been acquainted with his courage and virtue ; for
Telemachus, according to Mentor's advice, was
every where continually informing himſelf of the
good and bad qualities of all perſons who were in
any conſiderable poſt, not only among the confederate nations who ſerved in this war, but among
the enemy alſo.   His principal care in every place
was to find out and ſift the men who had any particular talent or virtue.

The confederate princes were at firſt a little unwilling to place Polydamas on the throne.   We have
experienced, ſaid they, how formidable a king of the
Daunians who underſtands and delights in war, is to
his neighbours.   Polydamas is a great commander,
and may bring us into great dangers.   But Telemachus replied, Polydamas indeed underſtands war, but
he loves peace ; and theſe are the two very things
which we ought to wiſh for.   A man who knows
the calamities, dangers and difficulties of war, is
much better qualified to avoid it than one who has
no experience of them. Polydamas has learned to reliſh the bleſſings of a quiet life ; he condemned the
enterpriſes of Adraſtus, and foreſaw their fatal conſe-

R 3   quences.

quences. A weak and ignorant prince is more to be dreaded by you, than a man who will enquire into and determine every thing himself. A weak, ignorant and inexperienced prince will see only with the eyes of a paffionate favourite, or of a flattering, turbulent, and ambitious minifter. He will therefore blindly engage himfelf in war contrary to his inclinations; you will never be fure of him, for he will never have it in his power to be fure of himfelf; he will break his word with you, and will quickly reduce you to fuch extremities, that you muft deftroy him, or he you. Is it not more advantageous, more fafe, and at the fame time more juft and noble to make a faithful return to the confidence of the Daunians, and to give them a king worthy of commanding?

This fpeech convincing the whole affembly, Polydamas was propofed to the Daunians, who were impatiently waiting for an anfwer. When they heard the name of Polydamas, they replied, we now plainly perceive that the confederate princes defign to deal fincerely and to make an eternal peace with us, fince they give us for our king a man fo virtuous and fo capable of governing. Had they propofed to us a cowardly, an effeminate and ignorant perfon, we should have thought that they only intended to deprefs us and to change the form of our government, and we should fecretly have retained a lively refentment of fo cruel and artful a conduct; but the choice of Polydamas is a proof of their real candour. The allies without doubt expect nothing from us but what is juft and noble, fince they give us a king who is incapable of doing any thing contrary to the liberty and glory of our country. We accordingly proteft in the fight of the righteous Gods, that rivers shall uproll to their fources, before we ceafe to love fuch beneficent princes. May your lateft pofterity be mindful of the benefit which we this day receive, and renew from generation to generation the peace of the golden age through the whole coaft of Hefperia!

Telemachus

Telemachus then propofed to the Daunians the giving the fields of Arpi to Diomed, to fettle a colony there. This new people, faid he, will be indebted to you for their eftablishment in a country which you do not cultivate. Remember that all men ought to love each other; that the earth is too large for them ; that you muft have neighbours, and that it is beft to have fuch as may be obliged to you for their fettlement. Pity the misfortunes of a prince who cannot return to his own country. Polydamas and he, being united together in the bands of juftice and virtue, which alone are lafting, will maintain you in a profound peace, and render you formidable to all the neighbouring nations that may think of aggrandizing themfelves. You fee, ye Daunians, that we have given your nation a king capable of raifing its glory to the heavens; do you therefore on your part give, at our requeft, a tract of land which is of no ufe to you, to a king who is worthy of all kind of fuccour.

The Daunians replied, that they could refufe Telemachus nothing, fince he had procured them Polydamas for their king. Hereupon they went to feek him in his defert, and to place him on the throne ; having firft given the fertile plains of Arpi to Diomed, to found a new kingdom there. The allies were over-joyed at this grant, becaufe this colony of Greeks might powerfully affift their party, if the Daunians should ever attempt to renew the ufurpations of which Adraftus had given an ill example.

And now all the princes prepared to take their leave of each other. Telemachus with tears in his eyes departed with his troop; having firft tenderly embraced the valiant Diomed, the fage and difconfolate Neftor, and the famous Philoctetes, the worthy inheritor of the arrows of Hercules.

End of the twenty-firft Book.

THE

ADVENTURES

OF

TELEMACHUS,

SON of ULYSSES.

BOOK the TWENTY-SECOND.

The ARGUMENT.

Telemachus arriving at Salentum is suprised to see the country so well cultivated, and to find so little magnificence in the city. Mentor explains the reasons of this change, points out the wrong measures which usually hinder a state from flourishing, and proposes the conduct and government of Idomeneus as a model for him. Telemachus afterwards opens his heart to Mentor concerning his inclination to marry Antiope the daughter of that king. Mentor joins with him in commending her good qualities, and assures him that the Gods design her for him; but that at present he ought to think only of departing for Ithaca, and of freeing Penelope from the persecutions of her suitors.

THE young son of Ulysses burnt with impatience to join Mentor again at Salentum, and to embark with him in order to return to Ithaca, where he hoped that his father might be arrived. When he approached Salentum, he was greatly astonished to see all the country round it, which he had left almost wholly waste and desert, cultivated like a garden, and full of diligent labourers. He knew that this must
be

be the work of the wife Mentor. As he afterwards
entered the city, he obferved that there were fewer
traders in the luxuries of life, and much lefs magnificence. Telemachus was not pleafed at this, for he
was naturally fond of every thing which is fplendid
and polite; but he quickly changed his mind. He
from afar beheld Idomeneus and Mentor coming
towards him, and his heart was immediately tranfported with joy and tendernefs Notwithflanding
his fuccefs in the war againft Adraftus, he was apprehenfive that Mentor might be diffatisfied with
him, and, as he advanced, confulted his eyes to fee
whether he had any thing to reproach him with.

Idomeneus immediately embraced Telemachus as
his own fon; Telemachus afterwards threw himfelf
on Mentor's neck, and bedewed him with his tears.
Mentor faid to him, I am fatisfied with your conduct,
you have committed great faults, but they have taught
you to know and to be diffident of yourfelf. · Men
often reap more fruit from their errors than from their
glorious actions. Great actions puff up the heart,
and infpire a dangerous prefumption; errors make a
man enter into himfelf, and reftore him the wifdom
which he loft while he was fuccefsful. What yet remains for you to do, is to praife the Gods, and not to
court the praifes of men. You have performed great
things, but own the truth; you can hardly be faid to
have performed them. Is it not true that the power
to perform them was infufed into you, like fomething
foreign to your nature? Were you not like to have
ruined all by your paffions and imprudence? Did you
not feel that Minerva as it were transformed you into
a perfon fuperior to yourfelf, to make you her inftrument of performing what you have done? She reftrained all your failings, as Neptune, when he ftills
a ftorm, reftrains the angry billows.

While Idomeneus was eagerly asking queftions of
the Cretans who were returned from the war. Telemachus was thus liftening to the wife counfels of Mentor. He afterwards turned his eyes with amazement

on every fide, and faid to Mentor, here is a change of
which I cannot comprehend the reafon: Has any
calamity befallen Salentum in my abfence ? Whence
comes it that one no longer fees that magnificence
which shone every where at my departure ? I now
fee neither gold, nor filver, nor precious ftones; the
habits are plain ; the buildings which are carrying on
are lefs fpacious and have fewer ornaments; arts languish, and the city is become a defert.

Mentor replied with a fmile, Did you obferve the
condition of the country round the city ? Yes, anfwered Telemachus, I faw that tillage is every where
efteemed, and that the fields are cultivated. Which is
preferable, added Mentor, a city proud of its marble,
gold and filver, with an untilled and barren country,
or a well-cultivated and fruitful country, with a city
that is modeft in its building and manners ? A great
city crowded with artifts, who are employed in cor-
rupting mens manners by adminiftring to their luxury, and furrounded with a poor and ill-cultivated
kingdom, refembles a monfter, whofe head is of an
enormous bulk, and bears no proportion to its ftarved
and meagre body : It is the number of the inhabitants and the plenty of provifions which conftitute the
true ftrength and the true riches of a kingdom. Idomeneus has now innumerable fubjects who are indefatigable in labour, and crowd the whole extent of
his country, which is now but one city, and Salentum no more than the center of it. We have tranfported from the city into the country, men who were
wanted in the country, and who were fuperfluous in
the city. We have moreover allured a great many
foreigners into the kingdom. The more thefe people multiply, the more are the fruits of the earth
multiplied by their labour ; this calm, this gentle increafe inlarges his kingdom more than a conqueft.
We have expelled from the city only fuperfluous arts,
which divert the poor from tilling the earth to fatisfy
their real wants, and corrupt the rich by plunging
them into pomp and luxury ; we have not done the
                                                    leaft

leaſt prejudice to the liberal arts, nor to men who really have a genius to cultivate them. Thus is Idomeneus much more powerful than he was when you admired his magnificence. That dazzling luſtre concealed a weakneſs and indigence which would ſoon have overthrown his empire: he has now a greater number of ſubjects, and he ſubſiſts them with more eaſe. Theſe men, inured to labour, pain, and a contempt of life through their attachment to good laws, are all ready to fight in the defence of a country which they have cultivated with their own hands. And this kingdom which you think decayed, will ſoon be the wonder of Heſperia.

Remember, Telemachus, that there are two evils in the government of a nation, which are hardly ever cured. The firſt is an unjuſt and too violent a power in the prince; the ſecond is luxury, which corrupts the morals of the people. When kings accuſtom themſelves to know no law but their own abſolute will, and no longer curb their paſſions, they may do any thing; but by their being able to do any thing, they ſap the foundations of their power. They have no certain rules or maxims of government; every one ſtrives who ſhall flatter them moſt; they have no longer any ſubjects; nothing is left them but ſlaves, whoſe number daily decreaſes. Who will tell them the truth? Who will ſet bounds to the torrent? Every thing gives way; the wiſe fly, hide themſelves, and mourn in private. Nothing but a ſudden and violent revolution can reduce this overflowing power into its natural channel, and the meaſures which might circumſcribe; often irrecoverably deſtroy it. Nothing is ſo near a fatal fall as authority ſtretched too far. It reſembles an over-ſtrained bow, which at length ſnaps of a ſudden, unleſs it be ſlackened; but who will preſume to ſlacken it? The very ſoul of Idomeneus was ſeduced by the allurements of this power; he had been dethroned but not undeceived. The Gods were forced to ſent us hither, to put him out of conceit with this, blind and exceſſive power, which does not

befit men; and a fort of miracles moreover were neceffary to open his eyes.

The other almoft incurable evil is luxury. As
too much power poifons princes, fo luxury poifons a
whole nation. It is faid that luxury feeds the poor
at the expence of the rich, as if the poor could not
get their bread more ufefully by multiplying the
fruits of the earth, without debauching the rich by
the refinements of voluptuoufnefs. A whole nation
habituates itfelf to look upon the moft fuperfluous
things as the neceffaries of life; new neceffaries are
daily invented, and men can no longer live without
things which were unknown thirty years before.
This luxury is called a good tafte, the perfection of
arts, and the politenefs of the nation. This vice,
which is the fource of an infinite number of others,
is commended as a virtue, and fpreads its contagion from the prince down to the very dregs of
the people. The near relations of the king imitate
his magnificence; the nobility that of the king's relations; the middle fort ftrive to come up to the nobility, (for where is the man who forms a right
judgment of himfelf?) and the loweft defire to pafs
for the middle fort. Thus every one lives above his
circumftances; fome through oftentation, and to
glory in their riches; others through a falfe fenfe of
shame, and to conceal their poverty: Even thofe who
are wife enough to condemn fo great a diforder, are
not enough fo to dare to be the firft to rife up againft
it, and to fet contrary examples. A whole nation is
ruined, and all conditions of men confounded. The
defire of getting money to fupport a vain expence,
corrupts the pureft minds; to be rich is the only
thing that is minded, and to be poor is infamous.
Let a man be learned, wife, virtuous; let him inftruct
mankind, win battles, fave his country, facrifice all
his own interefts; yet will he be defpifed, if his talents are not fet off with pomp and show. Even they
who have not money, endeavour to feem to have it,
and fpend as if they really had it: they borrow, they
cheat,

cheat, they use a thousand artifices to procure it. But who will cure these evils? The taste and customs of a whole nation must be changed, and new laws must be enacted. And who can attempt this but a king who is so much of a philosopher, and so prudent, as to put out of countenance, by the example of his own moderation, all those who are fond of ostentatious expences, and to encourage the wise, who would be very glad to be authorised in a laudable frugality?

Telemachus hearing this discourse, was like a man coming out of a profound sleep. He felt the truth of these words, and they were engraved on his heart, as a skilful statuary imprints what features he pleases on the marble, and gives it softness, life and motion. Telemachus made no reply; but revolving what he had heard in his mind, he surveyed the alterations which had been made in the city, and at length thus addressed himself to Mentor.

You have made Idomeneus the wisest of all kings; I neither know him nor his subjects again. Nay, I confess that what you have done here is infinitely greater than the victories which we have obtained. Chance and strength have a great part in the successes of war; we must share the glory of battles with our soldiers; but all you have done proceeds from a single head: You alone must have struggled against a king and all his people in order to reform them. The successes of war are always fatal and odious; here all is the work of an heavenly wisdom, all is calm, all is innocent, all is lovely, all discovers an authority more than human. When men thirst for glory, why do they not seek it by thus applying themselves to do good? O what wrong notions have they of solid glory, since they expect to obtain it by ravaging the earth and by shedding human blood! Mentor's countenance shewed that he was exceedingly glad to see Telemachus form so true a judgment of victories and conquests, at an age when it was so natural for him to be intoxicated with the glory he had acquired.

After

After this Mentor added, All that you see here is indeed laudable and good; but know that it is possible to do yet better. Idomeneus curbs his passions, and applies himself to govern his people with justice; but he still commits a great many errors, which are the unhappy consequences of his former errors. When men desire to forsake evil, the evil still seems to pursue them; they long retain bad habits, a weakness of nature, inveterate errors, and almost incurable prejudices. Happy they who never strayed! they may do good to a greater perfection. The Gods, Telemachus, require more of you, than of Idomeneus, because you have known the truth from your youth, and have never been delivered up to the seducements of too great a prosperity.

Idomeneus, continued Mentor, is wise and knowing; but he applies himself too much to particulars, and does not sufficiently consider the whole of his affairs to form judicious schemes. The art of a king, who is set over other men, does not consist in doing all himself; it is gross vanity to hope to do this, or to endeavour to persuade the world that one is capable of it. A king ought to govern by choosing and guiding those who govern under him; he must not descend to particulars, for that is doing the office of his agents; he ought only to make them give him an account, and to know enough to examine that account with judgment. He is an admirable governor, who chooses and employs those who govern, according to their respective talents. The highest degree and perfection of government consists in governing those who govern: they must be watched, tried, checked, reproved, encouraged, promoted, degraded, removed from one post to another, and always kept in dependance. A prince who pries into every thing himself, betrays a mistrustful narrow soul, he abandons himself to jealousy about trifles, which consumes the time and the freedom of mind which are necessary for affairs of importance. To form great designs the soul must be free and composed; it must

think.

think at its eafe, and be entirely difengaged from all
knotty and difficult affairs; a mind exhaufted by particulars, refembles the lees of wine which have neither ftrength nor flavour. Governors who defcend
to particulars, are always determined by the prefent,
without extending their views to remote futurity;
they are continually borne away by the affairs of the
day, which being the only object of their thoughts,
makes too great an impreffion upon and cramps their
minds; for men never form a right judgment of
things unlefs they compare them all together, and
range them in a certain order, that they may have
connection and proportion. Not to obferve this rule
of government is to refemble a mufician, who should
content himfelf with finding out melodious founds,
and should give himfelf no trouble to combine and
make them harmonize with each other, in order to
compofe a fweet and ravishing piece of mufic. It
is alfo to refemble an architect, who thinks he does
every thing when he heaps together large columns and
a great number of well-wrought ftones, without at-
tending to the order and proportion of the ornaments
of his edifice. When he is building the faloon, he
does not forefee that there muft be a fuitable ftair-
cafe; when he is at work on the body of the ftructure,
he never dreams of the court-yard nor the gate; his
work is only a confufed jumble of magnificent parts,
which are not made to fit each other. This perfor-
mance, inftead of doing him an honour will be an
eternal monument of his shame; for it is a proof that
the workman had not a fufficient reach of thought to
take in at once the general defign of his whole work,
which is the character of a bounded and fubordinate
genius. When a man is born with a mind thus limited to particulars, he is only fit to execute under
another. Be affured, my dear Telemachus, that the
government of a kingdom requires a certain harmony like mufic, and juft proportions like architecture.

1E

If you will give me leave to go on with my comparison from these arts, I will convince you what indifferent capacities those men have who descend to all the particular parts of government. A person in a concert who sings only particular things, though he sings them perfectly well, is no more than a singer; he who conducts the whole concert, and at once regulates its several parts, he alone is the master of music. In like manner he who forms the columns, or raises a side of the edifice, is no more than a mason; but he who designed the whole building, and has all its proportions in his mind, he alone is the architect. Thus they who toil, who dispatch and transact the most business, are those who have the least share in the government; they are but the under-workmen. The true genius that directs the state, is he who does nothing himself, and yet causes every thing to be done; who thinks, who contrives, who dives into the future, who reviews the past, who orders and proportions every thing, who makes early preparations, who continually bears up against and struggles with fortune, as a swimmer against a torrent of water, and who studies night and day to leave nothing to chance.

Do you think, Telemachus, that a great painter assiduously toils from morning to night, that he may dispatch his works the sooner? No, such constraint and drudgery would damp the fire of his imagination; his genius would work no longer! every thing must be struck off irregularly and by starts, as his fancy leads and his spirit prompts him. Do you think he spends his time in grinding colours, and in making pencils? No, that is the business of his scholars. He reserves himself for thought and design; he only studies to strike bold strokes, which may give a noble air, and life and passion to his figures; his head is full of the thoughts and sentiments of the heroes he designs to represent; he transports himself to their times, and puts himself in all the circumstances in

which

which they have been : To this kind of enthufiafm he muft join the curb of judgment, that the whole may be true, correct and proportionable. Do you think, Telemachus, that lefs elevation of genius and efforts of thought are required to make a great king than to make a good painter ? conclude therefore that the bufinefs of a king ought to be to think, to form great defigns, and to choofe perfons proper to execute them under him.

Telemachus replied, I comprehend methinks all you fay ; but if things were thus, a king not entering into particulars himfelf would often be impofed upon. You are miftaken, anfwered Mentor ; a general knowledge of government prevents their being impofed upon. Men who obferve no maxims in affairs, and who have no true difcernment of men, are always groping as it were in the dark, and it is a chance if they are not impofed upon. They do not well know what they look for, nor which way they ought to direct their fteps ; their knowledge extends only to miftruft, and they fooner miftruft men of pro-bity who contradict them, than traitors who flatter them. On the contrary, they who have certain principles to govern by and a knowledge of men, know what they are to expect of them, and the means of coming at it : They know, at leaft in general, whether the perfons they employ are proper inftruments for their defigns, and whether they enter enough into their views to hit the mark they aim at. Befides, as they do not burden themfelves with the weight of particulars, their minds are more at liberty to furvey at one view the whole of the work, and to obferve if it tends towards their principal defign ; if they are deceived, it hardly ever is in effentials. Again, they are above the little jealoufies which denote a narrow mind and a groveling foul. They know that it is not poffible to avoid being deceived in important affairs, fince they are obliged to make ufe of men, who are fo often deceitful. More is

lost

loft by the irrefolution which arifes from diffidence, than by fuffering one's felf to be a little impofed upon. Happy the man who is impofed upon only in things of little confequence; the more important may go on well, and a great man ought only to be in pain about them. Deceit muft be feverely punifhed when it is difcovered, but one muft expect to meet with fome deceit, if one would not really be deceived. A mechanic fees every thing in his fhop with his own eyes, and does every thing with his own hands; but a king can neither do nor fee every thing in a large kingdom. He ought to do nothing but what nobody elfe can do under him, nor ought he to fee any thing but what concerns the decifion of important affairs.

In fine, Mentor faid to Telemachus, the Gods love you, and defign you a reign of wifdom. Every thing you fee here is done lefs for Idomeneus's glory, than for your inftruction. All the wife inftitutions which you admire at Salentum, are but a fhadow of what you will hereafter do in Ithaca; if your virtues correfpond to your high deftiny. It is time for us to think of departing hence. Idomeneus keeps a fhip ready for our return.

Hereupon Telemachus, though with fome difficulty, opened his heart to his friend concerning an attachment which made him loth to leave Salentum. You will cenfure me perhaps, faid he, for too eafily conceiving paffions in the places where I go; but my heart would continually reproach me, fhould I not tell you that I love Antiope, the daughter of Idomeneus. This, my dear Mentor, is not fuch a blind paffion as you cured me of in the ifle of Calypfo. I have been thoroughly fenfible of the depth of the wound I received from love when I was with Eucharis; I cannot yet pronounce her name without diforder, nor have time and abfence been able to efface it. This fatal experience teaches me

me to be diffident of myfelf. But what I feel for
Antiope is quite another thing. It is not the phren-
zy of love, it is judgment, it is efteem, it is conviction. How happy should I be in paffing my life
with her! If ever the Gods reftore me my father,
and permit me to choofe a wife, Antiope shall be
mine. What charms me in her, is her filence, her
modefty, her referve, her affiduity in labour, her
induftry in works of wool and embroidery, her application to the management of her father's houfe
fince the death of her mother, her contempt of
gaudy apparel, her evident forgetfulnefs or rather
ignorance of her beauty. When Idomeneus bids
her lead the dance of the young Cretans maidens to
the melody of flutes, she is attended with fo many
graces that one would take her for the fmiling Venus; when he takes her with him to hunt in the
forefts, she feems as majeftic, and as skilful in hand-
ling a bow, as Diana in the midft of her nymphs:
she alone is ignorant of it, while all the world admires it. When she enters the temple of the Gods,
and carries the facred offerings in baskets on her
head, one would think that she herfelf were the
Divinity which inhabits the temple. With what
awe and what devotion do we fee her offer facrifices, and deprecate the wrath of the Gods, when
any crime is to be expiated, or any dreadful omen
to bo averted! In fine, when one fees her with a
company of maidens, holding a golden needle in
her hand, one thinks that she is Minerva herfelf,
who has affumed an human form here on the earth,
and is teaching the polite arts to men. She encourages others to work; she fweetens their toils
and wearinefs by the charms of her voice, when
she fings all the marvellous hiftories of the Gods;
and she excels the moft exquifite paintings by the
delicacy of her embroideries. Happy the man
whom gentle Hymen joins with her! He will have
nothing to fear but to lofe and furvive her. I here
callt

call the Gods to witnefs, my dear Mentor, that I
am ready to depart ; I shall love Antiope as long
as I live, but she shall not one moment retard my
return to Ithaca. Were another to poffefs her, I
should pafs the reft of my days in bitternefs and forrow ; but I will leave her, though I know that abfence may caufe me to lofe her. I will not fpeak to
her nor her father of my love ; for I ought to fpeak
of it to you only, 'till Ulyffes, re-feated on his
throne, gives me his confent to do it. You may
hereby know, my dear Mentor, how different this
attachment is from the paffion with which you faw
me blinded for Eucharis.

Mentor replied, I grant, Telemachus, that there
is a difference. Antiope is gentle, ingenuous, prudent; her hands difdain not labour : she forefees
things long before they happen, she provides for
every thing, she knows how to be filent, and to do
things regularly without being in a hurry ; she is always employed, but never in a confufion, becaufe
she does every thing at a proper time. The good
order of her father's houfe is her glory, and adorns
her more than her beauty. Though she has the
care of every thing, and is charged with the office
of reproving, denying, faving, (things which make
almoft all women hated) yet has she made herfelf the delight of the whole houfe; becaufe they
find in her neither paffion, nor obftinacy, nor levity, nor humour, as in other women. With a fingle glance she makes herfelf underftood. and they
are afraid to difpleafe her ; she gives precife
orders, she commands nothing but what may be
done, she reproves with gentlenefs, and encourages when she reproves. Her father's heart refts
itfelf upon her, as a traveller, fainting with the heat
of the fun, refts himfelf upon the tender grafs in
the shade. You are in the right, Telemachus ;
Antiope is a treafure worthy to be fought after in
the remoteft countries. Her mind, no more than
her

her body, is never decked with vain and gaudy ornaments; her fancy, though lively, is restrained by her judgment; she does not speak but when it is necessary; and when she opens her mouth, soft persuasion and native graces flow from her lips. When she speaks, every body is silent, and she blushes at it; she can hardly help suppressing what she designed to say, when she perceives that she is listened to with so much attention; we have scarcely heard her speak.

Do you remember, Telemachus, when her father one day sent for her? She appeared with downcast eyes, was covered with a large veil, and spoke no more than was necessary to appease Idomeneus's anger, who was going to chastise one of his slaves with severity. She at first joined in his resentment, then she calmed him, at length she intimated what might be alledged in the wretch's excuse, and without making the king sensible that he was too much transported, she inspired into him sentiments of justice and compassion. Thetis, when she sooths old Nereus, does not more gently calm the angry billows. In this manner will Antiope, without assuming any authority, or taking any advantage from her charms, one day manage the heart of her husband, as she now touches her lyre, when she would draw forth its sweetest melody. Once again, Telemachus, I own that your affection for her is reasonable; the Gods design her for you; you love her with a rational passion, but you must wait 'till Ulysses gives her to you. I commend you for not discovering your sentiments to her; but know that if you had by any indirect means acquainted her with your designs, she would have rejected them, and have ceased to esteem you. She will never promise herself to any body; she will leave her father to dispose of her, and will take for an husband none but a man who fears the Gods, and discharges all his duties. Have you not observed ferved as well as I, that she lefs frequently appears, and that she oftener bends her eyes on the ground fince your return? She knows all your fuccefs in the war; she is not ignorant of your birth, of your adventures, or of any qualification which the Gods have beftowed upon you! it is this that makes her fo shy and referved. Let us go, Telemachus, let us go to Ithaca; I have nothing more to do but to conduct you to your father, and to put you in a condition to obtain a bride worthy of the golden age: Were she a shepherdefs on the frigid Algidus, inftead of the daughter of a king of Salentum, you would be the happieft of men in poffeffing her.

End of the Twenty-fecond Book.

THE

THE
ADVENTURES
OF
TELEMACHUS,
SON of ULYSSES.

BOOK the TWENTY-THIRD.

The ARGUMENT.

*Idomeneus fearing the departure of his two guests, pro-
poses several intricate affairs to Mentor, assuring him
that he could not settle them without his assistance.
Mentor tells him how he ought to act, and persists in
his resolution to carry Telemachus home. Idomeneus
again attempts to detain them by exciting the passion
of the latter for Antiope : he engages them in a
hunting match, at which he orders his daughter to
be present. She would have been torn in pieces by a
wild boar, but for Telemachus who rescues her. He
is afterwards very unwilling to forsake her, and to
take leave of the king her father ; but being encouraged by Mentor, he overcomes his reluctance, and
embarks for his native country.*

IDOMENEUS, who feared the departure of
Telemachus and Mentor, made it his whole study to retard it. He represented to Mentor that he
could not without him adjust a dispute that was risen
between Diophanes, a priest of Jupiter Conservator,
and Heliodorus, a priest of Apollo, concerning the
presages which are drawn from the flight of birds
and

and the entrails of victims. Why, said Mentor, would you intermeddle in things sacred? Leave the decisions of them to the Etrurians, who have the tradition of the most ancient oracles, and are inspired, that they may be the interpreters of the Gods. Use your authority only to stifle these disputes in their birth. Show neither partiality nor prejudice; content yourself with supporting the decision when it is made. Remember that a king is to be subject to religion, and is never to take upon him the regulation of it: Religion comes from the Gods, and is above kings. If kings meddle with religion, instead of protecting they enslave it. Kings are so powerful, and other men so weak that every thing will be in danger of being changed, according to the fancy of princes, if they should be permitted to concern themselves in questions relating to things sacred. Leave therefore the free decision of them to the favourites of the Gods, and confine yourself to the quelling of those who shall not conform to their determination when it is made.

Idomeneus afterwards complained of the perplexity he was in, with regard to a great number of lawsuits between divers private persons, which he was importuned to determine. Decide, replied Mentor, all new questions, which may be the foundations of general maxims, and become precedents of law; but never burthen yourself with trying private causes: they would come and besiege you in crowds. You would be the only judge of all your people. All the other judges, who are under you, would become useless; you would be overburthened; trifling affairs would take you off from the important, and yet you would not be sufficient to adjust all the particulars of the trifling. Take care therefore not to plunge yourself into this perplexity; refer the causes of private persons to the ordinary judges; do nothing but what nobody else can do to ease you, and you will then discharge the real functions of a king.

I am

I am alſo importuned, ſaid Idomeneus, to interfere in certain marriages. The perſons of diſtinguiſhed birth, who attended me in all my wars, and who loſt large eſtates in my ſervice, aim at a ſort of recompenſe by marrying certain rich maidens; and I need but ſpeak one word to procure theſe fortunes for them.

It is true, replied Mentor, that it would coſt you but one word; but this word itſelf would coſt you too dear. Would you deprive fathers and mothers of the liberty and ſatisfaction of chooſing their ſons-in-law, and conſequently their heirs? This were to bring all families into the ſevereſt ſlavery. You would make yourſelf anſwerable for all the domeſtic evils of your ſubjects. Marriage is full enough of thorns without this addition of bitterneſs. If you have faithful ſervants to reward, give them uncultivated lands; to theſe add rank and honours in proportion to their condition and ſervices. Add likewiſe, if neceſſary, ſome money ſaved out of the funds appointed for your own expences: But never pay your debts by ſacrificing young maidens of fortune contrary to the inclination of their families.

Idomeneus ſoon paſt from this queſtion to another. The Sibarites, ſaid he, complain of our uſurping ſome lands that belong to them, and of our giving them as grounds to be cultivated to the ſtrangers whom we have lately allured hither. Shall I yield to theſe people? If I do, every one will think that he needs only to form pretenſions upon us to have what he claims.

It is not reaſonable, replied Mentor, to believe the Sibarites in their own cauſe, neither is it reaſonable to believe you in yours. Who then muſt decide the matter, replied Idomeneus? Neither of the two parties, continued Mentor. A neighbouring people whom neither ſide can ſuſpect of partiality, muſt be choſen as an umpire; ſuch are the Sipontines, who have no intereſt oppoſite to yours. But am I obliged, rejoined Idomeneus, to be determined by an umpire? Am I not a king? Muſt a ſo-

S   vereign

vereign submit himself to foreigners as to the extent
of his dominions?

Mentor thus resumed the discourse. Since you
persist in keeping the lands, you must necessarily believe that your title to them is good. The Sibarites, on the other side, abate nothing of their pretensions, and maintain that their right is incontesta-
ble. In this opposition of opinions an arbitrator
chosen by both parties must make up the difference,
or the fate of arms decide it; there is no medium.
Were you to go into a republic, where there are
neither magistrates nor judges, and where every family should think it had a right to do itself justice
by violence against all the pretensions of its neighbours; you would deplore the misery of such a nation, and be struck with horror at its dreadful disorders, where all families would arm themselves one
against another. Do you think the Gods would
with less horror behold the whole world, which is
the universal commonwealth, should every nation,
which is but as a large family, think it had a right
to do itself justice by violence, as to all the pretensions it had upon other neighbouring nations? A
private man, who possesses a field by inheritance
from his ancestors, cannot maintain himself in it but
by the authority of the laws and the decree of the
magistrates; he would be severely punished as a seditious person, should he attempt to maintain by
force what justice has given him. And do you
think that kings may immediately make use of violence to support their pretensions, without having
first tried all the ways of gentleness and humanity?
Is not justice much more sacred and inviolable in
kings with regard to whole countries, than in private
families with regard to a few plough'd fields? Is a
man unjust, and a robber, who seizes a few acres of
land? And is he just, and an hero, who seizes whole
provinces? If men are prejudiced, if they are deceived and blinded in the trifling concerns of private persons, ought they not to be much more afraid
of

of being deceived and blinded in the great concerns of ftate? Shall a man rely upon his own judgment in an affair wherein he has fo much reafon to miftruft it? Will he not dread being miftaken in cafes, wherein the error of a fingle perfon has fuch terrible confequences? The miftake of a prince whofe pretenfions are ill-grounded, often occafions devaftations, famines, maffacres, loffes, and depravation of manners, whofe fatal effects extend to the remoteft ages. Should not a king, who is continually furrounded with crowds of flatterers, fear his being flattered on thefe occafions? If he agrees upon an umpire to decide the difference, he gives a proof of his equity, fincerity and moderation, and publifhes the folid reafon on which his caufe is founded. The appointed umpire is a friendly mediator, and not a fevere judge. His decifions are not blindly fubmitted to, but a great deference is paid to him. He does not pronounce fentence like a fupreme judge; but he makes propofitions, and fome things are given up by his advice for the prefervation of peace. If a war happens, notwithftanding all the pains which a prince takes to preferve peace, he then at leaft has on his fide the teftimony of his confcience, the efteem of his neighbours, and the juft protection of the Gods. Idomeneus was affected by this difcourfe, and confented that the Sipontines fhould be mediators between him and the Sibarites.

The king then perceiving that all his attempts to detain the two ftrangers were in vain, tried to hold them by a ftronger tie. He had obferved that Telemachus loved Antiope, and he hoped to detain him by that paffion. With this view he ordered her to fing at feveral entertainments; fhe did it that fhe might not difobey her father, but with fuch a referved and melancholy air, that one eafily faw the pain fhe fuffered by her obedience. Idomeneus went fo far as to bid her fing the victory gained over the Daunians and Adraftus; but fhe could not prevail on herfelf to fing the praifes of Telemachus; fhe

excufed

excufed herfelf in a refpectful manner, and her father did not think fit to conftrain her. Her fweet and ravishing voice went to the very foul of the young fon of Ulyffes; he was quite tranfported. Idomeneus, whofe eyes were fixed upon him, took a pleafure in obferving his tranfport; but Telemachus feemed as if he did not apprehend the king's defigns. He could not help being moved on thefe occafions; but his reafon prevailed over his love, and he was no longer the fame Telemachus whom a tyrannical paffion had formerly enflaved in the ifland of Calypfo. While Antiope was finging, he would obferve a profound filence; as foon as she had done, he would turn the converfation on fome other fubject.

The king not being able this way to fucceed in his defign, refolved at laft to have a great hunting-match, and ordered his daughter to partake of the diverfion. Antiope wept, being unwilling to go to it; but her father's command muft be obeyed. She mounts a foaming fiery fteed, like thofe which Caftor broke for battle; she manages him with eafe; a troop of young virgins with eager joy attend her; and she appears in the midft of them, like Diana in the foreft. The king fees her, and cannot tire his eyes with the fight, which makes him forget all his paft misfortunes. Telemachus fees her alfo, and is more ftruck with Antiope's modefty, than with her dexterity and all her graces.

The dogs chaced a wild boar of an enormous bulk, and furious as that of Calydon. His lengthful briftles were hard, and ftood upright like darts; his glaring eyes were red and fiery; his breath was heard from afar, like the murmurs of feditious winds, when Æolus recalls them to his cave to ftill the ftorms: his tusks, long and crooked as the keen fcythe of the mower, cut the trunks of the trees. All the dogs, that ventured to approach him, were torn in pieces. The boldeft hunters were afraid to overtake him in their purfuit. Antiope, as fwift in

the

the chace as the winds, was not afraid to approach and attack him. She hurls a javelin at him, which pierces him above the shoulder; the blood of the fierce animal gushes out like a torrent, and makes him more outrageous. He turns towards her who has wounded him. Upon which Antiope's courser, notwithftanding his great courage, trembles and ftarts back. The monftrous boar rushes againft him, like ponderous engines which shake the walls of the ftrongeft cities. The courfer ftaggers, and is thrown down. Antiope lies on the earth, incapable of avoiding the fatal gripe of the fangs of the exafperated boar. But Telemachus, feeing Antiope's danger, had already leapt from his horfe; he, fwifter than lightning, darts between the fallen fteed and the boar, which was going to revenge his blood; he holds a lengthful fpear in his hand, and buries it almoft entirely in the flank of the terrible animal, which falls raging on the ground.

Telemachus immediately cuts off his head, which is ftill terrible when nearly viewed, and which aftonishes all the hunters. He prefents it to Antiope; she blushes, and confults her father with her eyes, who after his fright is tranfported with joy to fee her out of danger; and makes her a fign to accept of the prefent. As she took it, she faid to Telemachus, I thankfully receive from you a more valuable gift; for I owe you my life. She had hardly fpoken, but she feared that she had faid too much; she looked on the ground, and Telemachus, who perceived her confufion, ventured to fpeak only thefe words: Happy the fon of Ulyffes in preferving fo precious a life! but ftill more happy, could he pafs his with you! Antiope, without replying, immediately rejoined the troop of her youthful companions, and mounted her fteed again.

Idomeneus would that moment have promifed Telemachus his daughter, but he hoped to enflame his paffion the more by leaving him in fufpence, and even imagined that he should detain him longer at

Salentum

Salentum by his defire to infure his marriage. Thus reafoned Idomeneus within himfelf: but the Gods deride the wifdom of men. What was to detain Telemachus, was the very thing which haftened his departure; what he began to feel, gave him reafon to be diffident of himfelf. Mentor redoubled his af-fiduity to infpire him with an impatience to return to Ithaca; he urged Idomeneus at the fame time to let him go; the veffel was now ready. Thus Mentor, who regulated every moment of Telemachus's life, in order to raife him to the higheft pitch of glory, did not let him ftay in any place longer than was neceffary to exercife his virtue, and to make him gain experience.

Mentor had taken care to order the veffel to be got ready as foon as Telemachus arrived; but Idomeneus, who beheld it equipping with great reluctance, fell into a deadly melancholy and a deplorable ftate of grief, when he faw his two guefts, from whom he had received fo much affiftance, going to forfake him. He fhut himfelf up in the moft private parts of his houfe, where he eafed his heart by fighs and tears; he forgot his food; no flumbers foothed his fmarting grief; he withered, he pined away with his uneafinefs, like a large tree, which hides the earth with the fhade of its fpreading branches, whofe trunk a worm begins to gnaw in thofe curious canals, through which the fap for its nourishment flows: As this tree, I fay, which the winds could never fhake, which the fertile earth delights to nourish in her bofom, and the axe of the woodman always refpected, continually languishes without any apparent caufe of its malady, and withers, and is defpoiled of its leafy honours, and is but a trunk overfpread with cloven bark, and faplefs branches; fo Idomeneus appeared in his grief.

Telemachus was moved, but afraid to fpeak to him. He dreaded the day of their departure; he fought for pretences to put it off, and would have remained a long while in this uncertainty, had not

Mentor

Mentor said to him, I am very glad to see you so altered. You were naturally obdurate and haughty; your heart used to be touched only with your own inconveniency and your own interests; but you are at length become a man, and begin by the experience of your own misfortunes to compassionate those of others. Without this sympathy, a man has neither goodness, nor virtue, nor a capacity to govern others; but he must not carry it too far, nor sink into the weaknesses of friendship. I would willingly speak to Idomeneus to prevail on him to consent to your departure, and would spare you the confusion of so irksome a conversation; but I would not have a vicious modesty and sheepishness tyrannize over your soul. You must accustom yourself to blend resolution and firmness of mind with the warmth and softnesses of friendship; you must be afraid of grieving men unnecessarily; you must sympathize with them in the troubles which you cannot help occasioning, and soften as much as you can the stroke from which it is impossible to exempt them entirely. It is in order to soften it, replied Telemachus, that I should rather choose that Idomeneus should be informed of our departure by you than by me.

Mentor immediately answered, you are mistaken, my dear Telemachus; you are naturally like the children of kings, who are bred up in purple, and insist that every thing be done in their own way, and that all nature be obedient to their humour, and yet have not resolution enough to oppose any one to his face. It is not that they have any regard for men, or that they are tender of grieving them through any principle of goodness; but it is for their own case; they do not care to see sorrowful and discontented faces about them. The distress and miseries of mankind give them no concern, provided they are not under their eyes. If they hear them mentioned, the discourse is grating and saddens them; to please them they must continually be told that every thing goes well; while they are pursuing

S 4   their

their pleasures, they do not care to see or hear any thing which may interrupt their mirth. If there is a necessity to reprove, chastise, or undeceive any one, or to thwart the pretensions and unreasonable passions of some troublesome person, they will always commission others, rather than speak themselves with mildness and resolution on these occasions: they would suffer the most unreasonable favours to be extorted from them, and cause the most important affairs to miscarry, for want of courage to determine contrary to the sentiments of those with whom they have every day to do. This weakness, which is perceived in them, prompts all men to study to make their advantage of it; they teaze, they solicit, they tire them; and by tiring them obtain their ends. They at first flatter and praise them, in order to ingratiate themselves; but as soon as they have gained their confidence, and are seated near them in places of power, they lead them whither they please, and impose their yoke upon them. They groan beneath it, and often try to shake it off, but they wear it as long as they live. They are solicitous not to seem to be governed, and yet they always are so; nay, they cannot do without it; for they resemble feeble vines, which not being able to support themselves, creep around the trunk of some large tree.

I will not suffer you, Telemachus, to be guilty of a failing, which unfits a man for government. You, who are of so tender a disposition as to be afraid to speak to Idomeneus, will not feel his grief the moment you are got out of Salentum. It is not his grief which affects you, it is his presence which confounds you. Go, speak to Idomeneus yourself: learn on this occasion to be tender-hearted and resolute at the same time. Tell him how sorry you are to leave him, but tell him also with a peremptory tone how necessary your departure is.

Telemachus did not dare either to oppose Mentor, or to go to Idomeneus; he was ashamed of his fears,

but

but had not courage to overcome them; he paused,
he took a step or two, and immediately returned, to
alledge to Mentor some new reason of delay: but a
single look of Mentor deprived him of his speech,
and made all his fair pretences vanish. Is this then,
said Mentor with a smile, the vanquisher of the Daunians, the deliverer of the great Hesperia, and the
son of the wise Ulysses, who is after him to be the
oracle of Greece? He dares not tell Idomeneus,
than he can no longer put off his return to his own
country, to see his father again! O ye people of
Ithaca, how unhappy will ye one day be, if you
have a king who is a slave to a criminal modesty,
and who sacrifices his most important affairs to his
weaknesses in the veriest trifles! See, Telemachus,
what difference there is between valour in battle,
and courage in business: You were not afraid of A-
drastus's arms, and yet you fear Idomeneus's grief.
This is what dishonours princes who have performed
the greatest actions; having shewn themselves to be
heroes in war, they shew themselves to be the lowest
of mankind in common occurrences, wherein others
support themselves with vigour.

Telemachus feeling the truth of these words, and
stung with this reproach, hurried away without giving
his passions time to speak. But as soon as he entered where Idomeneus was sitting with downcast,
languid, and sorrowful eyes, they were afraid of and
durst not look at each other; they understood one
another without speaking a word; each feared that
the other would break the silence, and they both began to weep. At length Idomeneus, prompted by
his excess of sorrow, cried out, What profits it to
pay one's court to virtue, if she so ill requites her
lovers? I am made sensible of my weakness, and
then deserted! Well! I shall soon relapse into all
my former misfortunes. Let no man talk to me of
governing well; no, I am incapable of it. I am sick
of mankind. Whither would you go, Telemachus?
Your father is no more, you seek him in vain;

Ithaca is become the prey of your enemies; they will destroy you, if you return thither. Some one of them has married your mother. Stay here, you shall wed my daughter, and be my heir; you shall reign after me: Nay, during my life you shall have an absolute power here; my confidence in you shall be unbounded. But if you are unmoved by all these advantages, at least leave me Mentor, who is my only resource. Speak, answer me, harden not your heart, pity the most wretched of men. How! silent! Ah! I feel how cruel the Gods are to me; I have even a quicker sense of it than I had in Crete, when I slew my own son.

At length Telemachus replied with a disordered and timorous voice, I am not at my own disposal. Destiny recalls me to my country. Mentor, who is endued with the wisdom of the Gods, commands me in their name to depart: What would you have me do? Shall I renounce my father, my mother, my country, which ought to be yet dearer to me than they? As I am born to be a king, I am not designed for a life of pleasure and repose, nor to follow my own inclinations. Your kingdom is richer and more powerful than that of my father; but I ought to prefer that which the Gods have alloted me to that which you have the goodness to offer me. I should think myself happy, were Antiope my wife, without any hopes of your kingdom: but to render myself worthy of her, I must go where my duty calls me, and it must be my father who demands her of you. Did you not promise to send me back to Ithaca? Was it not upon this promise that I, with the allies, fought for you against Adrastus? It is time for me to think of repairing my domestic misfortunes. The Gods who gave me to Mentor, gave Mentor also to the son of Ulysses, that he might fulfill the decrees of fate. Would you have me lose Mentor, after having lost every thing else? I have now neither estate, nor place of retreat, nor father, nor mother, nor any certain country; nothing is

left

left me but a wife and virtuous man, who is the most
precious gift of Jupiter. Do you yourself judge if I
can renounce him, and consent that he should forsake me. No, I would sooner die. Take my life,
my life's a trifle, but take not Mentor from me.

As Telemachus spoke, his voice grew stronger,
and his fears vanished. Idomeneus knew not what
to answer, nor could he consent to what the son of
Ulysses said. When he could no longer speak, he
endeavoured at least by his looks and his gestures to
move his pity. The same moment he saw Mentor
appear, who made him this serious address:

Do not grieve; we quit you, but the wisdom
which presides in the council of the Gods will remain with you; believe that you are very happy,
in that Jupiter has sent us hither to save your kingdom, and to reclaim you from your errors. Philocles, whom we have restored to you, will serve you
faithfully. The fear of the Gods, a taste for virtue,
a love of the people, and compassion for the miserable, will always possess his heart. Hearken to him,
and employ him with confidence and without jealousy.
The greatest service which you can receive from him,
is to oblige him to tell you of all your failings without any softenings. The greatest fortitude of a good
king consists in his seeking for real friends, who
may point out his mistakes to him. If you are endued with this fortitude, our absence will be no
prejudice to you, and you will live happy; but if
flattery, which insinuates like a serpent, again finds
the way to your heart, and makes you mistrust disinterested counsels, you are ruined. Do not suffer
yourself to be dejected by grief; but exert yourself
in the pursuit of virtue. I have told Philocles every
thing which he ought to do to assist you, and never to abuse your confidence; I can answer for him.
The Gods have given him to you, as they have given
me to Telemachus; every one ought courageously
to follow where his destiny leads; it profits not to
grieve. Should you ever want my assistance, after

I have reſtored Telemachus to his father and his country, I will viſit you again: And what could I do that would afford me a more ſenſible pleaſure? I ſeek not riches nor power on the earth? I would only aſſiſt thoſe who ſeek after juſtice and virtue. Can I ever forget the marks of confidence and friendſhip which you have ſhewn me?

At theſe words Idomeneus became of a ſudden quite another man; he felt that his ſoul was calmed, as Neptune with his trident calms the angry waves and the moſt lowring tempeſts: There remained only a gentle peaceful ſorrow, which was rather a concern and a ſenſe of fondneſs than anguiſh. Courage, confidence, virtue, and a reliance on the aſſiſtance of the Gods began to revive within him.

Well then, ſaid he, my dear Mentor, I muſt loſe every thing, and not be diſcouraged! At leaſt be mindful of Idomeneus, when you arrive at Ithaca, where your wiſdom will crown you with happineſs; do not forget that Salentum is the work of your hands, and that you there left an unhappy king, whoſe only hope is in you. Go, worthy ſon of Ulyſſes, I detain you no longer; I am far from oppoſing the Gods, who lent me ſo great a treaſure. Go, Mentor, alſo, thou greateſt and wiſeſt of mortals, (if humanity can indeed perform what I have ſeen in you, and if you are not ſome Deity who have borrowed this form to inſtruct weak and ignorant mankind) go, be a guide to the ſon of Ulyſſes, more happy in the poſſeſſion of you, than in being the vanquiſher of Adraſtus. Go both; I dare ſay no more, excuſe my ſighs. Go, live, be happy together; nothing in the world is left me now but the remembrance of having enjoyed you here. O happy, thrice happy days! days of whoſe value I was not ſufficiently ſenſible! O days which are too ſwiftly fled, you will never return! Never will my eyes behold again what they ſee now!

Mentor laid hold of this moment to get away; he embraced Philocles, who bedeweed him with his tears

without

without being able to fpeak.   Telemachus would
have taken hold of Mentor's hand to get out of thofe
of Idomeneus ; but Idomeneus advancing towards
the port, interpofed between Mentor and Telemachus ; he gazed upon them, he fighed, he began to
fpeak fome broken words, but could utter none dif-
tinct.

And now a confufed murmur is heard on the
shore, which is crowded with mariners ; the cordage is ftretched, the fails are hoifted, a favourable
gale begins to blow.   Telemachus and Mentor take
leave of the king, who holds them along while
locked in his arms, and purfues them as far as he
can with his eyes.

End of the Twenty-third Book.

THE

ADVENTURES

OF

TELEMACHUS,

SON of ULYSSES.

BOOK the TWENTY-FOURTH.

The ARGUMENT.

During their voyage, Telemachus gets Mentor to explain
to him several difficulties concerning government ;
among others those of knowing men, in order to em-
ploy only the good, and not to be imposed upon by the
bad. Towards the end of their conversation a calm
obliges them to put in at an island where Ulysses was
just landed. Telemachus sees him there, and talks to
him without knowing him. But having seen him em-
bark, he feels a secret uneasiness of which he cannot
conceive the cause. Mentor explains it to him, comforts
him, assures him that he will soon be with his father
again, and makes a trial of his piety and patience, by
putting off his departure, to offer a sacrifice to Minerva.
At last the Goddess, concealed under the figure of Men-
tor, resumes her own form and discovers herself. She
gives Telemachus her last instructions, and disappears.
Telemachus departs, arrives at Ithaca, and finds his
father in the house of the faithful Eumæus.

THE sails already swell, the anchors are
weighed, the land seems to fly, and the skilful pilot descries at a distance the mountains of Leu-
cate,

cate, which hides its head in whirling storms of freezing snow, and the Acroceraunian hills, which still uplift their haughty brows to heaven, though they have so often been shattered by thunder.

During this voyage Telemachus said to Mentor, I now understand the maxims of government which you have explained to me. At first they appeared to me like a dream, but their obscurity gradually vanished, and I now view them in a clear light. So all objects look dark at the first dawnings of Aurora in the morning, but afterwards seem to come as it were out of a chaos, when the light, which insensibly increases, distinguishes them, and restores them, to use the expression, their figures and natural colours. I am thoroughly convinced that the essential point of government is to discern the different characters of men, in order to choose and employ them according to their respective talents; but I am still at a loss to know how one may obtain such an insight into mankind.

Hereupon Mentor replied, You must study men in order to know them; and to know them, you must often see and have an intercourse with them. Kings ought to converse with their subjects, to make them speak, to consult them, to try them by little employments of which they should make them give an account, in order to see if they are capable of higher functions. How, my dear Telemachus, did you in Ithaca acquire your skill in horses? It was by often seeing them, and by taking notice of their faults and perfections in the company of persons of experience. In the same manner speak frequently of men's good and bad qualities with other wise and virtuous men, who have long studied their characters, and you will insensibly learn the turn of their minds, and what may be expected from them. Who taught you to know the good and the bad poets? It was frequently reading and reflecting upon them with men who had a taste for poetry. Who procured you judgment in music? It was the same application

cation in obſerving ſkilful muſicians. How can any one expect to govern men well, if he does not know them? and how can he know them, if he does not converſe with them? It is not converſing with them, to ſee them in public, where nothing is ſaid on either ſide but what is indifferent, and prepared with art. The buſineſs is to ſee them in private, to draw out to view all the ſecret ſprings of their hearts, to probe them on all ſides, to ſound them in order to diſcover their maxims. But to form a right judgment of men, it is neceſſary to begin by knowing what they ought to be; it is neceſſary to know what real and ſolid merit is, in order to diſtinguiſh thoſe who have it from thoſe who have it not. Men are continually talking of virtue and merit, without knowing preciſely what merit and virtue are. They are only fair words and indefinite terms in the mouths of the generality of mankind, who take a pride in talking of them eternally. It is neceſſary to have certain principles of juſtice, reaſon, and virtue, to know who are reaſonable and virtuous. It is neceſſary to underſtand the maxims of a wiſe and good government, to know men who are furniſhed with them, and thoſe who depart from them through a falſe ſubtility. In a word, to meaſure ſeveral bodies, it is neceſſary to have a fixed meaſure; to form a judgment of men's minds, it is likewiſe neceſſary to have conſtant principles which may be the ſtandard of all our judgments. It is neceſſary to know preciſely what is the end of human life, and what end we ought to propoſe to ourſelves in the government of men. Now this ſole this eſſential end is never to covet power and grandeur for one's own ſake, for this ambitious purſuit would only tend to gratify a tyrannical pride; but a man ought to ſacrifice himſelf to the infinite toils of government, to make men virtuous and happy: he otherwiſe walks in darkneſs and at random as long as he lives: he drives like a ſhip on the open ſea, that has no pilot,

that

that does not confult the ftars, nor know any of the neighbouring coafts ; he cannot but be wrecked.

Princes many times, for want of knowing where-in true virtue confifts, know not what they ought to look for in men. True virtue has fomething of harfhnefs for them ; it feems to them too aufterc and too independant ; it affrights and fours them ; they incline to flattery. From that moment they can no longer find either fincerity or virtue ; from that moment they purfue an empty phantom of vain glory, which renders them unworthy of the true, and they foon habituate themfelves to think that there is no true virtue in the world. For the good do indeed difcern the wicked ; but the wicked do not difcern the good nor can they believe that there are any. Such princes fufpect every body alike ; they hide themfelves, they fhut themfelves up, they are jealous on the moft trifling occafions, they dread mankind and make themfelves dreaded by them. They fhun the light, and dare not appear in their natural co-lours. Though they would not be known, they always are fo ; for the malicious curiofity of their fubjects pries into and guefles every thing, but they themfelves know nobody. The felfifh crew which befets them, is overjoyed to fee them inacceffible. A king who is inacceffible to men, is inacceffible to truth alfo. They blacken by infamous tales, and remove every thing from him which might open his eyes. Such kings pafs their lives in a favage inhu-man grandeur ; they are continually afraid of being impofed upon, and yet they always unavoidably are and deferve to be fo. When a man converfes only with a fmall number of perfons, he neceflarily im-bibes all their paffions and prejudices: And even vir-tuous men have their failings and prepoffeffions. Be-fides, one is at the mercy of tale-bearers, a bafe ma-licious tribe, who feed upon venom, who poifon the moft innocent things and magnify the leaft, who in-vent the evil rather than ceafe to injure, and who for their own intereft play upon the jealoufy and bafe curiofity of a weak and fufpicious prince.

Gcc

Get a knowledge therefore, my dear Telemachus, get a knowledge of men ; fift them, make them fpeak of one another, try them by little and little ; deliver yourfelf up to none ; profit by your own experience when you have been miftaken in your judgment, (for you will fometimes be miftaken) and thereby learn not rashly to judge well or ill of any man. The wicked are too deep diffemblers not to impofe upon the good by their difguifes ; but your paft miftakes will be ufeful leffons of inftruction. When you find a man of ability and virtue, employ him with confidence ; for men of integrity are pleafed to fee others confcious of their uprightnefs : they prefer efteem and confidence to riches : but do not fpoil them by entrufting them with an unbounded power. Many a man would have continued virtuous, who is no longer fo, becaufe his mafter has given him too much wealth and power. A prince, who is fo beloved of the Gods as to find in a whole kingdom two or three real friends of a fteady wifdom and integrity, quickly finds by their means other perfons who are like them, to fill inferior pofts ; by the men of virtue in whom he confides, he learns what he could not of himfelf difcern in his other fubjects.

But is it right, faid Telemachus, to make ufe of ill men when they have talents for bufinefs, as I have often heard it is ? One is often, faid Mentor, under a neceffity to make ufe of them. In a convulfed and difordered ftate one often finds unjuft and crafty men who are already in authority ; they are poffeffed of important pofts which cannot be taken from them ; they have infinuated themfelves into the confidence of certain perfons of influence with whom one muft needs keep well : nay, one muft keep well with the villains themfelves, becaufe they are to be feared, and have it in their power to throw every thing into confufion. It is highly neceffary therefore to make ufe of them for a time ; but it is neceffary, alfo to have in view the rendering them by degrees un-

unneceffary. As for a real and intimate confidence, take care never to repofe it in them ; for they may abufe it, and hold you faft whether you will or not by your fecrets, a chain harder to be broken than any chains of iron. Employ them in temporary negotiations, treat them kindly, and engage them to be faithful to you by their paffions themfelves, for you have no other hold of them, but never admit them into your fecret counfels. Always have fome fpring ready to put them in motion whenever you pleafe, but never give them the key either of your heart or your affairs. When your kingdom is quiet, fettled, and governed by wife and upright men, on whom you can depend, the wicked men, whom you were conftrained to make ufe of, become ufelefs by degrees. You muft not then however ceafe to treat them kindly, for it is never allowable to be ungrateful even to the wicked ; but at the fame time that you treat them kindly, you muft endeavour to make them virtuous. It is neceffary to wink at certain human frailties in them; but you muft however by degrees affume more authority, and check the growth of evils which they would commit openly, were they fuffered to go on. After all, the doing good by wicked inftruments is an evil ; and though this evil is often inevitable, we muft proceed gradually to put an entire ftop to it. A wife prince, who aims only at good order and juftice, will in time be able to do without corrupt and treacherous men ; he will find good men enough who have fufficient abilities to ferve him.

But it is not enough to find good fubjects in a nation ; it is neceffary to make others fo. That, anfwered Telemachus, muft needs be very difficult. Not at all, replied Mentor; your diligence in feeking for able and virtuous men, in order to prefer them, excites and fpurs on all perfons of abilities and fpirit ; every one exerts himfelf. How many men are there who languifh in idlenefs and obfcurity, who would become great men, were they fpurred on to induſtry by emulation and hopes of ſucceſs! How many men are there whom indigence and an impoſſibility of riſing by virtue, attempt to raiſe themſelves by vice! If therefore you annex rewards and honours to genius and virtue, what numbers of your ſubjects will of themſelves become eminent and virtuous! But how many will you render ſo, by making them riſe ſtep by ſtep from the loweſt employments to the higheſt? you will exerciſe their talents; you will prove the extent of their genius, and the ſincerity of their virtue. The men who arrive at the higheſt poſts, will have been trained up under your eyes in the inferior. You will have followed them all your life ſtep by ſtep, and will form your judgment of them, not by their words, but by the whole courſe of their actions.

While Mentor was reaſoning thus with Telemachus, they perceived a Phæacian veſſel that had put in at a little iſland, which was deſert, wild, and ſurrounded with frightful rocks. The winds at the ſame time were huſhed, the gentle Zephirs themſelves ſeemed to hold their breath, the ſea was become as ſmooth as a mirror, the flagging ſails could no longer animate the veſſel, and the efforts of the weary rowers were vain; it was neceſſary therefore to land in this iſland, which was rather a rock than earth proper to be inhabited by men. In leſs calm weather it would have been impoſſible to have landed there without the utmoſt danger. The Phæacians, who were waiting for a wind, did not ſeem leſs impatient than the Salentines to proceed in their voyage. Telemachus advances towards them on theſe rocky shores, and immediately asks the firſt man he meets, if he had not ſeen Ulyſſes king of Ithaca in king Alcinous's palace.

The perſon to whom he accidentally addreſt himſelf was not a Phæacian, but an unknown ſtranger, of a majeſtic, but melancholy and dejected air. He ſeemed thoughtful, and at firſt hardly heard Telemachus's queſtion; but at length he anſwered, You

are

are not miftaken, Ulyffes was entertained in king Alcinous's palace, a place where Jupiter is revered, and hofpitality practifed ; but he is not there now ; you would feek him there in vain ; he is departed in order to revifit Ithaca, if the appeafed Deities will at length fuffer him to falute his houshold Gods again.

This ftranger had hardly fpoken thefe words in a melancholy manner, but he rushed into a thick grove on the top of a rock, whence he ftedfaftly viewed the fea, flying from every one he faw, and feeming uneafy at not being able to profecute his voyage. Telemachus looked ftedfaftly upon him, and the more he looked the more he was moved and afto- nished. This ftranger, faid he to Mentor, anfwer- ed me like one who does not much attend to what is faid to him, and who is oppreft with grief. I pity the unfortunate, fince 1 have been fo myfelf, and I feel that my heart is concerned for this man, without knowing why He was not over-civil to me, hardly vouchfafing to hear and anfwer me ; and yet I cannot help wishing that his miferies were at an end.

Mentor replied with a fmile, Lo the ufe of the evils of life ; they foften the hearts of princes, and make them feel the woes of others. When they have tafted only of the fweet poifon of profperity, they fancy themfelves Gods ; they will have moun- tains become plains, to gratify them ; they efteem mankind as nothing, and make all nature their fport. When they hear of fuffering, they know not what it means ; it is a dream to them ; they have never feen the diftance between good and evil : misfortune a- lone can teach them humanity, and change their hearts of ftone into hearts of flesh. They then find that they are men, and that they ought to be tender of others who are like them. If a ftranger excites fo much pity, becaufe he is a wanderer on this shore like you ; how much more compaffion ought you to have for the people of Ithaca, when you hereafter
fee

fee them fuffer! This people, whom the Gods will commit to your care, as a flock is committed to a shepherd, will perhaps be rendered miferable by your ambition, or pride, or imprudence; for the people fuffer only through the faults of princes, who ought to be watchful to prevent their fufferings.

While Mentor was fpeaking thus, Telemachus was overwhelmed with grief and trouble, and at length replied with fome emotion: if all thefe things are true, the condition of a king is very unhappy; he is the flave of all whom he feems to command; he is not fo much born to command as to ferve them; he owes himfelf entirely to them; he is burdened with all their wants; he is the fervant of all the people, and of every one in particular; he muft accommodate himfelf to their weakneffes, and correct them like a father, that he may render them wife and happy. The authority which he feems to have, is not his own; he can do nothing for his own glory or pleafure; his authority is that of the laws; he muft obey them, in order to be an example to his fubjects. Properly fpeaking, he is only the guardian of the laws, to make them reign; he muft watch and toil to maintain them; he has the leaft freedom and tranquility of any man in his kingdom; he is a flave, who facrifices his own repofe and liberty for the liberty and happinefs of the public.

It is true, replied Mentor, that a king is a king only to take care of his people, as a shepherd takes care of his flock, or a father of his family. But do you think my dear Telemachus, that he is unhappy in being obliged to do good to fuch multitudes? He corrects the wicked by punishments, he encourages the good by rewards, and reprefents the Gods in thus conducting all the human race to virtue. Has he not glory enough in caufing the laws to be obferved? That of placing him above the laws is a falfe glory, which infpires nothing but horror and contempt. If he is wicked, he cannot but be un-

unhappy; for he can find no peace in his paffions and vanity. If he is virtuous, he muft needs tafte the pureft and moft folid of all pleafures, in toiling in the fervice of virtue, and in the expectation of an eternal recompence from the Gods.

Telemachus, who had a fecret uneafinefs in his heart, feemed as if he had never underftood thefe maxims, though his mind was well ftored with them, and he had himfelf taught them to others. A melancholy humour infpired him contrary to his real fentiments, with a fpirit of contradiction and fubtilty, to oppofe the truths which Mentor explained. To thefe arguments Telemachus oppofed the ingratitude of men. What! faid he, take fo much pains to win the affections of men, who perhaps will never love you, and to do good to wretches who will make ufe of your benefits to your prejudice!

Mentor made him a calm reply: We muft expect men to be ungrateful, and yet we muft do good to them: we muft ferve them lefs for their own fakes, than for the love of the Gods who command it. The good which a man does is never loft: if men forget it, the Gods remember and reward it. Befides, if the multitude is ungrateful, there are always fome virtuous perfons who are affected with your virtue: nay, the multitude itfelf, fickle and capricious as it is, never fails fooner or later to do a fort of juftice to real virtue. But would you prevent the ingratitude of men? Do not labour folely to make them powerful, rich, formidable in arms, happy in their pleafures: this glory, this abundance, thefe pleafures corrupt them; they will only be the more wicked for them, and confequently the more ungrateful; it is making them a fatal prefent, it is offering them a delicious poifon: But apply yourfelf to reform their manners, and to inftill into them juftice, fincerity, a fear of the Gods, humanity, fidelity, moderation, and difintereftednefs. By making them good you will hinder them from being ungrateful, and confer virtue, a real good, upon
them;

them ; and virtue, if it be real, will for ever attach them to him who has instilled it into them. Thus by conferring the real good upon them, you will do good to yourself, and will have nothing to fear from the ingratitude. Is it any wonder that men are ungrateful to princes who never taught them any thing but injustice, unbounded ambition, a jealousy of their neighbours, inhumanity, haughtiness and treachery ? The prince should expect nothing from them but what he has taught them to do. But on the contrary, if he endeavoured by his own example and authority to render them virtuous, he would find the fruits of his labour in their virtues, or at least he would find in his own and in the friendship of the Gods, wherewithal to comfort himself under all his disappointments.

This discourse was hardly ended, when Telemachus hastened towards the Phæacians, whose ship was anchored on the shore. He addressed himself to an old man amongst them, and asked him whence they came, whither they were bound, and if they had not seen Ulysses. The old man replied, we come from our own island, which is that of the Phæacians ; we are going to Epirus for merchandize ; and Ulysses, as you have already been told, came into our country but is departed from it.

Telemachus immediately added, Who is that melancholy man who seeks the most solitary places, while he waits for the departure of your vessel ? He is, replied the old man, a stranger that is unknown to us. But it is said that his name is Cleomenes ; that he was born in Phrygia ; that an oracle foretold his mother before his birth that he would be a king, provided he did not remain in his own country ; and that if he did remain there, the wrath of the Gods would fall on the Phrygians in a dreadful pestilence. As soon as he was born, his parents delivered him to certain mariners, who carried him to the island of Lesbos, where he was privately brought up at the expence of his country, which had so great an in-

terest

reft to keep him at a diftance. He foon grew tall, robuft, handfome, and expert in all exercifes of the body. He even applied himfelf with great tafte and genius to the fciences and the liberal arts; but he was not fuffered to ftay in any country. The prediction concerning him became famous; he was prefently known wherever he went, and kings were every where afraid that he would wreft their crowns from them. Thus has he been a wanderer from his birth, and can find no part of the world, where he may have the liberty to fettle. He has often travelled into nations the moft remote from his own; but he hardly arrives in any city before his birth and the oracle concerning him are difcovered. He in vain hides himfelf, and choofes in every place fome obfcure kind of life; his talents for war, letters, and the moft important affairs fhine forth, they fay, whether he will or not; there always offers in every country fome unforefeen occafion which gets the better of him, and makes him known to the public. His merit is the caufe of his misfortune; it makes him feared, and excludes him from all places where he attempts to refide. It is his fate to be every where efteemed, beloved, admired, but expelled from all the known countries in the world. He is not young, and yet has he not hitherto been able to find any coaft, either of Afia or Greece, where they would fuffer him to live in peace. He feems to have no ambition, and does not aim at greatnefs; he would be very happy, had not the oracle promifed him a crown. He defpairs of ever feeing his country again; for he knows that he should carry nothing but mourning and tears into every family. A crown itfelf, the caufe of his fufferings, feems not defirable to him; he purfues it contrary to his own inclinations, through a fad fatality, from kingdom to kingdom, and it feems to fly before him, in order to mock this unhappy man even to his old age. Fatal gift of the Gods, which clouds his brighteft days, and caufes him nothing but pain, at a time when

T   feeble

feeble man needs nothing but rest! He is going, he says, to Thrace in quest of some savage lawless people, whom he may assemble, civilize, and govern for some years; after which, the oracle being accomplished, the most flourishing kingdoms will have nothing to apprehend from him. He designs then to retire to some village of Caria, where he will devote himself to agriculture, of which he is passionately fond. He is a wise and sober man, who fears the Gods, who has a thorough knowledge of mankind, and who knows how to live in peace with them without esteeming them. This is what is reported of this stranger, of whose fortunes you desired me to inform you.

During this conversation, Telemachus was continually turning his eyes towards the sea, which began to be in motion. The winds raised the waves, which beat against the rocks, and whitened them with their foam. The same instant the old man says to Telemachus, I must go; my companions cannot wait for me. As he speaks these words, he runs to the shore; the Phæacians embark, and nothing is heard but the confused clamours of the mariners, who were eager and impatient to be gone.

The stranger, who was called Cleomenes, had strayed some time up and down the island, climbing up to the tops of all the rocks, and from thence taking a melancholy survey of the vast expanse of the sea. Telemachus had not lost sight of him, nor ceased to watch his steps. His heart was moved for a virtuous, wandering, unhappy man, who was born to perform the greatest actions, and was made, far from his native country, the sport of rigorous fortune. I perhaps, said he to himself, may see Ithaca again; but this Cleomenes can never return to Phrygia. An instance of a man more unhappy than himself alleviated Telemachus's grief.

At length this man seeing the vessel ready, descended from the craggy rocks with as much speed and agility, as Appollo in the forests of Lycia, having
tied

tied his flaxen locks together, flies over the precipices, when he pursues the stags and wild boars
with his arrows. And now this unknown person is
on board the ship, which cleaves the briny wave,
and flies from the land.

Hereupon a secret impression of sorrow is made on
Telemachus's heart; he grieves without knowing
why; tears trickle from his eyes, and nothing is so
pleasant to him as to weep. At the same time he sees
all the Salentine mariners on the shore, lying fast a-
sleep on the grass; they were tired and quite spent;
gentle sleep had insinuated itself into their limbs, and
all the humid poppies of the night had been shed upon
them, by Minerva's power, in the middle of the day.
Telemachus is surprized to see this universal drowsi-
ness of the Salentines, while the Phæacians had been
so watchful and diligent to improve a favourable
wind; but he is more intent on viewing the Phæacian ship, which was ready to disappear in the midst
of the waves, than to go and awake the Salentines.
Amazement and secret anguish fasten his eyes on the
departed bark, of which he now sees nothing but the
sails, which look a little white in the azure waves;
he does not even hear Mentor who speaks to him;
he is quite beside himself, and transported like the
priestesses of Bacchus, when they hold the Thyrsus
in their hands, and make the banks of Hebrus and
the mountains of Rhodope and Ismarus ring with
their frantic howlings.

At length he recovers a little from this kind of in-
chantment, and tears again begin to stream from his
eyes. Whereupon Mentor says to him : I am not
surprised, my dear Telemachus, to see you weep;
the cause of your sorrow, which is unknown to you,
is not unknown to Mentor; it is nature that speaks
and works in you; it is she that melts your heart.
The stranger, who excited such lively emotions in
you, is the great Ulysses. What the old Phæacian
told you of him under the name of Cleomenes, is
only a fiction, the more securely to conceal your fa-

ther's.

ther's return to his kingdom. He is going directly to Ithaca; he is already near the port, and at length sees that so long wished for place again. Your eyes have seen him, as it was formerly foretold that you should, but without knowing him; you will quickly see him again, and know him, and he will know you. But at present the Gods do not permit you to know each other out of Ithaca. His soul was not less moved than yours; he is too wise to discover himself to any mortal, where he might be exposed to the treachery and insults of the cruel suitors of Penelope. Ulysses, your father, is the wisest of all men; his heart is like a deep well; his secrets cannot be drawn out of it. He loves truth, and never says any thing that wounds it; but he speaks it only when it is necessary; wisdom, like a seal, always keeps his lips shut against all useless words. How was he moved when he spoke to you! What violence did he do to himself, that he might not be known! What did he not suffer in seeing you! It was that which made him sad and dejected.

During this speech, Telemachus being greatly moved and troubled could not help shedding floods of tears, and his sobbings hindered him a long while from making a reply. At length he cried out, Ah! my dear Mentor, I felt I know not what in this stranger which attracted me to him, and moved all my bowels within me. But why, as you knew him, did you not tell me that it was Ulysses before his departure? Why did you let him go without speaking to him, and without seeming to know him? Pray what mystery is this? Shall I be wretched for ever? Will the angry Gods punish me with thirst like Tantalus, whom a delusive stream derides by its flight from his greedy lips. O Ulysses! Ulysses! art thou gone for ever? Perhaps I shall never see him more: Perhaps Penelope's lovers may cause him to fall into the snares which they laid for me! Had I went with him, I should at least have died with him. O Ulysses! Ulysses! if storms do not throw you on the rocks
again,

again, (for I have every thing to apprehend from
adverſe fortune) I tremble leſt on your arrival at
Ithaca you ſhould meet as dreadful a fate as Agamemnon did at Mycenæ.   But why, my dear Mentor, did you envy me my happineſs! I had now
embraced him, I had now been with him in the port
of Ithaca, we had been fighting to vanquiſh all our
enemies!

Mentor replied with a ſmile, See, my dear Telemachus, the temper of mankind.   You are now in the
greateſt diſtreſs, becauſe you have ſeen your father
without knowing him ; and yet what would you
not have given yeſterday to have been aſſured that
he was not dead? To day you are aſſured of it by
your own eyes, and this aſſurance, which ought to
overwhelm you with joy, fills you with anguiſh.
Thus does the ſickly ſoul of mortals eſteem as nothing what is moſt deſired, as ſoon as it poſſeſſes it,
and is ingenious in tormenting itſelf with regard to
what it does not yet poſſeſs.   It is to exerciſe your
patience that the Gods keep you thus in ſuſpence.
You look upon this as loſt time, but know that it is
the moſt uſeful of your whole life; for it exerciſes
you in a virtue which is the moſt neceſſary in thoſe
who are to command.   It is neceſſary to be patient,
in order to become maſter of one's ſelf and others.
Impatience, which ſeems ſtrength and vigour of ſoul,
is nothing but weakneſs and an inability of bearing
pain.   He that cannot wait and ſuffer, is like a man
who cannot keep a ſecret; they both want a firm-
neſs of ſoul to contain themſelves, like a charioteer
in a race whoſe hand is not ſtrong enough, when
it is needful, to ſtop his fiery courſes : they no longer obey the reins, they ruſh down a precipice, and
the feeble driver, with whom they run away, is
daſhed in pieces by his fall.   So an impatient man
is hurried by his fierce and unconquerable deſires into an abyſs of miſeries.   The greater his power is,
the more fatal to himſelf is his impatience.   He waits
for nothing, he does not allow himſelf time to weigh
                                                                any

any thing, he breaks through all things to gratify himself; he tears off the branches to gather the fruit before it is ripe; he breaks down the doors rather than stay 'till they are opened to him; he will needs reap when the wife husband-man sows; every thing which he does in a hurry and out of season is ill-done, and cannot last longer than his fickle desires. Such are the mad projects of man who thinks he can do every thing, who gives himself up to his impetuous desires, and abuses his power. It is to teach you to be patient, my dear Telemachus, that the Gods do so much exercise your patience, and seem to mock you in the vagrant life wherein they always keep you in doubt. The good which you hope for shows itself to you, and flies away like an empty dream, which a man's awaking causes to vanish, to teach you that the very things which you think you hold fast in your hands may slip away in an instant. The wisest lessons of Ulysses will not be so useful to you as his long absence, and the hardships you suffer in quest of him.

Mentor afterwards resolved to put Telemachus's patience to a last and yet severer trial. The moment the youth was running to urge the mariners to hasten their departure, Mentor stopped him on a sudden, and engaged him to offer a great sacrifice to Minerva on the shore. Telemachus readily executes what Mentor desires. Two altars of turf are erected, the incense smokes, and the blood of the victims streams around. Telemachus sends up tender sighs to heaven, and acknowledges the powerful protection of the Goddess. As soon as the sacrifice was ended, he followed Mentor into the gloomy paths of a neighbouring grove, where he suddenly perceived that the face of his friend assumed a new form. The wrinkles of his brow disappear, as shades vanish when Aurora with her rosy fingers opens the gates of the east, and enflames all the horizon. His hollow and severe eyes are changed into eyes of a celestial azure, and filled with a divine fire. His white and uncouth beard disappears.

Noble

Noble and majeſtic features, tempered with ſweetneſs and grace, preſent themſelves to the dazzled eyes of Telemachus. He ſees a woman's viſage with a complection more beautiful than a tender flower juſt unfolded to the ſun ; the whiteneſs of the Lilly is there blended with the crimſon of the opening roſe. Eternal youth blooms on her face, with a plain unaffected majeſty. An ambroſial odour is diffuſed from her flowing treſſes. Her veſtments gliſter like the lively colours with which the riſing ſun paints the dusky vaults of heaven, and gilds the clouds. The Goddeſs does not touch the earth with her feet, but glides with eaſe through the air, as a bird cleaves it with his wings. In her puiſſant hand she holds a glittering ſpear, that would terrify the moſt warlike cities and nations ; nay, Mars himſelf would tremble at it. Her voice is ſweet and mild, but ſtrong and inſinuating ; all her words are darts of fire, which pierce the very ſoul of Telemachus, and make him feel a pleaſing kind of pain. On her helmet is ſeen the ſolitary bird of Athens, and on her breaſt glitters the formidable Ægis. By theſe marks Telemachus knows Minerva.

O Goddeſs! ſaid he, it is you yourſelf then who have deigned to conduct the ſon of Ulyſſes for the ſake of his father! — He would have proceeded, but his voice failed him, and his lips vainly endeavoured to expreſs the thoughts which impetuouſly ruſhed from the bottom of his heart. The preſence of the Goddeſs overpowered him, and he was like a man who is ſo much oppreſt in a dream as to loſe his breath, and who by the painful agitations of his lips cannot form a ſingle word.

At length Minerva ſpoke theſe words : Son of Ulyſſes, hear me for the laſt time. I have never inſtructed any mortal with ſo much care as you ; I have led you by the hand through shipwrecks, unknown countries, bloody wars, and all the evils which can try the heart of man. I have shewn you by ſtriking examples the true and falſe maxims of government.

Your

Your faults have not been lefs ufeful to you than your misfortunes: For where is the man that can govern wifely, if he has never fuffered, and never profited by the fufferings into which his faults have plunged him? You like your father have filled the earth and the feas with your difaftrous adventures. Go, you are now worthy to tread in his fteps. You have but a short and eafy paffage to Ithaca, where he is this moment arrived; affift him in fight, obey him like the meaneft of his fubjects, and be an example to others. He will give you Antiope for your wife, and you will be happy with her; becaufe you fought for beauty lefs than for wifdom and virtue. When you come to reign, place all your glory in renewing the golden age; hear every body; believe a few; be fure not to rely too much on yourfelf; be afraid of being deceived, but never be afraid to let others fee that you have been deceived; love your people, and ufe all means of winning their love. Fear is neceffary when love is wanting; but like the moft violent and dangerous medicines, it should always be ufed with reluctance. Always confider at a diftance all confequences of what you defign to undertake; be careful to forefee the moft terrible evils, and know that true courage confifts in facing and defpifing dangers when they become neceffary. He that will not look upon them, has not courage enough to bear the fight of them with tranquillity; he who furveys them all, who avoids all thofe which may be avoided, and who calmly encounters the reft, he alone is wife and magnanimous. Fly luxury, pomp and extravagance; place your glory in fimplicity; let your virtues and good deeds be the ornaments of your perfon and palace; let them be the guards which furround you, and let every body learn of you wherein true honour confifts. Never forget that kings do not reign for their own glory, but for the good of their people. The good which they do, defcends to the lateft ages; the evil which they do, multiplies from generation to generation even to remoteft pofterity:

One

One bad reign is often the cause of ages of calamity. Be particularly upon your guard against your own humour, an enemy which you will carry every where with you as long as you live, which will intrude into your counsels, and betray you if you listen to her. Humour makes a man lose the most important opportunities; she gives him the desires and aversions of a child to the prejudice of his greatest concernments; she causes his most weighty affairs to be decided by the most trifling reasons; she obscures his talents, debases his courage, and renders him unequal, weak, mean, and insupportable. Be jealous of this enemy. And, O Telemachus, fear the Gods; this fear is the greatest treasure of the human heart; it comes attended by wisdom, justice, peace, joy, unmixed pleasures, real liberty, delightful abundance, and spotless glory.

I leave you, O son of Ulysses: but my wisdom shall never leave you, provided you are always sensible that you can do nothing without it. It is time for you to learn to go alone. I was separated from you in Egypt and at Salentum, only to accustom you to live without me, as children are weaned when it is time to take their milk from them, and to give them more substantial aliments.

As soon as the Goddess had ended this speech, she sprung up into the air, and involved herself in a gold and azure cloud, in which she disappeared. Telemachus sighing, amazed and transported, threw himself prostrate on the earth, and lifted up his hands to heaven. He afterwards went and waked his companions, departed, arrived at Ithaca, and found his father in the house of the faithful Eumæus.

End of the Twenty-fourth and last Book.

Peyton's Elements of the English language, explained in a new, easy, and concise manner, by way of Dialogues; in which the pronounciation is taught by an union of letters that produces similary-sounds in French, and the true quantity of each syllabe is determined, 12mo.

Boyer's Dictionary, French and English, by Prieur, 2 vols. 4to.

——————————— Abridged, 2 vols. 8vo.

Nugent's Pocket Dictionary French and English, and English and French, 12mo.

Addisson's Cato a Tragedy, 12mo.

——————— works, 4 vols. 12mo.

Fielding's works, 12 vols. 12mo.

——————— Amelia, 3 vols. 12mo.

——————— Adventures of Jos. Andrews, 2 vols. 12mo.

——————— Tom Jones, 4 vols. 12mo.

Richardson's Clarissa, 4 vols. 12mo.

——————— History of Grandison, 7 vols. 12mo.

——————— Pamela, 4 vols. 12mo.

Shakespear's works, 10 vols. 8vo.

Spectator, 8 vols. 12mo.

Robertson's History of Scotland, 2 vols. 8vo.

——————— Charles V. 4 vols. 8vo.

——————— America, 2 vols. 4to.

Pope's Works, 9 vols. 8vo.

——————— 6 vols. 12mo.

——————— Homer's Iliad and Odissey, 11 vols. 8vo.

Adventures of Roderick Random, by Smollet, 2 vols. 12mo.

Butler's Hudibras, 2 vols. 8vo.

The same, 12mo.

Chambaud's Grammar of the French tongue, 8vo.

——————— Exercises, 8vo.

Cyrus's Travels, 12mo.

Dryden's Dramatick works, 6 vols. 12mo.

——————— Miscellaneous works, 6 vols. 12mo.

Gay's Fables, 12mo.

Goldsmith's Grecian History, 2 vols. 8vo.

Johnson's Dictionary, 2 vols. folio.

——————— Abridged, 2 vols. 8vo.

www.ingramcontent.com/pod-product-compliance
Lightning Source LLC
Chambersburg PA
CBHW030940110726
47900CB00004B/1060